Angel Baby

A Novel by

Kris Williams

authorHOUSE®

AuthorHouse™
1663 Liberty Drive, Suite 200
Bloomington, IN 47403
www.authorhouse.com
Phone: 1-800-839-8640

First published by AuthorHouse   10/31/2008

ISBN: 978-1-4389-2450-2 (sc)

Printed in the United States of America
Bloomington, Indiana

This book is printed on acid-free paper.

To the men who inspired it...
and to Lory, who believed

Love hurts
Love scars
Love wounds and mars ...

- Nazareth

You're walkin' a wire
Pain and desire
Lookin' for love in between ...

- The Eagles

Chapter One

"He's watching you again."

Megan's furtive whisper drifted to my ears from the seat behind me, and I turned and gave her an exasperated look. At the same time, I couldn't help but notice she was right: he *was* staring, and making no secret of it, either. I hastily turned away from that insolent gaze, feeling an embarrassed blush stain my cheeks bright pink. Stuart Black always seemed to have that effect on me. Although I told myself I detested him, there was something about his attention that made my heart beat faster and my breathing quicken just a little. If I had been listening to Mrs. Greenbaum elaborate on the trials of Romeo and Juliet, I wasn't any longer. My mind was now on Stu and the interest he had always displayed in me.

Stu had never tried to hide that interest; his remarks and glances were blatantly sexual, almost insulting, and it drove my boyfriend crazy. Although Jason and I had only been going out a few months, I had already had to discourage him from instigating a fight, the prospect of which seemed to amuse Stu immensely. I knew Jason backed off out of respect for my feelings, but I had no idea what stopped Stu from fighting, if anything. I could never figure out what he was thinking, and I had no idea why he was so attracted to me. All I knew was that it made me nervous, and that was not a feeling I liked.

Now, I jumped as Megan poked me in the back. Reaching down and behind in an automatic gesture, I felt for the note she pushed into my fingers. I sighed inwardly, certain it would be more breathless speculation about the level of Stu's interest. Meg found the situation endlessly diverting, and I was tired of her always making a big deal about it. I unfolded the note and saw with surprise that it was from Stu, not Megan.

I want to talk to you after class, Ang. Meet me on the back steps, okay?

I half turned in my seat and looked at him curiously, and Stu gave me a lazy smile and winked. As usual, I felt the same confusing mix of apprehension and flattery, and I wasn't sure how to respond. I left the note on the corner of my desk and studiously ignored Megan, who kept poking me in the back, dying to know what Stu had written.

The bell rang, and I barely had time to close my books before Meg was all over me. "What did it say?" she hissed in my ear, and another blush warmed my face as Stu strolled casually by us. Tall and lanky, he was attractive in a dark, dangerous way, and the thought of a private conversation with him made me incredibly nervous.

"He says he wants to talk to me, satisfied?" My tone was sharper than I had intended, but Meg was looking at me in a fascinated way that was irritating.

"What could Stu possibly have to talk to you about?"

I scooped up my books and walked from the room by her side. I shrugged as we left the English room. "How should I know?"

We went toward the back door, and as I pushed it open that feeling of apprehension grew until it felt suspiciously like panic. When I saw Stu sprawled at the bottom of the steps, smoking a cigarette, I almost turned and went back inside, but Meg was right behind me and she gave me a push.

"Go on!" she whispered excitedly. "I can't wait to hear what he has to say!"

I looked at Megan with one raised eyebrow. "You're not going to be there," I told her, giving her a push back. "Go talk to Darryl and make sure if Jason comes out here he doesn't freak."

I left her and went down the stairs to where Stu sat, leaning back on one elbow and blowing smoke rings into the cool afternoon air. He looked at me with that insolent smile.

"The princess descends from her throne," he said, amused. I sat down beside him, resolutely pushing away the jitters that engulfed me every time I was around him.

"You wanted to talk to me?" I looked at Stu, noticing for the first time how beautiful his eyes were. So dark they were almost black, the desire in them showed plainly, and my heart gave an uncomfortable jog.

"Yeah, I did."

Stu sat up and tossed the butt of his cigarette onto the pavement in front of us, clasping his hands between his knees and looking down at the ground. He seemed almost nervous, and for a moment I was utterly confused. Then he looked up and into my eyes again, and the confusion vanished when I saw the determined look on his face.

"Ang, I want you to go out with me."

It wasn't a question, and I was so surprised that I couldn't think of a single thing to say. I just stared at him like an idiot, and Stu smiled at me. It was a different smile, not teasing or sarcastic at all, and my heart leaped for a reason that had nothing to do with nerves. Then logic took over, and I tore my gaze from his and laughed nervously. I said the first thing that came to my mind, and later, much later, I would look back on that statement and wonder if it had been the thing that had started it all.

"Stu, you can't be serious."

I glanced at him again. For a split second a look of pain crossed his face and I could have kicked myself. "I'm sorry," I amended hastily. "I didn't mean that the way it sounded – "

"Oh, I think you meant it exactly the way it sounded." Stu's eyes were cold now, and his voice was hard. "It's ridiculous to think that you'd want to go out with me. What's the matter, Ang? I'm not good enough for you?"

Dismay filled me, and I struggled to explain. "Of course you are. It's just that we're so different – "

"Different." Stu's tone was flat. "Yeah, I get it. You're a princess, and I'm definitely not a prince." He got to his feet and glared down at me, and for a moment I was intimidated. "Forget I said anything."

Stu turned and walked off, and I watched him go, his unique, loose-limbed stride almost graceful. Something stung me, and I tried to figure out what it was: surely not *regret*?

Then Megan was beside me, clutching my shoulder, and I tried to dismiss my garbled feelings and think up a plausible lie. I didn't know why, but I didn't want to tell her; it would have seemed like betraying Stu, somehow.

"What did he want?"

I pulled out of her grasp and gave her an annoyed look. "He wanted me to help him with English," I told her, smiling at the disappointed look on her face.

"That's it?" She looked so crestfallen that I laughed.

"What did you expect? A proposal?"

Meg shrugged philosophically. "Well, the way he always looks at you, I thought it might be something else."

I arranged my face into an expression of fond intolerance and got to my feet. "Sorry to disappoint you, Meg, but that was it."

The bell rang and we went back into the school, but for the rest of the day the look in Stu's eyes stayed with me, and I couldn't decide whether to feel sorry for him or afraid for myself.

Chapter Two

"Now, honey, you're sure you're going to be all right?"

Mom looked at me with fondness and concern at war in her eyes, and I smiled at her, trying not to let my frustration show. We'd been over this at least three times now: she was going to Calgary to visit her boyfriend, Ivan Romanovich, and I was finally being given the opportunity to stay by myself for the weekend instead of with her sister Jen. I had been pressuring her for the last six months, ever since I had turned seventeen, to let me show her I could handle the responsibility, and wonder of wonders, she had finally decided to let me prove it.

"Mom," I said with exaggerated patience, "I promise that I won't set fire to the house, kill myself, or end up pregnant. Satisfied?"

Mom reached out and gave my head a push. "Smartass." She pulled me close and hugged me. "Just because I think you can handle it doesn't mean I'm not going to worry."

"Worry all you want," I told her, hugging her back. "There isn't any reason to."

Mom pulled away and looked at me skeptically. "Are you telling me there isn't going to be a party?"

I took a deep breath and decided that honesty was probably the best policy. "Nooo … but not a very big one," I admitted, and Mom laughed.

"It's okay with me, as long as it doesn't get out of hand. I was young once, too, you know."

Mom knew all my friends, and she believed me when I told her that things weren't likely to get too wild. She put her hand under my chin and tipped my head up until I was looking into her eyes; her expression was serious. "No drugs."

I nodded. Drugs weren't my thing, and it wouldn't be a problem to let my friends know not to bring any. They were cool.

"No problem," I answered. Mom kissed me on the forehead and left the kitchen to finish packing. I smiled and hugged myself. I was looking forward to the party, of course, but even more, I was looking forward to showing Mom that I could be responsible and that her trust in me wouldn't be misplaced. Her opinion meant a great deal to me, and I had no intention of letting her down.

I went upstairs to my room to call Megan. "All right!" she cried when I told her the party was on. "Your mom is too cool, Ang. How did you get so lucky?"

"Genetics," I told her, and we fell to discussing who would be there, who was going with whom, who was breaking up, and so on. It was a fun conversation, and I had entirely forgotten the other day until Meg suddenly said, "Do you think Stu will show up?" Instantly my stomach was in knots.

Thanks for that, Meg. Just when I'd managed to forget him.

Aloud, I said, "I don't know. I hope not. Why the hell would he come to one of our parties?"

Meg let out a knowing laugh. "Come on, Ang, why do you think? Every time Stu watches you he looks like he has rape on his mind."

"Megan!" I was truly upset by her comment. The same thought had occurred to me more than once, and it wasn't a pleasant one. Meg must have heard the distress in my voice.

"Sorry, Ang," she said, sounding a little shamefaced. "That was a little crude of me. Seriously, though, he scares me."

"He scares *you*?" I exclaimed. "Meg, he terrifies me. What did I ever do to encourage him? Anything?" I sounded like a frightened child, and I told myself to grow up. The guy wasn't going to just jump me, for Christ's sake.

"Ang, you've never encouraged him, and I mean never." Meg's firm response made me feel better. "He's just got a case for you, don't ask me why." After a second she added, "Not that you're not attractive, but – "

I laughed shortly; it was a sound with little humor. "I'm not exactly his type, I know. No offense taken."

"What did Stu *really* say to you on the steps yesterday?" Meg's voice had taken on a wheedling quality I knew too well. She sensed something was up, and I briefly considered reiterating my earlier story but thought better of it. Why shouldn't I tell her?

"He asked me to go out with him." There was complete silence on the line for a moment, and I rolled my eyes: *Here it comes.*

"Omigod, you're *not* serious!" Megan sounded totally shocked, and I knew she was loving this. "*Stu Black* asked you to go out with him? I don't believe it! What did you say??"

"What do you think I said?" I asked her in exasperation. "I said no." When I remembered what I had really said (*Stu, you're not serious*) my face grew warm and that vague feeling of pity filled me again.

"Did he get mad?" Meg was breathless now, and I wished I hadn't told her.

"No, why would he?" I lied, anxious to change the subject. "Listen, are you and Darryl going to bring Jase tonight?"

"Uh, yeah, I guess so," Meg replied. "Unless he's going to come over early for some pre-party festivities, if you know what I mean. How about *you*?""

My face grew hot, and I resisted the urge to hang up on her. "Not quite yet," I said. "I've only known the guy for three months, Meg. Give it a chance."

"The perennial virgin," Meg said, amused. "When you finally lose it we're going to have to have a real rip-snorter, Ang."

"Fuck off," I told her in what I hoped was a good-natured tone. "See you later, hot pants."

Then I hung up the phone and started getting dressed for the party.

Chapter Three

By the time Meg and Darryl arrived with Jason I had forgotten all about Stu. We put on some great music, cracked open a case of beer, and got right down to it. I was in a great mood by the time everyone else arrived, immensely relieved that no party crashers had shown. I had asked everyone to keep the news of the party as quiet as possible, and it was good to know that my friends had taken my words to heart. There was no way I wanted the house destroyed on the first weekend Mom let me stay home alone.

When Jason and Darryl started playing a drinking game with their buddies, Meg and I went out on the front steps. It was getting hot and smoky inside, and the cool air felt wonderful on my flushed face. We sat in companionable silence for a moment, enjoying the night. September was fading into October, and while the days were still warm, the evenings had begun to have that nip in the air I particularly enjoyed. Fall was my favorite season, and it didn't last nearly long enough.

Once I was out in the fresh air I realized how much I had had to drink, and I leaned against Meg as a wave of dizziness swept over me. Pretty soon we were both giggling and swapping sips from the single beer we had brought out, and we didn't hear him come up the sidewalk until he was directly in front of us.

"Evening, ladies. Nice night, isn't it?"

I looked down, and when I saw Stu standing at the bottom of the steps my stomach did a somersault that made me feel queasy. Meg looked at him, and then at me, and I was certain we wore identical expressions of surprise. Stu mounted the steps slowly, giving me that lazy grin. When he reached us he took Meg's hands and pulled her to her feet.

"You don't mind, do you Meg?" She jerked her hands out of his grasp and stepped backward, looking outraged. "I want to have a word with Ang."

Meg put one hand on her hip, swaying slightly. "Actually, I *do* mind!" she declared, and Stu gave her a push. She tottered and almost fell over, and I started to rise to my feet. Stu put his other hand on my shoulder and stopped me, and at the touch of his fingers I froze.

"Go on inside, Meg," Stu told her, and she shot back, "Forget it, Stu! Anything you wanna say to Ang you can say in front of me."

I would have smiled if I hadn't been so nervous. Meg always defended me, even when I didn't want her to. "It's okay, Meg," I said, and she looked at me incredulously: *It is??* I gave her my best confident smile, and she frowned.

"Yeah?"

I nodded. "It's okay," I repeated. "He just wants to talk."

Stu gave Meg another push, and she started for the door, weaving. I thought of something, and called out to her. "Meg?"

Meg turned and almost fell, peering at me owlishly. "Don't mention this to Jase, okay?" Beside me, Stu laughed.

"Yes, *please*, don't mention this to Mister Iverson, Meg. I wouldn't want to have to fight him. Get it?"

Meg nodded doubtfully. "Scream if he tries anything, Ang."

I gave a weak chuckle and Meg turned and went into the house, the screen door slamming behind her. Behind me, I could hear music and the babble of voices; the sounds were vaguely comforting. Stu sat down beside me on the step and I moved away from the pressure of his thigh against mine. I looked at him uneasily, and he smiled at me. His expression softened.

"You're so beautiful," he told me, leaning forward and touching his lips gently to mine. "You're everything I've ever wanted. Won't you change your mind, Angel?"

My mind whirled; I was so surprised by his tenderness that I couldn't think of a thing to say. Stu took my hand and raised it to his lips, and I looked at his bent head.

Just do it better than last time, Ang … (sure you want to?)

I was conscious of my heart pounding furiously, and suddenly the beer made me feel nauseous instead of lightheaded.

"I'm already going out with someone, Stu," I said, and his head came up. "Besides, we have nothing in common, we have totally different friends, and frankly, I'm a little afraid of you."

That brief pain streaked through his eyes again, and Stu abruptly let go of my hand. My own gaze became worried, and he smiled, that insolent grin. His demeanor had shifted so quickly that the tender moment just passed might never have happened.

"I get it. Relax, Angel, I'm not going to attack you."

"Why doesn't that make me feel any better?" I retorted, and Stu's smile widened.

"You're learning," he said cryptically. "I still want you to know something, though." He leaned in close to me again and I backed up, regarding him warily.

"What?"

Stu reached out and captured my chin in his long fingers, tightening his grip as I tried to pull away. "I'm going to have you anyway."

He spoke matter-of-factly, his eyes darkening until they appeared black. Something rushed through me at his words, and I wasn't sure just what it was: fear, excitement ... desire?

"What are you talking about?" The most I could manage was a shocked whisper. "I just told you – "

Stu released my chin and made a dismissive gesture. I watched his slender fingers, fascinated. "I don't care what you told me, Angel. I don't care that you have a boyfriend. I don't even care if you want to. I'm going to have you anyway."

I struggled to focus. "Stu, you can't – "

He grabbed my chin again, and this time he turned my head to the side so he could whisper in my ear. "I can, and I will. I'm going to fuck you, Angel. Tonight."

I pulled away from him, my heart hammering, and summoned up all the anger I could, but underneath the fear lurked: fear, and a growing sense of unreality. I seized the anger and held onto it desperately, and to my relief it finally blotted out everything else.

"That's not funny, Stu." I tried to get up and make an indignant exit, but Stu jerked me back down, hard. He leaned toward me again, smiling in a predatory way that made me all too aware of how much bigger he was than me.

"I'm not joking." At the inexorable quality of his voice the panic broke through, and I jumped to my feet.

"I'm not listening to any more of this, Stu. I'm going back inside."

Stu rose quickly and grabbed my upper arms, his fingers digging into my skin.

"Don't make the mistake of thinking I'm not serious, Angel." His dark eyes bored into mine, and suddenly I was more than afraid; I was terrified.

"Stu – "

He cut off my reply by pulling me abruptly forward, and when his mouth slammed down on mine it sent a crazy shiver skittering down my back. Even as I tried to push him away I was aware of how he was making me feel: weak and dissolving, filled with an unnamable emotion I didn't want to call desire. Stu kept kissing me, taking all coherent thought away, and it wasn't until I felt his hand on my breast that I was able to pull away and slap him across the face with all my strength.

Instantly his hand flashed out and he slapped me back, hard. I toppled over and nearly fell down the stairs from the force of the blow, and I sat where I had fallen and stared up at him, my cheek burning and my head reeling. Stu sat down beside me again, and once more he grabbed me by the shoulders, shaking me hard.

"You don't want to hit me, Angel." His words, said in an icy, controlled voice that was worse than a shout, chilled me. "You don't *ever* want to hit me. Think you can remember that?"

My head bobbed like a puppet on a string, and Stu relaxed, letting go of my shoulders. He smiled at me, a lazy, sexy smile, and I thought faintly: *Who is this guy? Who the hell is he?*

"I'll be back at two thirty. Make sure everyone's gone by then."

I wondered if I had heard him correctly, and Stu laughed at the look on my face.

"What do you mean?" I whispered. Stu cupped my reddened cheek in one hand.

"What did I just tell you, Angel?" he said in a gently mocking tone. "I'm going to fuck you. Tonight. So make sure no one's around and

14

the door is unlocked. If you don't I'll come in anyway, but I won't be happy. You don't want that. Not after what you just did. Got it?"

"Are you threatening me?" I asked weakly.

Any minute now I'm going to wake up ... Then I can laugh, because it will all have been a dream ...

"Yeah." Stu's voice cut through my chaotic thoughts. "I'm threatening you, Angel. So be a good girl and do what I say."

He stood up and went down the steps, sauntering off into the night. I sat for a moment, dazed, unable to believe what had just happened. I jumped when a hand descended on my shoulder, and I jerked around to see Megan, looking at me in concern.

"You okay, Ang?" she asked, and I managed to nod and give a careless laugh.

"Sure," I told her, wondering why I was lying. "He just won't take no for an answer." Meg helped me to my feet.

"Well, he's gone now," she said, slinging an arm around my shoulders. "Let's get back to the party."

What party? I thought as the screen door closed behind us.

Chapter Four

For the rest of the party I was distracted and nervous, swinging between skepticism and terror. One moment I'd tell myself there was no way Stu could have been serious, and the next I'd want to curl up in a ball and hide. That ominous conversation was all I could think about, and I stayed out of the way, washing dishes and picking up after people, until finally Meg cornered me in the kitchen.

"Okay, what the hell is going on? " she demanded, hands on her hips, looking at me almost challengingly. "Ever since Stu was here it's like the party's over for you. What *happened* out there?"

I thought about trying to fob her off with a story but surprised myself by beginning to cry instead. A concerned frown on her face, Meg led me over to the kitchen table and pulled out a chair. I sank into it, sobbing, and she placed another chair close to mine and sat with her arms around me, letting me cry. When the storm had subsided somewhat, I pulled back and looked at her with an apologetic smile.

"I'm kind of freaked out," I said, and her expression changed from concerned to anxious.

"Did Stu do anything? What happened?" There was real worry in Meg's voice, and I loved her for it. I decided to tell her the truth.

"He hasn't done anything yet, but he says he's going to."

Meg's brow wrinkled. "What? What does that mean?"

"Meg, he says he's going to have sex with me. Tonight."

For a moment she looked astonished. "He can't be serious!'

"That's what I keep saying to myself," I said, nervously rubbing my thighs with the palms of my hands. "A guy doesn't just walk into a house and rape someone." I looked at her fearfully. "Does he?"

Meg hesitated only a second before making a face and shaking her head. "No! He knows you'd call the police in two seconds! Stu is a lot of things, Ang, but he's not stupid."

I tried to take comfort in her words, but it was hard. When I remembered that relentless determination in Stu's eyes, it filled me with panic all over again.

"You didn't see his face," I said, hating the quavering in my voice. "I'm scared, Meg. I'm really scared. What am I going to do?"

"Do?" Meg repeated, taking my hand and squeezing it. "You don't have to *do* anything, Ang. He's just trying to freak you out – you know, get back at you for turning him down. Don't take it seriously, for God's sake."

"You're probably right."

Meg knew I wasn't convinced, and she said, "Come on, Darryl and Jase and I are going to be here all night. What could happen?" Her words made sense, and I tried to relax.

"That's true," I said, wishing I could believe her. "What could happen? Hey, where is Jason, anyway? I haven't seen him in a while."

Meg rolled her eyes. "Too much quarter bounce. He passed out in the bedroom downstairs about an hour ago."

Great, I thought as we went back to the living room and I tried to join the party. *Some help he'll be if something does happen.*

By two o'clock, everyone was gone but Megan, Darryl, and Jason. Jason was still dead to the world, sprawled on a bed in the spare room, snoring, and Meg and Darryl had gone upstairs to my mother's room. I didn't get ready for bed myself, knowing that I wouldn't be able to relax until two thirty had come and gone.

As I tidied the house I kept up a running inner dialogue, telling myself there was no way Stu would come back. This was real life, not some cheap novel, and that things like that might make good reading, but they certainly didn't really happen. I almost had myself convinced, and by two forty-five I breathed a sigh of relief.

See, Ang? Meg was right. He was just trying to freak you out.

At that moment there was a loud pounding on the back door, and I froze in the act of picking up an empty beer bottle, my heartbeat cascading into a runaway frenzy. I heard it again, impatient pounding and what sounded like a good, solid kick against the door, and I hurried into the kitchen, barely able to breathe past the terror clogging my throat. I saw Stu through the glass panel in the back door, and he was angry. I went over to the door and stood in front of it, looking at him in disbelief.

"Open this goddamn door, Angie."

Stu's mouth was a thin line and I could see his hands at his sides, clenched into fists. I shook my head and his eye became dark slits. He stepped back and kicked the door as hard as he could, and it rattled alarmingly in its frame. I heard a faint splintering noise, and my heart leaped in a way that made me lightheaded. Was this really happening?

From somewhere behind me I could hear Meg's voice, but the words didn't register: "Ang? What's going on? Are you okay?"

"I said open the fucking door, or I'll kick it in." Stu's voice was low and threatening.

"Want to see me do it?"

He raised his booted foot again, and I shook my head frantically. I reached out and unlocked the door with trembling fingers, and he pushed it open and charged into the room, backing me up against the kitchen counter and grabbing my arms.

"I can see I'm going to have to teach you how to listen, Angel."

Stu's pelvis ground against mine and there was nowhere for me to go. I could feel him against my hip, hard and insistent, and the panic overflowed. I hitched in a breath and started to scream, but before I could make a sound he drew back his arm and slapped me across the face as hard as he could, so hard that I lost my footing and fell to the cold tile floor.

Stu was at my side in an instant, pushing me all the way down on my back, his hands on either side of my head. He kissed me with curious tenderness, and the sensation it provoked was totally at odds with the pain in my head and the ringing in my ears. He explored my mouth in a delicate, teasing way, and although I began to twist my head from side to side, I felt a response beginning in the pit of my stomach and spreading outward.

"What the hell are you *doing*? Get away from her!"

Stu raised his head at the sound of Darryl's voice, and I used the opportunity to push him away and get to my feet. Darryl and Meg were standing several feet away, and I went over to Meg. She put her arms around me and I began to cry, so glad they were there that I nearly broke down completely. Darryl repeated his question.

"What the fuck are you doing here?"

Stu looked back at him coolly. "None of your goddamn business, Anderson. This is between Angie and me."

Beside me, Meg exploded. "The hell it is, Stu! It sounded like you were breaking the goddamn door down, and it looked to me like you were attacking her!"

Stu looked at Meg with contempt. "Shut up, Meg. Good girls only speak when they're spoken to."

Darryl was across the room in an instant, and he grabbed Stu by the jacket. He was at least three inches shorter, but heavier and muscled, not afraid of Stu in the least.

"Don't fucking talk to her like that, you asshole. Angie didn't invite you in, so get the hell out."

Stu's eyes narrowed, and he looked at me. "I don't know about that," he said, breaking Darryl's grip on his jacket and stepping back. "You opened the door for me, didn't you, Angel?"

"Only after you threatened to kick it in!" I cried, fear seizing me once again at the renewed anger in his eyes. "Get out of here, Stu! Just go!"

I buried my face in Meg's shoulder and burst into tears, and Darryl said, "You heard her, Black. Get out. *Now.*"

"Sure. No problem." I looked up in surprise at the easy tone of Stu's voice, and he smiled at me, a cold smile that didn't reach his eyes. "I'll be back, Angel. Count on it. I *always* get what I want."

He turned and walked out the door, and I collapsed against Megan, crying so hard that I couldn't catch my breath.

"Holy shit," she breathed, as she turned and began to walk me toward the stairs. "Holy shit, Ang, oh my God …"

I could hear Darryl slamming and locking the door, and the only thing I could think was: *What good is that? He's going to get back in no matter what.*

Chapter Five

I had an instant of blessed amnesia when I woke the next morning, and for a moment the bright fall sunshine flooding through the blinds to puddle on the floor made it seem like any other Saturday morning. Then I remembered, and the anxiety came rushing back. I curled up under the covers, trying to make sense of what had happened.

I'll be back, Angel. I always get what I want.

I shivered at the memory of the flat, matter-of-fact sound of those words. I told myself he had just been trying to scare me, but it was hard to be convincing. Stu had seemed deadly serious, and all of a sudden I felt foolish for taking my safe, protected existence for granted. There was a tap on the door, interrupting my thoughts, and Meg poked her head in.

"You awake, Ang?"

I sat up, the covers pooling around my waist. "Come on in."

Meg entered the room and closed the door behind her. She came over to the bed sat beside me, looking at me with a worried expression that made the anxiety worse.

"What the fuck was *that* last night?" she asked.

I shrugged, trying to be nonchalant. "Stu told me he'd be back. He was mad because the door was locked."

Meg gaped at me. "You make it sound like he had every right to be here! Jesus, Ang, if we hadn't come in I think he would have – "

I interrupted her. "Come on, Meg, he was just being Stu Black, Mister Tough Guy. I think he likes me, yeah, but I have a hard time believing that he really would have raped me."

"*I* don't. You should have seen what it looked like from where me and Darryl were standing."

Meg's reply was emphatic, and I wanted her to drop it. I *needed* her to drop it - it was essential for my sanity that I keep up the pretense of skepticism, because the alternative was unthinkable. I held up one hand.

"I'm glad you guys were there. Really. But I don't want to talk about it, okay?" Meg looked puzzled, but she said, "Okay, Ang. You want me to hang around today?"

I nodded gratefully. "Would you? I'd feel a lot better if you did."

Meg reached out and gave me a hug. "Sure." Then her expression changed, and she gave an impatient exclamation. "Oh, shit! I can't. It's Sandy's birthday today, and Mom'll kill me if I'm not around to help out."

My heart sank at her words, and I realized how afraid I was of being alone. It made me angry. Safety was something I had never had to think about before, and everything felt different now. I forced a smile and said, "It's okay, Meg. I've got a lot of cleaning to do, anyway."

Meg rubbed my shoulder. "I'll keep in touch by phone. Just in case – well, just in case."

I got off the bed. "Jesus, calm down, will you? Stu's not a serial killer, for Christ's sake."

Meg got to her feet and took my shoulders in her hands. It reminded me of Stu's inflexible grip the night before, and I had to resist the urge to jerk away.

"Ang, I don't think the guy's exactly stable. I'm worried about you, you know?"

I stepped backward, relieved when her hands fell away. "Well, don't be. I'm a big girl, Meg. I can take care of myself." I bent down and scooped up my robe, pulling it on. "And don't tell Jason about this, okay? I don't want him and Stu fighting."

"I'd better go and tell Darryl not to talk to him, then," Meg said, walking across the room. "I'm sure he has some macho plan all worked out in his head by now."

She left the room, and I belted the robe around my waist, trying to quell the fear inside me. I went out of my bedroom and crossed the hall, on my way to the bathroom. I almost ran right into Jason, who was stumbling out as I started in, and I laughed in spite of how I was feeling. His hair was standing up in crazy whorls, his shirt was rumpled and stained, and his expression left little doubt about how he was feeling.

"You look like hell," I observed, and he looked at me sourly.

"Thanks. I feel like shit, too. Guess I'm a matched set."

I kissed him on the cheek. "I'm going to take a shower. Care to join me?"

Jason tried to smile. "I'm not up for it right now, Ang. I'll take a raincheck, okay?"

I reached out and ruffled his hair. "Go and lie down before you fall down."

Jason grimaced and turned away, and I went into the bathroom. As I showered I resolutely tried to push the whole mess with Stu out of my mind, but he was there no matter how hard I tried not to think of him. All I could see in my mind's eye were those, dark, dangerous eyes and unyielding hands, and my cheeks burned at the memory of his lips against mine.

Get it together, Ang! You have a boyfriend, and it's not Stu Black! After last night, you wouldn't exactly want it to be, would you?

Such thoughts were all very well and good, but I couldn't deny that behind the fear there was an undeniable attraction, and that upset me most of all. When I was dressed I went downstairs and into the kitchen. Darryl and Jason were slumped at the kitchen table, and Meg and I exchanged knowing grins.

"Awww, look at the poor beer babies," Meg crooned, going up behind Darryl and putting her arms around his neck. "Feeling a teensy bit hung over, are we?"

Darryl tried to shake her off and failed. "Fuck off," he grunted resentfully. "How come you never have a hangover, you bitch?"

"Because I throw up before I go to sleep," Meg answered, and I laughed. Darryl twisted around and looked at her.

"No shit?"

She nodded and kissed him on the nose. "No shit. Want some breakfast?"

He grimaced. "Ugh, don't mention food."

I went over to the sink and opened the cupboard beside it, taking down a glass and filling it with cold water. Coming over to the table, I offered it to Jason.

"Water, babe?"

He looked at me blearily and smiled. "Thanks." He chugged the glass in about three seconds, and I warned, "Watch it, chum. That's what got you in trouble last night."

This time even Darryl laughed, and I began to relax. Meg and I had some cereal, but the boys didn't even consider eating. After I had rinsed the bowls and put them in the dishwasher, Jason came over to me and put his arms around my waist. I leaned against him, enjoying his familiar safeness, and he squeezed me and kissed the side of my neck.

"I'm gonna go home and sleep for the next sixteen hours," he told me, and I turned around in his arms and kissed him.

"That's what you get for being an incipient alcoholic," I said lightly, and he slapped me on the behind.

"Ha, ha. You're a real laff riot, Ang, you know that?"

Jason looked over at Darryl, who was now resting his head on his folded arms. "You gonna give me a ride, man?"

"Only because your house is three minutes from mine." Darryl's voice was muffled. He raised his head and spoke to Meg. "You coming, babe?"

She nodded reluctantly, looking at me, and I frowned at her. "Yeah, I have to get home."

They made their way to the door, and before she went through it Meg hugged me quickly. "I'll call you."

I gave her a push. "Have the cavalry ready."

She made a face at me and followed Darryl down the driveway at the side of the house to his car. I waved at her, blew Jason a kiss, and shut the back door with an odd sense of relief. I didn't have to pretend anymore, and I could finally replay in my mind what had happened the night before without fear of interruption.

I was in the living room, picking up empties and dirty dishes, when I heard a voice come from the kitchen. The plate I was holding slid from my hand to the rug and my heart was suddenly in my throat again, making it hard to breathe.

"Knock, knock," Stu said, strolling into the living room and giving me that easy smile. "Anyone home?"

Chapter Six

"What are you doing here?" I fought to keep my voice steady and Stu came toward me, still smiling.

"You've got a lousy memory for such a bright girl, Angel. I told you I'd be back. I'm here to get what I should have had last night."

My heart gave a suffocating bound and I backed away as he came closer. "Stu, get out. I don't want you here."

Stu reached me and placed his hands on my shoulders, pulling me forward and giving me a gentle kiss. "That doesn't matter. I want to be here. I've waited long enough, Angel."

I looked at him in disbelief. "What the hell are you talking about?"

Stu laughed, a curiously gentle sound. "I've wanted you for the last year, Angel. You wouldn't believe how much. I'm not going to wait any more. I told you, I'm going to have you."

I pulled away from him, suddenly infuriated at the patient tone of his voice. "No, you're not! You've got about three seconds to get out of here before I call the police!"

Stu laughed again, but this time the sound was hard, and his eyes were angry as he seized my upper arms. He jerked me forward until our bodies were pressed together, and I could feel his erection against my belly.

"Really?" he asked. "Tell me, how are you going to do that when you're on your back and I'm between those gorgeous thighs of yours?"

He kissed me again, teasingly, and in spite of my terror I felt a tingle deep inside. I pushed against his chest and Stu released me. When I saw the determination in his eyes I began to cry.

"Please, Stu, just go. *Please.*"

Stu shook his dark head, and once more the fear threatened to overwhelm me. "Forget it, Angel. I'm going to fuck you. Come on, let's get on with it."

He took my arm and began to steer me toward the stairs, and I jerked away and stared at him. "No! *You* forget it, Stu! I'm *not* going to have sex with you!"

Tears slipped down my cheeks, and I hovered on the edge of hysteria. Suddenly, shockingly, Stu slapped me. Hard. I staggered from the force of the blow, my hand to my cheek, and Stu seized me, his fingers like iron.

"You don't seem to understand. This is about what *I* want. And I want you. Don't make this hard for me, or I'll hurt you."

I was literally speechless, more frightened than I had ever been in my life. My breath came in panicked gasps, and one of Stu's hands left my upper arm to caress my breast with casual propriety. His eyelids grew heavy, and he turned me around and wrapped both arms around me, urging me toward the stairs.

"Trust me, Angel. I'll have you screaming for more."

My feet seemed to move of their own accord, and before I knew it we were going up the stairs.

"Stu, please, you don't want to do this," I managed to say. "It'll be rape."

Stu's arms tightened around me, and he chuckled in my ear. "You're wrong on both counts. I *do* want to do this, and it won't be rape."

We reached the top of the stairs, and he glanced into my room before letting me go and pushing me inside. When the door had closed behind us I got as far away from him as I could, huddling on the far side of my unmade bed. Stu sat on the edge, looking at me with something like pity. "Come here, Angel."

I shook my head and a spasm of irritation crossed his face. He reached out and captured my ankle in one strong hand, pulling me across the bed toward him. His hands slid up my hips to my waist and lingered there, and he looked at me with reluctant admiration.

"God, you're beautiful," he said, low, and leaned over me. I turned my head away and Stu buried his face in my neck, inhaling deeply. "You even smell beautiful."

His voice was muffled, and his fingers reached for the front of my shirt and grasped the top button. Reflexively I pushed it away, and Stu sat up with a swiftness that frightened me still more. He looked at me warningly and hooked his fingers in my open collar, ripping the shirt down the front in one brutal motion. The buttons popped off and rolled in different directions, and he smiled at me, a cruel, mocking smile.

"Take off your clothes."

I blinked at him, and he repeated what he had said. It wasn't a request, and in spite of the fear I began to beg. "Stu, please, don't make me do this – "

Stu's hand snaked out again and tore at my bra, and before I knew what had happened he was holding it in his fist and my shoulders burned where the straps had dug into my skin.

"Want me to do the rest, Angel?" he asked softly. "I'm willing, believe me. I'm not going to be too happy when I get down to bare skin, though, and you might find yourself hurting. But say the word."

I sat up and removed what was left of my shirt with shaking fingers, crying. "Stu, please, you don't understand – " I got to my feet and began to unbutton my jeans, pleading with him.

"What don't I understand?" Stu asked in a tone of false concern. "Talk to your Uncle Stu."

I pushed the jeans down to my knees and then to my ankles, looking at him in despair. "I've never – I mean, me and Jason haven't – "

Stu smiled with real pleasure. "You've never what, Angel?"

My eyes begged him: *Please, don't make me say it. Please …*

He looked at me, expectant, and I said haltingly, "I've never … had sex before."

Stu's eyebrows shot up, and he smirked at me, leaning casually back on one elbow. "You're a *virgin*, Angel?"

He made it sound like a venereal disease, and I flushed, horribly embarrassed, and nodded.

"This is going to be even better than I thought," he said. "A virgin. That's a real bonus." Stu gestured to me. "Keep going."

I looked at him in disbelief. "Doesn't that mean anything to you?" I cried, and he laughed out loud.

"Sure. It means I'll be the first. I like that, Angel. No, scratch that. I *love* it. Now get the rest of your clothes off before I have to do it for you."

I began to cry again, stepping out of my jeans and standing in front of him with my arms crossed over my breasts. Stu caught me by one wrist and pulled me down onto his lap. In one easy motion he pinned both my arms underneath one of his, and his other hand skated lightly over my breasts. He smiled as my nipples hardened, then bent his head and took one in his mouth, his tongue teasing it playfully. An electric shock coursed through me and I stiffened against him.

"Oh, Angel-baby," Stu murmured against my breast. "You feel so goddamn good. I can't wait to be inside you." He eased me onto my back on the bed and covered my body with the length of his, pinning me under him.

"Stu, please – "

"That's what I want to hear," Stu told me, raising his head to look into my eyes. "Only how about if you wait until your legs are wrapped around me?"

I looked away in shame, my face hot. "Don't say things like that."

He took my chin in his long fingers and turned my face back to him. A sensuous smile lingered on his lips, and I looked into his eyes, breathless. "Why? I like shocking you, Angel – you being a virgin and all." He raised himself up on his elbows. "You ready?"

Panic flooded me and I shook my head. Stu laughed. "Doesn't matter," he told me. "I am."

He reached down and began to unbuckle his belt, and the sound, the tinkle of metal on metal, made it all real, galvanizing me into action. I began to twist from side to side, and Stu placed one hand on either side of my head, staring at me with smoldering eyes.

"Stop it. Right now. This is happening whether you want it to or not, Angel. Don't make me mad."

I responded out of blind terror, raising myself up and bucking him off in one convulsive movement. Stu fell off the bed, and I jumped up and ran for the door. I only made it halfway across the room before he caught me, and his hands were like steel as he seized me and threw me back onto the bed. He towered over me for a moment, then reached out and twisted a handful of my hair around his fist. Then he slapped me, first on one side of the face, then the other. He jerked my head back brutally, grabbing my breast in one hand. He twisted it, his fingers tightening on the nipple and pinching viciously, and the pain was immediate, incredible.

I shrieked and Stu slammed his palm over my mouth, hissing in my ear. "Shut up! You make another sound and I'll break your arm. I warned you, Angie. I wanted this to be good for you, but if you resist I'll take you anyway, and it won't be good at all."

I looked at him through tears of pain, my chest heaving as I gasped for air. I had never known such fear, and it occurred to me that he could actually kill me. I moaned against his hand and closed my eyes, wondering what I had done to deserve this.

Stu took his hand away from my mouth and stood up. He shrugged out of his leather coat, letting it fall to the floor, and then stripped off his shirt, tossing it aside. Then he finished with his belt, pushing his own jeans down and kicking them away.

I turned my head away as more and more of his skin was revealed, feeling lightheaded with terror. When Stu fell on top of me again I could feel his erection against my leg, flesh against flesh, and the thought of him inside me brought hysteria bubbling to the surface.

"Stu, please, oh God *please* don't, I don't want to I really don't want to – "

Stu placed his palm over my mouth again, gently this time, and shook his head. "*I* want to, Angel. That's all that really matters. You'll learn to love it, wait and see."

He took his hand from my mouth and braced it on the bed beside my head, getting between my legs. Then he got up on his knees and tore my panties on one side and then the other, pulling them out from under me and dropping them on the floor. He took one of my wrists in each hand, imprisoned them over my head, and looked down at me, helpless beneath him. A smile crossed his face, a satisfied, possessive smile, and I was filled with anger for a moment, in spite of the fear.

"Nice," Stu murmured. "Very nice. Ready, Angel?"

"No!" I cried. "No, Stu, don't – "

He responded by lowering his head to mine and kissing me, and when I felt the tip of him probing into me I panicked. Stu broke the kiss and grabbed my hips, his own pushing forward instinctively, and suddenly he was halfway inside me. I looked at his face, his eyes half closed and his mouth slack, and begged, knowing it was too late but unable to help it.

"Oh God, please stop, *please* – "

Stu smiled and looked right into my eyes. "It's way too late to stop now."

He gave another thrust and I felt a jagged pain deep inside that made me cry out. Stu dropped onto my chest and buried his face in my neck. "I've dreamed of this."

Later, I wouldn't be sure I'd even heard him say those words. It seemed far too vulnerable a thing for Stu Black to say, especially in the middle of a rape. Stu's hips continued to thrust, and as he moved rhythmically the pain increased until it felt like he was jamming a broom handle in and out of me.

I began to moan, twisting my head from side to side, and he put a strong palm against my mouth, muffling my cries. His breath began to come in ragged gasps, and the thrusts became harder and faster until I thought I would be torn apart. Finally Stu arched his back and cried out himself, and when he collapsed on top of me, his skin was warm and lightly filmed with sweat.

"Oh God," he gasped. "I've waited so long to do that. Christ, was it good. Angel, you're so amazing ..."

He buried his face in my neck again, and I could feel his breath on my skin. I lay motionless beneath him, aware that he was still inside me, feeling the weight of him, and suddenly I was filled with fury. I pushed against him, needing to be free of him, frantic just to have him gone.

"Get off me!" When he didn't move, I pushed harder. "Get off me, Stu! Get off!" My voice rose until I was nearly screaming, and Stu propped himself on his elbows and looked down at me.

"Why so upset, Angel? Wasn't it everything you dreamed it would be?" His mocking tone made me even angrier, and I beat against his chest with my fists.

"Get off me, you bastard!" The fury in my voice seemed to surprise him. "You got what you came for, now get off me!"

Stu obliged, withdrawing from me and getting off the bed to retrieve his pants. Before he pulled them on he looked down at himself. "Well, you didn't lie."

I realized what he meant and turned away from him, feeling used and violated. What had been so important to me seemed to mean nothing to him, and I vowed that I would die before I'd let him see how upset I was. I turned my back to him and pulled the covers up to my neck, waiting for him to leave.

I could hear Stu pulling on his boots, but instead of heading for the door he sat down beside me on the bed and placed a hand on my shoulder. I cringed and moved away.

"Get out of here. Just go." My voice trembled despite my efforts to control it, and it made me hate him even more. "I never want to see you again."

When he spoke, Stu's voice was matter-of-fact, as if we were discussing the weather or a science test.

"Sorry you feel that way, Angel, but you're going to be seeing a lot of me. This is only the beginning."

33

Chapter Seven

I sat up and turned around, clutching the blankets to my chest, staring at Stu in disbelief. "The beginning?" I choked out. "The beginning of *what*? You already raped me. What more could you possibly want?"

Stu's eyes hardened and he moved toward me, crowding me against the wall as I backed up to get away from him. "That wasn't rape," he ground out through clenched teeth. "Don't you say it was."

"What?" I thought I must have heard him incorrectly. "Did you just say that it wasn't rape?" He nodded curtly, and I let out a laugh that hovered on the edge of hysteria. "Funny, I thought that when the girl *isn't willing* it's called rape. What the fuck do you call it? Seduction?"

I continued to laugh, finding the entire situation so ludicrous that it was either laugh or scream, and I didn't want to scream. If I did, I might not be able to stop.

Stu slapped me again, and my head flew back and hit the wall. I came back at him a lot harder and a lot madder than he expected. I balled my hand into a fist and punched him just as hard as I could. I knew an instant of joyous satisfaction when I felt my fist connect with his jaw and saw his head snap to the side, but an instant later he grabbed my head and rammed it into the wall.

Lights and stars exploded just beyond my field of vision and dull agony flared at the base of my skull. Stu's hands circled my neck and he began to squeeze. My breath was cut off abruptly and panic filled me. I began to claw desperately at his fingers, but I couldn't budge them. I was becoming weaker with every passing second, and he kept squeezing, his face red, his eyes black. All I could see was the fury in those eyes; they became my entire world, and when the darkness began to descend I welcomed it eagerly, glad to escape. The need to breathe didn't seem so urgent any more, and as my muscles relaxed he suddenly let go.

The air that trickled down my throat initiated an instinctive response and I began to gag and cough, breathing in great, tearing gasps. Stu sat back, glaring at me resentfully, and to my astonishment he said, "Don't you *ever* fucking hit me again, Angie. Next time I'll kill you. I mean it." I struggled to draw air into my swelling throat, so terrified that my mind was utterly blank.

Stu placed one palm against the side of my face, a curiously tender gesture, and I just looked at him with wide, frightened eyes, feeling like I was mired in a nightmare. He leaned forward and kissed me, his lips as gentle as his hands had been brutal, and I couldn't react at all.

"Don't even think about going to the police, Angel," he said. "If you do I'll find out, and I'll make you sorry you were fucking born. Understand?" I nodded and Stu smiled at me, a normal, affectionate smile that was more frightening than that predatory grin. "Good girl. Because I love you, Angel. I always have."

He turned and left the room, closing the door softly behind him. As soon as I knew he was really gone I collapsed onto the bed and screamed into the pillow. I kept screaming, in spite of the pain in my throat and the sick throbbing in my head; at that point, it was scream or go crazy.

Finally, when the screams had tapered off and I was lying exhausted on top of the rumpled covers, a shrill ringing penetrated the harsh noises I was making, and I realized it was the phone. I picked up the extension that sat on my bedside table and pressed the "talk" button, hoping it wasn't my mother. If I sounded half as hysterical as I felt, I'd scare her to death.

"Hello?"

"Ang?" It was Meg, and she picked up on my tone immediately. "What's wrong? Are you okay?" I struggled for an answer.

Aside from the fact that Stu Black just raped me, yeah, I'm good ...

"No, I'm not okay, Meg." My voice was hoarse and trembling. "Stu just left, and he -" I couldn't bring myself to say it, but I didn't need to.

"Oh Jesus, Ang," Megan breathed, and it sounded almost like a prayer. "Jesus ... hold on, okay, hon? I'm coming right over."

"Thanks, Meg ..." Anything else I had wanted to say was lost in a renewed freshet of tears, and I dropped the phone on the floor and curled into a ball under the covers, hugging my knees to my chest and crying so hard I couldn't catch my breath.

Raped, I thought in agony. *I've been raped.*

It seemed to take hours for Meg to arrive, and when I finally heard a hesitant tapping at my bedroom door I jumped even though I knew it was her. Panic surged into my throat, and I told myself to stop being ridiculous.

"Ang?" Meg came over to the bed and sat down, and when I felt the weight of her beside me and the warmth of her hand on my back, my control broke yet again and I sat up and threw my arms around her.

She held me tightly, and when she spoke again it sounded as though she was crying, too. "How could he do that to you? Oh my God, Ang, I'm sorry, I'm so goddamn sorry …"

Meg rubbed my back and stroked my hair, and eventually I quieted and pulled away from her, suddenly aware that I was still naked and feeling absurdly ashamed. I pulled the covers up and clutched them around my chest, and Meg looked at me with wet eyes. I tried to smile.

"Thanks for coming, Meg." She smiled and touched the side of my cheek with her fingers.

"Try to keep me away. What are you going to do, Ang? Are you going to go to the police?"

I shivered, remembering Stu's parting words. "I don't know," I told her slowly. "Stu told me that if I did he'd find out, and he'd make me sorry."

"He'd make you sorry?" Meg repeated my words in disbelief. "Jesus Christ, Ang, he *raped* you! You have to report this!"

I knew she was right, but the fear was stronger than my sense of outrage, and before I could stop myself I said to her, "What are the cops going to do, Meg? Arrest him? Maybe they would, but they won't keep him in jail. And the second he got out, he'd find me."

I closed my eyes, the fear expanding inside me and stealing my breath as I thought of Stu's hands around my neck, squeezing …

"Well, we have to do *something*." I opened my eyes and looked at Meg, and at the righteous anger on her face something softened inside and I felt a little bit better. "He can't just get away with this!"

"He already has, Meg." I plucked at the blankets with nerveless fingers and forced out my next words. "He said it's only the beginning."

"*What?*" Meg nearly screamed the word, and I jumped. "What does *that* mean?"

"I think it means he considers me his girlfriend now."

Meg shook her head as if she hadn't heard me properly. "That's insane," she declared. "Stu can't *make* you go out with him, Ang."

My eyes filled with tears again and for a brief, bitter moment I hated myself; I felt like such a coward. "You know what, Meg? I think he can."

"No." Meg reached out and took me in her arms again. "No, Ang, he can't. And he isn't going to. Not if I have anything to say about it."

I surrendered myself to the safety of her embrace, wishing I could believe her.

You don't understand, Meg, I thought in despair as the tears rolled down my cheeks. *You really don't understand at all.*

Chapter Eight

Meg stayed with me the rest of the day. We cleaned up the house, and while I was grateful for the help and her company, there was a curious tension between us that I had never been aware of before. I knew she was baffled by my reluctance to go to the police, and I could tell she was dying to know more about what had happened between Stu and I. I deliberately kept myself busy, not wanting to even think about it, much less talk about it.

Images played over and over on the screen of my mind, and although anger surged through me at the possessive, unapologetic way Stu had taken me, I couldn't deny the response that happened inside me every time I remembered the way he had shuddered and groaned. It was a confusing combination of excitement and dread, and I wondered miserably what the hell was wrong with me.

How in God's name could I feel anything but disgust for Stu? He had *raped* me!

When the house was clean and the dishwasher going, Meg sat beside me on the couch in the living room, wiping the back of one hand across her sweaty forehead.

"We should have made Darryl and Jase help us," she commented. At the mention of Jason my stomach clenched into a slick knot, and I looked at her.

"What am I going to tell him?" I asked. "He's going to want to *kill* Stu."

"Let him." The flat sound of the words made me wince. "It's not as if Stu doesn't deserve it, Ang."

"Meg, you don't know what Stu is capable of." My voice was high and pleading, and Meg frowned at me and leaned forward.

"What did he do to you, Ang?"

My hand went instinctively to my throat, and I swallowed against the tears that wanted to escape again. "He told me that it wasn't rape," I began, disregarding the looked of shocked incredulity Meg gave me. "When I told him that it was, he hit me. I hit him back, and … " I trailed off, wondering how to explain without it sounding too bad.

Why are you protecting him?? He almost killed you, for Christ's sake! What is wrong *with you, Angie?*

Haltingly, I told Meg what Stu had done, and the look of horror that came over her face didn't make me feel vindicated, only more terrified.

"Oh my God, Ang, he's crazy," she breathed, and I wanted to scream at her to shut up.

Instead, I shrugged helplessly. "So you tell me, Meg. What am I supposed to do?"

Meg was saved from answering by the ringing of the phone, and I went into the kitchen and picked it up, sure it would be my mother. It was a terrible shock when Stu's voice greeted my ear instead, and I almost dropped the receiver.

"Hey there, Angel-baby," he drawled.

"Stu," I managed to say. "What do you want?"

Who cares what he wants? Tell him to go to hell!

"You, Angel. Always you." The intimate tone of his voice brought a furious blush to my cheeks, and shame filled me at his insinuation. "God, that was so fantastic this morning. You have no idea how long I've wanted to do that."

"If you've been waiting to rape someone, then I guess you got your wish," I said bitterly. I told myself I didn't care if he got angry; his feelings were the least of my concerns at the moment.

"Angel, Angel," Stu said in a dangerous voice. "I seem to remember telling you not to call it rape."

"It WAS rape!" I screamed. "I don't care what you think, you selfish bastard! It was RAPE!" There was absolute silence on the line for a moment, and in spite of my anger I began to be afraid.

"Do I have to come over there and teach you another lesson?" Stu's voice was emotionless, deadly and frightening, and the hand holding the phone began to tremble. "I can do that. Right now." I didn't say anything, trying desperately to show him that I wasn't afraid.

"ANSWER ME!" The intensity of the shout almost made me scream, and suddenly I was shaking all over, as terrified as I had been that morning.

"N – No," I stuttered, and Stu asked, "No what, Angel?"

"No, you don't have to come over here," I said, gripping the phone more tightly.

"Why? Why don't I have to come over there? Tell me."

I hated myself for playing his cruel game, but I was so frightened … "I don't need another lesson," I said, tears spilling down my cheeks. *Please,* I thought incoherently. *Oh God, please …*

"Why not?" Stu asked in a silky voice. "Why don't you need another lesson, Angel? What did you just learn?"

I had to force the words out through cold lips. "That it – it wasn't rape."

He chuckled, a low, amused sound. "What was that? I don't think I heard you, Angel."

"It wasn't rape."

I had hit rock bottom. I couldn't stand up to Stu; I couldn't stop being afraid; I couldn't even express my own opinion. In my own mind I had become a whore – *his* whore. I cried silently, wishing I could die and end this nightmare.

"I can't wait to fuck you again." I flinched at his words and cried harder. "You belong to me now, don't you?" His tone dared me to disagree, but I couldn't make myself say it.

"*Don't* you?" There was no mistaking the threat in his voice this time.

"Yes." I could only whisper.

"Yes what, Angel-baby?" I knew Stu was enjoying my pain, and it made me hate him even more.

Just say it. You know you don't mean it, so what does it matter?

It mattered, though. It mattered a hell of a lot, and I knew it.

"Yes, I – I belong to you."

Stu laughed, a sensuous sound that sent a chill racing down my spine. "That's right. You do. See you later, Angel."

He hung up and I hurled the cordless phone across the room, screaming. I collapsed to the floor and pounded my fists on the tiles, feeling like an animal in a cage. Suddenly Megan was beside me, and I shrieked at the touch of her hand on my shoulder. I looked at her in agony and said the first thing that came to my mind.

"I'm a hostage, Meg." I could hardly get the words out, but I knew she heard me. "Even when he's not with me, I'm a hostage."

Chapter Nine

Megan left reluctantly. I finally convinced her I needed to be alone so she would stop hovering around me like a hen with a single chick. I needed time before Mom came home to really think about what had happened and try to come to terms with it somehow. I didn't want her to know: there was nothing she could do about it, and getting her all worried seemed pointless to me.

I didn't want to think about *why* she couldn't do anything; that would have meant acknowledging the hold Stu already had over me, and I was unwilling to do that. It seemed unbelievable to me that one person could just imprison another, and every time I thought about my last conversation with Stu (*you belong to me now, Angel, don't you?*) my mind would reject the idea and that sense of unreality would come over me again.

I was lying on the couch, dozing, when I heard the back door open, and I wondered fuzzily why Mom was home already.

"Mom?" I called out as I sat up, and when I heard his voice I nearly screamed.

"Hi, beautiful."

Stu walked into the living room and my heart leaped. I couldn't move, and he came over and sat beside me on the couch, reaching for me as if he had every right to be there. He put his hand on the back of my neck and pulled my head forward, and when our lips met I fought the sensations that rose inside me.

Stu kissed me with barely restrained passion, and I tried to pull away but he wouldn't release me. Finally I jerked away from him and backed up, my breathing uneven and my heart racing.

Hmmm ... wouldn't be because you want *him, would it, Ang?* A nasty little voice in the back of my mind spoke up gleefully, the one that never hesitated to point out my worst mistakes and most obvious flaws. I ignored it and concentrated on Stu, who was looking at me with a knowing smile.

"You're going to want me before you know it, Angel. Come here."

I shook my head, getting to my feet. "No, I'm not. Get out of here, Stu. Right now."

Stu chuckled and stood up, coming toward me. He shook his head, and his black hair brushed against the collar of the denim shirt he wore.

"We've already been through this, Angel. You're mine, and I'm not going anywhere. Now come here."

Stu closed the distance between us in two strides and wrapped his arms around me, dipping his head and kissing my neck. At the touch of his lips on my skin a shiver snaked its way down my spine, and he trailed tiny, teasing kisses up the side of my face until he reached my mouth. I turned my head to the side, and Stu laughed deep in his throat.

"Come on, give in. You know you want to."

His satisfied, possessive tone sent sudden fury cascading through me, and I pushed against his chest with all my strength. Caught off guard, Stu stumbled and nearly fell, and when he faced me again his amused expression had vanished, replaced by anger.

"I *don't* want to!" I cried, darting away from him, toward the kitchen and the back door. "Don't you get it, Stu? I don't want to! I don't want *you*! Now GET OUT!"

Stu moved unbelievably quickly; in three seconds he had me in an iron grip, and his furious eyes glared into mine. I hadn't even made it into the kitchen, and I felt like a mouse in the talons of an eagle: helpless and about to be devoured.

"You're the one who doesn't get it, Angel," he said, shaking me so hard that my head bobbed back and forth. "I don't give a shit if you want me or not. I want you. And I'll have you whenever I feel like it. Get it?"

"Yes, yes, okay!" I was ready to agree to anything if he would just stop shaking me. "I get it." I looked into his eyes, chilled by their coldness. "Why are you doing this, Stu? *Why?*"

I began to cry, feeling that shame again, a self-deprecating loathing that told me I was a coward, and because of it, I deserved what I got.

Stu kissed me tenderly. "Because I love you, that's why." He began to drag me into the living room, and I struggled, edging closer and closer to hysteria.

Not again Oh God not again —

Stu stopped walking abruptly, seizing me in a merciless grip. "Don't make me hurt you, Angie. Fight me and I'll take you the hard way. I don't want to do that, you know. I want to make it good for you. But if you fight me you won't be able to walk for a week."

I sagged against him and sobbed, and Stu enfolded me in his arms. He kissed the top of my head and whispered, "Let me make love to you. You have no idea how good it can be."

I continued to cry as he urged me up the stairs, and when we were in my room and the door was closed Stu cupped my face in his hands and kissed me tenderly. "Get undressed, baby. I want to look at you."

I obeyed him automatically, and as each article of clothing dropped to the floor I could feel his gaze on me, his eyelids growing heavier and his breath coming faster, until I was naked in front of him. Stu ran his hands up and down my body, saying in a hoarse voice, "Jesus, look at you, Angel. You're the most beautiful girl in the world."

He eased me onto my back on the bed and stretched out next to me, caressing me with reverent hands, and in spite of the fear and misery I responded. A tingle began in my belly and grew, and as he explored every inch of me I fought the ache inside that insisted I wanted him, just as he had said. Stu's fingers slipped between my legs and my hips rose instinctively, my body reacting shamelessly, completely separate from my brain.

Oh God what's happening to me? No I don't want him I don't I swear I don't –

"That's right, Angel-baby," Stu whispered. "Open up for me, that's it – "

His fingers were inside me now, and I gasped. It hurt, just a little, a reminder of what he had done to me that morning. I moaned helplessly, and he kissed me, long and deeply. Then suddenly he was gone, and my body protested, the ache growing worse. I could hear Stu undressing, and I turned my head away and began to cry.

I'm a slut, I am, a cowardly slut and I deserve this, I really do –

When Stu returned to me he was naked, and he got between my legs, nudging them father apart.

"Please, Stu," I begged, my voice so clotted with anguish I barely recognized it as mine. "Don't do this to me again please don't do this – "

Stu laughed and lowered himself onto me, and I could feel him pushing inside me. "This is what you were made for, Angel. Just lie back and enjoy it."

His hips began to move, and then he was pumping in and out of me, making those same guttural noises, and this time strange emotions rushed through me. It didn't feel good, exactly, but listening to Stu and knowing I was bringing this out in him, this animal *need*, was thrilling in a way I didn't understand.

"Put your arms around me," he begged, and I did as he asked, holding him as he groaned and shuddered.

That's what it's like for a boy to have an orgasm, I thought, pushing away a pinprick of satisfaction. I lay still under him, hating him, but hating myself more for what he had made me feel. Finally Stu raised his head and smiled at me, and the tenderness of it took my breath away.

"I really do love you," he whispered, and I couldn't say a thing. How could rape possibly equal love?

Then the tenderness was gone as suddenly as it had appeared, replaced by that smug, gloating expression I detested. "Better?" he inquired, and I turned my head, refusing to answer. Stu buried his face in my neck. "You'll learn to love it. I'll have you begging for it, Angel-baby. Just wait and see." When I didn't respond, he lifted his head and looked at me. My tears seemed to irritate him, and he shook his head a little. "Jesus, it wasn't *that* bad. Come on."

I stared back at him, incredulous. Then I placed my palms against his chest and pushed. "You seem to keep forgetting that I *don't want this*, Stu!"

"You sure about that?" Stu pulled out of me and got off the bed. "You weren't putting up much of a fight." He crossed the room and began to dress.

I couldn't believe my ears. "*What*? You told me if I fought you you'd *hurt* me, Stu!"

I was so frustrated that I wanted to scream. I pounded my fists on the bed instead, and he laughed. It was that sound, more than any other, that finally pushed me over the edge. I flew out of the bed and over to where Stu stood, buckling his belt. Before my rational mind could think about what I was doing my hand flew out and slapped him across the face. The weight of my entire body was behind the blow, and he staggered to the side for a moment. He put one hand to his reddening cheek and for a moment I saw complete and utter surprise on his face. It filled me with a vicious sense of satisfaction, but it didn't last long.

Stu's grabbed my shoulder and punched me in the stomach as hard as he could. I dropped to the floor, strangling on the pain and the lack of air in my lungs. He kicked me savagely in the side, and a piercing agony flooded my ribcage. I curled into a ball, wanting to scream, but with no air in my lungs I couldn't make a sound.

Stu bent over and wound a handful of my hair around his fist, pulling me to a sitting position, and I managed to shriek, a thin, breathless sound. It felt like a section of my scalp was tearing away, and I held up my hands in front of me as he jerked me to my feet, trying vainly to protect myself.

When I was standing Stu slapped me, again and again, and my head snapped back and forth. When he finally released my hair I collapsed to the floor, every part of me blazing with pain. This time he left me there, and when he had finished dressing he knelt beside me. I tried to move away, and he placed a hand on my back, pinning me to the floor.

"You're a slow learner, Angel," Stu told me matter-of-factly. "What did I say about hitting me? You're lucky I just fucked you. I'm feeling generous, so that's as much as I'll give you. Was it enough?"

I nodded, gasping. My side was on fire, my ears rang, and my stomach ached fiercely. Stu patted my back and got to his feet. "See you on Monday, Angel."

I heard the snick of the door closing and lay where I was, struggling for every breath and wondering what sin I could possibly have committed to deserve this.

Chapter Ten

I managed to get myself onto the bed, and I just lay under the covers for what seemed like hours, shaking. Every breath was painful, and I wondered if Stu had broken one of my ribs when he kicked me. I drew my knees up to my chest and hugged them tightly, wanting to make myself small enough to just disappear. The phone rang but I ignored it, and I finally fell asleep, a restless sleep that was haunted by dreams of Stu, both savage and tender.

When I woke it was evening, and the phone was shrilling right beside my head. I picked it up, wondering why I was even bothering to answer; I knew it was him.

"Hello?"

"Hey, Angel-baby. Sleeping?"

I thought about just hanging up, but decided I had been through enough for one day. I sat up and stretched, wincing at the pain in my side. "I was."

Stu chuckled. "I hope you were dreaming about me."

For no reason at all tears filled my eyes and I began to cry, heaving sobs that hurt my chest. His voice brought it all back, and I wished hopelessly that I *was* still dreaming, and that none of it had really happened.

"What's wrong?" He sounded honestly puzzled, and I couldn't even respond. My God, was he crazy? Was *I*?

"Angel?" Stu's voice was more insistent. "Answer me. What's wrong?"

"What's wrong?" I repeated, gasping through my tears. "What's *wrong*, Stu? How can you even ask me that? It hurts to breathe because you kicked me, you pulled my hair so hard that my scalp is killing me, and you slapped me maybe six times. Does that answer your question?"

I stopped myself from bursting into hysterical laughter with only the greatest effort, and when Stu answered his voice was short. "That's not my fault, Angel."

I let out an exclamation that was more of a shriek, and before I could stop them the words spilled out. "What are you *talking* about? You *attacked* me, Stu! You raped me, and you beat me up! How can you say it's not your fault?"

"You want to watch the way you say things." Stu's voice was flat and emotionless, and I wanted to scream. Would this ever end? "I told you what would happen if you hit me again. Didn't I?"

I made myself answer: "Yes. You told me. Why are you calling, Stu?"

"I wanted to make sure you were all right."

That did it; the tears started again, and this time I couldn't make a sound. Such confusion filled me that I was dizzy with it. How could he hurt me the way he had and then turn around and express such tender concern? My mind couldn't make sense of it, and I just cried, holding tightly onto the phone as if it were a lifeline.

"Come on, Angel, don't." Stu spoke softly. "Lie down, baby. Just lie down, okay?"

For some crazy reason I did what he said, still gripping the receiver, and he continued to talk to me in that soothing voice. Little by little the tears tapered off, and when they had stopped entirely I felt absurdly grateful.

"Do you want me to come over?" he asked, and I whispered, "No, Stu, please, just leave me alone, okay? Please?"

"I will for tonight. You get some sleep."

"Okay." I took a deep, shuddering breath and pulled the covers up to my chin.

"Goodnight, Angel."

"Goodnight, Stu."

I dropped the phone on the floor and curled up again, wanting only to go back to sleep. This time, though, I didn't want to wake up.

The phone woke me again, and I let the voicemail pick it up, but when it kept on ringing I thought it might be Mom, so I finally picked it up and pressed the "talk" button.

Please don't let it be him please God –

"Ang?"

It was Megan, and she sounded so relieved to hear my voice that I smiled. "Hi, Meg. What's up?"

"I've been trying to call you for the last three hours! Jesus, where have you been? I've been worried sick!" She sounded so much like Mom that I laughed.

"I've been right here. Sleeping."

"Sleeping? It's only ten o'clock, Ang. How long have you been asleep?"

"Who are you, my mother? I needed to sleep because – "

I broke off – I had no idea what I was going to say. Why *had* I been sleeping? Because Stu beat the shit out of me? Because I never wanted to wake up again?

"Because why?" Megan sounded suspicious, and I sighed inwardly; why did I think I could ever keep anything from her? "What happened, Ang?"

"Stu was here again."

"Oh, God. I knew I shouldn't have left you alone." She sounded so guilty that it almost got me going again, and I forced down the tears with an effort.

"Meg, it's not your fault," I told her, trying to keep my voice even. "Stu does what he wants."

"Bullshit, Ang!" Meg's reply was so quick and fierce that I was startled. "He *can't* just do whatever he wants! That's why prisons exist, you know – for guys like Stu."

"Great. Why doesn't that make me feel any better?" I lay back down and placed an arm over my eyes.

"You have to go to the police. Otherwise he'll never leave you alone."

Her emphatic words made me feel desperate, and I said the first thing that came to my mind. "Meg, I slapped him and he kicked me so hard I think he broke one of my ribs. He punched me and pulled a handful of my hair out! I don't want to even think about what he'd do if I reported him to the police! Leave it alone, okay?"

"Jesus Christ, Angie!" Meg burst out. "I'm NOT going to fucking leave this alone!" She sounded incensed now, and I was sorry I had said anything. "I can't stand by and let this guy abuse you! Come on!"

I sat up again, despair filling me like a noxious poison. "What can I do, Meg? You tell me! What the hell am I supposed to do? Who's going to protect me?"

The reality of my situation tried to intrude, and I pushed it away. It was as if a dark chasm yawned in front of me, and if I took one wrong

step I'd fall into it, all the way down to a black, bottomless place I had
only glimpsed in my worst nightmares.

"I don't know," Megan said. "But I'm going to find someone. Don't
go anywhere, Ang. I'm going to come and get you. You're staying at
my house tonight."

"Okay. Thanks, Meg. I'll see you in fifteen."

I tossed the phone on the bed and stood up, grimacing at the pain
in my stomach. I went over to the mirror that hung over my dresser and
looked at my reflection, horrified when I saw the huge purple bruise on
my forehead. I leaned closer to the mirror, inspecting it, and noticed the
marks on my neck. Red and angry, they were the shape of his fingers,
and I grabbed the edge of the dresser, suddenly lightheaded.

Why is this happening to me? What did I do, God? What did I do?

I turned away from the mirror and stumbled out of the room when
I was dressed, going downstairs and sitting at the kitchen table to wait
for Megan.

Chapter Eleven

It was good to be surrounded by Meg and her family that night. I felt safe, and that was the only thing that mattered to me now. I refused to talk to Meg about Stu, and I knew it annoyed and worried her, but I didn't care. If I focused on what had happened to my life in one short weekend I was afraid I'd start crying and not be able to stop. We watched a movie, a comedy, and for a little while I was able to forget Stu Black and the control he seemed to have established over me. For most of the movie, Meg's German Shepherd Muffin was draped over my legs, and I took comfort in her heavy warmth and the love she lavished on me with her tongue.

When the movie ended and Meg had shooed her younger sister Monica out of the room, she turned to me. I knew that determined expression, and I held up a hand before she could even get started.

"Don't, Meg. I really don't want to talk about it." Muffin looked up at me quizzically, and I patted her head absently.

"Ang, you can't just pretend this isn't happening!" Meg exclaimed. Muffin got up and came over to her, nudging her with a wet black nose, and Meg pushed her away.

"I'm not," I said. I was beginning to get defensive, and I told myself to take it easy. "I just don't want to think about it right now. I *can't* think about it right now."

Meg came over to me and took both my hands in hers, sitting so close to me on their old sectional that our outer thighs were pressed together.

"Ang, I'm scared for you," she said, and I had to look away and take a deep breath, cursing the tears that hovered, waiting. "This is like something out of a movie!"

"Tell me about it," I said, squeezing her hands before letting them go. "Stu thinks I belong to him now. It's like he's ... *claimed* me, or something." I looked into her eyes. "I honestly feel like my entire life is out of my control right now, Meg. I don't feel safe anymore."

"Well, you will."

I frowned at her. "What do you mean?" A thought occurred to me, and I was suddenly terrified. "Oh God, you didn't go to the police, did you? Tell me you didn't!"

"Calm down, Ang." Meg put a hand on my shoulder. "No, I didn't go to the police. But I did tell Darryl and Jason. And they're going to take care of Stu."

Horror encased me up to the neck. "Oh Jesus, Meg, why did you do that? Why?"

She looked at me in amazement. "*Why?* Because *someone* has to do *something*! That's why! And they said they'd be happy to."

I pulled away from her and got to my feet. I began to pace around the room, struggling with the anger inside, anger that was growing stronger every second. How could she have told Darryl and Jason what had happened? How would I ever look at them again?

"Did you stop to think about whether *I* wanted them to?" I asked, getting angrier at the mulish look that came over her face.

"That's why I didn't tell you until now. I don't understand your reaction to this, Ang! It's like you think it's *okay* or something!"

That stopped me in my tracks, and I turned around and stared at her. How could she possibly *think* that?

"Have you looked at my forehead, Meg?" My voice was low, and I clenched my fists at my sides to keep from screaming. "What about my neck? That's what happens when I do something he doesn't like. How can you say I accept this? *How?*"

The last word dissolved into a wail, and the strength in my legs gave out. I collapsed to the floor, sobbing hysterically, and instantly Meg was beside me, her hands gentle on my back.

"I'm sorry, Ang, I'm sorry, I'm so sorry." She leaned her forehead against my shoulder and wept. "I just didn't know what to do. It was the only thing I could think of *to* do. Stu can't just rape you and hurt you like this! He can't!"

Suddenly we were clinging to each other and crying, and in spite of my anguish, it was so good to know that someone was in this with me.

The next morning Meg and I woke up to a loud pounding on her bedroom door.

"What?" she yelled. "We're trying to sleep here!"

Mrs. LeClair opened the door and put her head in. "Meg, Darryl's here." She raised an eyebrow at Meg and smiled at me.

"Sorry, Mom," Meg said sheepishly. "I thought it was Sandy."

Her mother left and she jumped out of bed, throwing off her pajamas and wiggling into yesterday's jeans. "I'll bet this about Stu!" she said excitedly. "Come on, Ang, get dressed! I want to know what they did to him!"

I got out of bed reluctantly and pulled on my own clothes.

"Why isn't Jason with him?" I asked her as we left her bedroom for the kitchen, and she shrugged. "I don't know. Let's find out."

When we entered the kitchen I heard Meg draw in her breath in a horrified gasp, and my heart sank. I knew why Jason wasn't there; if he looked as bad as Darryl, he was probably recovering at home. Darryl had a puffy, shiny black eye, and his lip was purple and swollen. There was a raised abrasion just over his cheekbone, and when I looked at his hands, folded on the table, I saw that his knuckles were scraped and raw-looking.

"Omigod, baby, what *happened?*" Meg went over to him, bending over and kissing his cheek, and Darryl looked at her with a half smile. It was all he could manage; one side of his mouth wouldn't move.

"Stu Black happened. That's what fucking happened."

Meg looked around frantically. "Shhh! My parents are around, you know. Let's go up to my room."

When we were back in Meg's bedroom she sat beside Darryl on the bed. I stood in front of them, waiting.

"What the hell happened? There were *two* of you!"

Darryl looked at her sourly. "Thanks for that, Meg. I feel like more of a loser now, and I didn't think that was possible."

Meg hugged him gently. "I'm sorry, babe. You know I didn't mean it that way." Darryl looked at her, carefully avoiding my gaze, and I felt anxiety seize me in a relentless grip.

"What happened to Jason?" I whispered, and Darryl looked down at his hands.

"Fucking Black broke his arm. I had to take him to Emergency last night."

He looked up at Meg again. "His parents freaked. They were acting like it was *my* fault, for Christ's sake."

The anxiety turned into terror, and suddenly it was hard to breathe. Darryl finally looked at me, and what I saw in his eyes surprised me: not condemnation, but an odd sort of pity.

"That guy's a maniac, Ang. All Jase had to do was mention your name, and he lost it. He fucking lost it like I've never seen anyone lose it in my life. Kept saying you were *his*, shit like that."

The color leached out of the world for a moment, and reality wavered. Meg got up and came over to me, and I leaned on her heavily: I felt faint. She helped me back to the bed, and I just sat staring straight ahead, my breath rasping in and out, unable to focus on anything but the fear. A sudden knock on the door made us all jump, and Meg called out, "Who is it?"

For the second time Meg's her mother popped her head in. "Phone for you, Ang."

"Is it my mother?"

Mrs. LeClair seemed taken aback at the urgency in my voice, and she shook her head. "No, it isn't. Are you all right, Angie? You look awfully white."

I made myself smile at her, and it was an effort; I had never been so conscious of the muscles in my face. "I'm fine, Mrs. LeClair. Thank you."

Meg handed me the phone, and when I looked at her my terror increased. For the first time, *she* looked frightened. I held the phone to my ear.

"Hello?"

"Tell me it wasn't your idea." Stu's voice was full of suppressed rage, and I had to lean over and prop my elbows on my knees; the world was fading in and out again. "And you'd better convince me, Angie. You don't want to face the consequences if you don't, believe me."

"It wasn't me, I swear to God Stu, it wasn't me – "

My voice was small and terrified, and I began to hyperventilate, more afraid than I had ever been in my life. Before I could hear Stu's reply Darryl snatched the phone from my hand.

"Angie had nothing to do with what happened last night, Black. Now fuck off and leave her alone."

I didn't want to think about what Stu was saying to him, and Meg put her arms around me. I could barely feel her holding me. I felt as though I was floating outside my body, watching the scene unfolding before me, completely detached.

Darryl just listened silently and then handed the phone back to me. I almost dropped it, holding it up to my ear with a hand that shook badly.

"I'm coming to get you, Angel." Stu's tone brooked no refusal, and I almost started to cry.

"Stu, you're not – you're not … mad at me, are you?"

I waited, and when I heard his response the relief that rushed through me left me weak. "No, I'm not mad at you. But I need to see you. I'll be there in a few minutes."

He hung up and I let the phone fall from my hand, sagging against Megan.

"Are you going to go to the cops, Ang?" Darryl asked, and I looked at him.

"Are *you*?"

He gave a sound that might have been laughter; it was hard to tell. "Guess not."

"I have to go." I stood up and began to look for Megan's brush. When I found it I pulled it roughly through my hair, unmindful of the tangles. "Stu's going to be here any minute."

"Ang, I don't want you to go with him." Meg sounded tearful, and again I gave that smile: a mere stretching of the lips, nothing more.

59

"I'll be okay, Meg. He's not mad."

Meg buried her face in Darryl's shoulder and burst into tears. He put an arm around her, awkwardly, as though he wasn't quite sure what to do. I looked at Darryl.

"I'm so sorry, Darryl – "

He interrupted me. "Stop it, Ang. Don't even say that. I'm the one who's sorry. I wish we could have stopped him from getting to you."

I swallowed hard; tears were crowding the back of my throat. "I'll manage. See you guys later."

Meg didn't even look up, and I left the room, closing the door quietly behind me. I went down to the kitchen and out the back door. Stu's car, an ancient black Rambler with red primer showing on the trunk and left fender, was just pulling up at the curb. Its engine idled noisily, and a billow of oily black smoke belched out of the tailpipe.

I forced myself to walk down the driveway toward him, feeling as though I was walking toward my own execution.

Chapter Twelve

I got into the car on the passenger side, slamming the creaky door hard. It was as old on the inside as it appeared outside: the vinyl dashboard was pitted with cigarette burns, and the seats were cracked, worn through in spots. Cluttered with fast food wrappers and odd pieces of clothing, it was very much a single guy's car.

I glanced over at Stu and he smiled at me, and it was as if I was seeing him for the first time. His hair hung around his face in wisps and tatters, but it was always clean, and his skin was smooth and unblemished. His eyes were dark, fringed with black lashes, and his nose was straight and proud. His mouth was beautiful, with a full lower lip that was impossibly sexy, and before I could stop myself I thought: *My God, he's gorgeous, he really is.*

I reminded myself fiercely of what he had done the night before (*and the night before that, Ang*), but it didn't stop a furious blush from warming my face. Stu leaned over and kissed me gently, and it was hard not to respond. There was little doubt of the attraction between us, but it only made me more confused. How could I feel anything for him other than fear and disgust?

"Hi, Angel," he said softly. He cupped my face in his hand for a moment, and I was afraid to say a thing. "Aren't you glad to see me?"

I blinked at the question, honestly wondering if Stu was really two personalities. At times he acted like he might love me, and other times he seemed to glory in hurting and frightening me.

"I don't know," I said hesitantly. "I'm scared of you, Stu."

Stu pulled the car away from the front of Megan's house, and I looked at his hands on the wheel. The fingers were long, slender and beautiful, but when I thought of what kind of power they had I shivered.

"You don't have to be scared of me, Angel. Just do what I want you to. That's all."

"Do I have any say in this?" I asked, and he shook his head and clicked on the turn signal.

"No. You don't."

I looked at him carefully as he twisted the wheel around a corner, hoping he wouldn't get angry at the next thing I said. "Why not?"

Stu took his eyes from the road for a moment to look at me, and his expression was calm and determined. "Because you're mine, Angel. You belong to me now. That means I can do what I want with you."

It was hard not to be sucked into the utter certainty in his voice, but I fought it. "But that's not up to you to decide, Stu. What about how *I* feel?"

Stu looked at me again, and this time there was a warning in his eyes. "You're going to feel how I want you to feel, Angel. You're going to want me as much as I want you. Just give it time."

I sank back against the seat, feeling trapped. We didn't talk for the rest of the ride, and when we got to my house I was surprised to see Mom's car in the driveway.

"My mother's home from Calgary," I said unnecessarily, and Stu nodded.

"What do you want, Angel?"

I was confused. "I don't understand."

He took my chin in those long fingers and looked into my eyes. "Do you want to go in alone, or should I come with you?" I tried to figure out what he meant, but I couldn't tell from his expression. "Ask me, Angel." My heart sank.

Control, Ang. This is all about control.

"Can I please go in alone?" I hated myself for giving in, but I didn't feel like I had much of a choice - about anything. Stu smiled gently and kissed me.

"Yes, you can. Get going, Angel. I'll see you tomorrow." I opened the door of the Rambler and began to climb out, and Stu spoke again. "And if you go near him, Angel, you'll be sorry. Understand?"

I knew who he was talking about, and I twisted around on the seat and stared at him, suddenly frightened again. Slowly, I nodded. "I understand."

"Good girl. See you tomorrow at school."

When I got into the house, I saw Mom right away; she was sitting at the kitchen table reading the paper. She looked up as the door opened and smiled at me, and I almost started crying again. I controlled myself, however, remembering my earlier determination not to let her know what was going on. She came over to me and I hugged her gratefully, reveling in the sense of security I always felt in her embrace, and she laughed as she pulled away.

"Wow," she said, kissing me on the cheek. "What did I do to deserve that?"

"I just missed you," I said, and she placed one palm against the side of my face.

"I missed you too, Peach. I always do." I smiled at the sound of my childhood nickname, given to me for my ravenous love of that particular fruit. I still liked peaches, but not as fervently as I had back then.

"How's Ivan?" I asked. "I miss him, too. When is going to come here?"

"Next weekend," Mom told me. "He promised."

I liked Ivan a great deal. He and my mother had been an item for almost five years, and the effortless way they dealt with living three hours apart never ceased to amaze me. Mom said it was like being on a honeymoon every time they saw each other, and she was a little afraid that if they lived in the same city the bloom would be off the rose.

Ivan Romanovich was everything that his name implied: large, bearded, and very Russian. He was a professor of Russian history at the University of Calgary, an opinionated, motivated, extremely intelligent man who happened to have the soul of a kitten inside his lion's body. He was gentle, sentimental, and incredibly sensitive, and it always made me smile when I thought about his students and how intimidated by him they were.

Now, I said to Mom, "Good. It's been too long since he was here."

Mom went over to the cupboard by the sink and took down two mugs. "How was the party?" she asked. I thought about how I should answer and finally decided to leave out anything about Stu altogether.

"Good," I said, sitting down at the kitchen table. "Jason got totally wasted and passed out by midnight." Mom looked at me with a rueful expression.

"Are you sure that boy doesn't have a drinking problem?" she asked, putting the kettle on the stove.

"Oh, he definitely does," I said with a grin. "He drinks, he gets drunk, he falls down. I'd say that's a problem."

"Ha, ha." Mom turned around and looked at me seriously. "There seems to be a lot of drinking at these parties, Ang. Should I be worried?"

Only about twelfth grade rapists, I thought before I could roadblock it behind the wall of denial I was trying to build.

"Not about me," I said lightly. "I had a few beers, that's all. Everyone else was cool, Mom. It was pretty mellow."

Mom brought the mugs over to the table and dropped a teabag into each. Then she filled them with boiling water, and the fragrant aroma of cinnamon filled the air. When she handed me the mug it was warm against my palms, and I smiled at her. Mom put the kettle back on the stove and sat down across from me. She stirred her tea for a moment and then asked, "What's on your mind, Peach?"

The question startled me. Was I that easy to read? I looked at her cautiously, but she just smiled over the rim of her mug. "You look like you want to talk about something."

"Wow, that's scary. Do all mothers have this frightening perception?"

"Yep," she answered easily. "It goes with the territory. Now out with it."

I decided to tell her about part of it: the least threatening part. "Well, there's this guy at school, and ..." I hesitated, and she raised her eyebrows. "He's always making sexual remarks and it makes me ... uncomfortable."

Mom put her mug down on the table and looked at me searchingly. "What kind of remarks?" she asked, sounding concerned, and I wished I hadn't said anything. I shrugged, trying to give the impression that it was nothing.

"Oh, just "Nice ass," stuff like that. Sometimes he pinches me. It drives Jason nuts."

"I can see why. Sounds like he likes you, Ang."

You could say that, Mom. He likes me so much that he —

I pushed thought away unfinished and said, "He asked me out and I told him no. I think he was a little pissed off."

Mom laughed. "Too bad. We can't always have what we want." She took another sip of tea. "Just avoid him, Ang. He'll move on to someone else, believe me."

"I don't know, Mom," I said weakly. "He's awfully ... persistent."

Mom smiled at that. "Well, persistent or not, he has to understand that you have a boyfriend and that you're not interested. You told him that, right?"

I nodded, feeling shame worm inside me, and suddenly I needed to be done with this conversation.

I tried, Mom, but he hit me ...

I pushed away my mug and stood up; if I didn't get out of the room I was going to burst into tears. "I'm going to do my homework."

Mom frowned. "Are you okay, Ang? Anything else you wanted to talk about?"

I shook my head and forced myself to smile at her. "That's okay. I'll see you later, okay?"

"Okay, honey."

I left the room as quickly as I could, running when I got to the stairs so I could make it to my room before the tears came.

Chapter Thirteen

The alarm buzzed me awake at seven o'clock the next morning, and for a moment it was another Monday morning. Then the panic hit, the panic that hadn't allowed me to fall asleep until four, and my stomach twisted.

Everyone's going to know now, Ang, that little voice whispered. *Everyone's going to know you're his...*

I tried to ignore it and threw back the covers, even though I felt like huddling under them all day and never going to school again. I made myself pull on my robe and go into the bathroom for a shower. When I was back in my room, I searched through my closet for another turtleneck. Until the marks on my neck faded, I had resigned myself to looking like a ski instructor. Thank God it was fall, or it would have looked odd, to say the least.

I looked closely at myself in the mirror as I brushed my wet hair, wondering what it was about me that Stu found so irresistible. I didn't think I was beautiful. My features were attractive and my body slim, but there were a lot of girls in my grade that were better looking, some of them in Stu's own group of friends. One in particular, Gin (so called because of her fondness for the alcohol, not because her name was Virginia), was really gorgeous, with lots of wavy red hair and a body that would stop a clock. I wished wretchedly that she were the target of Stu's dubious affections instead of me.

I had thought long and hard the night before about whether or not I had encouraged Stu without being aware of it. After much soul searching, I really couldn't remember ever doing anything that could have been construed as appreciation or acceptance. Deep inside I might have been flattered, just a little, but I was certain I had never let Stu see it.

I tried to push the entire thing out of my mind on the way to school, but it was impossible. By the time I got off the bus my hands were shaking and my stomach felt queasy, and when I saw the bulk of the brick school in the distance it was all I could do not to run in the other direction. As I got closer I could see Meg sitting on the front steps, craning her neck as she looked for me, and I ran up to her in relief.

"I've never been so glad to see you," I said breathlessly. "I'm scared out of my mind."

She looked at me sympathetically. "I'll be right beside you all day," she promised.

"You'd better be," I told her as she got to her feet and we went inside to go to our lockers before first period.

I didn't see Stu on my way to French, and by the time the class was over I didn't know which was worse, seeing him or not seeing him. Something in me just wanted to get it over with, but when it finally happened I was totally unprepared.

I was standing at my locker searching for my biology text when I felt an arm slip around my waist. I froze, my heart beginning to knock against my ribs, and I felt his breath against my ear as he whispered, "Hey, Angel-baby."

I turned around so suddenly that my head banged against the door of my locker, and for a moment I couldn't breathe as I looked into those dark eyes. Stu braced a hand on the locker beside mine and leaned over, smiling knowingly. He hooked one finger in the collar of my shirt and pulled it down a few inches, and when he saw the angry red marks he had put on my neck an expression crossed his face that looked curiously like regret.

"See what you made me do, Angel?" he murmured. I tried to duck out from under him.

"Please, Stu, just leave me alone," I said in a low voice, agonizingly conscious of the curious looks we were getting. "Everyone is staring."

Stu looked at me in amusement. "Do you really think I give a shit?"

I turned my back and tried to close my locker, but he put one hand on my shoulder and turned me around again. Then he had me back up against the locker and his mouth was on mine, and as he kissed me I could hear muffled giggles and sly remarks from passing students. I tried to focus on that, on the embarrassment of looking like I was making out in the hallway, but the sensations his lips provoked tried to drown that out and pull me down, begging me to kiss him back.

At last I placed my hands against his chest and pushed, and Stu obligingly stepped back, smiling at me with desire in his eyes. "See you later, Angel," he said, and walked away, his hips seesawing in a sexy way I tried to ignore.

Meg came hurrying up, and when she reached me I was trying to get myself under control, cursing Stu under my breath. "What happened?" she asked curiously. "Everyone's talking."

I slammed my locker shut with a little more force than necessary. "Nothing." I was a little light headed and I knew my face was red, but I wasn't about to explain why. "Let's go."

All through biology I struggled to focus, but all I could think about was Stu and the way he made me feel. Was he right? *Did* I want him?

It was certainly beginning to feel like I did, and it distressed me beyond all imagining. What was happening to me?

When the class was over Meg and I were just going out the door when I literally bumped into Jason. When I saw his arm I was horrified. It was encased in a white plaster cast up to the shoulder, and it hung on his chest in a sling. It was his left arm, so he could still write, but it didn't make me feel any less responsible. We stared at each other for a second, and then Jason stepped aside, out of my way, and motioned for me to follow him. When we found a clear spot in the hallway he gave me a lopsided smile.

"Nice, huh?"

I bit my lip and my eyes filled with tears. "God, Jase, I'm so sorry."

He shook his head and looked past me, at the wall over my shoulder. "Hey, Ang, *you* didn't do it. I went up against Stu because I wanted to." He looked at me again and made a small, bitter noise. "Guess I didn't know what I was getting into."

I tried to smile but it felt more like a grimace. A tear slid down my cheek and I brushed it away absently. "I'm sorry," I said again. It seemed to be the only thing I *could* say.

"Don't be," Jason told me. "But I think I'm gonna just steer clear, Ang, you know?" His eyes slid away from mine, this time down to the floor, and I nodded, tears blurring my vision.

"I don't blame you," I whispered.

Suddenly Meg nudged me, hard. "Oh Christ Ang – "

I looked up and saw Stu coming toward us. He looked furious, and my heart leaped. I began to pray.

"You'd better get lost, Jason," Meg said, and he left quickly. When Stu reached us he grabbed my arm, and I only had time for one frantic glance at Meg before he dragged me away.

"What did I tell you, Angie?" he said through clenched teeth, and I tried to keep up with his angry strides, practically running.

"I know, Stu, but *he* talked to *me* – " I hated the pleading sound of my voice, but I couldn't help it; I was too afraid to try and cover it up. We reached the back door and Stu jerked it open, pushing me out ahead of him.

"I told you if you talked to him you'd be sorry, didn't I?" His voice was a venomous whisper in my ear as he followed me down the steps, and I resisted the urge to beg. My arms tightened around my books as we walked over to his car, and when we reached it I stood by the passenger door and looked at the ground, resentful at being made to feel like a naughty child. Stu backed me up against the car, and I looked up at him, astonished when anger began to replace the fear inside me.

I don't deserve this! He can't treat me this way!

"You can't tell me who I can talk to, Stu," I told him, and I was rewarded by his look of surprise.

"Is that right?" he said, and despite the suppressed anger is his tone I nodded.

Now's the time, Ang! If you don't stand up to him now, you never will!

I squared my shoulders, pretending a bravery I didn't feel. "You can't *control* another person, Stu." I looked into his eyes, praying that my nerve wouldn't fail me. "You've had your fun. Can't you find someone else to torture?"

Stu grabbed my shoulders. "You don't seem to get it, Angel-baby. You're *mine*. And you're going to stay mine. How many times do I have to tell you?"

Desperation filled me. "Doesn't what *I* want count for anything?"

Stu leaned forward and brushed my lips with his, shaking his head. "No."

I dropped my books and pushed against his chest, feeling like he was suffocating me with his nearness. "Stop it!" I cried. "Just *stop it*, Stu! Why are you doing this? Can't you find someone who *wants* you?"

Stu's lips curved in a possessive smile. "You want me, Angel. You just don't know it yet."

"No I don't! Don't *you* get it, Stu? I *don't*!"

Stu didn't answer. He just pulled me into his arms and lowered his head to mine, and when he began to kiss me I stiffened and tried to pull away, but there was nowhere to go. His lips caressed mine and his tongue gently explored my mouth, and as his arms tightened around me I began to respond; I couldn't help it.

Before I realized what I was doing my arms went around Stu's waist and I found myself kissing him back, that ache beginning at the top of my pelvis and spreading downward. We stood there for what felt like forever, and when he finally released me my head was spinning and my breath was coming in short gasps. Stu's eyes were heavy with desire, and for a split second I saw something tender and vulnerable. Then the familiar insolence replaced it, and I was overcome with shame.

"See, Angel?" he asked. "If I'm not mistaken, you enjoyed that." He sounded inordinately pleased, and I couldn't bring myself to speak. Stu gripped my chin and forced my head up, looking into my eyes. "Didn't you?"

When I still didn't reply his fingers tightened. I nodded, hating him for this most of all. "Say it." I looked at him in dismay, and this time his smile was cruel and taunting. "Say it, Angel."

I closed my eyes and whispered the words. "I enjoyed it."

"What did you enjoy?"

I began to cry, hating myself now but unable to help it. How had my life gotten to this point? When had I become a prisoner? "Stu, please don't do this to me – "

Stu's hand dropped to my breast and he squeezed it. Hard. "You heard me, Angel. What did you enjoy?"

Tears slid down my cheeks, and I looked away, unable to face that satisfied gaze. "I – I enjoyed kissing you."

When I heard Stu's low chuckle, my face burned. "You want me, Angel. Don't you?"

I lost control completely and began to sob. "Why are you doing this, Stu? *Why?*"

Stu squeezed my breast again, viciously, and I wailed.

"Isn't it obvious by now?" His voice was a cold breath in my ear, and I could hear his darkness. "Because I can. And I want to."

"You *want* to hurt me?"

It seemed so important to understand, as if understanding would somehow give his behavior meaning. Stu placed his hands on either side of my face and kissed me gently, and my mind screamed in confusion. "Yes. I want to hurt you."

He bent his head to my neck, pulling my shirt out of the way, and when I felt his teeth fasten on my skin I shrieked. Stu slapped a hand over my mouth and bit down hard, and I screamed against his palm as I felt his teeth break the skin.

Stu raised his head and kissed me again, and I imagined I could taste blood on his lips, sharp and coppery. I was beyond protest now, in a twilight world where all the rules had changed and the possibility of escape was remote.

He whispered in my ear again, and I couldn't believe what he said. "I want to hurt you, Angel, because I love you."

Then he walked away, leaving me standing beside the car, my hand to my neck, wondering if I had heard him correctly but knowing it didn't matter.

Chapter Fourteen

I went home for the rest of the day - I couldn't even contemplate trying to act as though everything was normal. Suddenly everyone else's life seemed so simple and uncomplicated, while I was trapped in an unpredictable, never ending nightmare. All the way home on the bus I tried to push away the feeling of unreality that wanted to swallow me whole.

Things like this just don't happen. There must be something I can do. The guy's not the Antichrist, for heaven's sake.

There was only one problem; it *was* happening, and there didn't seem to be a damned thing I could do about it. The only option I could think of was going to the police, and I shied away from it. Not only did the entire situation sound like the plot of some late night television show, but what proof did I have that any of it was true?

Look at your neck, Ang, a cynical voice inside me whispered. *Sure looks like proof to me.*

Even though this made sense, something else kept me from seriously considering reporting Stu to the police for what he had done to me: fear. I knew what he was capable of, and if I went to the police I was honestly afraid he might kill me.

As I got off the bus a feeling of utter despair filled me, and once again I felt like a hostage. Oh, I might be able to move around freely, but the invisible ropes that bound me were every bit as real as the bonds securing a kidnap victim held in an underground cave. There was a pall hanging over my head that sucked everything positive out of me, and already it seemed like years since I had been my normal, carefree self. I cursed Stu again as I walked the rest of the way home, and I wished fleetingly that I had never met him, that I went to a different high school, that I lived in another city.

When I got home the house was quiet, and I dropped my books on the kitchen table and locked the back door. I hadn't even gone back into the school for my backpack, but I didn't care. I never wanted to go to school again.

I wearily mounted the stairs to my room, and once inside I lay down on the bed, curling myself into the tightest fetal position possible. Sharp pain stung my neck and I reached up and pulled my turtleneck away from the bite mark, wincing. Stu had actually said that he *liked* to hurt me. Remembering those words and the matter-of-fact way he had said them filled me with terror. I had never known anyone like Stu; I had never even dreamed that people like him existed.

What am I going to do? Oh, God, help me, please help me ...

I pulled the rumpled covers over my head and began to cry, and eventually I drifted off to sleep, exhausted. The insistent ringing of the phone woke me, and I sat up and looked around in confusion, momentarily disoriented. I reached for the cordless on the bedside table and pressed the "talk" button.

"Hello? Mom?"

"Afraid not, Angel." A chill ran through me when I heard his voice, and I resisted the urge to just slam the phone down.

"What do you want, Stu?" The lifeless sound of my own voice startled me, and I closed my eyes.

Go away, for Christ's sake. Can't you just go away?

"Missed you at school this afternoon."

I gave a bitter laugh. "Well, I thought like looking like an extra from "Buffy, the Vampire Slayer" wouldn't go over too well in gym class," I told him coldly.

Stu chuckled. "Get used to it, Angel. Next time I'll make sure it's in a spot that doesn't show."

I suppressed the scream that rose up in my throat with an effort. "Stop it, Stu. Can't you *please* stop?"

"Why would I want to do that? This is just starting to get interesting." His amused tone infuriated me.

"Goddamn you, Stu!" I shouted. "What will it take to convince you? You can't do this! I won't let you!"

"You won't *let* me?" He repeated the words in a sarcastic drawl. "Just what is it that you're going to do, Angel?"

There was an edge to his voice, but I ignored it. I was angry, tired of feeling helpless and afraid, and I blurted out the worst possible thing before I could stop myself.

"I'll go to the police! I mean it, Stu! I will!"

There was absolute silence on the other end, and as it stretched out the fear returned, growing stronger with every passing second.

What are you hanging on to the phone for, you idiot? Hang up!

I was about to pull the phone away from ear and press the "end" button when I heard his voice, low and furious, filled with deadly intention. "I'll be there in half an hour, Angie. You need a lesson. A really serious lesson."

I tried to think past the panic that was making me lightheaded.

Don't let him intimidate you, if you do you're sunk —

"Stu – " I got out, and he spoke over my protest without even acknowledging that I had said anything. "If you try to hide from me I'll find you. So just wait right there like a good girl. If you do that, maybe I won't hurt you too badly."

There was a click as he broke the connection and I sat frozen, literally unable to move. The terror that filled me was so immense I couldn't even think rationally, and the phone fell from my nerveless fingers to the floor. I let out a wail and collapsed on the bed, burying my face in the covers, my entire body trembling.

I don't know how long I lay there, but when I heard pounding at the back door I sat up with a shriek, terrified. I forced myself to get up, remembering what had happened the last time I hadn't been fast enough, but before I even got halfway across my bedroom I heard a splintering crash as Stu kicked the door in. The world went grey and flashing lights began to spin in front of my eyes.

I'm fainting, oh God, I'm actually fainting ...

I sat down hard on the floor, all the strength gone from my legs, and dimly I heard the angry sound of his boots on the stairs. My bedroom door flew open and banged against the wall and Stu was on me in seconds, grabbing my arm and pulling me to my feet.

He drew back his hand and slapped me so hard that he lost his grip on my arm and I fell to the floor again. This seemed to enrage him even more, and he kicked me in the stomach, the toe of his heavy boot slamming into me with shocking strength. The breath left my body in a rush, and I couldn't think past the pain. I struggled to draw air into my lungs and instinctively curled up on the floor, praying for survival.

Stu bent down and grabbed my hair, twisting a handful around his fist and pulling me into a sitting position. The roots of my hair screamed in agony, but I still couldn't make a sound. Stu punched me on the jaw and I grabbed his arms blindly as my head snapped back, trying to make him stop. He took my arm and yanked me to my feet, throwing me on the bed, and I scrambled away from him, pressing myself against the wall.

Stu ripped off his jacket and flung it across the room, then kicked his boots off. He turned around and glared at me, chest heaving, his eyes black and filled with rage. I could finally breathe but I only stared at him, terrorized, the pain stealing my words. He moved toward me with the stealth of a predatory animal and I began to make a whining noise deep in my throat, turning my head from side to side and holding out my hands in a futile warding-off gesture. Stu crouched in front of me on the bed and captured my head between his hands, forcing me to face him.

"Look at me, Angel."

I shrank away from his touch and squeezed my eyes shut, moaning. "No, I can't I can't I can't – "

"LOOK AT ME!"

My eyes flew open at the savage sound of the words and I screamed. I looked into his eyes, feeling my control slip another notch.

"Was that enough of a lesson for you, Angel?" Stu's voice was low and controlled, and I nodded hysterically, my head throbbing miserably and the agony in my stomach making me feel sick.

"Yes, yes, please don't hit me again, Stu, please don't hurt me anymore – "

He took one hand from the side of my head and placed a finger across my lips, a gentle gesture that stilled my frantic babbling. "I had to do that, Angel. You know what happens when you make me mad."

"I won't," I told him, tears running down my cheeks. "I won't make you mad just please, don't hurt me anymore – "

I began to cry in gasping sobs and Stu folded me into his arms and held me close, cradling me as if I were a precious child. At last he held me away from him and began to kiss me, softly at first and then more insistently. The pain faded away, replaced by a growing feeling of need, a fire that kindled in my belly and radiated outward. Stu eased me onto my back, his lips still working against my own, and when his hands began to explore underneath my shirt I didn't push them away. His fingers were gentle, caressing my breasts, teasing the nipples into stiff peaks, and I found myself arching my back, pushing myself into his palm.

Still kissing me, Stu's fingers trailed down to the waistband of my jeans and he skillfully undid the button, slid the zipper down, and slipped his fingers into the top of my panties. My breath coming in short gasps, I took his hand and thrust it between my legs, moaning as his fingers found me and explored. His thumb rubbed me gently, and my hips began to move as the sensation increased to an unbearable friction. I began to writhe and moan, and suddenly the friction peaked and spasms of exquisite pleasure carried me to a place I had never known existed.

I opened my eyes and found Stu looking at me with a tenderness that seemed curiously out of place, and confusion swirled in my head.

"Stu – " I whispered, and he shook his head.

"Shhh, Angel. We're not finished yet."

He got up from the bed and began to remove his clothes and I watched him, wondering why I was no longer afraid. I turned my head as he took his pants off, but when he joined me on the bed again I didn't protest as he pulled my jeans down to my ankles. Stu nudged my knees apart and got in between them, and I took a deep breath as he gripped my hips and entered me. This time there was no difficulty; he slid into me easily and I gasped, amazed at how good it felt. My arms twined around his neck and I buried my face in his shoulder as he began to move.

My hips rose up to meet each thrust, and Stu's fingers tightened as he pumped harder. His breath began to come faster and it filled me with that odd excitement, and when I looked at his face, it was twisted into an expression that was almost agony. Finally he began to groan and thrust harder, then harder still, stiffening as he climaxed. He opened his eyes and looked into mine, still breathing hard, and I felt a curious sense of power.

Stu dropped on top of me and I held him, conflicting feelings battling within me. Did I hate him? How could I, when I had allowed him to make love to me? Did he love me? How could he, and hurt me the way he did?

"See, Angel?" Stu breathed in my ear. "You belong to me. Don't you?"

When I didn't respond, he lifted himself onto his elbows and looked down at me silently.

"I don't know," I said truthfully, tears coming to the surface again.

His hand twisted itself in my hair and pulled savagely, jerking my head back painfully.

"You're a stubborn girl, Angel-baby," he whispered, dipping his head and kissing me. As the kiss intensified he pulled harder on my hair, and the pain intermingled with the passion until I couldn't tell them apart anymore. Finally Stu broke the kiss and murmured in my ear again.

"Say it. 'I belong to you, Stu.' I want to hear you say it." His grip on my hair tightened still more, and tears of pain ran from the corners of my eyes into my ears.

"I belong to you, Stu," I whispered, and his hand relaxed, caressing the place on my scalp where it hurt.

"That's right, Angel." His voice was calm and possessive. "You do."

Stu pulled out of me and got off the bed, gathering his clothes. He began to pull on his jeans and I pillowed my head on my arm and watched him, trying to figure out how I was feeling. I knew how I *should* be feeling, and part of me screamed: *What the hell is your* problem, *Angie? He's an abusive bastard! You should feel like killing him!*

Stu finished with his clothing and came back to the bed. He sat down on the edge and looked at me. "Every lesson I have to teach you will be harder." He spoke calmly, and suddenly I was frightened all over again. "You know that, don't you?"

I nodded wordlessly, and he reached out and caressed my cheek briefly. "Good. No more of this shit, okay, Angel? I like hurting you. Maybe too much. Get it?"

Tears slipped unnoticed down my cheeks. "Why does it have to be like this, Stu?" I asked in a trembling voice, and he looked surprised at the question.

"I thought I already told you that, Angel-baby," he said patiently. "Because I want it to be. See you tomorrow."

He stood up and left the room without looking back, and I turned over and began to cry in earnest, feeling more trapped than ever.

Chapter Fifteen

I heard the back door slam after Stu and sat up quickly, instantly sorry as my stomach muscles objected violently. My eyes jumped to the clock beside the bed and when I saw the time I panicked. It was after four, and I had to think of something to explain the condition of the back door before Mom got home.

I swung my legs over the edge of the bed and pulled up my jeans; he hadn't even bothered to take them all the way off. Wetness trickled out of me and I thought: *That's Stu. There's a part of him inside me.* A flash of something – desire? – went through me and my cheeks burned.

As I passed the mirror I stopped, transfixed by my own image. The girl staring back at me – hair tousled, face flushed, and bruises plainly visible on her forehead – was no one I recognized.

Who is that? Where did Angie go?

I tore my gaze from the mirror and gingerly lifted my turtleneck. There was a large, angry red mark where Stu's boot had connected with my stomach, and the area was already purplish with bruising from the last time he had hit me there. I touched the mark gently with my fingers, feeling that now familiar confusion rush through me. What *was* it that I felt for him?

I pulled the shirt off and searched through my closet to find another. I wondered how long I was going to have to hide bruises and marks from my mother, and I stopped in the act of pulling the clean shirt off the hanger as a harsh realization suddenly occurred to me.

I'm a battered woman. God help me, I really am. How many abused wives and girlfriends end up dead?

I banished those thoughts before they could take hold. I needed to act right now, not fall apart. After I had pulled the new turtleneck over my head I brushed my hair, carefully avoiding my own eyes in the mirror. I caught it up behind my head in a ponytail and left my bedroom, hurrying down the stairs and going into the kitchen.

I stopped in the middle of the floor when I got a good look at the remains of our back door. It was splintered and broken along the outer edge, and the part of the jamb that connected to the deadbolt lock was completely gone, leaving a ragged hole. I went over to the door and peered out at the side of the house; there were pieces of wood tossed carelessly over by the fence that separated our house from the neighbours', and I had no doubt they would fit neatly into that hole.

How in the hell am I going to explain this to Mom? She's going to freak!

I was struck all over again by the ludicrous nature of my situation. To explain this to my mother I was going to have to protect Stu, when what I really wanted to do was have him arrested for having done it in the first place. I paced the kitchen floor, feeling more panicked with every step, and when the phone rang I jumped. I went over to where it hung on the wall and picked it up, my heart thudding heavily in a way that made me feel nauseous.

"Hello?" The word was tentative and frightened, and Meg said, "Ang? Is that you?"

Relief flooded me at the sound of her voice. Was it really only that morning that I had last seen her? It seemed like another lifetime ago.

"Meg, thank God. I was afraid it might be Stu."

"Ang, what the hell is going on? You and Stu didn't come back after the first break, and everyone's been talking all day! Where have you been?"

"Here," I said weakly, knowing it wouldn't satisfy her for a second.

"Was he with you?" she asked, and the question came out sounding suspicious and disapproving.

"You could say that."

I began to laugh helplessly, and the laughter rapidly turned to tears, tears that I couldn't control. I tried to say something, anything, to avoid scaring Megan to death, but I was crying too hard.

"Angie?" Meg was on the verge of tears herself. "What happened? What did that bastard do to you? Talk to me, please!"

"Meg," I finally managed to choke out, "can you come over? I really need you right now." I slid to a sitting position on the floor, clutching the phone to my ear, still crying.

"I'll be there as fast as I can."

There was a click as she hung up and I dropped the phone, burying my face in my arms on my bent knees and wishing there was a way out of this nightmare. The phone shrilled beside me and I almost screamed. I picked it up, suddenly furious.

I'm not going to spend the rest of my goddamn life being afraid to answer the phone!

"Hello."

"Peach? What's wrong, honey? You sound upset." Mom's voice was worried, and I had to bite my lip hard to keep from crying again.

"Hi, Mom. There's nothing wrong, but I just got home and found the back door all broken, so I was kind of freaked out. It looks like someone kicked it in or something." I had decided I would tell her the truth: I would just leave out the fact that I knew *who* had kicked it in.

"*What?*" Now Mom sounded frightened, and I hated myself for bringing this on her. "You didn't go inside, did you, Ang?"

"There was no one here, Mom, and nothing is gone. The house looks fine."

What a cool liar you are, Angie. Ever consider an acting career?

"I'm calling the police and then I'm coming right home, honey." The only thing I heard was the word "police", and I panicked.

"Don't!" I cried before I thought about what I was saying, and Mom said in a puzzled voice, "Don't? Don't what? Call the police, or come home?"

"Don't call the police, Mom," I said, knowing how weird the words must have sounded the second they were out of my mouth. "I mean, nothing's gone, and – "

Mom interrupted me. "Of course I'm going to call the police. What a strange thing to say, Ang. I'll be there as soon as I can."

A sudden, primitive longing filled me, and all I wanted in the world at that moment was to have her arms around me, protecting me the way they had when I was small.

"Mom?" My voice wavered in spite of my effort to control it, and she sounded alarmed at my change of tone.

"What, Peach?"

"Hurry, okay?"

"I will, sweetheart." She broke the connection and I got to my feet and hung up the phone, struggling to get myself under control. I went upstairs to wash my face, going into the bathroom and rummaging in one of the drawers for a headband. I slipped it over my head and used it to hold back my hair, and for the first time since this had all begun I took a good look at my face.

My cheeks were red and chapped looking, and the bruise on the side of my forehead stood out harshly, vivid purple mixed with shades of yellow and brown. My eyes dropped lower and I pulled the turtleneck away from my neck and examined the bite mark. The marks of Stu's teeth were clearly visible, and I shuddered at the pinpricks of blood. I grabbed a facecloth and soaked it with warm water, applying it carefully to my neck and wincing as I washed the brownish streaks away. Then I scrubbed my face, patting it dry and staring at myself in the mirror. I felt like I was looking at a stranger. Was it really *my* face anymore, or did it belong to Stu, like the rest of me?

"Ang?" I heard Meg's voice and I came out of the bathroom to stand at the top of the stairs.

"Up here, Meg!" She appeared at the foot of the stairs and smiled, running up to me with nimble grace. She hugged me gently and then stood back to look at me. I pulled the shirt away from my neck and when Meg saw the bite mark she gave a little cry and her eyes filled with tears.

"Oh my God, Ang," she whispered, one hand to her mouth. "What's he doing to you?"

"Meg, don't," I urged her. "If you cry I'll start again, and I've been crying all afternoon." We went into my bedroom, and Meg sat cross-legged on the bed.

"What the hell happened to the door?" she exclaimed.

"Stu kicked it in. I guess I didn't answer it fast enough."

Meg stared at me in disbelief. "You're not serious."

I nodded and sat down beside her. "Yeah, I am. He was pretty angry."

"Angry?" Meg echoed, her eyes taking in the bruise on my forehead. "Ang, this is *beyond* angry! The guy is nuts! Really, sincerely nuts!"

I rose and began to pace restlessly around the room. "I don't know about nuts," I said, "but he's certainly … obsessed with me."

Meg got up from the bed and came over to me, taking my shoulders in her hands. "You have to do something. *Right now.* Before he really hurts you."

I pulled away from her, desperation rising inside me. "What?" I almost screamed the word, and Meg looked taken aback. "What am I supposed to do, Meg?" On an impulse I didn't understand, I yanked up my shirt and showed her my stomach. "This is what he did when I *threatened* to go to the police!"

Meg's eyes widened in horror, and she took an unconscious step backward. "Jesus Christ," she breathed, and I felt a grim sense of satisfaction. *Now* would she believe there was nothing I could do? We looked at each other, my pain mirrored in her eyes, but before she could say anything we both heard my mother's voice.

"Ang? Where are you?"

"I don't know who broke down the door," I said to Meg with a meaningful look, going over to the door and yelling, "Up here, Mom!"

I went over to my dresser and took a bottle of foundation, applying it carefully to my forehead. When the bruise was covered, I went over to the door. Mom rushed inside, looking scared and out of breath. She pulled me into her arms and hugged me tightly and I clung to her, so glad to feel her comforting presence that I wanted to cry again.

"Oh God, Peach," she said against my neck. "I'm so glad you're all right. The back door looks like a tornado hit it."

A tornado named Stuart Black, I thought, and when I looked at Megan over Mom's shoulder I knew she was thinking the same thing. I stepped back from Mom and adopted a surprised tone.

"I know. I wonder why nothing is gone? I mean, they went to all that trouble to get in."

Mom gave a short, humorless laugh. "Maybe we have nothing worth stealing. I'm going to go and call the police. At least I can get the insurance process going. We can't leave the door like that." She patted my cheek, smiled at Meg, and left the room.

The instant she was gone I looked at Megan fearfully. "Stu will kill me if he finds out!"

Meg's brow wrinkled in confusion. "If he finds out what, Ang? What are you talking about?"

"The reason that Stu … hit me today was that I threatened to go to the police. If he finds out they've actually been here, what's he going to do?" Fear washed over me in a suffocating wave, and I began to hyperventilate.

"Calm down!" Meg grabbed my hands and looked into my eyes. "We'll think of something." She pulled me over to the bed and we both sat down. "What if you told him that your mom called the cops and not you? Maybe then he wouldn't get mad."

I thought about that for a second and then nodded my head. "Okay, yeah," I said, my breathing slowing down. "That might work."

Megan got up. "I'll go and get the phone book."

While she was gone I thought about what I was going to say to Stu, praying that he wouldn't get angry. Megan returned clutching the telephone directory, and she sat cross-legged on the floor with it in her lap, turning to the 'B' section.

"Jesus, there are a lot of Blacks in here," she muttered, running her index finger down the side of a page. "Good thing I know his mother's first name."

"You do?" I asked, surprised.

Megan nodded. "Yeah. It was an assignment in Social last year. We had to do a family tree and I remember looking at his and thinking that his mother's name sounded a lot like yours." She looked at me apologetically. "Sorry."

"What is it?"

Meg bent her head to the book again. "Evangeline. Here it is: 467-8392." She reached into her bag and pulled out her cell phone. "Use this. Your mom is probably on your phone."

I took the cell from her and unfolded it, feeling as if I was in a dream. "What was that number again, Meg?" She read it to me and I punched it in nervously.

"Yeah?" His voice was laconic and bored, and for a moment I couldn't speak. Then I cleared my throat and said, "Stu?"

"Angel-baby," he said with real pleasure. "Can't get enough of me, can you?"

"I – uh … have to tell you something."

"Yeah?" His voice sounded interested, but it had that edge to it that I had come to dread. "What's that?"

"When my mother came home and saw the back door," I began, so terrified that I could barely get the words out, "she called the police." There was that black, dreadful silence again, and I began to cry.

"Stu, please …" I managed to say through the tears. "It wasn't me, I didn't say anything about you, I promise, don't …"

"Don't what, Angel-baby?" His voice was just threatening enough to prolong my fear, and I cried harder.

"Don't hurt me again, Stu," I whispered, and I heard Meg gasp and begin to cry, too.

"I'm not going to hurt you, Angel." It was a moment before the words penetrated, and the relief that flooded me was so great that I almost dropped the phone. "I'm very pleased with you, actually."

"You are?" I sounded like a surprised child, and Stu chuckled, a warm, sensuous sound.

"Yeah, I am. I knew your mother would call the cops, but I *love* the fact that you called to tell me you didn't say anything. You're a good girl, Angel. I'm going to give you a special treat the next time I've got you on your back." His voice lowered intimately, and the sexual timbre in it provoked an immediate response; my stomach quivered and I could feel my nipples hardening. Shame swept through me, and my face burned.

"Stu, the only reason I called is that I'm afraid of you."

"Angel, fear and love are very closely connected, you know."

"Do you believe that?" I really wanted to know.

"Of course." Stu spoke matter-of-factly, as if it were established truth. "The same way that pain and lust are connected. But you already know about *that*, don't you, Angel?" My face grew hotter, and I didn't reply.

"*Don't* you, Angel?" Teasing, but slightly menacing: he demanded a response, and I whispered, "Yes, I know."

"What do you know, Angel?" Stu sounded amused, and I hated him again.

"Yes ... I know that pain and lust are connected." I mumbled the words, conscious of the outraged expression on Megan's face.

"You're such a good girl, Angel," Stu crooned. "I'll see you tomorrow."

I closed Meg's phone and handed it to her silently, so ashamed that I couldn't even meet her eyes. "What a controlling bastard!" she burst out, and I nodded.

"You're telling me. I'm so afraid of him, Meg … "

Meg got up and sat on the bed beside me, putting her arms around me. I leaned my head on her shoulder, telling myself that I wouldn't cry again, I wouldn't, I wouldn't …

"This is so fucking wrong, Ang," she said softly, beginning to rock me back and forth, and I lost the battle and let the tears come.

Chapter Sixteen

The next morning I was unbelievably stiff, and it hurt like hell to get out of bed. My stomach muscles felt like they had been pulverized. I managed to stand up straight and went over to the mirror, lifting my nightshirt. My eyes widened when I saw the spectacular bruising. It was much worse than yesterday, now that Stu's boot mark had had a chance to really sink in to my skin. The intensity of the color shocked me, and I ran my fingers over it carefully, wondering how I was going to survive this.

I pulled on my robe and left my room, intending to cross the hall to take a shower, but before I could duck into the bathroom Mom came out of her room, dressed to the nines and smelling great. Quickly I clutched the neck of my robe tightly in one hand, hiding the bite mark, and she came over to me with a fond smile. She brushed the hair back from my forehead, and when she saw the bruise she looked shocked.

"What happened, Ang? That's the worst bruise I've ever seen."

No, it isn't, Mom. You should see the ones on my stomach.

"Gym class," I lied effortlessly. "We're playing soccer and I ran right into one of the goalposts." Mom patted my cheek and looked at me in amusement, all concern gone.

"You get that from your father's side of the family," she told me with a smile. "That man could have tripped over a pattern on the floor."

I smiled back and gestured to the bathroom door with my free hand. "Gotta take a shower," I mumbled, and she gave me a light slap on the rear.

"Hurry up and I'll give you a ride to school."

I showered quickly and dressed - another sweater/turtleneck combination. When I came downstairs I wasn't surprised to discover that my appetite was absolutely nil.

"Aren't you going to eat?" Mom asked when she saw mw grab my coat, and I shook my head.

"I'll get something at school."

"Okay, but let me give you money for the cafeteria. You can't get anything decent from a vending machine." I accepted ten dollars from her and we left the house.

The police had come by the night before and taken our statements about the door, and I had sweated throughout mine, certain they would know that I wasn't telling the truth. They had merely written down what I said, however, and had given Mom a card with a file number on it. She had already contacted the insurance company about replacing the door, and when she slammed it behind us she looked at me ruefully.

"Guess I don't need to worry about locking it."

Once again guilt stabbed me as I got into her car. Even if I hadn't broken the door myself, it was still my fault it had happened, and there didn't seem to be a damned thing I could do about it. On the drive to school Mom glanced over at me.

"You okay, Ang?" she asked lightly, but I could sense her worry; that was part of *my* radar. "You've been acting sort of funny ever since I got back."

"What do you mean?" I said, a little too quickly. "Funny how?"

"I don't know, sort of … spooked." Her accuracy was amazing, and the desire to tell her everything was overwhelming. I suppressed it with an effort.

"Everything's fine, Mom. I'm a little freaked out by the break in yesterday, but otherwise everything's cool."

Mom gave me a speculative look as she stopped for a red light. "You're not a very good liar, kiddo," she told me, and for a moment I really began to panic, thinking she was going to pry the truth out of me. "What's really going on – is it you and Jason?"

I sagged against the seat in relief; she had given me an out and she didn't even know it. "Yeah," I said, looking down at my hands, which were twisting restlessly in my lap. "We broke up the night of the party. He just … " I thought hard for a second, and then inspiration struck. "Well, he drinks too much. We had a huge fight about it and decided maybe we'd better not see each other any more."

"Well, it's too bad, honey, but I can't say I'm sorry." Mom pulled the car up in front of the school and looked at me with such love and approval that I felt guilty all over again. "I think you made a wise decision. Too much drinking isn't good for anyone, especially a kid like Jason. If it's as much of a problem as you say, I'd rather you didn't go out with him."

I gave her a halfhearted smile and opened the car door. "Thanks, Mom." I hefted my backpack onto my shoulder and leaned in to give her a kiss on the cheek. "See you later."

"Okay, Peach. Have a good day."

I went up the steps and into the school, feeling horribly self-conscious, as if everyone knew what had happened to me yesterday. By the time I got to my locker it wasn't just my imagination. Kids were staring and whispering behind cupped hands, especially the girls, and once or twice a knowing giggle brought a miserable flush to my face.

There was a white envelope taped to my locker. It had one word on it, written in a bold hand: **Angel**. The word looked almost accusatory, and even if it hadn't been the name only Stu called me I would have known it was from him. I pulled the envelope off and tore it open. It was a card with a single perfect rose on the front and one word written inside, in that same angry slash: **Mine**. My face grew hot and I hastily closed it, feeling like all the kids walking by were watching me. Meg came up to me and looked curiously at the card.

"From Prince Charming?" she inquired, and I smiled at her, my first real smile of the day. I nodded and showed it to her.

"Just in case I forgot," I said sarcastically, and that was when Stu's arms slid around my waist and his dark voice whispered into my hair.

"I'd be happy to remind you with a lot more than that card." He kissed me on the neck, in the same spot he had bitten me the day before. "Morning, Angel-baby." His lips traveled up to my cheek, and I tried to pull away, but he tightened his grip.

"You smell wonderful," he murmured in my ear, and a shiver ran down my spine. I glanced at Meg. She was looking distinctly uncomfortable, and Stu raised his head and asked her lazily, "What's the problem, Meg? See anything green?" This time he kissed my temple, and Meg made a rude snorting noise and turned away.

"If that's the only way you can get it," she muttered under her breath, and my eyes widened as her implication became clear. I could feel Stu stiffen and then he let me go, striding over to Meg's locker and leaning over her.

"What did you say, Meg?" he asked softly, and she stared up at him. His voice was smooth and calm, but the undercurrent was plain, and after a moment she shook her head.

"Nothing."

She tried to turn away but Stu stopped her. "No, you meant something by that. What was it?"

Meg's expression changed from anxiety to outrage. She pushed Stu aside and slammed her locker door. "Fuck you, Stu! I don't have to explain *shit* to you!"

Stu caught her arm in a bruising grip and pushed her back against the lockers, hard. "Then let me explain something to you." His voice was low and menacing, and neither of us could move. Meg looked up at him in sudden fear, and Stu shook her, just a little. "I get *what* I want, *when* I want. Angel is mine now. And if you want to see more of *this* – "

He turned around and grabbed my arm, pulling me toward them roughly. He jerked down the neck of my turtleneck to expose the bite mark he had left on my skin, and I said a brief prayer of thanks that the halls were virtually deserted. "Just keep talking. Am I making myself clear, Meg?"

Megan looked from Stu to me, horrified, her eyes full of tears, and when I opened my mouth to comfort her Stu squeezed my arm warningly.

"Get it, Meg?" he asked, and she nodded, a tear escaping from one eye and dripping down her cheek.

"I get it, you bastard," she whispered, tearing her arm away. "Stay the hell away from me." She ducked out from under him and ran down the hallway, and I blinked back my own tears, knowing how useless they were.

"Did you have to do that?" I asked him, and Stu rounded on me, his eyes black and furious.

"I'm going to teach you a lesson for both of you," he ground out, and jerked hard on my arm. "Come on, Angie."

I resisted him, trying to stand my ground. "What?" I cried, that now familiar, sick fear coming over me. "I didn't do anything, Stu!"

Stu leaned over to hiss in my ear. "You'd better fucking walk, or you'll be sorrier than you've ever been in your life."

All the fight went out of me at the lethal promise in his voice, and I began to walk beside him, my limbs feeling wooden, not even attached to me. When we reached the back door I knew we were going to his car, and if we were leaving the school it meant he wanted to get me alone, where he could do some damage. I began to cry as he pushed the door open, and Stu grabbed my arm and shook me.

"Stop it. Just get over to the car." He sounded like a brutal, angry stranger, and my mind howled in confusion.

Why is this happening? What did I do?

When we were at the bottom of the stairs Stu pushed me, and I nearly lost my balance. He dragged me the remaining distance to his car, wrenching open the passenger side door and throwing me inside, then stalking around to the driver's side and getting in himself. I pressed myself against the door, trying not to make any noise, but the terror that filled me needed to come out, and small whimpering sounds began to escape my lips.

With no warning Stu slapped me hard across the face, and my head flew back and struck the window.

"Why are you doing this?" I wailed. "*Why?* I didn't DO anything!"

In a second Stu was across the bench seat and right in front of me, so close that our noses were nearly touching.

"Because I can," he ground out. "And I want to. Shut the fuck up, Angie, or you'll make it worse."

He slid back across the seat, keyed the Rambler's engine, and tore out of the parking lot.

How could this get any worse? Just how the hell could this get any worse?

Chapter Seventeen

I seriously considered opening the door and jumping out of the car, but Stu was driving too fast. It didn't matter, anyway - before I knew it he had roared into a carport on the side of a small, run down house. The paint was faded and peeling, the windows opaque with dirt, and the lawn had definitely seen better days.

Stu got out of the car and came around to my side, opening the door and pulling me out. He dragged me to a door on the side of the house and let go of my arm to pull a key from his pocket. I stood beside him in a daze, feeling the same way I had when he had charged into my bedroom, all righteous fury: the world seemed dreamlike, swimmy and far away, and my head reeled. Stu unlocked the door and pushed me through it, and I went sprawling on a cold linoleum floor.

I crawled away from him and got to my feet, backing up against the counter. The sight of Stu coming toward me, his eyes furious and his mouth grim, made me delirious with terror, and I screamed at him: "Stop!"

Stu was so astonished that he did stop, and I burst into hysterical tears. "Oh God Stu please don't hurt me, please *please* don't hurt me again... "

I covered my face with my hands to shut out the sight of him, feeling like the worst kind of coward, but I had to beg. If he hit me I would shatter, just break into thousands of unmendable pieces. I felt his hand on my shoulder and I flinched and screamed again, trying to crawl up onto the counter to get away from him. "Don't, oh don't Stu *please* – "

Stu put his hands on my shoulders and gave me a little shake. "Look at me, Angel."

I forced my eyes open and looked at him, and at the speculative expression on his face a faint hope dawned. I forced myself to stay quiet. The fear wanted to make me beg again, but I sensed it would anger him if I continued, so I just looked at him, trembling all over, tears drying on my cheeks.

"Why shouldn't I give you a lesson, Angel?" Stu asked quietly, and my mind scrambled for a response. Finally I blurted out the only thing I could think of: the truth.

"Because I didn't do anything."

Stu looked at me, still with that considering expression, his hands light on my shoulders, and to my relief the anger faded from his eyes. He dipped his head and kissed me.

"I guess you didn't," he acknowledged, and my knees grew weak and rubbery. I grabbed the edge of the counter behind me to keep from falling, afraid to say anything else. Stu took my chin in his hand and tipped my head up. "But you'd better tell that bitch to keep her mouth shut. Understand?" I nodded frantically, and the corner of his mouth turned up.

"Jesus, you're even beautiful when you're scared," he said in a low voice, and lowered his head to kiss me again. This time he put his arms around me, holding me close to his body, and I could feel his erection pressing against my belly as my arms slid around his waist. I gave in to the sensations his lips were creating, feeling an ache begin deep inside me and move down my pelvis to rest between my legs.

When Stu raised his head again we were both breathing hard, and without a word he took my hand and led me into the small living room just off the kitchen. He took his coat off and kicked off his boots, and I slid out of my jacket as well, letting it drop to the floor. He put his hands on my shoulders again and pressed gently, and we both sank to the floor, me on my back, Stu next to me on his side. He began to kiss me again, his hands touching me everywhere, and the ache grew stronger, pulsing inside me until I thought I would scream from the need it was bringing out.

When I was certain I couldn't stand it another moment, Stu was gone from my side, and I raised my head to see where he was. He was kneeling between my legs, those long fingers undoing my jeans and working them down my hips. He was still fully dressed, and I felt incredibly vulnerable when he pulled my jeans off and tossed them aside. Then he hooked his fingers in the sides of my panties and began to pull, and I felt helpless in the face of his determination. "Stu, what are you doing?"

He cast the panties aside as well, and then he was prone, lying on his stomach with his upper body propped on his elbows. Stu looked at me with a smile, an indolent smile so full of sexual promise that I had to resist the urge to moan out loud.

"I told you I had a treat for you, remember?" He lowered his head again and my breath left me in a rush as his mouth found me, his tongue teasing me apart and exploring hidden crevices with delicate expertise. My head began to toss from side to side, and my hips rose involuntarily as words escaped my lips unnoticed.

"Oh God, Stu, oh God, Oh Stu, Ohhhh ... "

His tongue continued to caress me in the most intimate way imaginable, and the sweet pressure built to an unbearable pitch and exploded, sending wave after wave of sensation through me, leaving me weak and drained.

Stu raised his head and smiled at me, such a tender and satisfied smile that tears stung my eyes again.

Am I crazy? Why does he affect me this way?

He got to his knees long enough to unbuckle his own jeans and push them down, and when he returned to me it was as if we were made to fit together. Stu moved slowly, sliding in and out with long, deliberate strokes, until I raised my legs and wrapped them around his waist, bucking my hips to get him farther inside me. He braced his hands on the floor on either side of my head and moved faster, and I could feel his need building.

"Christ, Angel," he groaned, and I squeezed him tighter, glorying in the power I had in that moment, the power that made him utterly mine, although he would never admit it. His movements created a feeling of need inside me that grew rapidly, and as my arms tightened around his neck his entry became an exquisite kind of torture, culminating in an incredible sensation of release that left me with no strength at all.

Stu let out a guttural cry as he climaxed, and as he lowered himself onto me, gasping, he said hoarsely, "God, I love you, Angel, I really do."

I held him tightly as his breathing slowed, wondering if I was really as trapped as I thought.

Chapter Eighteen

Stu took me back to school after we dressed, and as he pulled the Rambler into the parking lot I could see several of his friends standing around in front of another car, smoking and laughing. They all looked over as Stu got out of his car, and I wanted to shrink down and hide. He came over to my door and opened it.

"Come and meet my friends, Angel."

It wasn't a request, and I grabbed my backpack and followed him reluctantly. There were three guys and a girl grouped around an old Trans Am. The boys were all dressed in black, with stringy hair and raucous laughs, but the girl was a vision. This was Gin, and when I got a good look at her I immediately felt small and plain.

She had gorgeous, perfectly balanced features that made her look more like a model than a high school senior, and her hair was a flame-red color so blatant that it had to be genuine. She laughed, displaying even white teeth, and I wondered again why Stu wasn't with her instead of me. We walked over to them, and the guys looked at me with interest. Stu wrapped an arm around my shoulders, pulling me close to him.

"Hey, guys. This is Angel."

He kissed me on the temple, and I felt my face grow warm. I glanced at Gin and she gave me a grin and winked; it made me feel less awkward. Stu introduced his friends. "Angel, this is Tim, Keith, Jordan, and Gin."

I smiled in what I hoped was a confident way. "Hey. Nice to meet you all."

To my relief, my voice came out sounding casual, and Stu squeezed me as if he was pleased with what I had said. Tim, Keith, and Jordan mumbled greetings and immediately went back to their conversation, but Gin smiled and said, "Are we finally gonna have another girl in this group? Sweet!"

Stu looked at her with a cocked eyebrow. "Didn't seem to be much of a problem for you before, Gin. I thought you liked being the reason for everyone's hard-ons." Gin rolled her eyes and I felt my face burn. Stu noticed and laughed.

"Virgin Angel," he murmured in my ear, and a shiver skittered down my spine at the feel of his warm breath on my skin.

"Well, it's great to meet you, Angie," Gin said, and I was surprised at her use of my real name. She grinned again and jerked her head toward Stu. "Yeah, I know your name. Mister Black here is the only one that calls you Angel, right?"

Stu answered for me. "That's right," he said lightly. "She's *my* Angel."

Gin whistled. "Jesus, you've got it bad, Stuart," she said, laughing at the way he frowned at her. I looked up at Stu and he gave me a long, lingering kiss.

"I sure do," he whispered against my lips and at the sound of the words I smiled and lifted my hand, placing it on the back of his neck and pressing my mouth hard against his. I could feel him smile back, and one of his friends joked, "Hey, man, get a room!" Stu raised his head and looked at them in amusement.

"You dogs should be so lucky," he said, and one of them punched him in the shoulder. The bell rang loudly, and Stu began to steer me toward the school.

"Wouldn't want you to be late for class," he said, waving lazily at his friends. As we went up the stairs and into the school I could feel the weight of myriad stares. We were obviously the topic of the week, and everywhere I looked there seemed to be a girl with an openly envious look on her face. Stu walked me to my locker, and when I had gotten it open and shoved my backpack inside, he smiled at me and said, "See you later, Angel."

He kissed me again and then ambled away, striding in that lazy, hipshot way that made me think of how his hips moved against my own. I turned hastily back to my locker, feeling too warm all of a sudden, and when Meg came up she startled me. I whirled around, dropping my Biology text on the floor, and she looked surprised.

"Nervous?" she inquired, and I bent to pick up the book, glad to hide my flushed face.

"Not exactly."

Meg peered at me. "What's wrong with you, Ang?"

I straightened up, pulled a binder out of my locker and slammed the door shut. "Nothing. You coming?"

Meg closed her own locker, looking suspicious. "Where were you during first period?" she asked as we began to walk down the hall, and I hesitated.

"Um, I was – I mean … "

Meg stopped in the middle of the hallway. "You were with Stu, weren't you?" She said it almost accusingly, and I grabbed her arm and pulled on it frantically.

"Shut up!" I hissed at her, and she shook her head.

"He must really be something in the sack," she said. "I've never seen your face that color before."

I smiled before I was aware of it, a sappy, dreamy smile. "He's really incredible," I said, and Meg's eyes grew round.

"What? Is this Angie Swanson talking? *Virginal* Angie Swanson??"

I reached out to slap her and she laughingly evaded my reach. We went into the classroom, and my heart sank when I remembered that this was the day we dissected frogs. I could see them, splayed out in plastic trays at intervals along the long lab tables, and I looked at Meg in dismay. She shook her head.

"I'm in the same boat as you, Ang. We can't be partners – we'd throw up on each other."

Kevin Sanchez came up to us. He was a dark, good-looking boy with olive skin, and Meg was forever teasing me about the crush he had on me.

"Want to be partners, Angie?" he asked, and Meg nudged me knowingly. I pushed her back and smiled at Kevin.

"Sure. As long as you do all the cutting."

Thankfully the experience wasn't quite as disgusting as I had feared, and when the period was over I walked out of the classroom with Kevin, laughing. Meg had gone on ahead, muttering something about a French test.

"You were almost as green as I was," I said, and a charming flush spread across his cheeks. He shrugged.

"I guess I better get used to a lot worse than that if I want to be a doctor," he told me, and I looked at him, impressed.

"Really?"

We were standing just outside the classroom, the rest of the students swirling around us. Kevin nodded. "Yeah. Everyone in my family's a doctor. My dad, my uncle, my grandpa ..."

"Just make sure it's what *you* want," I advised, and he looked pleased at my concern.

"It is," he assured me. "Hey, Ang, I heard you're not going out with Jason anymore."

I nodded, feeling suddenly uncomfortable. "Yeah, that's right. We ... er - decided to call it off."

Kevin looked at the floor for a moment, and I knew what he was trying to get up the nerve to say. I wanted to stop him before the words came out, but as it turned out, I didn't have to. I saw Kevin's eyes widen a second before I felt a strong hand clamp around my upper arm, and when Stu jerked me backward I uttered a gasp of fear.

"Hey! What the hell are you doing?" Kevin looked outraged, and I shook my head at him.

"No, Kevin, it's okay – " I began, and Stu shook me, hard.

"Shut up, Angel. He has something to say." He glared at Kevin, who suddenly looked unsure of himself. "Go ahead, Sanchez. You wanted to say something to my girlfriend?"

"Angie's *your* girlfriend?" Kevin asked, and Stu nodded.

"Yeah. Anything you want to say about it?"

Kevin shook his head and stepped around us. "No, I guess not. See you later, Ang."

I was too frightened to reply, and as soon as Kevin had gone Stu pulled me toward him so hard that I lost my grip on my books and they went skidding across the floor.

"You want to explain that to me, Angie?" he hissed, and my heart contracted.

Angie ... he only calls me Angie when he's so angry ...

"We were – partners, and Kevin was talking to me – " Stu jerked me over to the side of the hallway, ignoring the curious looks we were getting.

"Partners?" His voice was low and deadly, and I had to resist the urge to burst into tears. "That sounds pretty cozy. Partners."

"Stu, it was *biology!*" I whispered desperately, blinking rapidly to keep the tears back. "We were *lab* partners! I was just talking – "

Stu squeezed my arm, his fingernails digging into my skin, and I gave a little moan and closed my eyes. "He wanted to do more than talk. I guarantee you that. And it didn't look to me like you had much of a problem with it."

My eyes flew open and I stared at him in disbelief. His gaze was flat and angry, and I began to pray. "What are you saying? We were just *talking* – "

Stu placed his hand deliberately over my mouth, cutting off my words, and the tears spilled over, running down my cheeks and over his fingers. "You say that one more fucking time and I'll let you have it right here."

My throat was closed in terror, and I could hardly breathe. Stu's eyes never left mine, and the fury in them pinned me more effectively than his hands ever could. "You get the fuck home and stay there, Angel. You hear me?"

I nodded, more tears running down my face, and he smiled, a grim, satisfied smile that had no warmth or humor in it. "I'll be calling in half an hour to make sure you're there. Now go."

Stu released me and I stumbled away from him, going into the now empty hallway to pick up my books. I turned around and looked at him before I ran to my locker, and he just stared at me, his face expressionless.

Oh God, help me, please ...

I cried all the way to my locker, wondering what I had done that was so bad, and scared to death of the punishment I knew was coming because of it.

Chapter Nineteen

When I got home the house was eerily quiet, and it was so much like the day before that I fought an overwhelming sense of déjà vu the moment I stepped inside. I tossed my backpack on a kitchen chair and went into the living room, trying to calm myself. I couldn't sit still and I paced the room, feeling like an animal in a cage.

I didn't do anything! Oh my God, am I going to have to be careful about who I talk to? What I say? What I do?

The longer I paced, the more desperate my thoughts grew.

I didn't even choose this! He just took me, and now he's controlling my life! What am I going to do? Why is this happening to me?

It was hideous and unfair, and the more I thought about it, the more I felt like a hostage. When the phone finally rang I almost screamed, and I scrambled to answer it, feeling panic rise in my chest.

"Hello?"

"Angel-baby. You're home – good girl."

I took a deep breath and decided to try to placate him. It was the last thing I wanted to do, but I didn't want him to hurt me again.

"Like you told me to be. I didn't do anything wrong, Stu. I was just talking to Kevin."

I knew immediately I had said the wrong thing when he answered in a cold and angry voice. "You were enjoying it just a little too much, Angel. Remember what I told you? You're *mine*."

"I know, Stu, I remember." I closed my eyes, feeling like I was trying to reason with a lunatic. "If I'm yours, why does it matter if I talk to someone else? I – I belong to you." I had to force the words out. They stuck in my throat, and for a moment I hated him, a dark, bitter emotion that was totally unlike me.

"I think I need to teach you how to remember that."

"No!" The word was out before I could stop it. "This is so unfair!"

"Unfair, Angel?" Stu repeated in a dangerous voice, and all of a sudden I was angry. I didn't want this, I hadn't asked for this, and I knew I didn't deserve it.

"Yes, unfair!" I told him. "I don't have a *choice* in any of this! I didn't choose to go out with you, I didn't choose to have sex with you, and I sure as hell didn't choose to be hurt by you!"

"I'd shut up right now if I were you, Angel." At the lethal undercurrent in his voice my courage evaporated and I began to cry, but he continued as if he couldn't hear me. "You're going to find out what happens when you talk back to me."

"Jesus, Stu, please – " I sobbed, and he yelled, "SHUT UP!"

I almost dropped the phone, crying harder. *What did I do what did I do oh Christ what did I do that was so wrong –*

"I'll be there at two o'clock tonight, Angel. Leave the door open."

There was a click and he was gone, and I stood stupidly by the kitchen table, holding the dead phone to my ear. Then I hurled it across the room and collapsed in a heap on the floor, giving in to the hysterics that had only been waiting to claim me.

Mom commented on my tense, nervous mood that evening, but I told her I was worried about a French assignment and she seemed to believe it. I couldn't relax; I kept replaying what Stu had said in my mind, and when I remembered the fury in his voice I wondered what he was going to do to me. I finally managed to fall asleep around twelve thirty, but jerked awake with a start an hour later, gasping and looking around my dark room in a panic. I realized that I had been dreaming, and fell back against the pillows, sweating.

In the dream, I had been wandering in a dark, empty, echoing place, totally disoriented and scared to death. All I had wanted was to hear another voice or feel the touch of a warm hand, anything to tell me I wasn't totally alone in the world with nothing but the menacing blackness. Suddenly I had become aware of a sound, a threatening, sibilant hissing that seemed to be coming from everywhere. I had spun around and around, looking for the source of the noise, growing more and more frightened, and the hissing had transformed into words, a word, *one* word, and the sound of it filled me with terror.

"Angel ... Angel ... *Angel ...*"

I lay awake in the darkness, trying to calm the rapid pounding of my heart, the covers pulled up to my chin.

I can't even escape from this in my dreams ...

I turned my head and looked at the luminous numbers of the clock: 1:45. I threw back the covers and sat up, momentarily surprised at my own nudity. I searched on the floor for my robe and pulled it on, belting it tightly around my waist.

I opened the door to my bedroom and stepped out into the hallway, and the stillness of the house surrounded me. I made my way downstairs and went into the kitchen, staring silently at the ruin of our back door.

Kind of symbolic. That's my life, shattered and torn apart, only I can't just get a new one. God, I wish I could.

I went out onto the back step, wishing I had thought to wear slippers; the night air was cold. I sat down on the step and drew my knees up to my chest, resting my chin on them and staring at the fence on the neighbours' property without seeing it. I wondered again what Stu was going to do, what punishment he had in store, and fear wrapped loving arms around me, squeezing tightly.

I wished the situation was black and white, that I could just hate Stu for what he did, but whenever I thought of his arms around me, his lips against mine, and the feel of him inside me I would grow weak. That was how he made me feel – weak and cowardly, as trapped by my own desires as I was by his fists, and I was struck all over again by the lunacy of the whole thing.

I raised my head when I heard what sounded like footsteps coming toward me. I looked to my left and Stu materialized out of the darkness, his loose-limbed stride familiar. I looked up at him as he reached me and he stopped in front of me, his face unreadable. He raised his hand and I flinched; it was an automatic response, and I couldn't have stopped it if I had wanted to.

"Angel, Angel," Stu said softly, his voice caressing the word. "Are you that afraid of me?" I nodded, wishing I could tell him the opposite. Stu squatted in front of me and took my face in his hands.

"You're so beautiful," he murmured, pulling me toward him and kissing me. I slipped my arm around his neck and tangled my fingers in his hair, kissing him back hard, and he slid a hand inside my robe and stroked my breast. "Christ, I want you," he gasped, and it was my turn to feel powerful. I kissed him again in response, my tongue exploring his mouth this time, and when I felt him shudder it made me smile. At last Stu pulled away and got to his feet, taking my hand and pulling me up with him.

We went into the house and silently up the stairs, and when my bedroom door had closed behind us he undid the belt of my robe and opened it to reveal my naked body. To my astonishment he sank to his knees in front of me and ran his hands reverently down my hips, reaching around to cup my buttocks. Then he pressed his face into my stomach and just held me, and I looked down at his dark head, curiously vulnerable from this vantage point.

"Stu – " I began, and stopped; I had no idea what I wanted to say. Stu released me and stood up, holding my shoulders and looking down at me with a half smile.

"What, Angel-baby?" I shrugged helplessly as he pushed the robe from my shoulders. I felt it slide to the ground behind me and kicked it away with my foot.

"I don't understand you," I told him, and he smiled again and kissed me.

"You don't have to," he whispered, pulling me over to the bed. "Just give yourself to me."

"I've already done that," I said, closing my eyes as he pushed me gently backward and ran loving hands over my body. He left me for a moment, and when he returned to lie beside me we were skin to skin.

"No, you haven't," Stu said into my hair as he kissed my neck. "I want your heart, Angel. Tell me you love me."

The words came out easily, and later I would be stunned that I had been able to say them at all. "I love you, Stu."

He covered my body with his, entering me gently, so gently that it was impossible for me to believe that he was the same boy who had thrust into me that first time with no tenderness at all. He began to move his hips, kissing me at the same time, and my arms came around him as we rocked together in an exquisite rhythm that left us both shaking and gasping. Afterwards he held me, and I struggled against the languor that stole over me.

He beat you up, Angie! He punched you and kicked you! What are you doing?

We lay together in silence, and after a few minutes I asked, "Stu, why do you hurt me?"

I thought I had gone too far when he raised himself up on one elbow to look down at me, but there was no anger in his eyes. "I have to hurt you, Angel. Pain helps you understand."

My mind couldn't make sense of his response, and I just stared at him in confusion. "Understand what?" I finally got out, and Stu answered me with that same eerie calm.

"Understand that you belong to me. That you have to do what I tell you."

"But it's awful for me," I told him, tears coming to my eyes yet again. "Don't you care about that?"

He shook his head. "No. I don't. You need to be what I want, Angel."

"Why?" The question came out sounding more like a wail, and Stu leaned over and kissed me tenderly.

"Why doesn't matter. Just accept it, because if you don't, I'm going to have to keep on hurting you." I hid my face in the crook of his arm; if I looked into his eyes for another moment I would go crazy, just as crazy as he sounded.

"It's so unfair, Stu," I said, knowing I was on dangerous ground but needing him to know how I felt.

Stu leaned over me and put his lips against my breast, taking the nipple in his mouth. His hand slid over my mouth, and before I could react he bit down as hard as he could. As his teeth ground the tender flesh to pulp I screamed against his palm, again and again. When he raised his head again there was blood on his lips, and as I watched through a veil of agony, he licked it away. Then he shrugged.

"Who said life was fair, Angel?" Stu leaned over me, looking right into my eyes. "Don't you *ever* talk back to me again. Understand?"

I nodded, unable to speak. The world was fading away again, and I would have agreed to anything, anything at all, to make this incredible pain go away. My hand came up and touched my breast, and when I looked at my fingers I was horrified to see smears of blood.

I twisted away from him, my hands cradling the wounded breast, shattered. Stu allowed me to pull away, rising from the bed and beginning to dress, watching me cry with detached interest. When he was finished with his clothing he came back to me and eased me over onto my back again. He knelt beside the bed and pulled my hands away from my chest, holding them by my sides while he leaned over me again.

"Oh God, Stu, no, *don't –* "

"Hush, Angel-baby."

Stu covered my nipple with his mouth again, but this time his tongue licked it gently, the way a mother cat would cleanse a kitten, soothing the torn flesh and washing the blood away with his saliva. When he was done he kissed me, and once again I could taste my own blood on his tongue. He cupped the side of my face briefly with one strong hand, got to his feet, and walked across the room. He left without saying a word and I rolled over, pulled my knees up to my mangled breast, and cried myself to sleep.

Chapter Twenty

The next morning I dressed carefully, wincing as I put on my bra. My nipple was hideously swollen, the torn flesh raw and ugly; it looked like a malignant growth. The marks of Stu's teeth were clearly visible around the areola, and I shuddered as a vision of him bent over me, those teeth tearing into me, came into my mind. I slipped the cup of the bra carefully over the breast and held it protectively in my hand for a moment, wishing I could still its sharp aching. Even after four extra strength Tylenol, the pain had kept me awake the rest of the night, and the exhaustion and fear that swept through me made me want to go back to bed, pull the covers over my head, and stay there until this nightmare ended.

My eyes rose to the bruise on my forehead, just starting to fade, and as my gaze slid down the rest of my body, past the oddly swollen breast and the spectacular bruising on my stomach, I suddenly felt like a prisoner of war.

War, right. There's only one enemy, and you know damn well who it is.

The thought brought desperation with it, that helpless certainty that I wasn't going to survive this, and my eyes filled with tears.

You don't deserve this, Ang! How could anyone deserve this?

I wondered once again what I was going to do. I had never been in a situation even remotely like this before: with no choices, no protection, and no way out. The worst part of it was not being able to tell Mom. I longed to run to her, to dump it in her lap and let her find the solution the way she had when I was younger, but I was terrified of what Stu might do if he found out. His capacity for violence seemed to know no boundaries, and I had no intention of testing his limits.

I brushed my hair, sweeping it up behind my head in a ponytail, and applied subtle makeup for the first time that week. As I carefully smoothed on light foundation and dusted a faint suggestion of blush on my cheeks, a nasty little voice inside me asked snidely: *Tell the truth, Angie. You're doing this for* him, *aren't you?*

I tried to ignore that voice, but deep down I knew it was right, and the realization filled me with shame. There was no denying that Stu brought out a passion in me I hadn't known existed, and the thought of him being pleased with how I looked created a pleasurable tingle of excitement in my belly, whether I wanted to acknowledge it or not. I deliberately chose a tight tee shirt, tucking it into my lowest pair of hip huggers.

It's the only control I have. I might as well use it.

I threw a zippered sweatshirt over my shoulders and went downstairs to the kitchen, where I grabbed an orange before heading out the back door. I hadn't even gotten to the end of the front walk before I spotted Stu's Rambler coming up the street, and a reluctant thrill went through me when I saw him behind the wheel. I waited on the sidewalk until he pulled up in front of me, and he cocked his elbow out the driver's side window and gave me that lazy smile.

"Hi, Angel-baby," he said, devouring me with his eyes. "You look good enough to eat." I came over to the window and bent over to kiss him.

"Hi, Stu," I said, trying to gauge his mood. Stu gestured to the passenger side with a jerk of his head and I went around the car and got in beside him. He slid over to me and kissed me hard, his hand deliberately cupping my injured breast. I stiffened against him as pain radiated outward, filling my chest and making it hard to breathe. His fingers brushed the nipple and a bolt of agony stabbed me. I brought my hand up instinctively, trying to protect the breast, but Stu pushed it away and rubbed his thumb roughly over my nipple, every movement making it hurt more. I tore my mouth from his and cried out, tears of pain filling my eyes, and at last he stopped and looked at me, a satisfied smile on his face.

"Good morning, Angel," he said softly, and bent his head to kiss the breast gently. He jammed the car into gear and roared up the street, leaving me to cradle it in one hand and try to get the tears under control before we got to school.

At lunchtime Meg and I wandered out of the school and sat on the back steps, enjoying the sun. Even in mid-October it was hot and strong, and I turned my face up to it, feeling it bake my cheeks and forehead. Suddenly, I felt a presence behind me and I opened my eyes and turned my head to the side. Stu took my shoulders in his hands and buried his face in my neck, kissing it lightly. He sat down on the step behind me, his thighs on either side of my hips. He pulled me back against his chest and wrapped his arms around me, and I looked at Megan with an apologetic little shrug. She seemed uncomfortable, and before I could say anything she got to her feet.

"See you later, Ang." She ran up the steps and into the school, and I watched her go, sadness tugging at me. I felt like Stu was beginning to come between us; if he hadn't already, he was sure to in the days to come, and it was one more thing I had no control over. I sighed, and he asked, "Something wrong, Angel?"

I shook my head and then surprised myself by saying, "My chest hurts." Stu kissed my neck again, bringing his hand up to cup the breast tenderly. His fingers were as gentle now as they had been rough earlier, and I had to struggle against the urge to cry.

"I know," he said, and his voice was soft and soothing. "Listen to me, Angel, all right? Then those things won't happen."

I didn't reply, and he turned me halfway around and kissed me. "I love you," he murmured, and I made a choked noise in the back of my throat. I slipped my hand around the back of his neck and pulled him toward me, kissing him again and again with barely disguised passion. Finally Stu pulled away from me, his breathing rough and unsteady, and the lust in his eyes was almost frightening.

"Angel – " He sounded angry now, and his hand tightened painfully on my shoulder. I reached up and traced the line of his jaw with one finger.

"Now you know how it feels," I whispered, amazed at my own audacity. He stared into my eyes, his dark with wanting me.

"What the fuck are you talking about?" he growled, and I smiled.

"To have no control," I elaborated softly, and he grabbed my chin with iron fingers.

"You're walking a fine line, Angel." Stu's expression was half anger, half lust, and I sensed he was barely in control of himself. It sent a thrill of power through me that almost erased the fear. "Watch where you're stepping."

"Hey, you two, nice free show!" I was startled by an amused female voice that came from directly behind us.

Stu looked around in annoyance, and when he saw Gin he got to his feet and stalked off, his hands thrust into the pockets of his black jeans. I watched him go, feeling lightheaded but stronger, somehow. Gin sat down beside me on the step.

"Figured I'd get you out of that," she said. "Looked like he was getting pissed off."

I smiled at her and she grinned back; it made her look like a mischievous child. She was as effortlessly beautiful as always, even with her hair pulled carelessly back and clipped behind her head and her face innocent of makeup. She nudged me with one shoulder. "I know about Stu's temper. He can be a pretty scary guy when he gets mad."

Gin looked at me searchingly, and I wondered how much she knew. I could feel my face getting warm and I glanced away quickly, embarrassed.

"Has he been hitting you, Angie?" Gin asked, and I jerked my head up and stared at her. I was so startled by the question that I couldn't reply for a long moment, and when I wanted to talk I couldn't get the words past the tightness in my throat. Gin put an arm around my shoulders and nodded.

"It's okay. You don't have to tell me. I should keep my big mouth shut – I usually talk first and think later."

Hot tears blurred my vision and I shook my head. "No, it's okay," I whispered, looking down at the fingers twisted together in my lap. "I want to talk about it with someone who knows him."

Gin squeezed me briefly. "Has it been bad?" she asked quietly, and I nodded. Tears dripped onto the knee of my jeans and made tiny wet spots, and she sighed. "Jesus, what's wrong with him?" The question sounded like it was directed more to herself than to me.

"I was hoping you could tell me that." I looked at her, and Gin shrugged.

"I don't understand it," she said. "Stu's been in love with you since the beginning of last year." My heart gave an unpleasant leap, and I could feel my eyes widening.

"Last year?" I echoed helplessly, and she nodded.

"Yep. I was going out with him at the time – nothing serious, but I was hoping. Then he saw you, and it was game over."

I frowned. "What do you mean?"

Gin laughed, but it was a sound without humor. "What I mean, little Miss Angel, is that he fell for you. Hard. Harder than I've ever seen any guy fall for a girl." I was dizzy with confusion.

Last year? Last year?? *What was he waiting for?*

"Why didn't he ever say anything?" I asked.

"Let me answer your question with a question." Gin's direct green gaze was unsettling, and I forced myself not to look away. "What did you say when he finally did ask you out?"

(*Stu, are you serious?*)

Gin saw the expression on my face and nodded. "That's why. He was scared shitless you'd shoot him down, and that's exactly what happened."

"Is that why he – " I broke off, unwilling to say it out loud.

"Hits you?" Gin asked, and I winced at the words and nodded.

"Yeah. Is that why? Because he's angry at me for turning him down?"

Gin considered the question, and then shook her head. "No. I don't think so. You should hear the way he talks about you, Angie. He loves you more than anything."

She met my eyes squarely again, and I had no doubt that she meant what she was saying. "I don't know why he hits you. I think it's probably fear more than anything else."

That made no sense to me. "Fear? How could *Stu* possibly be afraid of *me?*"

Gin smiled at me sadly. "He's afraid of how he feels about you. He's afraid of losing you."

Frustration welled up inside me. "He never had me in the first place, Gin! He – he *took* me!"

"What?" It was her turn to stare at me. "What do you mean, he took you?"

I looked down at my hands again. Why was I telling all this to a stranger? A stranger who might take it right back to Stu?

"Maybe I'd better not – " Gin grabbed my shoulder, and I shrank away from her instinctively.

"Sorry," she said, withdrawing her hand. "You can tell me, Angie. It won't get back to Stu, I promise."

I hesitated and then gave in to the impulse to tell it to someone who might actually be able to make sense of it for me. "The night of the party I had, Stu came over and told me that he was going to ... have me." I took a deep breath, cursing the shame that rushed through me.

Why are you ashamed? This isn't your fault, Angie!

"He said he didn't care that I had said no, and that he didn't care that I didn't want to. He told me he was going to have sex with me and he came back later, when everyone was gone."

I had to stop and compose myself, and Gin took my hand. I looked at her gratefully, and she smiled, such a gentle, understanding smile that I had to look away again. "He came back," I continued. "And he – well, he – raped me."

I could hear the hiss of Gin's indrawn breath. "Jesus. I never thought he'd ever do anything like that."

I could feel her gaze on me but I couldn't look up; if I did, I would burst into tears. "He says I belong to him now," I told her in a low voice, and Gin squeezed my hand. "And I guess – I guess I do. Not just because he ... hits me, but because – " I began to cry, and Gin slipped an arm around me again, murmuring nonsense words of comfort.

"Because why, Angie?" she asked at last, and I wiped my eyes and tried to explain it to her.

"Because of how he makes me feel. He hits me, he terrifies me, and he controls me, but … I want him. He *makes* me want him! And I can't help it! Jesus, I *can't* … "

I dropped my head in my hands and sobbed uncontrollably, and Gin just held me, there on the school steps in the late October sunshine. She held me, and I was finally able to let go of a little of it, a little of the pain and confusion that was tearing me apart.

Chapter Twenty One

Talking to Gin helped. I didn't feel quite so alone, and she told me a lot about Stu. She said that his older sister, Amelia, had been a legend at the junior high school they had all attended: an eerie, out-of-touch girl that had drifted through the school oblivious to her own weirdness while whispers and catcalls had dogged her every step. Stu had been a natural target after that, Gin said, a shy, painfully awkward boy who had taken every criticism to heart and had burned with anger and resentment during those endless three years. I tried to picture Stu as lonely and insecure, but I just couldn't do it.

"He seems so totally sure of himself," I said to Gin, remembering that look of relentless determination I always saw in his eyes.

"Don't kid yourself, Angie." Gin looked at me seriously. "He's still a scared kid. He just hides it really well. Once he grew into that anger of his, he became a pretty dangerous character."

"You don't have to tell me that," I said. "What about his parents?"

Gin's expression turned grim, and she shook her head. "Stu's mother took Amelia and left him."

I looked at her in disbelief. "Left him?" I repeated. "What do you mean, left him?"

"I mean she just took off one day." Gin sounded angry, and her hands clenched themselves into fists. "He woke up one morning and they were gone. He's been alone ever since."

An unexpected feeling of pity gripped me, and I was surprised by its depth and strength. "Holy shit," I said softly. "No wonder he's mad at the world." I looked at Gin. "You love him, don't you?"

She flushed and looked away from me, out at the yellowing grass of the back field. After a moment, she nodded. "Yeah, I do. But not just ... that way. I love him as a friend, too. I think I'm the only real friend he has."

Gin turned back to me, and her eyes were pleading. "I know it sounds crazy, Angie, but be good to him, will you? He's been hurt so much in his life."

I blinked at her, wondering if I had heard correctly. "Be good to *him*? What about me, Gin? Do you know what Stu *does* to me?" As her words really sank in, I grew more and more angry. "He's kicked me in the stomach, pulled my hair out, and last night he – " I stopped; I couldn't tell her that. It was just too freakish. Gin looked at me anxiously.

"What, Angie? What did he do?"

I shook my head, taking a deep breath. "I can't – I can't talk about it," I whispered, and shame filled me again, the insidious shame that relentlessly whispered that I deserved it.

"I'm sorry I said that," Gin told me. "I just don't know what to say to you. I'm so torn – on one hand, I love him, and on the other, I really feel for you." A suspicion began to dawn in my mind.

"Did he beat up on you?" I asked, and Gin nodded slowly.

"He tried. I gave it right back to him, and after a while he stopped." Despair filled me.

See? She stood up to him, didn't she? You're such a coward ...

"Great. I guess I'm the perfect victim then, huh?"

"No, Angie, you're not," Gin told me. "Stu didn't really care about me. I was something to pass the time. He was waiting for you." She looked unbearably sad as she said this, and I resisted the urge to comfort her.

"So what does this mean?" The frustration was back, and it made me want to scream. "Stu cares about me, so that gives him the right to beat the shit out of me? That's nuts, Gin. He's just … obsessed. I don't understand it. Look at you, and look at me. Who do *you* think a guy would rather be with?"

Gin made an impatient noise. "You know what? Sometimes looks have nothing to do with it. I'm telling you, Stu loves you. He *really* loves you. I've watched him for a year now. You're all he talks about. Christ, I hated your guts for a while."

I gave her a half smile. "Because you wanted him," I stated, and she nodded. Anger filled me, an irrational, desperate anger. "Then *you* have him, Gin! I don't want this! I didn't ask for it!"

"I know, Angie. But you've got it, and now you have to deal with it. I'll try to help you if I can. Okay?"

I nodded then, my eyes full of tears, and she comforted me as best she could until Stu came back.

As the days and weeks went by, I tried to accept my new role as Stu's girlfriend, but it was hard. He continued to be volatile and unpredictable, and I never knew what would set him off. He continued with the "lessons", never hesitating to mete them out if he thought he needed to "teach" or "correct" me, and the inconsistent nature of these episodes of abuse began to take its toll on me.

I became agitated and nervous, unable to really enjoy anything, and the people who cared about me most began to notice. Mom tried to get me to talk to her, but all I would tell her was that I was having trouble in school and that it would work itself out. I knew she wasn't convinced, but there was nothing else I could do. Telling her the truth was out of the question. Meg tried to stand by me, but her hatred of Stu was a constant sticking point, and it got to the point where we could only spend time together if we didn't talk about him at all. I knew she thought I should just go to the school counselor, my mother, or the police, but she had no idea how abusive Stu could be and I wasn't going to tell her.

Something else was happening to me, as well. I was beginning to believe that I must be doing something wrong; that I must be responsible for what he did to me. My mind couldn't cope with the feelings I was beginning to have for Stu, and it was easier to blame myself for the abuse than to believe I could possibly love someone so twisted and brutal. There was just enough tenderness, just enough times when Stu worshipped me, to make me believe that he honestly loved me. And if he loved me, why would he hurt me, unless I was somehow to blame? This dilemma ran around and around in my mind, wearing an exhausted groove, until I deliberately stopped thinking about it and concentrated on just surviving.

The constant fear I lived with kept me on edge. It prevented me from trusting Stu and reinforced my position in our relationship – firmly under his thumb. I didn't think love could exist under conditions like these, but it wasn't genuine love - it was Stu's version of love, and I had no choice but to deal with it. I wouldn't have chosen him as a boyfriend, but now that I was with him I wanted to get to know him, to have a chance to relax around him, but that wasn't what he wanted. He told me he loved me, but he didn't seem interested in *me*: what kind of person I was, what my thoughts and dreams were, what I wanted out of life. I knew very little about him, either, except what I learned from Gin. Stu was reluctant to talk about himself, and I knew better than to press him.

The sex, however, had gotten better and better, and Stu overwhelmed me completely with his constant passion, bringing out responses that he seemed to pull from a secret place inside me that I wasn't even aware of. Was *this* love? It confused and upset me that I thought it might be, and I was beginning to need him in a way that was truly frightening.

One afternoon, on our way back to my house from his, I stared out the car window, wrapped up in pensive thoughts. Stu startled me by asking, "Why so quiet, Angel?"

"Do you really want to know?" I hated that everything I said to him came out sounding so timid, but I never knew if he would get upset, and it seemed safer to be hesitant. Stu slid his hand possessively between my legs, resting it against my crotch.

"Sure," he said expansively. "Lay it on me."

"I'm wondering why it is you want to be with me," I said, adding quickly, "Other than sex. You really don't know me at all."

Stu looked at me intently after he stopped for a red light, and at the depth of feeling in his eyes a shiver traced its way down my back. After a moment he smiled, caressing my cheek.

"You just do it for me, Angel. There's something about you that makes me want to possess you."

"But possession isn't the same as love," I said, choosing my words carefully. "Don't you want to know who I am?"

Stu stepped on the gas again and rubbed the side of his finger gently against me. I shifted in my seat and thought about removing his hand, but decided against it. We were finally having a real conversation, and I didn't want to spoil it by making him angry.

"Oh, I intend to find out everything about you, Angel," Stu told me, his hand continuing that maddening caress. "I've just been laying out the ground rules until now. Breaking you in, so to speak."

Anger rose up in me at his words. I wanted to tell him indignantly that I wasn't a slave. I wanted to say that I had a mind of my own and should be an equal partner in any relationship, but as usual, I was afraid. I was always afraid; it was what he wanted.

"Breaking me in?" I asked in what I hoped was merely an inquiring tone. Stu's hand stopped moving and he answered shortly, "Making sure you understand the rules."

I decided to chance one last question. "Do I understand the rules, Stu?"

Stu's jaw tightened, and his hand clenched on my thigh. "Are you trying to piss me off, Angel?"

Anxiety began at the base of my spine and crawled up my back, and I shook my head. "No. I just want to know where I stand."

Stu jerked the wheel of the car to the right, pulling the Rambler over to the side of the road we were on. He stepped hard on the brake and then looked over at me, his expression dangerous.

"Where you stand, Angel?" He gave a short, humorless bark of a laugh. "You don't stand. You lie on your back. Does that answer your question?"

His words hurt more than I would have believed. I just sat quietly, looking out the window at the grey December afternoon, trying not to cry. Stu reached over and took my chin in one hand, turning my face toward his, and my eyes met his reluctantly.

"I said, does that answer your question?" He spoke coldly, and I nodded. A tear escaped and ran down my cheek, and he kissed it lightly from my skin. I closed my eyes, feeling a yearning inside I couldn't put a name to, and when his lips touched mine I began to cry in earnest.

"Angel-baby," Stu murmured against my mouth, and I slipped my arms around his neck and pulled him closer to me. He broke the kiss and looked into my eyes.

"Tell me," he whispered, and I knew what he wanted to hear.

"I love you, Stu."

Chapter Twenty Two

One afternoon something happened that made me realize how deep my feelings for Stu really were, and it was far from a positive experience. Meg and I had just stowed our books in our lockers and were walking through the school toward the gym. I hadn't seen Stu since first period, and although I was more relaxed when he wasn't around, in an odd way I had missed him.

Meg and I had almost reached the gym when I saw him, and he wasn't alone. He was standing by the door to the chemistry classroom, talking to a short, dark girl with a pointed face and closely cropped hair. She was tiny, with gamine features and a kaleidoscopic way of dressing: everything she wore was mismatched, but it was a curiously good look on her. She was hanging on every word Stu was saying, and he was looking down at her with amused indulgence, one arm around her waist.

A totally unexpected bolt of jealousy shot through me, and I stopped walking, more upset by my reaction than by seeing Stu cozying up to some other girl.

You should be glad! Maybe now he'll leave you alone!

"Ang?" Meg looked at me. "What's wrong?" She followed my gaze and an expression of disgust crossed her face. "Nice." Her voice dripped with sarcasm, and I forced myself to look at her instead of Stu and the girl. "He treats you like his personal property, but that doesn't stop *him* from – "

I interrupted her, wanting desperately to convince her - and myself, if I was going to be honest - that it didn't matter. "Whatever," I said, starting to walk again, studiously ignoring them. We were almost past them when Stu caught sight of me and called me over.

I stopped, and Meg hissed, "Forget it, Ang! Ignore him!"

"I can't." She shook her head and continued on to the gym, and I went over to Stu, trying to hide the confusion and pain I was feeling.

"Hey, Angel-baby," Stu drawled, letting go of the other girl to slide a long arm around my shoulders. He pulled me toward him. "I want you to meet someone."

He gestured to the girl, who glared at me with poorly disguised animosity. "This is Delaney. Del, this is Angel."

Delaney looked me up and down, and her gaze was frankly insulting. "Angel?" she said rudely. "What is this, Stu? A *girlfriend*? Or is she your piece of the week?"

I was so astonished at her attitude that I just stared at her without speaking, but Stu reacted immediately. His hand shot out and grabbed Delaney's upper arm, and he jerked her forward.

"That's fucking crude, Del." Delaney looked momentarily frightened, and Stu smiled. "Let's try this again. This is Angel. She's my girlfriend. Angel, this is Delaney."

Stu looked at me expectantly, and I said, "Hi," glancing quickly at Delaney and then away.

Stu's hand tightened on Delaney's arm, and she muttered, "Yeah, whatever." She looked at Stu, and I was surprised to see that the expression on her face mirrored what I was feeling inside: pain and confusion. "Let go of me."

Stu obligingly released her, and Delaney walked away without another word. He squeezed me and kissed my temple, and I resisted the urge to pull away from him. He must have noticed my reluctance, because he asked, "What, Angel?"

Suddenly my eyes filled with tears, and I looked down at the ground, feeling foolish and angry with myself, but so utterly vulnerable that I wanted to scream. I shook my head. "Nothing."

Stu's fingers burrowed under my chin, and he lifted it until I was looking into his eyes. He smiled, and I knew he was aware of the reason I was upset. I also knew that it pleased him immensely, and I hated him for it.

"Did it bother you?" he asked. "That I was talking to Delaney?"

"Why would it bother me?" I tried to be offhand, but he saw through me at once. Stu chuckled, kissing me.

"You wear your heart on your sleeve, Angel. It bothered you. Admit it."

Goddamn him! Why is he doing this to me?

"Okay, it bothered me, all right?" My voice was angry, and he looked surprised. I pulled away from him and gave in to the anger I seldom expressed. "You get to hang all over some girl, and I can't even *talk* to another guy without you threatening me! That's really fair, Stu!"

Stu's arm shot out and he grabbed me, imprisoning my shoulders in both his hands. I tried to hold on to my resentment, but I couldn't, and when I saw the look on his face, I knew I was going to regret my outburst.

"Let me tell you about fair, Angel." Stu's face was inches from mine, and his eyes were black and furious. " 'Are you serious, Stu?' " How fucking fair was *that*?"

He shook me, mocking me with my own words, and I wanted to scream back at him that it hadn't mattered, that I hadn't had a choice anyway, and I still didn't. But I was smart enough not to; I was in enough trouble already. Stu began to pull me down the hallway, and I knew where we were going.

"Stu, please – " I began, and he stopped walking so suddenly that I ran into him. The bell had rung and the halls were deserted, and I prayed for a teacher to walk by.

Someone save me oh please someone save me –

"Please, Angel?" Stu said in a low, threatening voice, and his eyes bored into mine. "You'd better save 'please' for when we get back to my house. You're going to need it."

He clamped his hand around my arm and pulled, and I knew better than to fight. I just walked along beside him, hoping his anger would burn itself out by the time we got there.

Chapter Twenty Three

When Stu took me home that afternoon I could hardly walk to the car. He had been in an ecstasy of rage, much more angry than usual, and my legs were covered with ugly red welts where his belt had connected with my skin.

After getting me into the house and tearing the clothing off my body, Stu had pulled the leather belt out of the loops of his jeans and wielded it savagely. After a while I had just collapsed on the floor, huddled with my arms over my head, waiting until his fury was spent. He had been frenzied, yes, but never out of control. He was careful to hit me only where it wouldn't show, and although my legs and stomach were studded with red streaks and bruises, my face and arms remained untouched.

After Stu had exhausted himself and dropped the belt to the floor, he had jerked me to my feet, thrown me on the bed, and raped me, not once but twice. The first time had been painful; I was dry and unready when he battered into me. The second time I had responded in spite of the pain and clung to him as he emptied himself inside me. It was a hideous sort of irony that I would seek comfort from the very person who brutalized me, but I needed some small indication that he cared, that I was worth more than the pain he inflicted on me.

The ride back to my house had been quiet, with Stu brooding and me struggling to contain my tears. After these episodes it upset him when I cried, and I was learning to keep it inside and let go when he wasn't around. Now, as he pulled the car into the driveway at the side of the house and shut off the engine, I just stayed where I was, waiting for permission to leave the car. Stu reached for me, taking me into his arms and holding me tightly, and that wretched confusion rose up again: how could he be so cruel and then so loving?

Stu tipped my chin up and kissed me with such tenderness that the tears overflowed and ran down my cheeks between us. He pulled back and wiped them away with the tips of his fingers.

"Stay here," he whispered, and then he left me to get out of the car and come around to my side. He opened the door and helped me out. I moved slowly, like an arthritic old lady, every movement agony. Stu put a supportive arm around me and led me into the house. He closed the back door behind us but made no move to leave, and I asked him, "Don't you have to go?"

He shook his head and kissed my temple. "Not yet."

He helped me up the stairs and into the bathroom, easing me down to sit on the closed toilet. As I watched in confusion he swept back the shower curtain and turned on the faucet in the bathtub, adjusting the water temperature until it was pleasantly warm. Then he turned to me and began to remove my clothing, his hands as careful and tender as a nurse with an injured patient. He unclasped my bra and drew it off, and when my ragged and bitten nipple was exposed he bent his dark head to it and kissed it gently.

Stu pulled me to my feet and took off my jeans and panties, working the denim carefully over the myriad slash marks, and I drew in my breath as the material brushed the painful spots. He ran his hands over my legs lovingly, and as he worked the jeans over my feet I began to cry.

What is this? Who is this? You're not the Stu I know …

When I was naked, Stu lifted me gently and placed me in the bathtub, urging me into a sitting position in the warm water. After he turned off the faucet he proceeded to bathe me as if I were a precious infant, soaping my skin with smooth, comforting strokes and rinsing me over and over. Then he took the shower attachment, turned on the water again, and carefully wet my hair. He poured shampoo into his palm, working it into my scalp with expert fingers, and I cried helplessly the entire time; glad, so pitifully glad, that he wasn't hurting me.

When I was clean, Stu helped me to my feet and wrapped me in a towel, then lifted me into his arms and carried me to my bedroom. He put me down on the bed and eased me onto my back, unwrapping the towel and patting my body dry. I watched his face as he worked; his expression was serious and absorbed, and my heart ached with – what? Confusion? Gratitude? Love?

"That feels nice," I told him softly, and Stu looked at me and smiled, such a beautiful, adoring smile that it took my breath away. He reached for the bottle of lotion on my bedside table and squeezed some into his palm. Then he rubbed both hands together to warm it and massaged it into my skin with skillful, gentle fingers. I closed my eyes and lost myself in the exquisite sensation, the exact opposite of the agony I had suffered less than two hours before. Stu's hands moved in circles, soothing the stinging marks his belt had left earlier, and he bent his head to kiss my stomach.

"I love you, Angel," he murmured. "I love you so much …"

He left my side to remove his clothing, and when he lay down beside me his skin was warm and smooth. I opened my eyes and found him looking at me, his dark eyes depthless, and he kissed me over and over until I was breathless with desire. I pressed myself against him, running my hands down his back to cup his muscular buttocks, and when he whispered, "Tell me, Angel," against my lips, I didn't hesitate.

"I love you, Stu."

Stu slipped inside me, moving in a tender and almost hesitant way until I raised my hips hungrily and made a passionate noise deep in my throat. He abandoned all pretense of my fragility and began to pound into me roughly, and as I reached a shattering climax I finally said it of my own volition: "Oh God, I love you Stu, I really do ..."

He spent himself inside me, shaking with the force of his own orgasm, and we faded into sleep wound around each other in a lover's embrace.

Stu woke me an hour later, his hands on either side of my face and such love in his eyes that I was utterly overwhelmed. "Say it again, Angel," he entreated softly. "Please, say it again."

I kissed him gently, glorying in the feel of his body against my own. "I love you, Stu," I whispered. "I really love you."

He held me tightly, and when I felt his body begin to tremble I realized, to my amazement, that he was crying. "Don't leave me, Angel," he sobbed hoarsely. "Christ, please don't ever leave me."

"I won't," I whispered, and the love in my heart tried to strangle me. "I won't, Stu, I promise, I won't ..."

Chapter Twenty Four

After Stu left I cleaned up my room, trying to concentrate on what needed to be done instead of the chaotic thoughts that whirled through my mind.

I love you, Stu. I really love you ...

I was alternately elated and terrified at the memory of saying those words, and when I remembered the way Stu had reacted to them I was more confused than ever. It seemed that the more he cared for me, the worse the "lessons" became, so this unexpected vulnerability made no sense to me at all. He had been completely overwhelmed with emotion, and it had astonished me. I had never seen him so defenseless, and I couldn't help wondering whether I would pay for it later.

I couldn't think about having fallen in love with him at all. It filled me with so many conflicting emotions that panic was the only thing that rose to the surface, and I resolutely pushed the whole mess from my mind. It was Friday, and Ivan was coming to town. I wanted to enjoy being with him and Mom, and take comfort in the normalcy his being with us provided.

I had just finished putting a load of my clothes into the washer when I heard the back door bang open and a rich baritone voice drift up the stairs. "Where is my Angie? Why has she not come to see me?"

I descended the stairs two at a time, running to the kitchen and into Ivan's open arms. He hugged me passionately, the way he did everything, and when I finally pulled away he placed his large, warm hands gently on the sides of my face and kissed me first on one cheek, then the other. Then he held me at arm's length and regarded me fondly.

"You grow more beautiful every time I see you, my Angie," he told me, his accent caressing the words and turning them into something exotic and sensual. "It has been far too long since we have been together, milaya."

I loved the way my name rolled off Ivan's tongue: Ahn-jee. It always made me feel like a foreign princess, and it suddenly occurred to me that when I was around him I always felt safe and well loved.

"I'm so glad to see you, Ivan," I said, and for no reason at all tears came to my eyes. Ivan frowned and took my chin in his hand, a gesture reminiscent of Stu but so gentle with him, with so much more tenderness.

"What is this?" he asked in concern, peering into my eyes. "You are upset? What is wrong, my darling?"

I shook my head and blinked the tears away rapidly, giving him another quick hug. "I've just been missing you, that's all."

Ivan laughed and patted the side of my face. "You make an old man feel young again," he told me fondly.

At that moment my mother shouldered the back door open, her arms loaded with groceries, and Ivan hurried over to help. When they had brought all the bags inside Mom came over to me and put an arm around my shoulder. She kissed my temple and smiled.

"Here he is, as promised."

"And she is so happy to see me that she has the tears in her eyes!" Ivan proclaimed, looking up from the bag he was taking things out of. Mom looked at me, puzzled.

"Are you all right, Peach?" she asked gently. "There seems to have been a lot going on in your life lately."

Oh Mom, if you only knew ...

I had to push that away before I started to cry for real. I shrugged and began to help Ivan put the groceries away. "I'm seeing someone new – " I began, and Mom let out a laugh.

"That's a pretty poorly kept secret, Ang."

I almost dropped the box of rice I was holding. "What do you mean?"

Too late I realized that my voice had a high, panicky note in it that was totally out of keeping with Mom's playful tone, and she and Ivan both stared at me. I smiled awkwardly. "I mean – you know that I'm seeing someone else?"

"Of course." Mom took the rice from my hand and put it in the cupboard. "All the signs are there, honey. You're distracted, you're always gone, you take off first thing in the morning ... and what kind of car does he have, anyway? It's louder than hell."

She smiled, and an ache began inside me: why couldn't this just be a normal situation? I wished so much that I could brag about Stu the way I had about Jason, but it wasn't the same at all.

"It's an old car," I said weakly. Mom looked at me with raised eyebrows. "What?" I asked her defensively.

"Aren't you even going to tell us his name?" Ivan chimed in, "Yes, milaya, who is this young man who has captured your heart?"

Captured ... that's a good way to put it, Ivan ...

"His name is Stu Black," I told them, annoyed when an immediate flush warmed my face. "He's in grade twelve." Mom nudged me with her shoulder.

"Wow, looks like he has quite an effect on you, Peach." My face burned as Ivan laughed, and I nodded.

"Yeah, he's really … something." (… *especially when he's got me on my back …*)

"So, when do we get to meet him?" Mom asked, turning to put the empty plastic bags under the sink. "Or is he one of those guys who doesn't like parents?"

I was at a loss; I'd never thought to ask. I had assumed that I would have to keep Stu hidden, like a shocking secret only I really knew the truth about.

"Soon, I guess," I said, wondering what Stu would say when I told him about Mom's interest.

Mom laughed again at the look on my face. "Relax, Ang. I'm not going to give him the third degree."

Ivan took her by the shoulders and began to steer her out of the kitchen. "Out, my lovelies! I must prepare dinner!"

"I love it when he visits," Mom said to me as we went into the living room. "I don't have to cook." She drew me over to the couch, and I looked at her determined expression with a sinking sensation in the pit of my stomach.

"So tell me about Stu," she said, too casually. I thought hard for a moment: what could I tell her?

Oh, how about that he used a belt on you this afternoon? Or that he kicks you? Or bites you? How about —

I pushed the nasty little voice away and forced myself to smile at Mom.

- the good stuff just think about the good stuff -

142

"Well, he's really tall, and he has dark hair ..." My voice trailed off as I pictured Stu in my mind, and a different sort of ache began inside me, one that was becoming all too familiar. My face grew hot again at Mom's knowing laugh.

"You should see the look on your face, Ang," she teased. "He's gorgeous, isn't he?" I nodded, surprised at the warmth that went through me.

"Yeah, he really is," I said. "We – er, got together the night I had the party here."

"The night that you broke up with Jason?" Mom asked, and I nodded.

"I guess we didn't really get together, but that was when I knew that Stu was ... interested in me. We've been going out ever since."

Mom frowned. "Why didn't you tell me?"

I stared at her, nonplussed. "I don't know," I finally answered, a little irritated at her insistence. "I don't want to spill my guts about everything the way I did when I was ten, Mom. Give me a break."

"I guess you don't." Mom looked a little wistful, and I immediately felt guilty. "I keep forgetting that you're not my little girl anymore, Ang." I reached over and hugged her.

"I'll always be your little girl," I told her, and she held me tightly.

Chapter Twenty Five

I slept late the next morning, and when Mom knocked on my door I had to shake myself out of a dream. It was an erotic dream about Stu, and when she poked her head in the door I felt as though she tell just by looking at my face. I burrowed under the covers, and when she came into the room I smiled at her halfheartedly, my heart racing from the vivid images that were still clear in my head.

(*Oh God Stu, Jesus, oh yes, Ohhh don't stop*)

"Phone, Peach," she told me. "If it's Stu, he sure has a sexy voice."

I reached for the cordless on the bedside table, knocking it to the floor. "Mom!" She picked it up and handed it to me.

"What?" Mom tousled my hair and gave me an amused smile. "Old doesn't equal dead, Ang." She walked out of the room and I brought the phone to my ear.

"Hello?"

"Hey, beautiful."

God, he does have a sexy voice, doesn't he?

"Hi, Stu. What's up?"

"Do you really want to know?" His insinuation was plain, and I was glad he couldn't see my red face.

"I can guess," I told him. "Is that why you called?"

144

Stu chuckled. "I can't believe what you do to me, Angel. Sex with you is all I think about." Heat rushed through me, and my eyes closed as I remembered my dream.

"I had a dream about you last night," I found myself telling him, and he said, "Really. Why don't you tell me all about it?" A wave of desire washed over me and I had to catch my breath.

"Let's just say you were doing what you do best," I told him softly, and he groaned.

"Don't make me come over there. I'm pretty fucking horny right now."

"After yesterday?" I asked, and he laughed.

"I'll never get enough of you, Angel. You bring out the animal in me."

Animal, right. The smile disappeared from my face as I remembered the fury with which he had wielded his belt the previous afternoon. *Animal is a good way to describe you, Stu ...*

"What are you up to this weekend?" he asked, and I was surprised at the question.

"Mom's boyfriend Ivan's in town and we're going to the opera tonight," I told him.

"Sounds thrilling," Stu replied in a bored voice. The remark cut me, and I spoke without thinking.

"Well, I guess it's a good thing you're not going, isn't it?"

"You want to watch the way you say things, Angel." The flat and threatening tone of his voice startled me, and I didn't respond.

"*Don't* you, Angel?" Stu said meaningfully, and I said, "Yes, I do, Stu. I'm sorry."

It was these little exchanges that reminded me I had to be forever on my guard, always careful to say the right thing in the right way. No matter how well things went between us, Stu never hesitated to put me in my place, and I knew he loved doing it. Those times made it seem so wrong to love him, and it always made me want to scream with frustration. Why couldn't I be an equal?

"Well, I'll let you get back to your family bliss, Angel." Stu's voice was sarcastic now, and all the enjoyment had evaporated from the conversation. "I want you home by two o'clock tonight. You know why."

My treacherous body responded immediately to the lust in his voice, and I said dutifully, "I know, Stu. I will be."

"I'm going to fuck you until you're begging for mercy, Angel. Make sure you're naked under that robe again. Understand?"

"I understand, Stu. I will." I swallowed against the tears that suddenly crowded my throat, feeling like an object. How well he knew how to subjugate me, and how willingly I let him do it.

"Good girl, Angel. I'll see you later."

"Bye, Stu."

I pressed the 'end' button and dropped the phone on the bed, pushing the entire exchange from my mind. Ivan was only going to be here for a little while, and I wanted to enjoy it.

Mom, Ivan and I had a good time that Saturday. We went to the university district and walked around Whyte Avenue, a long stretch of unique shops and businesses that had a definite bohemian flair. With names like 'The Funky Pickle', 'Death by Chocolate', and 'When Pigs Fly', it was fun and interesting to browse. We had lunch at Yianni's Taverna, a popular Greek restaurant, and Mom even let me have a glass of wine. It was so nice to just be myself and not have to worry about what I said or did that by the end of the day I was relaxed and almost happy again.

When we got home we had a pick-up supper and then began getting ready for the opera that evening. As I undressed for the shower, I examined the marks on my body almost dispassionately. The latest crop of bruises were fading - although there were always new ones to replace the old - but the angry red marks left by Stu's belt still stood out clearly, and I would have to wear dark pantyhose to hide the ones on my legs. My nipple was healing, but it looked oddly distorted, puckered in a way I suspected nothing but surgery would be able to correct. The bite mark on my neck had faded considerably, but I decided to wear a dress that had a high neckline to avoid any questions Mom and Ivan might have.

As I pulled the black dress out of my closet I thought about Stu, and an aching sadness filled me. I wondered for what seemed like the millionth time why our relationship couldn't be normal, and that voice in the back of my mind spoke up immediately.

You wouldn't be with him if it were, Ang! You seem to be forgetting that it wasn't your choice to be with him in the first place!

I told the voice to shove it, placed my dress carefully on the bed and pulled on my robe to go across the hall to the bathroom. I remembered what Stu had said that morning about wanting me naked underneath it and my face burned.

Think of something else besides him, for Christ's sake! He's not your whole life!

I tried to convince myself of that, but I couldn't. Stu *was* becoming my whole life, and it scared the hell out of me. Every time I looked in the mirror I would hear his voice (*you belong to me, Angel*), every time I closed my eyes I would think of his touch, and everywhere I went I looked for him, as though he might be following me, watching to ensure I was behaving myself. It upset me terribly, but there didn't seem to be a thing I could do about it, especially now that I loved him. His opinion, his approval, his happiness, was becoming more and more important to me, and the abuse was tearing me down in a way that it hadn't before.

It was so much more personal now that I cared about Stu, so much harder to understand and harder to endure, and every time it happened I felt worse about myself. I was losing the confident edge I had always possessed, becoming timid and uncertain, and there were times when I hated myself for my weaknesses.

Hiding all these changes from my mother was taking a toll. I had to put on an act around her, and behaving like the old Angie was becoming more and more difficult. I began to spend a lot of time alone; my friendships were falling away, and I realized that Stu had imprisoned me in more ways than one. I felt like I was losing myself, and becoming what *he* wanted me to be (*Angel*), and I wondered constantly what I could do to stop it.

After I showered I returned to my room to get dressed. I slipped the short black dress over my hips, noticing that it was looser than it had been the last time I had worn it. I had lost weight, and I hadn't even noticed. I smoothed the material over my hips, running my fingers over the bones that jutted out on either side. It was a pretty dress with a high neck, but it left my shoulders bare and my back exposed to the waistline. I applied my makeup, putting on a little more than usual, but loving the results when I surveyed the entire look.

I left my room in search of Mom. I wanted to get her to put my hair into a French braid, and just as I got to the door of her bedroom I heard my name. I stopped in the doorway, knowing I shouldn't listen but unable to help it.

"I tell you, my Joy," Ivan was saying, "there is something different about her. I have never seen her like this. She is so nervous, so – how do you say – not all there."

"Distracted?" My mother asked him, and I could picture Ivan nodding vigorously.

"Exactly!" he exclaimed. "What could be the matter, do you think?"

"I don't know, Ive," Mom answered. "I think it's just this new guy she's going out with. He's got her head in the clouds."

"I do not think that is it." Ivan's tone brooked no disagreement, and I could hear Mom make an impatient noise. "If our Angie was 'in the clouds', as you say, she would be happy, would she not? I am not seeing a happy girl, my Joy. Nervous, yes. Distracted, yes. But not happy."

"Oh, for God's sake, Ivan!" Mom said. "I'm with her every day! Angie has a lot going on right in her life. She's seventeen now. Relationships are getting more serious."

"You need to ask her about this boy, milaya," Ivan told her, and I smiled at the fatherly tone of his voice, even though his concern made me cold inside. What was he seeing that Mom wasn't?

"I'll talk to her, all right? Now stop playing the worried father and get dressed."

I decided to step in at this point, and when I walked into the bedroom the guilt on both their faces made me feel momentarily ashamed. "Did I interrupt something?" I asked lightly, and Mom's face grew slightly pink. She shook her head.

"Of course not, honey," she said. "What is it?"

"Will you do my hair?" I asked her, and a relieved expression softened her features.

"Sure. Sit down." I smiled at Ivan, and he leaned over to kiss me on the forehead before leaving us to go into the ensuite and dress. I looked at Mom in the mirror as she picked up her brush.

"I heard you and Ivan talking about me," I told her. "There's nothing to worry about, Mom." Mom began to brush my hair; long, slow strokes that felt good against my scalp.

"Ivan's right, though, Ang," she said. "You *have* been nervous and distracted lately. Anything you want to talk about?"

I had to look away from her at that. There was so much I wanted to talk about, so much I needed to tell her, but I couldn't. Instead, I shook my head.

"Not really. School's just wearing me out right now. All the teachers have decided to give massive assignments at once."

Mom put the brush down and began to divide my hair into sections. "Maybe you'd better spend a little less time with Stu and more time with your books," she advised, and I could feel myself flushing.

"Stu likes to spend time with me," I said, and she looked at me oddly.

"Well, what about you? Do you have a say in this?"

I went cold at the question. Of all the things she could have said, that made me the most nervous.

Does she know? Oh my God, does she know anything??

"Of course I do," I said, laughing. "I love being with Stu. He's really a fantastic lover."

I clapped a hand over my mouth, unable to believe I had said this last out loud, and Mom laughed at the look on my face. "Come on, Ang. I know you're having sex. I just hope you're using protection."

Terror seized me in a cold and panicky grip. It had never even occurred to me, and Stu certainly never brought the subject up. I covered the feeling, however, and made an impatient face at Mom in the mirror.

"Well, duh," I said. "I'm not totally clueless, Mom."

It was a neat way of responding in the affirmative without actually saying yes, and I tried frantically to remember when my last period had been.

"I knew I could count on you, Peach," Mom said fondly, squeezing my shoulder. She finished braiding the sections of my hair together and stood back to admire her work. "You're so beautiful, Ang. When did you grow up on me?"

She bent over and hugged me, and I leaned my head back against her arm. "That doesn't mean I don't need you."

Mom kissed me on the cheek. "Glad to hear it."

Ivan came strolling toward us, looking distinguished in his formal black suit. He wore a crisp white shirt and a bow tie, even though Mom told him it wasn't necessary. Ivan insisted: he proclaimed that the opera was one of the few occasions left where he could dress up, and he relished the opportunity. When he saw us, he burst out into a boisterous Russian song, and Mom and I looked at each other and smiled.

"I am the luckiest man in the world tonight!" Ivan declared, and Mom kissed him.

"Let's get going, lucky man. We don't want to be late."

Chapter Twenty Six

In spite of the fact that the opera was in Italian, it was very exciting and dramatic. As we filed out of the auditorium during intermission I said to Ivan, "It doesn't even matter that I don't understand the language. The acting and the vocal intonation tell the story on their own."

Ivan's eyes lit up at this and he kissed my cheek enthusiastically. "You are the most perceptive of young women!" he exclaimed proudly. "I will make opera a love of yours yet, my Angie!"

I kissed him back. "I'm going to go and get in line for the bathroom," I told him and Mom. "If I'm not back in time for curtain, just go in ahead, okay?"

"Okay, hon." Mom took Ivan's arm and they strolled off in search of refreshments.

I descended the huge, curving staircase that was a focal point of the auditorium, knowing that the washrooms on the lower floor were always less crowded. As I made my way through the crush of people toward the ladies' room, I was astonished to see Stu leaning against the wall right next to it. He was wearing an old leather coat and his customary black jeans, and when he saw me the corner of his mouth turned up in a lazy grin. He was getting some strange looks from women waiting to use the washroom, but he ignored them and came toward me.

My heart began to race and I stood where I was, feeling like we were the only two people in the entire building. Stu reached me and placed his hands on my bare shoulders, his fingers caressing my skin gently.

"You look absolutely gorgeous," he said, dipping his head and kissing my shoulder lightly. I smiled at him, confused.

"What are you doing here, Stu?"

He wrapped his arms around me, oblivious to the stares we were getting. "Just checking to see that you're where you're supposed to be," he said into my ear, his warm breath sending a shiver down my spine. A cultured voice over the loudspeaker announced that the performance would resume in two minutes, and the crowd began to head for the stairs.

"Stu, I have to get back inside," I told him. I tried to pull out of the circle of his arms, but he tightened them around me.

"Wait a minute, Angel-baby," he whispered. He pushed his hips into mine and I could feel his hardness against my belly. A furious spark of lust shot through me and my control began to dissolve. When the majority of the people had gone up the stairs, Stu urged me toward the ladies' room. I looked at him in confusion.

"This was where you were headed, wasn't it?" he asked, and I nodded.

"Yes, but – "

Stu gave me a gentle push toward the door. "Then get in there."

I did as he said, and went into a stall while two other women primped in front of the mirror. When I had finished the room was empty, and I was standing at the sink washing my hands when Stu came through the door.

"What are you doing?" I asked him, beginning to giggle. "You can't come in here, Stu."

Stu reached out and grabbed me, running his hands over my thinly clad breasts. "Actually, Angel," he said into my hair, "I have every intention of coming in here."

He pushed me into the wide handicapped stall and locked the door behind us. Then he pulled me into his arms and began to kiss me, overwhelming me so thoroughly that when he finally stopped and turned me around, I had no idea what he meant to do.

"Bend over," he ordered in a voice heavy with desire, and his hand lifted my skirt and searched between my legs.

"What?" Stu hooked his fingers into the top of my pantyhose and began to pull. "Stu, you can't – "

He jerked the tight material over my hips and pushed it down. His hand thrust between my legs again, and I let out a gasp as his fingers found their way inside me.

"Don't tell me what I can't do, Angel." Stu withdrew his fingers and pulled the pantyhose down to my knees. "Now bend over."

I did as he said, bracing my hands against the tile wall opposite the toilet. Stu flung my dress up over my buttocks and grabbed my hips. With no warning he rammed himself into me, and I barely managed to stifle the cry that rose to my lips. He thrust into me again and again, harder and harder, and as I felt orgasm approaching my breathing quickened, coming in short pants.

Just as I climaxed, Stu removed one hand from my hip and reached around for my breast, taking the injured nipple in his fingers and pinching as hard as he could. Intense pain and incredible pleasure shot through me at the same time, and the sensations melted into one another as the spasms rocked me. Stu continued to hold my nipple in that cruel grip as his own orgasm burst out of him, and his fingers tightened unbearably as he shuddered. By the time his hips stopped moving tears of pain were running from my eyes, and when he finally released me I almost fell over as my hand left the wall to go to my breast. Stu leaned over me, his breath harsh in my ear.

"Pain and lust, Angel," he whispered. "Pain and lust." He pulled out of me and I could hear the sound of him buckling his belt. I leaned against the wall of the cubicle, one hand braced on the tile, the other cradling my breast.

"I couldn't wait until later," Stu told me as he opened the cubicle door. "Have a good night's sleep, Angel."

He left the room, and I straightened up as the door closed behind him, wiping away the tears and pulling my pantyhose back up. I repaired my makeup in front of the mirror, being careful to avoid looking into my own eyes.

When I returned to my seat in the auditorium, I whispered to Mom that the lineup for the bathroom had delayed me. Then I sat and stared unseeingly at the rest of the performance, feeling him dripping out of me and knowing that whatever it had been, I couldn't call it rape.

Chapter Twenty Seven

The next morning I woke feeling upset and out of sorts. The night before, I had been quiet and subdued for the rest of the opera, and although Mom and Ivan had noticed, they didn't remark on it. I went straight to bed when we got home, and although I had tried hard not to, I had ended up crying myself to sleep. I had felt so used, like a receptacle for Stu's lust, and the fact that I had enjoyed it made it seem so much worse.

You're a slut. You loved it and you know it.

I turned over and pillowed my head on my arm, trying to ignore the nasty, judgmental voice that never hesitated to point out my shortcomings. Stu was changing me, and not for the better. I felt like I didn't know myself at all anymore, and the more I cared for him, the more of me, of *Angie*, I seemed to lose. I lay silently, willing myself to remain in control. I was so goddamn tired of crying.

There was a light tap on the door, and Mom poked her head in. "Are you awake, Peach?"

I raised my head and tried to smile. "Just. Come in, Mom."

Mom entered the room and sat beside me on the bed. "What happened last night?" she asked, smoothing the hair from my forehead.

"You were like night and day during the first and second acts." Her voice was light, but I sensed concern beneath the surface.

"I had a headache," I said. "It came on really suddenly. It was one of those ones that feel like it's trying to burst out your skull. I could hardly focus on the second act."

Mom looked dubious, but she didn't call me on it. She leaned over and kissed my forehead. "Well, come on down for breakfast," she said. "Ivan made pancakes just for you."

That brought a genuine smile to my face. "I'll be right down."

Mom left the room and I sat up, stretching. I got out of bed and threw on some sweats, twisted my hair up into a careless knot, and went down to the kitchen. Ivan was standing at the stove, flipping pancakes and humming under his breath, and I sneaked over to him and slipped my arms around his waist, no mean feat considering how broad he was around the middle.

"Aha," he said in a wondering tone, "Who is it that we have here?" He put down the spatula he was holding and reached behind him, and I darted out of the way. Ivan laughed and spun around, placing his hands on his hips and smiling at me.

"My Angie," he said expansively. "I thought perhaps you would not get up today."

"Hardly," I said, sitting down at the table across from Mom. "I wouldn't miss seeing you before you go, Ivan. You know that." A pleased smile creased Ivan's bearded face.

"I do indeed," he said, picking up the pan and bringing it over to me. He slid three wonderfully fragrant pancakes onto the plate in front of me.

"Thanks."

He bowed to me solemnly and returned the pan to the stove. He sat beside Mom, sipping his coffee, and we talked desultorily about the opera while I ate. I was about halfway through my breakfast when there was a tapping at the back door, and Mom twisted around in her seat.

"Who could that be?" she wondered. She got up and went to the back door, opening it and greeting the person standing there, and my fork froze halfway to my mouth when I heard Stu's voice. I lowered the fork to my plate, watching as he sauntered into the kitchen behind Mom. She smiled at me.

"It seems I've met Stu," she said, and Stu winked at me.

"Hey, Angel-baby," he said, and Mom exchanged an amused glance with Ivan: *Angel-baby. Isn't that sweet?*

"This is Ivan Romanovich," Mom said, and Stu reached out and shook Ivan's hand.

"Nice to meet you, Mr. Romanovich."

"The pleasure is mine," Ivan said gravely, looking at Stu closely. I managed to find my tongue at last, and I said weakly, "Hi, Stu. What are you doing here?"

Stu slid into the chair beside me and kissed me chastely on the cheek. "That's a nice way to welcome your one and only. Aren't you glad to see me?"

He slid an arm around my shoulders and squeezed, and I looked at Mom and Ivan with an embarrassed smile. "Of course." I turned my head for a real kiss, and he whispered, "I'd like to fuck you right now, in the middle of this table." My face burned, and I slapped him on the knee.

"Stop it," I hissed out of the side of my mouth, and Mom laughed.

"So, Stu, you're in grade twelve?" she asked, and Stu nodded.

"Graduating in June."

"Do you have any plans?" I frowned at her: *Don't give him the third degree! You just met him!* Stu chuckled, as if he had been expecting the question.

"Well, I'd love to run off with Angel, but I think I'll wait until the six month mark to propose." Ivan's mouth fell open and I looked at Stu in disbelief.

"Stu!" I protested, and Mom laughed.

"You're a sharp one, aren't you? Just give me a little notice, you two, before you get the license." Stu squeezed me again and kissed me on the temple.

"You got it," he said to Mom. "Actually, I'm thinking of getting into mechanics. I've always liked working on cars, and God knows there's a market for it."

I just sat beside him, amazed. Who *was* this friendly, humorous young man sitting beside me? It was yet another side of him, and I marveled that there seemed to be so many.

"It's certainly a practical choice," Mom said. "Does it pay well?"

"Pretty good," Stu replied. "Enough for me to live on, at least." He nuzzled my neck briefly. "Until I get married, that is."

I jerked away from him as Ivan burst into laughter. "Stu!" I cried again, giving his shoulder a push. "Shut up!"

He grinned at me, a mischievous little boy, and something in that smile made my heart sing. "What can I say?" he told me. "You've got me, Angel."

Mom rose and began to clear the table. "Would you like some breakfast, Stu?" He shook his head.

"No, but thanks, Mrs. Swanson." He turned and looked at me. "Want to come for a ride, Angel?"

I shrugged helplessly. "Uh – sure. Is it okay, Mom?"

Mom paused in the act of loading the dishwasher. "Sure. As long as you don't run off and get married."

I rolled my eyes as Stu laughed. "You guys are regular comedians," I muttered. I got up and went over to Ivan, putting my arms around his neck. "Have a good trip back, Ivan."

I stepped away as Ivan pushed out his chair and got to his feet. He enfolded me in his strong arms and held me tightly, and I hugged him back.

"I love you, milaya," he told me, and tears filled my eyes.

"I love you, too." Ivan kissed me soundly on both cheeks, and I turned to Stu.

"Should I change?" I asked him, and the corner of his mouth turned up.

"I don't care what you wear. I like it better – "

I hurried over to him and placed my hand over his mouth; I could guess what he had been about to say.

"Okay, let's go. See you later, Mom."

"Have a good time, Peach. It was nice meeting you, Stu."

"You too, Mrs. Swanson."

We turned and walked out of the kitchen, and Stu murmured in my ear. "Peach?"

I could feel myself turning red again. "Family nickname," I explained briefly, and he chuckled.

"Cute." I got my coat and we walked out the front door. As soon as we were at the car I turned to him. "What are you really doing here, Stu?"

He looked confused at the question. "I wanted to see you. Why? Shouldn't I be here?" It was such a strange thing for him to ask that I just stared at him for a moment. Stu put his arms around me. "What's wrong with wanting to see the girl I love?"

Confusion filled me, confusion and something else: anger. How could he say that after what he had done the night before? I jerked away from him.

"After last night, I would have thought you'd had enough of me for a while."

Stu grabbed my arm. "What the hell is that supposed to mean?" His voice was angry, too, but I didn't care. I remembered how I had felt after he was done with me in that bathroom (*slut you know you're a slut*) and it kept me from being afraid.

"I felt like a whore last night." My voice was low and I fought to keep it from trembling. "You used me, Stu."

Stu didn't say anything, and I chanced a look at him. Anger and shame fought for control of his expression, and when the anger won my heart sank.

"I've got news for you, Angie," he said, pulling me forward against his chest. "You *are* my whore. And I'll use you any goddamn time I want." He glared into my eyes, and I knew that look all too well.

Jesus, Ang, why didn't you just keep your mouth shut?

"Stu, please – "

Stu shook his head. "Please isn't going to do it. I want you to say something for me, Angel. Do you think you can do that?"

I nodded, and tears spilled out and rolled down my cheeks.

"Ready?" Stu asked, and I nodded again. " 'Please give me a lesson, Stu.' Can you remember that?"

I didn't reply, and Stu ran his finger gently over my lower lip. "I'm waiting, Angel."

"Please – please give me a lesson, Stu," I whispered, and he smiled, letting go of me to open the Rambler's passenger side door.

"Anything you say. Get in."

I got in and he slammed the door behind me.

All the way to his house I prayed, asking God for the strength to get me through it somehow.

Chapter Twenty Eight

At school the next morning I ran into Megan at our lockers. When she got a good look at my face she was shocked. Stu had slapped me so hard that there was a visible bruise on my left cheek, and she reached out and touched it gently.

"Oh, Ang," she said in a trembling voice. "What can I do? Please, tell me what I can do for you."

I had to bite my lip hard to keep from bursting into tears right there in the hallway. "Thanks, Meg, but there's nothing anyone can do. I just have to put up with it."

Meg slammed the door of her locker so hard that I jumped. "That's bullshit!" she exclaimed, and I made a frantic gesture to get her to lower her voice. "You shouldn't have to put up with being abused, Ang." Meg said this last in a low, furious voice, and I smiled at her tiredly.

"What would you suggest?" I asked, and the smile that curved her lips was anything but cheerful.

"A bullet in that bastard's head comes to mind."

I opened my locker and stowed my backpack. "That's not terribly helpful."

"I'm not even sure I'm kidding." I looked at Meg in concern. Her eyes were full of tears, and I was touched beyond words at her distress for me. "I really want to hurt him, Ang. I want to give him back everything he gives you. In spades."

The bell rang and we began to walk toward the French classroom.

"Seriously," Meg continued. "There must be *something* we can do."

I stopped walking. I had to make her understand, and there was only one way to do it. It would probably make her despise me, but I couldn't listen to any more of this.

"Meg, stop. I love Stu. I'll deal with it somehow."

Meg stared at me as if I was a lunatic. "You *love* Stu?" she repeated. "Ang, are you crazy? How can you love someone who beats the shit out of you?"

Shame filled me at her incredulous tone, and I was achingly conscious of the fissure between us that was widening every time Stu's name was brought up.

"I guess I'm crazy, then. Just leave it alone, okay?" I turned and walked away, leaving her standing in the middle of the hallway.

I couldn't concentrate on any of my classes that day. Meg and I were growing farther and farther apart, and there didn't seem to be a thing I could do about it. It made me unbearably sad. We had been best friends since the fifth grade, and to lose her made me feel even more dependent on Stu. My entire life was out of my control, and I felt like a puppet, going through the motions while he moved the strings.

After the last bell rang I went out on the back steps. I knew never to head for home without checking with Stu. I had made that mistake more than once and had paid dearly for it. He was standing beside his car, talking to Gin. I watched her face; the way she looked at him gave me a strange feeling inside. I went down the steps and over to them, realizing what it was: I felt possessive.

He belongs to me.

The thought surfaced before I could block it, and it wasn't a positive one. I didn't want to feel like this. It trapped me, this love for Stu. It wasn't a good thing, and it should have been. I had wanted my first love to be wonderful, fun and magical, not this cornucopia of pain and passion, this desperate need that only seemed to lead to misery and confusion.

I walked over to the Rambler, and the moment he saw me Stu left Gin's side and came toward me. I looked into his eyes, and when I saw the eagerness in them, my overwrought emotions suddenly overflowed. I stopped walking and began to cry, and Stu closed the distance between us and put his arms around me.

"What's wrong, Angel-baby?" I shook my head and buried my face in his chest. I could never explain it to him, and I didn't want to try. I just stood in the circle of his arms, sobbing like a child, and he held me, resting his chin on top of my head. At last the tears began to taper off, and Stu lifted my chin. He kissed me gently.

"All done?" he asked, and I had the feeling he knew exactly why I'd been crying. He tilted my head to the side and looked at the bruise on my face.

"You need to be a good girl, don't you, Angel?" Tears filled my eyes again at that, and I nodded.

"I don't know how," I said in a low voice. "It seems like no matter what I say, it's wrong."

Stu dipped his head toward mine, his expression serious. "You're learning, Angel," he said. "You're learning."

We walked over to his car; Gin was leaning against it, filing her nails.

"Finished?" she inquired, and Stu raised an eyebrow.

"Never," he told her, kissing me on the temple, and envy in her eyes was palpable. He opened the passenger side for me and I got into the car. "I'm going to take Angel home," he told Gin. "We still on for tonight?"

"Sure, I guess," Gin said. "Why don't you ask her to come with us?"

I wondered what they were talking about. Stu got into the Rambler and started it, and I asked hesitantly, "What was that about?" Stu rammed the car into reverse and backed carelessly out of the parking lot.

"We're going to the Cellar tonight," he said shortly.

"The Cellar?"

"It's a bar downtown." I decided to drop it; it didn't sound like he wanted to talk about it. I wasn't involved in Stu's social life, and it hurt me.

You're good enough to fuck, but not good enough to be included with the rest of his friends.

We didn't talk on the ride home, and I tried to think of something other than how low and miserable I was feeling. I glanced over at Stu, and my heart contracted at the sight of his profile. He was so attractive, with that black hair falling over his brow and those eyes that could alternately fill me with passion and terror. My gaze dropped to his hands, and a flash of heat went through me as I thought about how they touched me. I looked away, suddenly certain I was going to cry again and not wanting him to see. I jumped when I felt his hand on my thigh, and I reached down and placed my hand over his.

"I really do love you, you know." The quiet certainty of those words made the tears fall freely, and I choked out, "Then why, Stu? Why do you hurt me all the time?"

Stu squeezed my thigh. "You already know that, Angel. The lessons are how you learn. Pain is how I teach you."

I took a shuddering breath. "I don't understand that, Stu. If you love me, how can you hurt me?"

Stu looked over at me, and there was something speculative in his eyes; I knew I had to be careful. "To make you understand what I want from you."

I didn't even want to try to make sense of such twisted reasoning. Instead, I asked the questions I thought he might want to hear. "Do I understand now? Am I finished learning?"

Stu turned down the street I lived on; he seemed to be considering what I had said. He pulled the car up in front of my house and sat for a moment, his hands on the wheel, looking out the windshield.

"Not entirely," he said. He turned his head to look at me, and I was chilled by his flat expression. He grasped my chin and pulled my face toward his. "You belong to me, Angel. That means doing what I want you to do. Without questioning me, and without talking back."

All my instincts told me to pull away, to tell him that he was an abusive control freak and I wasn't going to do any such thing, but I was stopped by two things: love, and fear. Part of me wanted nothing more than to please him, to see that look of adoration in his eyes, to feel loved and fulfilled; and part of me cowered, afraid, so endlessly afraid, of what he would do to me if I showed anything less than total surrender. I looked into his eyes: the love was hidden behind his relentless determination to possess me utterly and completely.

"All right," I said, hating myself for my cowardice. "I'll try, Stu. I promise I'll try."

Stu kissed me, and I slipped my hand around the back of his neck and kissed him back, hard. He put his arms around me and held me tightly, and when we finally broke apart we were both breathless and gasping.

"Jesus, I want to fuck you right now," Stu said, and I smiled at his sleepy, desire filled eyes.

"Why don't you?" I suggested, and he groaned.

"I've got something I have to do. I'll take a raincheck, Angel."

I wondered whether he would ask me to come along with him and Gin that evening, but he didn't mention it. Disappointment filled me, and I pushed it aside. I knew I would have to take what I got, and if it wasn't much, well, I would have to make the best of it. I opened the passenger side door and was about to get out of the car when Stu spoke.

"I'll pick you up at seven." I turned and looked at him inquiringly, and he gave me a crooked smile. "About time I showed you off. Wear something slutty."

An absurd sense of happiness filled me, and I leaned over and kissed him. "I'll see you later, then."

I got out of the car. "Angel-baby?"

I ducked my head and peered back inside the Rambler. "Yes?"

"Tell me, okay?" This time the smile was tender, almost shy, and I leaned back in, reaching over and placing my hand against the side of his cheek. "I love you, Stu."

He smiled back. "See you later."

I slammed the door and he drove off in a squeal of tires and a cloud of oily smoke. All the way into the house I was smiling, and I wasn't sure my feet even touched the ground until I got there.

Chapter Twenty Nine

When I got into the house the phone was ringing, and I snatched it up before voicemail could get it, hoping it was Megan.

"Hi, Peach, how was your day?" I dropped my backpack on the floor and began to take off my coat.

"It was okay, Mom. Are you still at work?"

I could hear laughter and the clink of glasses and silverware in the background, and Mom laughed. "Actually, I'm in a bar. I'm going out for drinks and dinner with a couple of girls from the office. Can you get your own dinner?"

"What if I said no?" I teased. "Go on, have fun. But I want you in at a reasonable hour, young lady."

"Very funny. I'll see you around nine, sweetheart."

"Okay, Mom. Have a good time."

I grabbed my backpack and went into the living room, determined to get some homework done. Since I had been with Stu he had been pulling me out of class at regular intervals, mostly to go to his house and have sex, and while I loved it, I was getting woefully behind in almost everything. I was engrossed in a social assignment, struggling to come up with an ending to a mediocre essay, when I heard the back door open and Stu's voice call out, "Anyone home?"

"In here!" I called back, and he strolled into the room, looking great in a burgundy button down shirt tucked into black jeans. I smiled at him and Stu grinned back, coming over and sitting beside me on the couch. "You've got horny eyes, Angel," he told me, and I stuck my tongue out at him.

"Takes one to know one," I retorted, and he laughed and reached for me. I evaded his grasp, getting to my feet and starting toward the stairs.

"I have to get dressed."

Stu sat reluctantly back against the couch. "Want some help?" he asked with a wicked smile, and I shook my head.

"You just want to help get my clothes off, not put them on," I said, and he raised an eyebrow.

"You're getting pretty mouthy, you know that?"

I made a face at him and went up to my room, stripping off the jeans and sweatshirt I had worn to school. Naked except for bikini panties, I searched through my closet until I found my tightest pair of jeans, the ones that barely came halfway to my belly button. I threw them over my shoulder and went over to the dresser to find a shirt. Smiling to myself, I pulled out a tiny pink tee shirt and a pushup bra.

I dropped the rest of the clothes on the floor and put on the bra, loving the way it raised my breasts up and out until I looked like a model for 'Victoria's Secret'. I ran my hands over them and stuck my chest out, giggling like a little girl. Then I bent down and picked up the jeans, stepping into them and slipping them over my hips, turning sideways to admire the new flatness of my belly.

As I reached for the shirt I caught a glimpse of Stu, leaning against the doorjamb and watching me, his lips curved into a smile. I flushed and held the tee shirt to my chest, embarrassed. He shook his dark head and came toward me, his eyes heavy with desire.

"Christ, Angel, you're so hot," he said hoarsely. "I've never seen anything so gorgeous in my life." He pulled me into his arms, his hands sliding down my back to cup my buttocks, and I smiled and slipped my arms around his waist.

"You're not so bad yourself," I told him, and he kissed me. I kissed him back hard, and his hands tightened on my behind.

"You'd better finish with that shirt or I'll fuck you right here," he said, letting go of me and stepping back reluctantly. I slipped the shirt over my head, deliberately smoothing it over my breasts and giving them a sensuous little squeeze.

"Jesus." Stu couldn't take his eyes off me, and his hands clenched into fists at his sides. "You could give a monk a hard-on."

I went over to him and placed a hand on his erection, amazed at my own boldness. "I'll settle for yours," I whispered, and his arms came around me convulsively, his breathing harsh in my ear.

"You're pushing it, Angel," he told me, and I smiled and squeezed him, reveling in my own power. Stu groaned and kissed me brutally, his tongue exploring my mouth without tenderness, and I wrapped my arms around his neck and pressed myself against him. He continued to kiss me roughly, his hands roaming over my body, and at last I broke the embrace and pushed him away, giving him a teasing little smile.

I picked up my hairbrush and began to apply it to my hair, watching him in the mirror. He took off his jacket, tossing it on the bed, and then began to unbuckle his belt.

"Stu, don't we have to – "

"The only thing you have to do right now is bend over," Stu said in a hard voice. He hooked his thumbs in the sides of my jeans and jerked them down, pulling me toward him. He placed a hand on my back and pushed, and I bent over, bracing my hands against the dresser. Stu thrust into me roughly, climaxing quickly, and when he had pulled his own jeans back up he grabbed me and turned me around.

I was dismayed by the anger in his eyes, and before I could react he slapped me hard across the face. I brought my hand up to my burning cheek and cried, "Stu! What was that for?"

Stu seized my shoulders and looked into my eyes. "You don't touch me unless I say you can. I don't like it when you act like a slut. Got it?"

All I could do was nod, and he stepped away from me and scooped up his jacket. "I'm sorry, Stu," I whispered, blinking back tears, and Stu reached out and caressed my cheek briefly.

"Finish up. I'll be waiting downstairs."

He walked out of the room and I pulled up my jeans, trying not to burst into tears. I finished with my hair, resisting the urge to change. I didn't feel sexy now, just overexposed, and like he had said, slutty. When I came downstairs, Stu noticed the change in my mood. As we walked out of the house to his car, he put his arm around me.

"Just do what I want you to, Angel."

He opened the passenger side door for me and I nodded and got into the car, staring out the windshield and wishing I knew what it was he did want from me.

Chapter Thirty

The ride downtown was quiet. I watched the lights of houses and streetlights flash past the window, feeling small and chastised. I had almost achieved an even footing with Stu, but he had unhesitatingly pushed me back down into submission, and it upset me more than I had ever thought it could.

No matter how I looked at it the situation was hideous and unfair, the opposite of everything I had once believed a loving relationship to be. I felt like a prisoner of my own body when I reacted so shamelessly to his touch, and a prisoner of my heart because I loved him in spite of what he did to me.

Stu pulled the Rambler into a tiny parking lot behind a decrepit building. The street was narrow and dark; two of the four streetlights were burned out, and the buildings seemed to close in on us as we got out of the car. Stu came around to my side, taking me in his arms and kissing me, and I held him tightly, wanting so much for him to be good to me that it was an ache in the pit of my stomach. His lips brushed my ear, and he whispered, "I love you, Angel."

I melted against him and squeezed him tighter. "I love you, too."

Stu tipped up my chin and kissed me again. "That's what I like to hear," he told me, smiling.

We went to the back door of the ancient building and Stu yanked it open with difficulty. Dirty cement steps descended into total darkness, and raucous strains of music drifted toward us. I could smell the sweet, pungent odor of marijuana mixed with cigarette smoke, and I wondered what kind of club this was.

Stu nudged me downward, and when we reached the bottom of the stairs the music was much louder and I could hear the babble of voices. Dim light led the way around a corner, and a guy dressed entirely in leather leaned casually against a wall, smoking a cigarette and looking bored. He had dyed black hair and so many piercings on his face that it was hard to know where to look first.

Stu went up to him with a grin. "Hey, Gideon. How goes it?"

Gideon raised one corner of his mouth in a parody of a smile and gave Stu a lazy salute. "Hey, man," he said in a slow, inflectionless voice. "Haven't seen you in a while. What's been?"

Stu took my arm and pulled me forward. "She's been keeping me pretty busy."

Gideon's gaze traveled up and down my body in a frank, almost insulting appraisal. He nodded. "Nice," he drawled, finally looking at my face. "What's your name, gorgeous?"

"Angie." I spoke flatly, resentful at being trotted out in front of this freak like a horse at auction. Stu's hand descended on my shoulder and squeezed warningly.

Gideon raised one pierced eyebrow and motioned us inside. "On the house, man," he said, winking at Stu.

We went into a smoky, overcrowded room and were immediately surrounded by a crush of people. Stu kept one hand possessively on my waist, and I was glad. He seemed to know where he was going, and I couldn't even see three feet in front of me. We finally reached a table at the very back, and I smiled when I saw Gin, sitting with three other people. She was drinking a beer and singing along to the music, and she jumped up and began to gesture wildly when she saw Stu and me.

She had her hair pulled tight against her skull and bound at the base of her neck, and the severe style only served to emphasize the loveliness of her features. She wore a skintight back body suit with numerous chains around her waist, and a filmy slip of red fabric was knotted at one hip; it barely covered her behind.

Stu cocked an eyebrow at the outfit as and she made a face at him. "Hey, you gave this up, remember?"

He looked at her, amused. "What time do you hit the street again, Gin?" Gin reached out to hit him and he evaded her easily, chuckling. I squeezed into a seat beside her and looked at her ruefully.

"I feel like a boy next to you," I told her, and she laughed delightedly.

"And I feel like a hooker next to you, little Miss Collegiate Cheerleader."

From his seat beside me, Stu wrapped his arm around my shoulders and kissed my neck. "I prefer cheerleaders," he murmured in my ear. "Fun to see what's under those short little skirts."

The three other people at the table just stared at us. I noticed that one was Delaney, the girl I had seen Stu with in the hallway, and I was taken aback at the frank hatred in her eyes. Her closely cropped hair was spiky, and she wore a torn tee shirt and a denim skirt with fishnet stockings and pink high top sneakers. One of the guys had shaggy blond hair and a thin face studded with acne; he had a ring in his nose and wore an Iron Maiden tee shirt. The other was a carbon copy of Gideon, except there was a chain hooked to the ring in his nose that attached to his left earring. He had an unbelievably pale face and blood red lips I suspected were painted.

Stu gestured at each one in turn. "Delaney you've met. Angel, this is Keenan and Slash." The two guys nodded at me, and Delaney said nothing. Stu leaned across the table. "You're not being very polite, Del. Don't you want to say hi to Angel?"

"Hi, *Angel*," Delaney spat, getting to her feet and pushing rudely past Keenan and Slash. She disappeared into the crowd, and I looked at Gin and shrugged.

"She's had a case for Stu forever," Gin whispered in my ear. "He's never been interested."

"Saving myself for you, Angel-baby," Stu said in my other ear, and a shiver traced its way down my spine. He looked at me, amused. "Want a beer?"

I smiled. "Sure."

Stu got to his feet and addressed the others. "Anyone want anything?"

Keenan and Slash shook their heads, but Gin piped up: "Yeah, get me a gin and tonic, would you, sweetie?" Stu looked at her and shook his head, and then winked at me and turned to make his way toward the bar. As soon as he was gone Gin turned to me.

"So how's it been going, Angie?" I knew exactly what she meant, and I could feel my face growing warm.

"Okay, I guess," I said weakly, and that didn't satisfy her for a second.

"You know what I mean," she whispered, and I glanced over at Keenan and Slash; they appeared to be deep in their own conversation, so I decided to tell her.

"It comes and goes," I said. "I never know when he's going to get upset. Just before we left to come here he slapped me because I … touched him."

Gin blinked at me, confused. "You touched him? Touched him how? Did you hit him first or something?"

I shook my head, lowered my voice still more, and explained what had happened in my bedroom. By the time I finished the look on her face was thunderous.

"That's just fucking ridiculous!" she exclaimed, forgetting to whisper, and I made a frantic gesture. "Sorry," she said, waving dismissively at Keenan, who was looking at us curiously. "It's just that this is so ... so bloody unfair!"

"You're telling me." I looked down at my lap and shame washed over me in a noxious wave. "I love him, Gin. I really do. Why does he do this to me?" I looked up at her, and the expression on her face surprised me: pity, rather than the envy I had expected. Gin shook her head sadly.

"I don't have a clue," she answered. "I've known Stu since the fifth grade, and I've never seen him act like this. I mean, he's always had a temper, but this violent streak ... I just don't get it. All he ever does is tell me how much he loves you."

A confusing mixture of happiness and regret filled me at her words, and I wondered if my relationship with Stu would always have these opposing feelings attached to it: pleasure and pain, hope and despair, love and hate.

"I wish he loved me enough to stop it," I said, and she squeezed my arm sympathetically. I looked around the small, oppressively crowded room. There was a postage stamp of a dance floor off to one side, and lots of small tables scattered around it. Most of them were filled with kids my age, laughing, drinking, or making out. The bar against the far wall was a plain wooden table with a skinny bearded guy behind it mixing drinks from bottles and cans on a cart behind him. A small refrigerator stood next to the cart, and every now and then he would open it and take out a beer or a soft drink.

"Pretty bare bones, huh?" Gin said, laughing, and I nodded. "There isn't supposed to be alcohol but everyone sneaks it in anyway. The cops do a raid every six months or so and we're shut down for a month, then city hall relents and reopens us. They like to pretend they're giving us underage kids a "safe" place to party." Gin crooked her fingers as she said "safe", and I laughed.

"Lousy neighborhood for a safe place to party," I observed, and she shrugged. "Hey, we take what we can get."

"Why don't you guys party at Stu's?" I asked her. "I mean, if he lives there alone – "

Gin shook her head at me. "Shhh, he's coming back. We just don't, that's all."

Stu returned to the table, carrying two cans of beer and a glass, and he looked at Gin suspiciously. "What are you telling her, Gin?" he asked, and she gave him an innocent smile.

"Not a thing but what a fabulous guy you are, Stuart."

He looked pained at the use of his full name and put the drinks down on the table. "Come on, Angel," he said, extending his hand to me. "Dance with me."

Gin looked at me with raised eyebrows (*dance?*) and I smiled at Stu and got to my feet. He led me around the people scattered in front of our table and over to the dance floor, finding a tiny square in one corner. He put his arms around my waist and I reached up to clasp my hands around his neck. His face was close to mine, his lips inviting, but I found myself hesitating.

"I don't know if I'm even allowed to kiss you," I said to him, and Stu smiled and lowered his head.

"Go ahead," he told me, pleased that I was deferring to him. I kissed him, lightly at first and then harder as his arms tightened around me. Lazy ribbons of desire curled inside me, and when he pulled away he looked amused at the expression on my face.

"You look like you could use a good fucking." His voice was low and sensuous, and I bit my lip, unsure of how to respond. Finally I nodded, and he laughed out loud. "I love it. I've got your number, Angel-baby."

I was saved from responding by the voice of the DJ, loud in the enclosed space. "Here's a golden oldie from the Stones," he announced. "From Stu to his Angie, here's 'Angie.' "

I looked up at Stu with a pleased smile as Mick Jagger began to sing. Stu pulled me close to him and began to sway back and forth, and I closed my eyes and gave myself to the moment.

" 'Angie, you're beautiful ...' " Stu sang softly in my ear, and tears came to my eyes as I struggled once again to reconcile this Stu and the one who hurt me with such murderous abandon. I clung to him until the song was over, and when it ended I looked up at him again.

"Thank you," I whispered, and he kissed my temple. "I'm going to go and find the bathroom, okay?"

Stu jerked a thumb over his shoulder. "It's over there," he told me. "Don't get lost."

He patted my behind and I began to wind my way through the crowd. When I finally reached the washroom I had to wait in line. It was a tiny room with two small cubicles, and there was a crush of girls in front of the spotty mirrors, adjusting their hair and applying makeup. I washed my hands after I had used the toilet and left, but before I had gone two steps I was confronted by Delaney, who blocked my way by standing in front of me with her arms crossed defiantly. There was a heavyset girl with her, and they both looked at me with contempt.

"Excuse me," I said, and tried to step around them. Delaney planted herself directly in my path.

"Isn't she just precious?" she said to her friend in a sarcastic voice.

"Just like a little prep-school girl," her friend agreed, and they both laughed. Delaney only came up to her companion's shoulder. The other girl was an inch taller than me and at least thirty pounds heavier. She had unattractive orange hair and her makeup was black and heavy. Her hips oozed over the top of the low-rise pants she wore, and she had a low, scratchy voice. I decided to try the polite way one more time.

"Excuse me, *please*," I said, trying once more to get by them. This time the bigger girl blocked my way while Delaney looked on and snickered behind a cupped hand. My temper began to rise, and I willed myself to keep cool.

"What's your problem?" I looked Delaney right in the eye and she laughed harshly.

"You're my problem, prom queen," she hissed at me in a low, threatening voice. "You slumming or what? You don't belong here."

Her words brought me back to that day on the steps of the school, that day when Stu had told me he wanted me to go out with him. (*What's the occasion, Ang? Felt like slumming?*) For some reason the memory ignited a fury in me that I couldn't control. I remembered what Gin had told me earlier, and I spoke without thinking, wanting only to get the smug, self-satisfied look off Delaney's face.

"You're just jealous," I told her, gratified to see shock replace the venom in her eyes. "I've got the guy you want, and you can't stand it."

Delaney sucked in her breath, momentarily at a loss for words. "You nasty little *cunt*!" she swore at me. "I'll bet you wanted to try something different, didn't you? Thought all your country club friends would be impressed with the bad boy!"

She was so far off the mark that I wanted to burst into hysterical laughter, but I couldn't; I was far too angry. "Get the hell out of my way, you bitch."

I looked at her through a red haze, afraid of what I might do if she stood there a second longer. I was aware that an interested group of spectators had gathered around us, and that made me even more furious.

Delaney looked at me with a sneer on her face. "Or what?"

I didn't even bother replying. I just balled my hand into a fist and punched her as hard as I could. She was totally unprepared and fell over backwards, skidding several feet on her backside. I felt fierce joy well up in me: for once, I was able to defend myself, and it sure felt good.

"Or that," I said, beginning to walk around her. The hum of reaction reached a feverish pitch, but I ignored it; I only wanted to get back to Stu. Before I could get by her Delaney leaped to her feet and intercepted me. She struck out wildly and her sharp fingernails raked down the side of my face, digging furrows in my cheek. At the same time her other hand connected with my temple, hard, and I saw stars for a moment. I cried out and pushed her away, one hand to my bleeding cheek, and that was when Stu charged through the crowd and over to us, his eyes blazing.

I felt a tremor of fear when I saw him coming toward me, but it faded quickly as he passed me, grabbed Delaney by the arm, and pulled her out of the bar. Her sneakers barely touched the floor as she struggled to match his long strides and I hurried after them, afraid of what he might do to her. Irrationally, part of me was rejoicing at the same time: he was defending me!

Stu stopped at the bottom of the stairs, still holding tight to Delaney's arm, and the fear in her eyes disturbed me.

Is that what I look like? Is that the expression on my face right before he hits me?

Stu drew back his arm and slapped Delaney brutally across the face. The force of the blow twisted her halfway around, and her head hit the grimy cement wall. She collapsed to a sitting position on the stairs, her hand to her cheek, staring up at Stu like a hunted animal. Stu grabbed the front of Delaney's shirt and hauled her to her feet, pulling her forward until her face was inches from his.

"You come near her again," he ground out through clenched teeth, "you so much as *look* in her direction, and I'll show you pain like you've never known." When Delaney didn't answer right away Stu shook her. "You hearing me, you slutty little bitch?"

Delaney nodded frantically, obviously terrified, and Stu relaxed his grip on her shirt and smiled at her benignly. He cupped the side of her face in one hand and slapped her cheek gently. "Good girl. Now go find your dyke friend and the two of you get the fuck out of here. If I see you again tonight you'll get more of the same."

Stu let go of her shirt and Delaney almost fell over in her haste to get away from him. She darted into the bar, and I watched her go, feeling a sadness I hadn't expected. It was as though I had been a witness to my own pain, and I couldn't help but feel sorry for her.

Stu turned to me. "Are you okay, Angel?" He came over to me and examined my cheek, his brow knitting in concern as he looked at the marks left by Delaney's nails. "Christ, you're bleeding."

He pulled his shirt out of the waistband of his jeans and pressed it gently against my cheek. My eyes filled with tears and I placed my hand over his, wondering why it was that he could react with such fierce protectiveness when someone else hurt me, but mete out the same punishment himself and enjoy doing it. Stu put a strong arm around my shoulders.

"I meant what I said, Angel," he told me seriously. "I'll fucking take her apart if she touches you again."

I began to cry; I couldn't help it. Stu smiled and kissed the top of my head and I collapsed against him, sobbing helplessly.

"Stu," I managed to say through the tears, "why did you do that when – "

I made myself stop, knowing it would only redirect his anger toward me if I said anything more. The frustration and grief welled up inside me and overflowed, and all I could do was what I always did: cry. Stu tipped my chin up and removed his hand from my cheek to gently wipe away my tears.

"That's different and you know it, Angel," he whispered. "Then, it's me, and you deserve it." His words only made me cry harder, and I buried my face in the front of his shirt.

"I don't want it to be you, Stu," I choked. "I don't want it to be anyone."

"You know it doesn't matter, baby," he told me, and I continued to cry because I knew what he said was the truth.

Chapter Thirty One

Mom was waiting up for me. When Stu dropped me off it was after two, and I knew she was going to be angry. When I came in the back door I saw her sitting at the kitchen table, her chin in her hands and a cup of coffee in front of her. She looked up when the door opened and I smiled at her half-heartedly; I didn't have a leg to stand on and we both knew it. She looked back at me silently, her eyes dark and serious, and suddenly I was filled with guilt.

"Do you have any idea how terrible it is to not know where your child is?" she asked quietly, taking the wind out of my sails before the boat even got out of the dock. If she had come at me angry and resentful it would have been easy to react in kind, but this sad, matter-of-fact question made it almost impossible for me to want to defend myself. I came over to her, feeling like an insensitive bitch.

"I'm really sorry, Mom. It was sort of a spur of the moment thing."

That made her angry. "*What* was a spur of the moment thing?" she demanded, twisting around in her chair to glare at me accusingly. "You waltz in here reeking of smoke at two o'clock in the morning on a school night, and that's the best you can do?"

"Stu wanted me to go downtown with him," I offered hesitantly, knowing how lame it sounded. Mom looked at me more closely, and when she noticed my cheek she blanched.

"What happened to you?"

I instinctively reached up to cover the marks with one hand. "Uh – I sort of got in a fight. With another girl."

Mom stared at me in disbelief. "A *fight*?" she repeated. "What the hell are you talking about, Ang? You don't fight!"

"Well, I did tonight," I said sheepishly. "It was a girl who likes Stu, and she was giving me a hard time, acting like I shouldn't be going out with him. She just wouldn't let up, and finally ... I punched her."

"You *punched* her?" I had to laugh at the look on Mom's face. I nodded.

"Yeah. Then she came at me, and ... did this to me."

Mom shook her head and looked up at the ceiling, smiling reluctantly. "I swear, Ang, sometimes I don't know who you are anymore." She looked at me, and all the amusement faded from her face. "Is there anything you want to talk about, honey? I've been kind of worried about you."

Warning bells began to ring in my head, and I forced myself to smile at her quizzically. "Worried?" I asked in what I hoped was a light voice. "Worried about what, Mom? Other than being in shit right now, things are fine."

Mom's eyes narrowed and she shook her head. "You're tense all the time now. You always seem ... I don't know, nervous. Are things with Stu getting to be too much for you?"

I had to fight down a hysterical laugh at the question. Things with Stu had been too much from the first moment he had taken me, but I couldn't tell her that. Instead, I put on an expression of fond impatience and shook my head.

"No. It's just hard to juggle school and a relationship, that's all."

She nodded. "Forty has a way of forgetting what seventeen is like, I suppose." Mom got to her feet and carried her coffee cup over to the sink. "Well, let's get to bed."

She went over to the back door and locked it, and then turned off the light. As we left the kitchen, she slung an arm around my shoulders and pulled me close to her.

"We'll get to spend a lot of time together in the next two weeks, anyway," she told me, and I frowned.

"We will? How come?"

Mom laughed and slapped me on the rear as we began to mount the stairs. "Because that's how long you're grounded for, sunshine."

The next morning Stu was waiting at my locker when I got to school. He smiled at me lazily and I went up to him and stood on tiptoe to kiss him.

"You got me in trouble last night." I began to open my locker, and Stu wrapped his arms around me, one hand reaching up to cup my breast.

"Yeah? How so?"

I pushed his hand away, my face growing warm as I intercepted several surprised looks from passing students. "Stu, stop it! People can see you!" He reached up again and squeezed my breast roughly.

"So?" His breath was warm on my neck, and I resisted the urge to melt against him. "What kind of trouble are you in, Angel?" He released me and I stuffed my backpack into my locker.

"The kind of trouble where I'm grounded for the next two weeks." I pulled out a binder and my English grammar book. "Mom was pretty ticked off when I got home last night."

Stu leaned against the locker beside mine and chuckled. "What did she say when she got a look at your face?" My fingers went to the red furrows on my cheek. I had tried to conceal them with makeup but it was a poor attempt at best.

"She freaked. When I told her what happened she freaked even more."

Stu leaned over and kissed my forehead. "You're a wild one, Angel," he said, his hand tracing the marks gently. "What the hell did you say to Del to get her so riled?"

My face burned and I turned away from him to close my locker. I didn't know exactly why, but it was embarrassing to tell him. "She was hassling me about being with you and I told her she was just jealous because I had you and she didn't."

Stu put his hand on my shoulder and turned me around, and when I looked up the expression in his eyes surprised me. He looked both pleased and proud, like a little boy who had gotten exactly what he wanted for Christmas.

"You don't know how true that is," he said to me softly, putting his arms around me and pulling me close to him. "You had me the second I saw you."

Tenderness rushed through me and I reached up and traced the line of his jaw with one finger. "That's really sweet," I whispered, and he kissed me.

"You know me, Angel. Sweet is my middle name."

The bell rang loudly and we began to walk down the hallway to the English classroom. Before we reached it Gin came running up to us, breathless and excited. "Hey, you guys!" she said, her eyes wide. "Guess what I heard from Reggie!"

Reggie, or Regina, was another of the girls in Stu's group of friends. Stu looked at Gin, bored. "Do tell," he drawled.

Gin ignored his tone and leaned toward us conspiratorially. "Apparently Delaney told Des what happened last night and now he's out for blood!"

Stu's expression didn't change. "Am I supposed to be scared?" he asked Gin in a flat voice, and she shrugged.

"Hey, the guy's built like a brick shithouse, but it's up to you, Stuart."

I smiled at her used of his full name and asked, "Who's Des?"

"Desmond," Gin elaborated. "He goes to Ainlay with Delaney. He's kind of whacko."

Stu made an impatient noise. "The little bitch got what was coming to her," he stated. "If Des has a problem with that I'd be happy to set him on the straight and narrow." He put an arm around my shoulders and squeezed. "A guy has to take care of his girl, doesn't he?"

A reluctant smile curved Gin's full mouth and she shook her head. "You two are pretty cute together."

I flushed and smiled at her, embarrassed, and Stu kissed me on the temple. "We're *perfect* together," he murmured in my ear as Gin waved and ran up the staircase to our left, and that shiver ran down my spine again.

We went into the English classroom and sat down at desks in the back, and a moment before the bell rang Meg rushed in and took a seat beside me. Her eyes widened when she saw my face, and she glared at Stu. He held up his hands and laughed.

"Don't look at me," he said in amusement. "I'm a little more subtle than that."

Meg's expression turned to disgust, and she looked back at me. "What happened?"

"Cat fight," I told her, and her eyes almost popped out of her head.

"What??" she hissed at me, but before I could go into the details Mrs. Greenbaum walked in and the class began. Meg passed me a note and I briefly described what had happened. When she passed it back she had written:

I can't believe this!! What's happening to you??

Stu put a possessive hand on my thigh and I knew he was reading the note.

I wrote: Hey, I couldn't let her walk all over me, could I?

I passed it back and watched Meg's face as she read it. She gave a quizzical little shrug and left it on the corner of her desk, and I felt as though she had slapped me across the face. The dismissal in the gesture was unmistakable, and I felt the growing gulf between us widen still more. When the class was over Meg scooped up her books and left without waiting for me, and I watched her go, my heart aching.

For the rest of the morning my mood was low and somber, and when lunchtime came I went to Meg's locker and waited for her. She smiled when she saw me, looking behind me for Stu. "Where's the prison guard?"

Thin anger cut through me at that, but I pushed it aside and shrugged. "He doesn't own me."

Meg cocked an eyebrow at me and looked skeptical. "That's not what he says."

Real dismay filled me, and I said pleadingly, "Let's not let this come between us, Meg." Meg opened her locker and pushed her books inside, taking her lunch bag out and closing it again.

"I don't know if that's possible, Ang," she told me. "I can't stand the way Stu treats you. It's as if you're his ... *property*, or something. And I haven't even gotten to the fact that he beats the shit out of you."

I gestured at her frantically and looked around to make sure no one had overheard. "Shhh!"

Meg just looked at me, and shame swept through me again. It never really left me anymore, but hovered in the background, always ready to pop up and remind me yet again what a coward I was. I looked at the floor, and my eyes filled with tears. Meg put an arm around me.

"I'm sorry, Ang. I really am. I'm sorry about this whole goddamn situation. It's like Stu is taking you away from me bit by bit, and there isn't anything I can do about it."

We began to walk toward the back door of the school. "I know what you mean," I said. "I feel like Stu is taking me away from *me*, too. It's getting to the point where everything is about making him happy."

Meg looked at me in disbelief. "Making *him* happy?" she repeated. "Do you know how crazy that sounds, Ang? Who the fuck cares whether *he's* happy? He makes you miserable!"

"Not all the time," I said. "Sometimes he makes me feel like the most precious person in the world. He really loves me, Meg."

"No, he doesn't." Meg's voice was implacable. "If a guy loves a girl he doesn't beat her up. Period."

We had reached the back door, and I pushed it open, trying not to resent Meg. It was so easy for her: she wasn't trapped in this confusing, brutal situation. We stepped outside and the first thing I saw was Stu, standing in the parking lot with his friends gathered around him. He caught my eye and crooked his finger at me, and beside me, Megan made a disgusted noise and turned to go back inside.

I caught her arm. "Wait, Meg, please. Just let me see what he wants. Okay?"

Meg sighed. "Okay."

She sat down on the top step and I ran down the rest of them and over to Stu, who walked several paces away from his friends to meet me.

"Where are you going, Angel?" There was an edge to his voice, and sudden anxiety twisted my insides. I looked up at him; his eyes were hard, and I swallowed nervously.

"Uh – I was going to eat lunch with Megan – "

Stu interrupted me. "You need to ask me first."

I blinked at him in surprise. "Ask you?" I said. "Why?"

Stu's hand descended on my shoulder, and he squeezed it. Hard. "Because I want you to, that's why. I want to know where you are, Angel. *All the time.* Understand?"

I stared into his eyes, feeling trapped. Stu cupped my chin, giving my head a gentle shake. "I said, understand?"

I nodded automatically. "Yes, I understand."

He looked at me expectantly, and I was acutely aware of his friends behind us, standing and listening.

"Now?" I whispered, and his hand came up between us and slid into my coat to grasp one breast. He twisted it, and I gasped in pain.

"Right fucking now. Ask me, Angel."

"Could – could I go and eat lunch with Megan, Stu?" I had to fight to keep my voice from trembling, and Stu smiled.

"Sure, you can eat with her, but stay here at the school."

I looked at him in dismay. "Why?"

The word was out before I could stop it, and this time his fingers closed on my nipple and pinched viciously. I flinched and began to cry, and it didn't affect him in the least.

"Because I told you to. Now go."

Stu let go of me and stepped away, giving me a push, and I stumbled back over to the steps. It was hard to see where I was going through the tears, but I managed to climb the steps back up to where Meg was standing. She watched me, concern puckering her forehead.

"What did he do? Are you okay, Ang?"

I shook my head at her without speaking, brushing past her to yank the door open. Meg followed me inside, but it was a while before I was able to talk about it. This time all she did was listen, and I was absurdly grateful.

Chapter Thirty Two

For the next two weeks I had no choice but to stick close to home, and to my surprise Stu was there with me a lot of the time. He seemed to be making a concerted effort to get to know Mom, and it confused me. The more time he spent at our house the more taken she seemed to be with him, and she began to make comments to me: "Stu sure is devoted to you, isn't he, Peach?" or "Stu certainly knows his own mind, doesn't he?"

I didn't know whether to be pleased or dismayed. While I thought it was a good thing that Stu was so interested in my family, it also made me feel more trapped. Mom may have been raving over him, but she had no idea what he was doing to me.

The abuse continued to be sporadic and unpredictable; I never knew when I would say or do the wrong thing. If my glance lingered on another boy a fraction of a second too long, or I spent more time on the phone with Megan or Gin that he thought I should, Stu would punish me without hesitation. It was his lack of remorse more than the physical pain that truly hurt me, however. He was never sorry for what he did, even when I was screaming and begging him to stop, or huddled on the bed or the floor, crying uncontrollably. Stu would insist at these times that the lessons were necessary, and all I needed to do was learn how to behave and they would stop.

I didn't believe this. There was a small part of me that saw the pleasure Stu took in his domination of me, and that part would bring this relentlessly to the forefront every time I tried to convince myself he would stop, that one day he would just love me for who I was and not who he wanted me to be. It was my mind's way of coping, I suppose, of keeping me from descending into a black pit of self-recrimination and despair. If I believed it was me, that I was the reason Stu hurt me, emotional collapse was inevitable, but if I reminded myself that there was a part of him that enjoyed it, that he abused me because he liked to do it, then it was somehow easier to cope with.

Meg and I continued to grow apart, and I discovered that Gin was more than willing to step in and fill the void. She was a quirky, cheerful, amazingly supportive person who became more and more important to me as the weeks passed. Because she knew Stu, she tried to put his behavior into some kind of perspective for me, although I didn't see what could have happened in his past that would be bad enough to explain the way he treated me.

Gin insisted that Stu was insecure and afraid, and covered these feelings with violence. I would listen to her talk about it, but when I thought about Stu, about his absolute certainty and the way he talked and behaved, it was impossible for me to believe. There may have been hints of a softer side every once in a while, but I had never seen anything to make me believe that Stu was less than totally self-assured.

That changed, however. One evening toward the end of my grounding, Stu and I were curled up on the couch together, watching a movie, and Mom came in and just stood for a moment, smiling at us. I noticed her and said pointedly, "Yes?"

She laughed. "You two look so good together," she said. "It's nice to see, that's all."

I smiled at Mom, a little embarrassed, and when I looked at Stu I was surprised to see him staring at the opposite wall, his head turned away. Mom came over and kissed me on the cheek.

"I'm going to go and get my prescription. I'll be back in about half an hour." She grinned at me. "I trust I can leave the two of you alone together that long?"

I felt my face grow warm. "Mom, give it a rest," I muttered under my breath, and she laughed and squeezed Stu on the shoulder. When she had gone, I looked over at Stu again. His head was still turned away, his jaw clenched, and I thought for a moment that he was angry.

"Stu?" I asked timidly. "What's wrong?" He finally turned toward me, and I was astonished to see the sheen of tears in his eyes. My own eyes widened and a rush of tenderness swept through me. "What is it?" I asked, and he reached up and put his hand in front of his eyes. I waited, and after a moment he took a deep breath.

"I wish I'd had a mom that was more like yours." Stu's voice cracked; it sounded close to breaking, and I could only stare at him. "It's really great how you two get along."

I placed my hand on his thigh, not sure if I should say anything. The muscles were rigid with tension, and all of a sudden all I wanted was to make him feel better, to make him feel *loved*.

I slipped my arms around him and kissed him gently on the cheek. "I really love you, Stu," I whispered, and he broke down. His arms came around me, and he held me so tightly that for a moment I couldn't breathe. He tucked his face into the hollow of my neck and shoulder, and I could feel his tears on my skin. His body shook with the force of his emotions, and I just held him, feeling completely overwhelmed.

What the hell happened to him? What did his mother do??

"Stu?" I finally asked. "Are you all right?" Stu clung to me for another moment, then took me by the shoulders and jerked my body away from his. The look in his eyes was anguished, and when I saw his wet lashes, spiky with the tears he had cried, something twisted inside me. I started to smile at him, but when I saw anger overtake the misery I stopped. Stu shook me, lightly at first and then harder, and I was completely bewildered.

"Stu, what – " I began, and he pulled me forward until our noses were nearly touching.

"Don't you think about leaving me, Angel." His voice was low and threatening, in total opposition to his tone of not five minutes earlier. "Don't you *ever* fucking leave me. You hear me?"

"I hear you," I whispered, but *he* didn't hear *me*. Stu got up, pulling me to my feet, and before I knew what was happening he had slapped me hard across the face. I backed away from him, my hand on my cheek.

"What's wrong with you?" I cried, and his expression darkened. He came toward me purposefully, and it took every bit of control I had not to turn and run.

"*You're* what's wrong with me." Stu grabbed my shoulders again, and his fingers bit into my flesh. "Goddamn you, Angel." He began to steer me toward the stairs, and panic erupted in my belly.

"What are you doing?" My voice was high and frightened, but Stu didn't seem to notice. He pushed me ahead of him up the stairs, and when we reached my bedroom he took my arm and dragged me inside, slamming the door behind us.

"Take off your clothes."

I gaped at him in disbelief. "Stu, if you'll only tell me – " I didn't get a chance to finish the sentence. Stu drew back his arm and slapped me again, and I nearly fell over. I began to remove my clothes, trying

195

my hardest not to cry. Stu sat on the edge of the bed and watched me, and when I was naked he ordered, "Get over here."

Trembling, I went over to him and he reached out and grabbed my arm, pulling me face down across his lap. He began to spank me, and as his palm slammed down against my buttocks harder and harder I twisted and wailed. "Stop! Stu, stop!"

He ignored me and continued to hit me, and the pain grew worse and worse. Finally he muttered, "My hand hurts like hell," and pushed me off his lap onto the floor. I stayed where I landed, afraid to move, my face wet and my nose running. I buried my head in my arms and cried helplessly, and when I felt Stu's hand on my shoulder I jumped and jerked away.

"Don't!" I cried, and he sat down on the floor beside me and placed a warm hand on my back. I looked up at him, my face red and my eyes raw.

"Why, Stu?" I choked out, not even caring about the answer. "*Why?*"

Stu gathered me into his arms and held me tightly, and that wretched confusion washed through me again. "Because I need you, Angel," he whispered into my hair, and I felt like screaming. "You have no idea how much I need you."

Chapter Thirty Three

The next day at school I talked to Gin at lunchtime. She looked at me in dismay when I told her what had happened. "Jesus, Ang," she said, putting one hand on my shoulder, and I nodded.

"Even when he loves me he hurts me," I said in a low voice, and her response surprised me.

"But it kind of explains things."

I couldn't believe my ears. "Explains *what?*" I asked. "That Stu's a sadist?"

Gin shook her head. "Stu associates love with loss of control," she said. "When he feels something strongly, he feels vulnerable. Feeling vulnerable makes him angry. And when he's angry ..."

"He hits me," I finished. "That's great, Gin. That's just fucking great. The more Stu feels for me, the worse he's going to treat me." I took a deep breath to suppress the tears that wanted to come out with a vengeance. "What am I going to do?"

Gin put her arm around me. "It's nuts," she said. "Somehow we've got to get him to realize that loving you is safe, that he's not going to get hurt."

"I've tried, Gin, believe me." My shoulders sagged, and she squeezed me briefly before letting go. "I try to do what he wants, be where I'm supposed to be, say what he wants to hear … it doesn't do any good."

"That's because it's not you," Gin told me gently. "It's how *Stu* feels that's scaring him. He can't control love, and it's making him crazy."

Frustration filled me. "So what do I do?" I cried. "Just put up with it?"

Gin shook her head. "Let me try talking to him, okay? Maybe he'll tell me why he's so scared."

I tried to picture Stu confiding in her and couldn't do it. "Good luck," I said. She smiled at me and took a bite of the wrap she had brought for lunch, and I finished my sandwich. We were sitting in a corner near the stairs, and when Megan came rushing down them she almost fell on top of us.

"There you are!" she gasped, her chest heaving as she gulped air. "I've been looking everywhere for you, Ang!"

I looked at her with raised eyebrows. "Well, you found me. What's going on? You look like you're bursting with something, Meg."

Meg reached for me and grabbed my arm. "Come on! You've got to see this!"

"What?" I asked, getting to my feet. She pulled me along excitedly, and Gin got to her feet as well, brushing crumbs from her lap. "Mind if I tag along?" she asked, and Meg barely glanced at her.

"Sure, but hurry! We don't want to miss it! This is really gonna make your day, Ang!"

I followed her out the back door, and as soon as I stepped out onto the concrete step I saw what she meant. On the snow covered lawn to my right I could see a crowd of kids gathered around two boys who were embroiled in a fight. The atmosphere was tense and strained, and there appeared to be two distinct camps: one grouped around a huge young man with slablike muscles and a flattop haircut, the other gathered around Stu. Stu had his jacket off, and the black tee shirt he was wearing had come untucked from his jeans; his hands were clenched into fists and his hair hung in strings in his eyes.

The other boy was enormous, at least three inches taller than Stu and probably forty pounds heavier. He wore a loose fitting basketball shirt and oversized jeans that hung low on his hips. I assumed that this was Desmond, and when I caught sight of Delaney standing in the group behind him sudden fury filled me.

As I watched, horrified, Desmond lunged forward with incredible speed, one hamlike hand grabbing Stu by the upper arm and the other, a huge fist, slamming into his stomach. Stu doubled over in pain but managed to stay on his feet, and beside me, Megan cheered.

"Isn't it great, Ang?" she crowed. "You gotta love watching *him* get it for a change!"

Desmond jerked Stu toward him and punched him again, this time squarely in the face. Blood jetted from Stu's nose in a thin stream, and I felt my breath catch as I saw his expression.

"How's that, big man?" Desmond sneered as Stu wiped the back of one hand carelessly under his nose, smearing blood in a wide swath from cheek to chin. "You like to hit girls, eh? Lemme show you what happens to pricks who hit girls."

Desmond drew back his arm again and Stu jerked out of his grasp just in time. He stepped nimbly back and Desmond's swing missed him entirely. Gin was down the stairs and over to Stu's side in seconds, and I was frozen, watching Stu respond.

"The bitch had it coming," he said in a furious voice. "She clawed up my girl's face. She let you in on that, Des?"

Desmond was unimpressed. "Where I come from, man, we let chicks fight their own battles."

He stared at Stu intently, sizing him up, and my stomach clenched painfully. I began to descend the stairs, leaving Meg staring after me, and when I got to the bottom she followed me and grabbed my arm. I turned around furiously, glaring into her confused eyes.

"I thought you'd love this, Ang!" She looked disbelieving at the expression on my face. "He's finally getting some of his own medicine!"

I looked over at the fight again as I heard startled exclamations, and this time it was Desmond doubled over; Stu had evidently gotten in a shot of his own. I looked at him, standing in a graceful crouch, his eyes dark slits and his hands curled loosely in front of him, and a wave of desire swept through me that was as unsettling as it was unexpected. I looked at Megan.

"You were wrong," I told her, and I left her standing at the bottom of the stairs to join the crowd around Stu. He looked at me briefly and I thought I saw the corner of his mouth turn up, but I couldn't be sure. I stood beside Gin, who whispered, "Oh, Ang, I think he's gonna get — "

She broke off abruptly as Desmond moved forward again. Stu raised his hands in preparation, but this time Desmond's foot shot out and hooked Stu's ankle, pulling Stu's feet out from under him and sending him tumbling to the ground. Desmond's foot drew back swiftly and when it swung forward again it connected with Stu's side hard enough to move his body several feet. Desmond kept going; his next kick caught Stu in the side of the head, and I could bear it no longer.

"Stop!" I screamed, rushing forward. Desmond swung around and stared at me, and so did everyone else watching. "Stop it!" I told him frantically. "Leave him alone!"

Desmond's face took on the sneer it had worn before, and he looked me up and down insultingly. "What have we here?" he asked in a sarcastic voice. "You Stu's piece, honey?"

"Fuck you," I spat at him, and Delaney glared at me with hooded, baleful eyes. "If anyone's a piece of ass, it's *her*." I jerked my head at Delaney, who drew in her breath in a hiss.

"All right!" I could hear Gin call gleefully. "That's telling him, Ang! Too cool!"

Desmond went over to Stu, who had gotten to his feet. He spat on the ground in front of Stu and fixed him with a contemptuous stare. "Guess I'll take pity on you, seeing as how your little *girlfriend* is so anxious to protect you, Stuart."

The scornful way he drawled Stu's name made the cronies around him erupt into derisive laughter, and Stu's expression hardened into something ominous and deadly. "This isn't finished, *Desmond*." He said the other boy's name in the same tone of voice, and Desmond looked at him with emotionless eyes.

"Sure it is," he said, turning away. "Good thing the little woman was here to save his ass, huh Del?" He slung one apelike arm around Delaney's shoulders and they walked away, most of their friends going with them. The crowd around Stu dispersed as well until it was only Gin and I standing there with him. Gin took one look at the glare he gave me and left hastily, giving me an apologetic glance over her shoulder.

I stood about twenty feet away from Stu, wishing I had kept quiet. He stalked over to where his jacket lay and scooped it up in a savage gesture, and I knew in that moment that there was a lesson coming, a hard one. He came over to me and stood directly in front of me.

"What the fuck was that, Angie?" His voice was low and furious, and I began to tremble. When I didn't say anything Stu grabbed my chin with iron fingers, forcing my head up. "Answer me, you stupid little bitch."

I looked into his cold eyes and began to pray. "I – I didn't want him to hurt you," I whispered, and his fingers tightened on my chin.

"You'd rather I look like a pussy-whipped loser, is that it?" His voice was ominous, and I began to cry.

"No," I said through the tears. "Of course not – "

Stu released my chin and grabbed my arm. "Then you should have kept your goddamn mouth shut." He began to drag me toward the parking lot, and the tears came faster.

"Stu, please – "

Stu jerked me forward and hissed in my ear, "Shut the fuck up, Angie. You say another word and I'll break your fucking arm."

I subsided into terrified silence, and when we reached his car Stu wrenched open the passenger side door and threw me inside. When he got into the driver's seat he sat behind the wheel for a moment, gripping it so hard his knuckles were white, his breath coming hard. I huddled against the passenger door, trying not to make a sound, but my breathing was shallow and terrified, and Stu turned his head slowly and looked at me, blood spread across his face like war paint.

"I have to give you a lesson, Angie." His voice was flat and matter-of-fact. "You know that, don't you?"

I nodded, tears spilling down my cheeks; there was no need to talk. Stu reached out and placed the palm of his hand against my face for a moment, a gentle gesture that surprised me.

"Let's go." He keyed the engine and roared out of the parking lot, and as the school faded behind us the fear inside me increased until I felt like it had swallowed me whole.

Chapter Thirty Four

When we were at his house and in his bedroom, Stu paced around the confines of the small room like a caged tiger. "Why won't you learn?" he said under his breath, and I wondered if he was talking to me or to himself. I perched on the edge of the bed, my arms wrapped around myself. I tried to get a handle on my fear, which wanted to rage out of control. Suddenly Stu stopped in front of me and reached down, jerking me to my feet.

"What do I have to do, Angel-baby?" he asked softly, his fingers biting into my shoulders. "What do I have to do to get you to listen to me?"

He let go of me without warning, and I almost fell at his feet. A moment later I was sorry I had kept my balance, because his hand flashed out and slapped me across the face, again and again. Finally he stopped, pulled me into his arms, and when his mouth slammed down on mine I was filled with confusion.

That's it? That's all??

Stu kissed me roughly, edging me toward the bed, and when the backs of my knees bumped it he pushed my shoulders. I fell onto the bed on my back and in an instant he was on top of me, his fingers already undoing the buttons on my shirt. He continued to kiss me as he worked my clothes off, and before I knew it I was naked, writhing under him as he touched me everywhere. Stu raised his head and looked at me with eyes now dark with lust rather than anger.

"Do you want it?" he growled, reaching between my legs. I nodded, and he brought his hand up and slapped my cheek lightly. "Answer me, Angel. Do you want it?"

"Yes, I want it," I breathed, kissing him over and over. He left me for a moment to get his pants off, and then got between my legs. I could feel him against me, hard and ready, and I lifted my hips, wanting him inside me. Stu tangled his hand in my hair and jerked my head back.

"I'll only fuck you if you tell me when you're going to come," he said roughly, and I stared at him through a haze of desire.

"Okay, whatever you say," I told him breathlessly, and he slid into me slowly. I cried out and bucked my hips, and he began to thrust hard and fast. I clung to him as the sensations climbed toward the peak I was craving, and just as I was about to climax I groaned in his ear, "Now, Stu, I'm going to come now – "

Stu looked at me with a cruel smile and abruptly pulled out of me, leaving me on the edge of orgasm, shaking and gasping. "Stu, what – "

He kissed me brutally and pressed his erection against my thigh. "You're not going to come now, Angel," he murmured. "You're not going to come at all unless I say you can."

My body was tingling, and an ache began deep inside me that cried out for fulfillment.

"Please," I begged, reaching down for him. "Don't stop – "

Stu slapped my hand away and looked into my eyes. "Do you want to come, Angel-baby?" he asked, and I groaned again, the ache intensifying.

"Yes, yes …" I tried to kiss him but he pulled away.

"Then ask me, Angel. Ask me if you can come."

I stared at him, my breath coming in short pants. Was this a new kind of torture? "Please, Stu," I pleaded. "Please, can I come?"

Stu smiled at me again, that cruel, self-satisfied smile. "Only if you tell me when," he whispered in my ear, and I nodded desperately.

"Okay, okay, please ..."

He rammed himself into me and I let out a cry and raked my nails down his back, throwing my head back as that sweet climb began again. Once more, I was on the verge of orgasm and gasped, "Oh God, now, right now ..."

Stu pulled out of me and again I was left hanging, my body screaming for release. "What are you doing?" I cried; the frustration was bringing tears to my eyes. Stu trapped both my wrists in his hand and pinned my arms over my head.

"Giving you a lesson, Angel," he told me. He leaned over to kiss me lightly and I twisted my face away; he laughed deep in his throat. "Lessons don't always have to be painful, you know. There are different ways I can teach you."

My chest heaved as I struggled to control my breathing and I looked away, feeling humiliated. Stu lowered his head and whispered in my ear, and at the feel of his warm breath on my skin desire surged to the surface again. "I decide when you feel pleasure, Angel, and I decide when you feel pain."

He began to trail teasing kisses down the side of my face and I tried as hard as I could not to respond, but the feel of his mouth and the rigidity of his erection pressing against me were overwhelming. I turned my head and he captured my mouth with his, using his tongue in the way he knew I loved. When Stu raised his head at last he looked into my eyes, and the desire I saw in his took my breath away.

"Do you want to come, Angel?" he whispered, and I began to cry; I couldn't help it. My body was aching, every part of me wanting him inside me desperately, but my mind didn't trust him, knowing the punishment wasn't finished. Stu's hands tightened on my wrists, and I knew he was expecting a response. "Answer me. Do you want to come?"

"Yes," I moaned. "Oh God, yes ..."

"Then you know what to do." He slid into me again and I fought the sensations as he moved back and forth, fought them with everything I had, but of course they had their way with me until once more I was on the edge of release.

"Oh now, Stu, please, please, now ..."

Stu pulled out of me again and I let out a shriek and struggled wildly against his restraining hands. "Stop it!" I cried, close to hysteria.

Stu grinned and dipped his head until his lips were inches from mine. "I did," he said teasingly, and I began to cry again, so frustrated that I felt like I was going to go crazy. Stu finally let go of my wrists and I pounded the bed on either side of me.

"Why are you doing this to me?" I sobbed, trying to sit up and get away from him. He grabbed my hips and pushed them into the mattress. "Where do you think you're going, Angel?"

I cried harder. "Please, Stu, don't do this to me any more, please ..." Stu's hands tightened on my hips and he slid his body down until his head was level with my pelvis.

"I think I'll do this instead," he said, lowering his head between my legs and beginning to explore me with his tongue. My hips bucked and I let out a cry as he caressed my swollen flesh with delicate expertise.

"Oh God, Stu, please – "

Stu raised his head and smiled at me, a gentle smile with just a hint of cruelty. "Please what, Angel? Ask me."

Tears came to the surface again, and I turned my head, refusing to answer. Stu bent his head to me again and took my clitoris between his teeth. I gasped as conflicting feelings filled me: pleasure at the gentle yet unaccustomed touch; fear at what those teeth were capable of. Stu released me and raised his head again. "I think I made myself clear, didn't I, Angel? Ask me."

I drew a deep, shuddering breath. "Can I come, Stu?" I whispered. "Please, please, can I come?"

His tongue began to tease me, and my treacherous body responded yet again, the sensations sharper and stronger. This time I was determined not to tell him when, but as the feelings spiraled up and up I felt his hand descend on my belly, fingers splayed in an unmistakably possessive and threatening gesture. Just as I reached the peak, but seconds before inevitability, I gasped, "Now, oh Jesus, please …"

Stu stopped instantly, raising his head and propping himself on his elbows, and before I realized what I was doing my hands pounded his shoulders. I was surprised when he just smiled and sat up, looking at me sprawled in front of him, my face red and my expression twisted with anger and frustration.

To my astonishment he reached down, and with three quick pumps in a closed fist he climaxed, shooting semen onto my belly. The amused look on his face made me suddenly furious, and I sat up and backed away from him, getting off the bed. Stu regarded me with fond tolerance.

"You look a little hot and bothered, Angel."

I tried to get past him. "You could say that." My entire body was thrumming with the need for release, and I fought back tears yet again. Stu grabbed me and pulled me onto his lap, and his hand reached between my legs and began to stroke lightly.

"Going somewhere, Angel?" His tone was calm, but there was menace in the way he held me.

"I want to go home," I told him in a shaking voice, and he laughed.

"Really? Well, guess what? You don't decide those things. I do. You're not going anywhere, Angel. We're going to be playing this little game all night."

I struggled against the restraint of his arms. "Come on, Stu, I've got to go home – "

Stu's arms tightened, cutting off my breath. "What will it take to convince you that I mean what I say?" He spoke into my ear in a deliberate voice, and a shiver snaked its way down my spine. "Now get on the goddamn phone and call your mother. You're *not* going home tonight."

"What am I supposed to tell her?" I asked, trying to twist away from his fingers; they were still between my legs, caressing me gently. Stu held me tightly.

"I don't give a shit what you tell her. Just do it."

He finally released me and plucked a cordless phone from a table beside his bed. He thrust it into my hand and I punched in Megan's number, praying she would answer.

"Hello?"

I sat down on the bed, weak with relief. "Hi, Meg, it's me."

"Hey, Ang." Meg sounded subdued, and I could guess at the reason. "What's up?" Suddenly the back of my throat was aching and it was hard to talk, but I said the first thing that came to my mind.

"I miss you, you know that? I'm sorry about this afternoon."

When Meg answered she sounded close to tears, too. "I miss you, too. What happened after the fight? You never came back to school."

I was morbidly aware of Stu beside me, listening, and I said carefully, "Oh, Stu and I went back to his place. Did you see what happened?"

"Yeah." Now her voice was flat. "Why the hell did you bother sticking up for him, Ang? He isn't worth it." Stu leaned over and began to kiss my neck, and I tried to push him away.

"To me he is," I told her, and Stu raised his head, looking at me curiously. "Listen, Meg, can you do me a huge favor?"

"What?" She sounded suspicious, and guilt filled me: why was I making her a part of this?

Because you don't have a choice, that's why.

"Can you cover for me if Mom calls you? Stu wants me to stay at his place tonight." Instantly Megan was up in arms.

"Christ, Ang, I hate the fact that you've even going out with him! How can you ask me that?"

I swallowed my pride. "Because I need you. I don't – I don't really have a choice about staying." I knew I'd said the wrong thing when Stu released me abruptly and got to his feet.

"Shit. Okay. I just hope she doesn't call."

Stu pulled on his jeans and zipped them, but began to remove his belt. My heart sank, and I said hastily, "Thanks, Meg. You're the best. I'll talk to you tomorrow, okay?"

"Okay, Ang. See you."

I hung up the phone and looked over at Stu, who was holding the belt in one hand. His face was set and determined, and I knew there was pain in store, a lot of it, when he reached for a straight chair standing behind an old desk and set it on the floor in front of him.

"Get over here."

I rose from the bed and went over to stand in front of him, and he looked down at me, shaking his head. "Angel, Angel. You just don't learn, do you?"

Stu reached out and jerked me forward, against the back of the chair. "Bend over it."

I chanced a look over my shoulder and panic filled me as I put two and two together. "Oh Stu, you're not – "

Stu slapped me on the side of the head. "Shut the fuck up and do what I tell you, Angel, or you're going to be really goddamn sorry."

I bent over the back of the chair, my hands clutching the sides. I had never felt so exposed and vulnerable in my entire life. I waited, trembling, and when the belt snapped against my bare buttocks it hurt every bit as much as I thought it would.

I tried not to beg and cry, to wail, and to scream, but eventually the pain overwhelmed me and I just wanted him to stop. When the belt finally dropped to the floor Stu grabbed my ass, and at the sting of the sweat on his palms against the raw marks he had put there I began to cry again, in ragged sobs that hurt my chest.

At last he helped me up and took me in his arms, holding me gently until I quieted. We lay down on the bed again, and Stu began to touch me, teasing out a response in spite of the misery and pain.

When I was on fire with desire once again, he took a pair of handcuffs out and secured them to a short length of chain, imprisoning my hands over my head.

"Time for your next lesson, Angel," he told me, and went to work on me with a vengeance.

It was two o'clock in the morning before he finally brought me up and over the edge, and I came in mindless, screaming ecstasy, telling him over and over again how much I loved him.

Chapter Thirty Five

Early the next morning I stirred uncomfortably. My arms were aching and numb, and I had to go to the bathroom badly. Stu lay on his back beside me, snoring, and I nudged him with my knee. He turned over but didn't wake, and I nudged him again, harder. This time he grunted and looked over at me.

"Fuck off, Angel. It's the middle of the goddamn night."

"Stu, I have to – "

He turned over and put one hand around my throat. "You have to shut the hell up. I'm going back to sleep." He released me and turned away, and I knew I would have to try again or I would wet the bed.

"Stu, please, I have to pee."

Stu didn't miss the urgency in my voice, and he chuckled. "What if I tell you to wait?" That note of cruelty was back in his voice, and I closed my eyes in despair. Surely he wouldn't be that inhumane – would he?

"I can't wait, Stu," I told him in a trembling voice. "I really can't."

Stu turned over again and smiled at me knowingly. "You can't, huh?" He placed a hand on my lower belly and pushed, and I managed to hold it in, but just barely. I began to cry, and Stu relented. He reached for the key and unlocked the handcuffs, and I scrambled off the bed and darted into the bathroom.

When I was finished I started the shower and stepped into the dirty tub, and as the hot water hit the raw skin of my buttocks I flinched at the pain and began to cry again. I stood still, leaning into the water, the sobs coming harder and harder until I had to brace myself on the wall with my hands to keep from falling.

Why is this happening to me? Why?

I cried harder as I realized there was no answer. It all seemed so unbelievably cruel and fickle, and I raised my fists and pounded them on the tiled wall in frustration and misery.

I just want to love him and be loved in return! Is that so wrong?

The unhappiness welled up inside me until I wailed out loud from the force of it, and that first cry led to another, and then another, until finally I slid down into a sitting position in the tub and wrapped my arms around my knees, rocking back and forth and keening.

I didn't hear the bathroom door open or the sound of the shower curtain being drawn back, so intense was my anguish, and when Stu's hand descended on my shoulder I uttered a thin scream and jerked away.

"Don't!" I cried. "Leave me alone!" The sound of my own voice, clotted with fear and agony, frightened me badly. I put my head down on my knees and wept silently, wishing he would disappear, wishing *I* could disappear. I wondered when I had lost myself and sobbed as I realized that it didn't even matter. Every day a little more of Angie vanished and a little more of the frightened creature named Angel took her place.

How long? How long until Angie is gone for good?

Stu climbed into the tub and sat down behind me, slipping his arms around my wet body and holding me tightly. He rocked with me, back and forth, back and forth, not saying anything, and after a little while the hysteria began to recede. I leaned against him, exhausted, and he poured shampoo on my head and began to wash my hair gently, working it into lather with tender fingers. The tears began again as Stu massaged my scalp lovingly, and as he pushed me into the spray the drops of water mingled with the tears on my cheeks. He helped me to my feet, washing my body with the same careful consideration he had shown before, and I relaxed and let him do it, wanting so much for him to be good to me that I ached with it.

Finally the water grew cool and we stepped out of the tub. Stu wrapped me in a large towel and I went back into his bedroom and lay down on the bed. The phone rang suddenly, right beside my head, and I started violently. Before I thought about what I was doing I picked it up.

"Hello?"

"Ang?" It was Megan; she sounded small and frightened, and I smiled in spite of how I was feeling.

"It's me, Meg."

"Are you okay, Ang?" Her voice was worried, and the genuine affection in it made those never ending tears come to my eyes again. "I kept thinking about what you said last night — about how it wasn't your choice to stay — "

"That wasn't the smartest thing I ever said," I told her wearily. "Stu got pretty mad when I told you that."

"Oh Jesus, what did that bastard do to you?" She sounded near tears, and I took a deep breath.

"I really don't want to talk about it, Meg. Did my Mom call you?"

"No. She trusts you, I guess." For some reason these words made me begin to cry, so hard that I couldn't talk. "Ang?" Meg asked in a panicky voice. "You're scaring me, girl. Talk to me, Ang, please, talk to me."

"Why doesn't *he* trust me, Meg?" I said, barely able to get the words out. "What do I do that's so wrong?"

"Nothing, Ang." I could tell that Meg was keeping her own tears back through brute force of will, and it made me love her all the more. "You don't do *anything* wrong. You're one of the best people I know."

"Then *why?* Why can't he just love me? *Why??*" My voice was high and pleading, and Meg's control broke. She began to cry.

"I don't know, Ang," she choked out. "There's something wrong with him. No guy who really loves a girl beats her up. You don't deserve this. *No one* could deserve this."

"Then why is it happening to me?" I knew the question would only upset her more, but it had to come out; just the act of saying it got rid of some of the pain, like lancing a boil to release noxious pus.

"I don't know," Meg whispered. "But we have to get you away from him before – "

I interrupted her before she could say it; that particular truth was too harsh and bitter for me to hear right then.

"I know." The bedroom door opened and Stu came into the room. "I have to go, Meg. I'll see you at school later, okay?"

"Okay, Ang. I love you, you know?"

I smiled through my tears. "I love you, too." I pressed the 'end' button just as Stu sat down beside me on the bed.

"Who was that?" he asked, smoothing the wet hair back from my forehead. I put the phone down on the bed and tried to smile at him.

"Meg. She wanted to see how I was."

Stu cupped the side of my face in one strong palm. "And how are you, Angel?" His voice was gently inquiring, almost worried, and I struggled against an overwhelming wave of emotion. "Angel?" Stu looked into my eyes, and the concern I saw there in his pushed me over the edge.

"How can you ask me that, Stu?" He looked so honestly puzzled that I almost laughed. I started to turn away and he caught my shoulder. I decided to be straight with him; right then, I wasn't up to lying. I sat up and hugged my knees to my chest, looking down at the rumpled bed. I didn't think I could look him in the eye and saw what I needed to, but I wanted to get it out.

"How can you treat me this way?" I spoke in a low voice. "How can you tell me you love me and then do the things you do?" I risked a glance up and saw him watching me, his eyes troubled. "What do I do? What do I do that's so bad, Stu?"

Stu took my shoulders and kissed my forehead. He pulled me to his chest and held me, and I fought the part of me that wanted to just melt into his embrace.

"I need you to listen to me, Angel," he whispered. "I need you to be what I want." I tried to pull away, but he wouldn't release me.

"I can't, Stu!" I cried. "I can't seem to make you happy, no matter what I do!"

"God, Angel, just having you near me makes me happy," Stu said in a hoarse voice, his arms desperate. "You don't know how much I love you."

"Then stop!" I began to fight him in earnest, pushing against his chest, and he finally let go of me. "Stop hurting me!" I looked into his eyes, mine wet and anguished, his dark and calm, and Stu took my face in his hands.

"If you do what I need you to, then I will," he whispered, and the frustration that filled me was boundless. It wasn't that simple: why couldn't he see that? I sagged against him, all the fight draining out of me, and when he urged me onto my back and began to unwrap the towel, I let him do it, knowing I was a coward but not having any other choice.

Chapter Thirty Six

When we go to school later that morning I had only missed one class. Stu walked me to my locker during the break, and as I stood in front of it and tried to get the stubborn lock to open he slid his arms around my waist and squeezed. I leaned back against him and closed my eyes, and Stu kissed my neck and murmured in my ear, "I love you, Angel-baby. I really love you."

My throat tightened and tears came to my eyes. I wished so much that our relationship was that simple, that it was a normal adolescent romance, but I felt as alien from the kids milling around us as though I had come from the surface of the moon. I knew we looked like any other couple, but only I knew the truth about how twisted and dark things were: about Stu's need to hurt me and my increasing dependence on pleasing him. I turned around in his arms and put my head on his chest.

"I love you, too," I whispered, a single tear sliding down my cheek. We stayed that way for a moment, wrapped up in each other, garnering curious looks from the students that passed us, and at last Stu released me and gave me a perfunctory kiss.

"See you later, Angel."

He turned and walked away, going toward the stairs that led to the lower floor. I watched him, loving his lean slim-hipped body and the fluid way he moved. As I turned back to my locker, a wave of the bleakest depression I had ever known washed over me and sapped all my energy. Suddenly my entire body seemed to cry out at once: my shoulders ached miserably, my ass was still stinging, and the rawness between my legs reminded me of the many times Stu had taken me in the last eighteen hours.

The bell rang but I ignored it. It was unthinkable to go to class and pretend it mattered, that my life was normal. I slammed my locker shut, not bothering to lock it, and walked toward the back door. I pushed it open and went out onto the steps, pulling my coat more tightly around me. I sank onto the third step down, unmindful of the cold, and dropped my chin into my hands. Darkness settled over my mind, and as my gaze wandered over the parking lot I saw Stu's car and burst into tears.

How can I love him? How?? He's sadistic and cruel, and he doesn't care how much he hurts me! What is wrong with me? Don't I deserve something better than this?

Not really, Angel, that nasty little voice in the back of my mind piped up. *I think you deserve exactly what you're getting, you stupid little slut.*

I lowered my head onto my knees and wept helplessly, wishing I had the courage to kill myself and end this torture. It occurred to me that I was close to my emotional breaking point and that made me feel desperate. There didn't seem to be any way out of this unbearable situation.

I stayed on the step, unmoving, for the rest of the hour, and when the bell rang I got up hastily and wiped my face with one hand. I went quickly down the steps and over to Stu's car, opening the door and getting in on the passenger side. It was strange to be sitting there without him in it, and I sagged against the seat, feeling like a prisoner.

I looked over at the driver's side and noticed a white sticker in the middle of the steering wheel. It was round and had a single word on it in flowing black script: **Angel.** I didn't know whether to laugh or cry, so I did both. I rested my head against the window while the tears slid listlessly down my cheeks and thought wearily: *I'm so goddamn tired of crying.*

At that moment there was a sharp tap on the glass that scared the hell out of me. I jumped and looked around, and to my surprise Gin and Megan were standing outside the car. Gin opened the door and looked at me in concern.

"You okay, Ang? Why are you sitting in here?"

I gave her a halfhearted smile and shrugged. "Nowhere else to go." At the forlorn sound of the words the tears surged to the forefront again, and I added in a poor attempt at humor, "Pretty pathetic, hey?"

I lowered my head and cried, and Gin took my hands and pulled me gently out of the car. She put her arms around me and I rested my head on her shoulder. "I don't think I'm going to get through this, Gin," I sobbed. "I really don't."

Gin hugged me tightly. "We're here for you, Ang," she whispered in a choked voice, and Meg reached out and put a hand on my shoulder. I raised my head and tried to smile at her, but I couldn't quite manage it.

"I can't stand this any more," she whispered. "I feel like I'm watching Stu destroy you bit by bit, and there's nothing I can do."

I blinked back tears and nodded. "That's how I feel, too. Like he takes a little more of me away every day. Sometimes I don't know who I am anymore, Meg."

"Well, *I* know who you are, Ang." Meg's voice was suddenly strong, and a thread of strength wound its way through me, too. "You're Angie Swanson, you're my best friend, and he's not going to fucking come between us any more!"

Gin released me and stepped back, and Megan hugged me fiercely.

"Thanks, Meg," I said. "I think I really needed to hear that."

"Let's go somewhere else," Gin suggested. "We're getting some strange looks."

We walked out of the parking lot, me between the two of them, and for the first time in a long time I actually felt safe and truly loved. We left the school grounds and went down a side street, stopping when we came to a popular café where everyone went when they skipped class. We hurried inside and got the last available table, and I looked around at the other kids there: laughing, smoking, arguing, talking. That feeling of being an outsider washed over me again, and suddenly it was as if I had no right to be there, like the only place I belonged now was in Stu's bed or at the mercy of his fists. Gin put an arm around my shoulders and gave me a little squeeze.

"What can we do, Ang?" she asked softly. "Please, tell us what we can do for you."

I raised my head and looked at her. "How can I tell you that when I don't even know what to do for myself?" I asked. "The way I feel is starting to scare me, Gin. There's no hope – none at all."

Meg looked alarmed. "What do you mean? Oh God, please tell me you're not thinking of hurting yourself."

I gave a bitter laugh. "No, Stu does a good enough job of that already," I said, and she reacted as though I had slapped her. "I'm sorry, Meg. I don't mean to take it out on you. I just feel so trapped. To be honest, I *have* thought about how good it would be to just kill myself and be out of this for good."

Meg reached for my hand, and Gin squeezed me tighter. "Don't say that, Ang," Gin told me. "There has to be another way."

I looked at her pleadingly. "You guys just don't get it! You don't know what he does to me!"

Gin shrugged helplessly. "I just can't figure it out," she said. "Stu's always had a temper, but I've never seen him act this way. He loves you, Angie. He really does."

"Bullshit." Megan's voice was flat, and Gin looked at her with faint resentment. "You don't beat the shit out of someone you love, Gin. That's not love, it's abuse."

"Maybe in your fairy tale world," Gin snapped. "Maybe things with you and your boyfriend are all moonlight and roses, but it doesn't always work that way."

Meg stared at her in disbelief. "Are you saying that Stu has the *right* to treat Angie the way he does?" Her voice rose, and I motioned at her to keep it down.

"Of course not!" Gin hissed. "What I'm telling you is that the first time he saw her, Stu fell for Angie, and brother, he fell hard. It was unbelievable."

"That doesn't give him an excuse for what he does. There is no excuse, Gin. None."

"And what does that make me for staying with him?" I asked Meg in a trembling voice, and her eyes cut away from mine.

"A prisoner," she said at last, and across the table, Gin nodded. "That's exactly what you are, Ang," she said. "A prisoner."

"In more ways than one," I told them. "I love him, too, Gin. I don't know why, but I do."

Gin's expression grew more serious. "But you can't stay with him, Ang. Sooner or later he's going to really hurt you."

"I can't get away from him!" I cried. "He'll hurt me worse than you can possibly believe."

"Ang, you have to do something to save yourself." Megan's voice was flat and determined. "You have to get some help. Go to the police, *please*. They can protect you."

I looked at her in disbelief. "You're so wrong about that, Meg. Don't you think I've already thought about it? Even if I told the police that Stu raped me, it's my word against his, and it happened months ago. And if for some reason they did charge him, do you really think they'd keep him in jail? He'd make bail in less than a day, and then he'd find me." Meg looked at me silently during this speech, and her eyes filled with tears.

"She's right, Meg," Gin said reluctantly. "That's why so many women don't press charges. They have every right to, and these men should pay for what they do, but it just doesn't work out that way."

"Why?" Meg cried, pounding her fist on the table. Several people around us looked at her curiously, but she ignored them. "What the fuck good are the cops if they can't protect you?"

"They just can't throw every guy in jail that hits a woman," Gin explained patiently. "I watched my mother go through this for years. My stepdad would beat the shit out of her, and the first few times she went to the cops. After he got out he'd come back and beat her worse than ever. She learned to just keep her mouth shut and try not to upset him."

"Fuck!" Meg exclaimed. "That's just so wrong, Gin! It's so goddamn wrong!"

"It sure as hell is," I agreed. "But I can totally understand it. Stu would kill me if I went to the police. I'm serious, Meg. I'm really afraid he would kill me."

"So what the hell do we do? Just sit back and watch him destroy you, Ang? I can't take this!"

I gave her a bitter smile. "You're telling me. I just need you guys to be there for me, okay?"

Gin gave me a sad smile and squeezed my hand. "We will, Ang - both of us," Gin told her. She gave Meg a significant look. "We're all on the same team, Meg."

"I know," Meg mumbled. She tried to smile at me, and then her gaze shifted toward the door of the cafe and she sucked in her breath, looking frightened. "Oh shit, Ang – "

I knew without her even saying it; my heart was suddenly racing, and my hands began to shake. When his hand descended on my shoulder I closed my eyes, and Gin let out an instinctive protest. "Jesus, Stu, what – "

Stu spoke right over her words as if he hadn't even heard them. "Where the fuck have you been, Angie?"

I forced myself to look up at him. His eyes were black and angry, his mouth in a thin, tight line.

Oh, I'm in trouble ... I'm in so much trouble ...

"I've been ... here, with Gin and Megan," I said in a small voice, and Stu's fingers tightened on my shoulder.

"I don't like it when I can't find you," he ground out through clenched teeth. "Didn't we have a little talk about this?"

I nodded frantically, and Megan burst out, "Leave her alone, Stu! You don't own her, you know!"

Stu let go of my shoulder and stalked around the table, leaning over Meg and getting right into her face. "This is none of your fucking business," he said in a low, threatening voice, and Meg's eyes widened. She scraped her chair back to get away from him, and Gin said, "Come on, Stu, relax. We're just having coffee."

Stu rounded on her as well. "This is between me and Angie. Back the fuck off, Gin." He took my arm and pulled me to my feet. "Come on."

Gin stood up beside me. "Stop it, Stu."

I shook my head at her: *Don't, Gin. Please, don't.* I wanted to get out of the restaurant before we attracted more attention, and I forced myself to smile at both of them.

"It's okay," I said, and Gin touched my shoulder, her eyes filling with tears.

"No, it's not," she whispered. "You know damn well it isn't."

As she sat back down I turned away and left with Stu, knowing I was leaving any safety I had managed to acquire back at that small table with her and Meg.

Chapter Thirty Seven

I looked over at Stu as we strode rapidly down the sidewalk toward the school. He still held my arm in an iron grip, and I could barely keep up with him.

"Where are we going?" I asked, and he looked over at me and smiled. It wasn't a pleasant smile, and the fear inside me turned into numbing dread.

"Where do you think, Angel?" Stu answered, his voice caustic, and the desperation overflowed. All the guilt, shame and misery that had been my constant companions on this dark and torturous journey reared their heads at once, and I was simply overcome. It was as though a plug had been pulled, and all the color and hope disappeared from my life and my heart, replaced with terror and hysteria.

I stopped walking abruptly, and Stu was forced to stop with me. He jerked my arm, hard, but I held my ground, staring at him with eyes that swam with those ceaseless tears.

"Can't you stop?" I begged in a cracked voice. "You're killing me, Stu. Don't you understand that? You're killing me!"

Stu's brow creased, and for a moment guilt fought with the anger in his eyes. Then he gave his head an impatient shake. "What the fuck are you talking about?" he demanded.

I pulled my arm from his grasp and stepped back, knowing that I was on the edge of a steep and fatal precipice. If I were to allow myself to fall, there was a good possibility I wouldn't survive.

"All I want is to love you and have you love me!" I cried, not even recognizing the voice that came out of me as my own. "That's all! Why can't you just love me, Stu? *Why?* I'd rather die than keep on living like this!" I stepped toward him and grabbed his hands, squeezing them as tightly as I could to keep from losing control completely. "Do you get it, Stu? I'd rather you kill me than keep hurting me the way you do!"

Stu ripped his hands out of mine and grabbed my shoulders. Unbelievably, he looked furious, and I was consumed with utter despair.

It's no use … no use at all …

"Don't you fucking try to make me feel guilty." He jerked me toward him until our noses were nearly touching. "Everything I do to you is what you deserve, Angel. You know it, and I know it."

I heard a wavering shriek, and it took a moment for me to realize that it had come from my throat.

Did I make that sound? Dear God, was that me?

"Oh God, Stu stop please please stop – "

"Let me tell you something, Angel." Stu's voice was emotionless and determined, and I held onto my sanity by a narrow tether that was fast slipping through my fingers. "You're *mine.* You belong to me. I can do anything I want to you, and if you try to leave me, I'll kill you. Period. Is that clear enough for you?"

I would have collapsed if he hadn't been holding me, and I could no longer speak, or even think rationally. I let go, abandoning all control, and began to scream. Stu drew back his arm and slapped me brutally across the face, and I fell to the ground at his feet, gasping and sobbing. He bent down and jerked me to my feet.

"Let's go, Angel. I have another lesson to give you."

All the way to Stu's I was mercifully numb, and when he pulled into the carport he got out of the car immediately, coming around to my side and wrenching open the door. I didn't protest as he grabbed my arm and yanked me out, and after he had gotten the door to the house open he pushed me roughly inside. I went sprawling on the kitchen floor, and Stu stepped in after me and slammed the door. He came over to me and tangled his fingers in my hair, pulling savagely, and I let out a shriek and brought my hands up instinctively.

"You're where *I* want!" he yelled. "When *I* want! You hear me?" He shook my head back and forth by the hair, and tears of pain streamed down my face. "You *ask* me! *Whenever* you want to go somewhere! *You ask!*"

"Okay, Stu, okay!" I tried desperately to placate him but knowing the effort was useless. "I'm sorry, please give me another chance I'm *sorry* – "

"Not as fucking sorry as you're going to be." Stu let go of my hair and pushed me toward the bedroom. "Get in the bedroom. Take your clothes off and wait for me."

I knew there was no point in protesting. Something in me broke, and I turned and walked through the living room, shrugging out of my coat and tossing it onto the couch. Once inside his bedroom I closed the door and began to remove my clothes automatically, trying not to think about what might be in store for me. When I was naked I sat on the bed, drawing my knees up to my chest and hugging them tightly to keep from trembling.

The door opened suddenly and I could barely keep from screaming. Stu came into the room and over to me, sitting beside me and taking my face in his hands. He kissed me gently, and I held back the tears with an effort.

"What should I do with you, Angel?" he murmured against my mouth, and I said in a shaking voice, "Love me, Stu. Please, please, just love me."

Stu eased me onto my back. "I want to, Angel," he told me regretfully. "But I have to teach you first." Before I was aware of what he meant to do he bent his head to my belly and took a fold of my skin between his teeth. He bit down hard, and I uttered a thin, strengthless cry. Stu kissed the spot and raised his head.

"Shhh," he whispered. "Quiet, Angel." I stared at him through the prisms in my eyes, wondering if he was as crazy as he sounded. Stu lowered his head to my breast, and when his teeth closed around my skin this time, he bit down much harder. I arched my back and screamed, and he shook his head at me reproachfully.

"Now I'll have to do it again," he told me, and I began to twist from side to side.

"No! *NO!* Stop it! God, Stu, *please* – " Stu kissed the broken skin on my breast.

"Shut up, Angel," he said tenderly, and his head dipped again, swift as a striking snake. He fastened onto my side this time, and as the pain ripped through me I could feel my hold on reality slipping.

"It hurts!" I wailed, my voice high and wavering. "It hurts, Stu, it *hurts!*"

"I know, Angel," Stu whispered. "It's supposed to." His hands pinned my shoulders to the mattress, and I bucked and thrashed, hysterical.

"Stop! Stop oh God *STOP* – "

Stu's mouth descended on mine, and when I felt the touch of his lips I wrapped my arms around his neck and clung to him desperately. He kissed me over and over, his hands caressing me eagerly, and I surrendered pain for pleasure, although I could hardly tell the two apart anymore.

At last he left me to take off his own clothes, and I waited for him to return to my arms in a fever of impatience, ignoring the insistent throbbing of the bite marks. When he slid into me, filling me in a way no one else ever could, I lost myself in the sensation and tried to believe that it could be good enough, that his loving could make up for the brutality.

Chapter Thirty Eight

When Stu pulled the Rambler into my driveway he sat for a moment behind the wheel, the engine rumbling noisily. I was exhausted and hurting, and I really didn't want to talk about anything. He had made himself very clear to me, and I was still struggling to accept the way things were obviously going to be. If I really stopped and thought about it, I was afraid I would break down again. I moved to open the door and Stu put a hand on my arm.

"Wait, Angel," he said, and I looked at him without expression. His eyes were pleading; his grip desperate, and I closed my eyes.

Not again. Please God, not again. I can't take this any more.

Stu tugged on my arm, and I surrendered reluctantly, sliding across the seat until I was right next to him. He put his arms around me and held me tightly, and I could feel his unsteady breath on the top of my head.

"Do you know how much I love you, Angel?" he said hoarsely, and I bit my lip to keep back the tears and shook my head. Stu took my shoulders and held me away from his chest so he could look into my eyes. His were dark and shiny, so serious that my breath caught in my throat.

"I need you." The words went straight to my heart and I stared at him, unable to say a thing. "I can't live without you, Angel. Knowing you love me is all that keeps me going." His hands cupped my face tenderly, and his touch was loving, so loving it was balm to my wounded soul.

"I can't help who I am," Stu continued, holding my gaze, and a single tear snaked its way down his cheek; I reached up and wiped it away with my thumb. "I love you more than my own life. I could never let you go. Please, Angel, please, don't ever leave me. I'd die without you."

I was utterly incapable of replying; the gravity with which he spoke convinced me beyond all doubt that he meant what he said. I reached up again and placed my palm against the side of his face, and Stu closed his eyes and leaned into it.

"Oh God, Stu," I finally managed to whisper, and he captured my fingers with his and kissed the tips of them gently. "What am I going to do?" Stu wrapped his arms around me again and held me.

"Love me, Angel," he said softly. "Just love me, and I'll love you back the best that I can."

When Stu had gone, I went straight up to my room and lay down on the bed, not even bothering to take off my coat. I must have fallen asleep, because the next thing I knew Mom was shaking me gently.

"Peach? Are you okay, honey?" I was taken off guard; still sleepy and vulnerable, I began to cry, and her brow furrowed with worry as she stroked my hair. "What is it, Ang? You can tell me, you know that."

Those words hurt more than I would have believed possible. I couldn't tell her; that was one of the worst things about the entire situation. I should have been able to go to her with this, to share it and let her help me with it, and instead I was forced to keep it inside, where it festered like an untended wound.

"It's everything," I sobbed, putting one arm over my eyes. "School, friends, Stu ..." Mom smoothed the hair from my forehead, and at her affectionate touch I cried harder. Would I always feel this absurd gratitude now whenever someone touched me with love?

"I thought things were going really well between you and Stu," she said. "What's happening?"

I wanted so badly to tell her, to let it all spill out. But I couldn't, as much for her safety as for my own. Finally I looked at her and shrugged helplessly.

"He's just getting so ... serious. I think I love him, Mom, but he hardly lets me breathe." I sat up and pulled off my coat, and Mom took my hands in hers, looking at me with a concern I found a little alarming.

He hardly lets you breathe?" she echoed, and I hated myself when I saw the worry she was trying to hide. "What do you mean?"

I told myself to be careful; it would be so easy to tell her too much. "He just wants to know where I am all the time, and he wants to be with me every second," I said, feeling a small measure of relief at being able to reveal this much, at least.

"Sounds like he's getting too possessive, Ang," Mom told me, and I pressed my lips together to keep from bursting into hysterical laughter.

You could say that, Mom. I belong to him. How's that for possessive?

"A little," I said, looking away from her, and she took my chin in her hand and turned my face back toward hers, a gesture so reminiscent of Stu that it took all my self-control not to jerk my head away.

"Ang, you need to show Stu that you're your own person," Mom said seriously. "You don't want him telling you what to do. That's not healthy."

Neither is beating the shit out of me, but what can I do?

"I know, Mom," I forced myself to say. "It's just gotten so serious so fast. Stu says he can't live without me. It sort of scares me."

Mom shook her head. "This doesn't sound good, honey. Stu obviously has some issues he needs to deal with. Don't make them yours."

I smiled at her, but it was an automatic gesture, not real in the slightest. "He's had huge issues with his mother," I told her. "Gin said that she and his sister left last year."

"Left? What do you mean, left?" Mom's expression was close to panic now, and I cursed myself for revealing too much.

"He just woke up one morning and they were gone. He's all alone now." I found myself filled with sudden pity for Stu, and it made me want to protect him. "I'm all he has, Mom. I need to be there for him."

Mom put her hand over mine. "Ang, you're not responsible for Stu's emotional well-being. You can't possibly be everything to him. That's not good for either of you."

"I know, but I love him – "

She interrupted me. "You've only been with him a few months, Ang. How can you be sure of that?"

"I'm sure. I've never felt this way about anyone, Mom. Never."

Mom smiled at me in a tolerant way I found a little insulting. "You're seventeen, honey. Stu is your first serious boyfriend. There'll be plenty more, trust me."

I pulled my hand out of hers and got off the bed, pushing past her. "Stop talking to me like I'm a little kid!" I stopped when I reached my bedroom door and turned around. "Believe it or not, I do know my own mind."

Mom rose from the bed and came over to me, and I let her hug me. "I'm sorry, Ang. I don't mean to make light of how you feel. I just want to make sure you're not getting in over your head, that's all."

I pulled away from her and left the room. "I'm not."

As I ran down the stairs, however, I wondered how I was able to tell her such a lie. I was in so far over my head that every day was a struggle just to keep from drowning.

Chapter Thirty Nine

After Mom and I had dinner that night I went back to my room and tried to get some homework done: I was woefully behind in almost everything. I finished writing an English essay and was just beginning on Biology when Mom knocked briefly and stuck her head in the door.

"Stu's here, honey," she told me, and my heart leaped, although whether it was from dread or excitement I couldn't have said.

"Okay, Mom, I'll be right down."

I got up from my desk and went over to the dresser, where I ran a brush through my hair. Then I stripped off the sweatshirt I was wearing for a lighter, more form fitting tee shirt. I ran my hands over my breasts, noticing that they seemed to stand out more than usual. *Must be the new bra,* I thought, and then promptly forgot about it.

I went down the stairs and when I saw Stu sitting on the couch, his hands between his knees and that sexy black hair falling over his forehead, I knew the feeling in my stomach was definitely excitement. There was something about him that really got me going, and while it bothered me, it was impossible to ignore. Every time I looked at him I felt a rush of heat in my belly and I wanted to feel his hands all over me.

Get it together, Swanson. You're turning into a slut.

Stu looked over at me as I came into the room, and the smile that blossomed on his face matched my lustful thoughts exactly. He got up and came over to me, holding me around the waist and sliding his hands down from my hips to my behind.

"Jesus, Angel," he said in my ear. "I can't believe how much you turn me on. I get hard just looking at you."

I slipped my arm around his neck and pulled his head down to mine. "I was just thinking about how much I like feeling your hands on me," I told him softly, and he squeezed me tightly and groaned.

"Let's go for a ride," he said, and I smiled into his eyes.

"Where do you want to go, Stuart?" I asked primly, and he brought his hands up to my chest and cupped my breasts.

"It doesn't matter," he whispered. "As long as you're with me, I don't care where we are."

It was such an unexpectedly sweet thing to say that I stood on tiptoe and kissed him. "I love it when you say things like that."

Stu hugged me briefly and grabbed my hand. "Let's go."

We walked into the kitchen, where Mom was sitting at the table, books and papers spread out in front of her. She was taking a course in business management from a local community college, and she had an exam the next evening.

"Hey, don't hit them too hard, Mrs. Swanson," Stu said to her with a grin. "You'll give yourself a headache."

Mom looked up and made a face at him. "Ha, ha. Unlike you guys, I'm actually doing this because I want to."

Stu laughed. "It's bad enough studying because you have to," he said. "I can't imagine doing it because you want to."

Mom raised an eyebrow at him. "Well, if you want to work somewhere other than McDonald's the rest of your life, Mr. Black, you'd better change your attitude."

I nudged Stu with my shoulder. "You asked for it." To Mom, I said, "We're going to go for a ride, Mom, okay?"

She glanced at the clock. "Okay, Peach, but be home by ten."

"Peach," Stu murmured in my ear as we left the house, and I elbowed him in the ribs. When we were out in the frosty air we walked down the sidewalk to his car, and before I could open the door Stu wrapped his arms around me and just stood for a moment, holding me tightly.

"Do you love me, Angel?" he asked, and I looked up at him in surprise, smiling slightly.

"You know I do."

Stu touched my cheek with one finger, and his answering smile was curiously sad. "Do I scare you?" Shock blazed through me, and I wondered if I could tell him the truth. I just looked at him hesitantly, and he shook his head. "You don't even have to answer, Angel. It's obvious from the look on your face."

I rested my head against his chest; I didn't know what to say. "I don't want to be scared of you, Stu," I told him softly, and he pulled back and looked down at me.

"Am I too hard on you, Angel?"

Another shock. Why was he asking me these things? I wanted to believe that he honestly wanted to know, but I didn't allow myself to trust the feeling; I was too afraid it might be a trap.

"Sometimes," I said, hoping I wasn't making a terrible mistake. Stu looked at me seriously.

"I'll try not to be, okay?"

He kissed me then, and such gratitude and love filled me that my heart overflowed. It was as if he had given me a wonderful gift, and in that moment I would have forgiven him anything. If such gratitude was hideously misplaced, it didn't occur to me, not then. I was so happy that Stu seemed to be thinking of *my* feelings for once that it seemed suddenly, deliriously possible that things might change between us.

The next morning at school Megan commented on my mood; I was upbeat and positive for a change, and it felt wonderful.

"You seem unreasonably happy today," she observed, and I smiled at her.

"Stu told me last night that he thinks he's being too hard on me," I said, and her expression soured. I was immediately sorry I had said anything. How could she possibly understand what this acknowledgement had meant to me?

"Well, that's big of the bastard," she said, shaking her head. " 'Too hard', Ang? Come on! He's a fucking sadist!"

I turned away from her and slammed my locker door. "I knew you wouldn't understand," I said under my breath, and Meg grabbed my arm.

"Ang, there's nothing to understand! Stu abuses you!"

I tore my arm from her grasp. "Forget I said anything."

Meg's face fell. "Ang, come on. I just can't stand to hear you make excuses for him."

I whirled and got right into her face. "Stu loves me, Meg, and I love him. And he seems to be more aware now of what he's doing to me! I think that's a *good* thing. I'm sorry you don't see it the same way."

"I don't." Meg's voice was stiff, and when she turned away my heart tore. "I think he's brainwashing you or something. Either that or he's got you so afraid you'll say anything to keep from making him sound like the bad guy."

The look she gave me was pitying, and I resisted the urge to scream at her. Instead I grabbed my books and walked away, fighting tears.

My first class was English, and the moment I walked in the room I saw Stu sprawled at a desk at the back. His mouth curved in that familiar slantwise grin, and he crooked his finger at me. I walked over to the desk beside his and put my books on it, and Stu reached out and pulled me onto his lap, wrapping his arms around me and kissing me thoroughly. I knew everyone in the room was staring and I tried to pull away, but he wouldn't let me go.

"Stu," I finally murmured against his mouth, "Class is about to start."

"That's okay," a red haired kid sitting in front of us said with a grin. "This is way more interesting."

My face turned red as a chorus of laughter greeted this remark. Stu smiled lazily and gave me a push. I got off his lap and sank into the chair attached to the desk beside his, dying of embarrassment as the entire room applauded. I glanced at Meg; she had a reluctant smile on her face and I stuck my tongue out at her.

I looked at Stu and frowned, and he gave me a wink and smiled again, a knowing smile that made me bite my lip and look away. A girl leaned over from the desk on the other side of Stu's and whispered, "How did she get so lucky?"

Stu laughed out loud at that. "Timing, Steph," he told her. "It was all in the timing."

Mrs. Greenbaum came in at that moment and class started, but I wasn't able to concentrate. For some reason what Stu had said resonated in my head, and it made me wonder. What exactly had been Stu's agenda when he had taken me? Was there significance to his timing?

When class was over I gathered my books and waited for Stu, watching Meg leave the room ahead of us. He slung an arm around my shoulders and pulled me close to his side, kissing me on the temple, and I clearly heard the girl named Steph say to her boyfriend, "How come you never treat *me* like that?"

I looked at Stu and smiled. "You're getting to be a hard act to follow, Stuart."

Stu reached down and pinched me on the behind, hard. "Watch it with that 'Stuart' stuff," he told me, and we started out of the classroom. When we were out the door and into the crush of students making their way to their next classes, I took a deep breath and said, "Gin and I are going out tonight."

I forced my voice to remain casual, as though I was only mentioning something in passing, but inside, my heart was thumping heavily. I had done a lot of thinking about what Mom and I had talked about the night before, and I had decided to try to regain a little of my independence. Now, however, as I looked at Stu, who had stopped walking and was looking at me with one raised eyebrow, I realized it wasn't such a good idea. Why had I thought it might be?

"Really." Stu's voice was deceptively light, but his hand on my shoulder was tight and hard. "Since when do *you* tell *me* what you're doing, Angel?"

I gathered my courage and plunged ahead, ignoring the voice inside that was screaming at me to stop, stop *right now*.

"Stu, I have the right to make my own decisions," I said, and a shutter came down over his face. He grabbed my arm and jerked me out of the flow of other students, looking down at me with a dangerous expression.

"What did I tell you, Angel? You *ask* me. Every time. That's not negotiable."

Frustration filled me, and in spite of my anxiety it spilled over. "Jesus, Stu! I'm not your fucking slave, you know!"

Stu's eyes narrowed into furious slits and he began to pull me toward the back door. I tried to maintain my indignation, trying desperately to believe that I was doing the right thing in standing up for myself, but when we reached the door and he yanked it open and pushed me through I began to panic.

"I'm sorry," I said, hating myself for my cowardice and wishing I'd never started this in the first place. Stu ignored me entirely, and as we went down the steps my heart hammered so hard that I began to feel nauseous.

"Stu, please," I begged, "I'm sorry – "

Stu dragged me across the parking lot to his car, and when we reached it he stopped, crowding me against the passenger side door. When I saw the black, determined look in his eyes I almost came undone.

"I'm sorry," I told him again in a shaking voice. "I'll never talk to you like that again – "

Stu grabbed my chin. "You bet your fucking ass you won't, Angie," he hissed at me.

Angie, oh no, oh God, Angie …

"Please, Stu," I pleaded, losing the battle not to cry. "I'm *sorry*. Please – "

"You really need another lesson, Angie. You seem to be having trouble understanding what I want from you."

I shook my head frantically, tears spilling down my cheeks. "No, I don't," I whispered. "I know what you want from me, Stu. I really do."

Stu grabbed my shoulders and slammed them against the car. "Then why are you always talking back?" he asked, and I reached up and touched his cheek.

"I'll never do it again, I promise. I know you're in charge, Stu. I do."

His face softened a little, and he placed his hand over mine. "That's good, I like that. Tell me again. Who's in charge, Angel?"

Thank you, God, thank you thank you thank you –

"You are, Stu. You're in charge."

Stu pulled me toward him and kissed me hard. "You'd better remember that, Angel." The relief that rushed through me was so great that I slipped my arms around his waist to keep from falling.

"I will," I told him, resting my head on his chest. "I promise."

"Do you need a lesson, Angel, or do you think you can remember that?" The hardness was back in his voice, and I looked up at him in dismay.

"I don't need a lesson, Stu," I whispered. "I really don't."

"I think you do, Angel." The fear raved inside me, and I began to shake. "I'll tell you what, though," Stu continued. "I'll let you choose."

I stared at him. Choose? What was he talking about?

"What – what are my choices?"

My voice trembled, and I didn't want to hear the answer. Stu had to bend his head close to mine to hear me, and at the question he smiled. "The belt, a nice hard spanking, or a couple of bites."

My breath rushed in and out, and I struggled to concentrate: was this really happening? Stu shook me gently. My mind was completely blank, and he seemed amused by the terror on my face. "I'm waiting, Angel."

"A – a spanking, I guess."

My voice was almost inaudible, and I hung my head in shame. Stu lifted my chin and smiled into my eyes. He kissed me gently and moved me away from the passenger door so he could open it. I got inside, and all the way to his house I cried without stopping.

Chapter Forty

He spanked me so hard and so long that by the time it was over I was in hysterics. Stu finally pushed me off his lap and I lay on the floor where I fell, wanting to die. I didn't care that I was naked; I didn't care that he had left me alone; I didn't care about anything except the shame that burned inside me, the awful feeling that I deserved it, that if I was a decent girlfriend he wouldn't have to hurt me this way.

The door to the bedroom opened and Stu returned. When he came over to where I was lying and squatted beside me, putting one hand on my bare shoulder, something snapped inside me. I sat up and crawled away from him, my eyes wide and feral, my face wet with tears and my nose running. I reached the bed and climbed onto it.

"Get away from me!" I screamed at him, beyond caring what he would do by then. "Don't touch me!" I pulled the covers over my head and huddled underneath them, wanting to disappear. I began to scream, over and over, every cry releasing more anguish, until I felt that I would truly lose my mind.

At last there were no more screams inside to come out, and I cried until my head ached and I felt like throwing up. Stu left me alone, and when I quieted at last he sat down on the bed and spoke to me gently. "Feeling better, Angel-baby?"

I began to laugh, edging dangerously close to hysteria. I uncovered my head and looked at him, hating him with everything in me, but loving him too, so much that I loathed myself. "Feeling better?" I repeated in a high, breathless voice. "Why do you care, Stu? Isn't my pain what turns you on? Jesus, make up your fucking mind! Do you want to love me or kill me? I'm getting tired of guessing!"

Stu's expression became flat and icy, and he grabbed a handful of my hair and jerked me toward him. "You want to watch that mouth of yours, Angel, or I might not be finished with you."

I began to laugh again; my mind was breaking loose and drifting. "Oh, please, go ahead!" I cried, not even recognizing my own voice. "I live to please you, don't I? Maybe this time I'll get lucky and you'll kill me!"

Stu let go of my hair so suddenly that I fell against him, my head in his lap. I began to cry again, the agony in my heart far worse than the pain in my body, and he stroked my back, his fingers gentle and comforting.

"I love you, Angel," he murmured. "I do, I love you, I've never loved anyone else, not ever – "

I sat up and threw my arms around his neck, clinging to him with all my strength. "Why can't that be enough?" I whispered, strangling on the tears that wanted to drown me. The anguish that filled me was like a living thing, twisting and squirming inside, and I gave myself up to it. "Can't you just love me, Stu?"

Stu unhooked my arms and held me away from him so he could look into my eyes. Then he kissed me, his lips working tenderly against my own. "I will, Angel," he whispered, easing me onto my back. "I will - forever."

I did get to go out that evening, but Stu insisted on coming with me. When I called Meg to let her know, she told me that if Stu was going, she wasn't, and when Gin saw his car pull up in front of her house she came outside, looking upset. To my astonishment, she lit into him as soon as she opened the back door on the driver's side.

"What the hell are *you* doing here, Stu? This was supposed to be girls' night out! Jesus!" She got in and slammed the door, and Stu said over his shoulder, "Angel wanted me to come along. Right, Angel?"

Before I could respond Gin snapped, "Oh, bullshit! You just don't want her doing anything without you!" She looked at me. "Is Meg coming?"

I shook my head, and Stu chuckled, pulling the Rambler carelessly away from the curb. "Meg doesn't like me for some strange reason. Go figure." He looked at me and winked, and I managed a weak smile. "So, where would you ladies like to go?"

"Let's go to the Strath," Gin suggested. "That okay with you, Ang?"

I shrugged. "Sure. I don't even know where it is."

"It's on Whyte. On the corner of Gateway Boulevard," Stu put in. He placed a hand on my thigh and squeezed. "If that's where you and Gin were going to go, then I'm glad I'm along. Rough characters there sometimes, Angel."

I covered his hand with mine, feeling a frustrating mixture of irritation and affection. I was glad when Gin piped up again from the back seat. "Oh for Christ's sake, Stu! We're not thirteen, you know! We don't need you around to protect us."

"Gin, you're starting to piss me off," Stu said curtly, and I smothered a grin when she muttered, "So what else is new?"

When we got to the bar, I could see bikers coming and going, and for a moment I *was* a little intimidated. Then we walked inside, and when I saw all the university students I relaxed. The staff appeared to be solely made up of older men: they looked like retired pro wrestlers, with tight tee shirts showing bulging biceps and graying, slicked back hair. One of them raised a hand to Gin as we sat down, and my mouth fell open when he said in a gruff voice, "Hey, Ginger. Haven't seen you for a while."

I stared at her, and at the horrified expression on her face I burst into laughter.

"Ginger?" I gasped when I had caught my breath. "Your real name is *Ginger?*"

Gin regarded me sourly, giving Stu a vicious jab in the ribs when he began to chuckle. "Watch it, Angel-face," she said to me warningly. "I've been known to take people out for saying it."

I struggled to maintain a properly respectful face. "I'm sorry for laughing," I told her, ignoring Stu, who was smiling slyly. "I'll forget I ever heard it."

"You'd better," Gin muttered darkly. The man who had greeted her came over to the table. "Kiss any tips you were ever going to get from me goodbye, Harry," she said to him coolly, and he roared with laughter. He gave me a wink.

"She hates it when I do that," he told me. "Dunno why. Ginger's a pretty sexy name, *I* think." This time Stu began to laugh, and Gin's face turned as red as her hair.

"Just bring us a pitcher of draft and get lost," she told Harry, and he laughed again and walked away, going toward the bar at the far end of the room.

It was a huge place, much bigger inside than it had looked from the outside. Pool tables stood in a line in the center of the room, all of them occupied by laughing, arguing men. Some looked like bikers, some hippies, but there was no sense of rowdiness, just a camaraderie that increased in volume every now and again.

At the long bar that ran along the back wall there were more bikers congregated, most wearing leather jackets and bandannas, one or two sporting astonishing tattoos. They bantered with the men who worked behind the bar, and one or two women circulated among them. I wondered whether they were hookers or girlfriends, and Stu followed my gaze and gave a knowing laugh.

"Working girls," he said, and I was embarrassed when my face grew hot. He leaned over and whispered in my ear. "You're such an innocent, Angel-baby. It really gets me hot." He grabbed my hand and placed it in his lap, and I could feel his erection against my fingers. I jerked it away, feeling like everyone in the bar knew exactly what I was doing.

"Stu!" I said to him, and he laughed. Harry arrived with three tall beer glasses and a pitcher of draft, and Gin waved a hand at Stu, who had started to reach for his wallet.

"Forget it, Stuart," she told him. "I have a job, remember?"

She gave Harry a twenty-dollar bill and then held out her hand silently, waiting for the change. When he gave it to her she flipped a dime deftly onto the tray.

"That's for saying Ginger," she informed him, and Harry walked away, laughing and shaking his head. Stu poured beer into our glasses, and after Gin had taken a long swallow she sat back in her chair and looked at him intently.

"You know, maybe it's a good thing you're here," she told him, and Stu raised an eyebrow at her.

"Yeah? How come?"

Gin pushed her glass out of the way and leaned forward, planting both elbows on the tiny round table. "So we can talk about the way you're treating Angie." Her gaze locked with his, and I felt suddenly faint. What the hell was she doing?

"What the fuck are you talking about?" Stu asked, and at the tone of his voice, flat and resentful, anxiety twisted my stomach. I gave Gin a frantic look, but she ignored me.

"I'm talking about how you beat the shit out of her."

Stu looked completely taken aback, but just for a moment. Then his face went blank, and I could tell he was angry by the way his fists were clenched on his thighs. Suddenly he rounded on me, and I shrank back in my chair.

"What have you been telling her, Angie?" he said, and at the furious look in his eyes the anxiety turned to terror. I shook my head, forcing my response out of a throat so dry it was a wonder I could talk at all.

"Nothing, Stu," I whispered. "Nothing – "

Stu grabbed my arm, and I winced at the pressure of his fingers. "Doesn't fucking sound like nothing to me," he said, his voice threatening, and it was a struggle for me not to burst into tears.

Gin leaned over the table and grabbed Stu's wrist. "Let go of her. Right now."

Stu was so surprised that he actually did as she said. Gin pinned him with her own furious gaze, so angry her body trembled. "Angie didn't have to tell me a damn thing, Stu. Did you think no one would notice the bruises on her arms and neck? The way she cringes when you get mad at her? The way you tell her what to do and push her around if she doesn't do it? What the hell is *wrong* with you?"

Gin finished and sat glaring at Stu, her chest heaving with the force of her breathing. He held her gaze for a moment and then looked away, down at the surface of the table. It took all the self control I had not to move my chair away from his, and all I could think was: *Oh God, Gin, how could you do this to me? I'm going to pay for this; I'm going to pay so much …*

"I need to, okay?" When I heard what Stu said I looked at him in disbelief. He met Gin's eye for a moment and then returned his gaze to his hands, his long fingers interlocked on the table in front of him. "I need to control her. I need her to do what I want."

"Stu, you don't *need* to control her," Gin pleaded. "Can't you see what you're doing? You're *hurting* Angie. Not just physically, but deep down inside, where the scars take a lot longer to heal. You're being cruel. I've never seen you like this - it's like I don't know you."

For just a moment, Stu looked ashamed, so deeply ashamed that it cut me to the quick. I wanted to reach out to him, but I was afraid. I was so afraid of his anger that I didn't dare try.

"She doesn't stop me," he said, low, and that seemed to infuriate Gin.

"How could she? *How,* Stu? You're a foot taller than she is and about fifty pounds heavier! Jesus Christ, what would happen if she tried? You tell me!"

I looked from Gin to Stu, terrified. I knew that no matter what was said, no matter what kind of understanding was reached, I would be the one to bear the brunt of his anger. And there would be anger later, a lot of it; I was certain of that. I wanted to scream at them to stop, but I was too frightened of directing Stu's attention toward me. He glared at Gin, and she gave it right back to him, not giving an inch. How I wished I had the courage to do the same.

"Let it go, Gin. It's none of your goddamn business."

Gin pounded the table with one fist, and I had to grab my glass of beer to keep it from tipping over. "You're wrong about that, Stu. Angie is my friend. That *makes* it my business."

"Stop it, Gin. I'm not going to tell you again." Stu's voice was flat and deadly, and her eyes narrowed.

"You know what, Stu? I know damn well that Angie won't go to the police, but maybe I will. I can't stand knowing what you're doing to her and not doing anything about it."

"Stop it!" They both looked at me in surprise, as if they had forgotten I was there at all. I forced the tears back and said to Gin, "Just stop! Don't sit there and discuss me like I'm some kind of ... social problem! Do you know how humiliating this is?"

Gin's face fell, and she reached for my hand. I allowed her to take it, but only because I didn't want to draw any more attention to our table.

"Ang, I'm just trying to help – " she began, and I let out a sound that was halfway between a laugh and a sob.

"You're not helping," I told her, and the tears began to run down my cheeks. I dashed them away angrily: I was so tired of crying. "How is this going to help? How? If you make him feel bad *I'm* going to pay for it! Don't you understand that?"

Stu placed a hand on my shoulder, and I jerked away and got to my feet, pulling on my coat. "Don't! Either of you! Just leave me alone!"

I turned and walked quickly out of the bar, into the chilly night. Whyte Avenue was noisy and colorful, as always, and I weaved in and out among the many people on the sidewalk, noticing only that everyone else in the world seemed to be happy. I wondered what it was like. It seemed like years since I had been happy, and I marveled that I had ever taken the life I had lived before Stu for granted. I continued to wipe my eyes as I walked, my head down, and the desperation that filled me made me want to scream out loud.

Oh God he's going to be so furious and he'll take it out on me I know he will the way he does everything –

When a hand closed around my upper arm and stopped me I let out a shriek and tried instinctively to pull away. A couple directly in

249

front of me turned around, and the young man looked at me. "Are you all right?"

He was a tall, thin guy with a black knit cap pulled low on his forehead, and his eyes narrowed as he locked gazes with Stu. "You wanna let go of her, buddy? Doesn't look like she wants to go with you."

Stu pulled me toward him and wrapped his arms around my shoulders, my back against his chest. "Look, I appreciate your concern, but we just had a fight, that's all." He dipped his head and whispered in my ear, "Right, Angel?"

I forced myself to smile at the young man and his girlfriend. "It's okay, really. I just walked out of the bar. I needed to calm down, I guess."

The guy nodded. "Okay, if you're sure. Take it easy."

He and the girl with him turned and walked away, and Stu's arms tightened around me. I began to cry, unable to help it. I was so afraid of the lesson I knew would be coming that I wanted to just give up.

Kill me, Stu, please, this time just kill me –

"Come on, Angel-baby, don't cry," Stu murmured in my ear, and I twisted around in his arms and stared at him. He smiled gently and wiped away a tear from my cheek with one finger.

"But what about … the – the lesson?" I said, low, and he shook his head and held me tightly.

"There is no lesson, Angel. Maybe this time *I'm* the one who needs a lesson."

I pulled back, so astonished that I forgot all about crying. "What? Aren't you upset about what Gin said?"

Stu nodded reluctantly. "Yeah, but not with you." He kissed my temple. "I feel like a major asshole right now, if you want to know the truth." My eyes widened and he reached out and closed my open mouth with the tip of his index finger, a crooked half smile on his face. "Close your mouth, Angel, you're catching flies."

Stu let go of me and took my hand, pulling on it to get me to walk with him. We started up the street, and my mind was whirling. Were things going to change? Was it even possible?

While we waited for a light, I asked him where Gin was, and he told me she had stayed to have a drink with some other friends. He leaned over and kissed me, and I reached up and touched the side of his face.

"I really love you, Angel," Stu whispered. "That's all you need to understand."

I nodded, and a feeling of sadness gripped me, so strongly that the sensation was close to physical agony.

"I know, Stu," I told him, and we began to cross the street. "I know you do."

Chapter Forty One

For a while, my relationship with Stu actually *was* different. He seemed to take what Gin said that night to heart, and he was less controlling and much more affectionate. The level of violence diminished considerably, and I began to hope that it might stop entirely. Mom was pleased that I was more relaxed and happy than I had been in some time, and Stu spent a lot of evenings with us, watching TV, movies, or just talking. He was conversant on an amazing array of subjects, and I knew Mom was impressed with his intelligence. He was careful never to tell me what to do or mistreat me in any way around her, and she remained unaware of the true nature of our relationship.

Ivan, however, never quite unthawed. He was friendly, as always, and he and Stu had some intense debates, but I sensed that Ivan didn't trust him. I would often catch him watching us, and the expression on his face was serious, as if he was seeing something in Stu that Mom didn't. He only spoke to me once about Stu, but the conversation stood out in my mind; it was as if he had been privy to things he couldn't possibly have known.

He asked me gently if Stu was treating me as he should, and I made a show of being confused and told him that of course Stu was treating me properly: why would he, Ivan, think otherwise? Ivan had merely patted my cheek in his fatherly way and said that if I ever needed to confide in him, he would be there for me with no hesitation. While I appreciated his concern, it also worried me. He suspected something, but why?

Gradually, however, I began to notice that Stu was becoming increasingly possessive, less tolerant, and more angry, and when he gave me the first lesson I had had in a month, I despaired of us ever having the relationship I longed for so much. When he finished with me that afternoon I huddled on the floor of his bedroom, my face stinging from the force of his slaps, my scalp aching where he had pulled my hair, and my stomach cramped from the punch he had given me without warning.

"Why?" I asked him in a gasping voice. "Things were different, Stu. They were *different!* What – "

I didn't get the chance to complete the sentence. In seconds he was beside me, pushing me down onto the floor on my back and putting one hand around my throat. "Why?" he said in a sarcastic mimic. "Let me tell you *why*, Angel. You belong to me. I fucking *own* you. That's why. Any more questions?"

Stu's fingers tightened around my neck, and for a moment I couldn't breathe. I shook my head, my eyes swimming with tears, and he let go and got to his feet, grabbing my arm and pulling me up with him. He shoved me roughly toward the bed, and I knew what was coming.

I lay down and stared at the ceiling, and when he had shed his clothes he got on top of me and used me like a whore, with no consideration for my feelings or comfort. I listened to the harsh grunting noises he was making and turned my head to the side, trying to cry without making a sound, all my newfound hopes shriveling and dying.

One Saturday morning about a week later I woke feeling like something was wrong, but not really sure of what it was. I stirred uncomfortably, the feeling of unease growing, and as I became fully awake I realized that I was incredibly nauseated. I jumped out of bed and ran for the bathroom, vomiting into the sink; I hadn't even had time to make it to the toilet. I wondered what was wrong with me as I turned on the tap and rinsed my mouth.

I didn't have that much to drink last night! What the hell?

I grabbed the edge of the sink as a sudden wave of dizziness swept over me. As I stared at myself in the mirror, face white and strained, my eyes wide, a terrible realization began to dawn. My breasts had definitely gotten bigger and they were tender to the touch, and when I cast my mind back frantically I wouldn't for the life of me remember when my last period had been.

"Oh, my God," I whispered to myself. "I think I'm pregnant."

A test from the drugstore confirmed it. I gave Mom some story about needing to buy makeup so I could get one, and after I had done it I took the test strip with me into the bedroom and stared at the plus sign, gripped by the deepest feeling of panic I had ever known.

A baby … I'm going to have a baby.

Reality faded in and out as I struggled to come to terms with that thought, and when Mom opened the bedroom door I jumped. I shoved the test strip under my pillow and stood up as she came into the room.

"I'm leaving now, Peach."

I went over to her, giving her a hug. "Have a good time, Mom," I told her. "Give Ivan a kiss for me."

She smiled and kissed me on the cheek. "Are you sure you're – "

I interrupted her. "Come on, Mom, let's not go through this again. I'm a big girl, remember?" She nodded and patted my cheek; no trace of Delaney's nail marks remained.

"Just make sure Stu doesn't move in while I'm gone." She looked at me meaningfully, and at the sound of his name fear rose up inside me in a nauseating wave.

I forced myself to smile at her. "Ha, ha. Now get lost, would you?"

"Very funny. I'll call when I get there, Ang." Mom turned and left the room, and I could hear her going lightly down the stairs. I closed the door and went back to the bed, putting my head in my hands and fighting the panic that wanted to overwhelm me.

How am I going to tell him? He's going to kill me!

Just pick up the phone, you chickenshit. Do it now, before you lose your nerve altogether.

I listened to the nasty little voice for once and picked up the cordless with a shaking hand. I punched in Stu's number and listened to it ring, my stomach heaving.

"What?" Stu sounded irritated, and I realized that it was only nine thirty - early for him on a weekend. "This better be good."

"Stu?" My voice came out sounding amazingly calm, and it gave me a little more confidence.

"Angel-baby. I thought you knew better than to call me before noon on a weekend."

The idle threat in his voice went right by me; I had to tell him, right now, before I became too afraid to do it at all.

"I have a good reason," I told him, and he sounded considerably more awake when he answered.

"Yeah? What is it?"

"Maybe I'd better tell you in person," I stammered, suddenly terrified at having to say it out loud.

"Angel. You're starting to piss me off."

I knew from the warning tone of his voice that I'd better spill it, and fast, so I just blurted it out and then held my breath. "Stu, I'm pregnant."

There was utter silence for a few seconds, and then: "You've got to be fucking kidding."

He sounded more annoyed than angry, but I didn't let if fool me. More than once I had assumed that he wasn't really mad, and more than once I had paid a heavy price.

"I'm not," I said, my voice growing softer with every word. "I just did the test, and it's positive."

"Jesus Christ, Angel, how could you be so stupid?"

The coldness of his words stung me, and I responded without thinking. "Me? It takes two people to make a baby, Stu. You had a little something to do with it, you know."

There was another moment of ominous silence, and then he said, "I'll be right over. Be ready when I get there."

"Stu, you're not – " I began, and he cut me off immediately.

"I'd shut up right now if I were you, Angel. Got me?"

"Okay," I whispered, and he hung up. I dressed quickly and paced the floor, unable to sit still. One thought ran through my mind until it wore a groove: *What am I going to do? What am I going to do? Jesus help me, what am I going to do?*

I wandered through the house, my mind racing. The options, as I saw them, were threefold: abortion, adoption, or keeping the baby. I rejected the first one: I didn't believe in abortion. It was my opinion that an unplanned pregnancy was the responsibility of the people who had let it happen, and I didn't think killing the fetus was the answer. I also knew that I didn't want to keep and raise a baby at my age.

That left adoption, and the more I thought about it, the more sense it made. I would be doing the responsible thing by giving the child a chance at life, and I would also have the opportunity to enrich another family beyond measure. It felt like the right decision, and I wondered how to let Stu know that.

As if the thought had summoned him, I heard the choppy motor of the Rambler, then silence and the slam of a car door. Before I could even prepare myself he charged into the kitchen, yelling, "Angie? Where the fuck are you?"

God help me. He's mad. He's really, really mad.

I came into the kitchen and the second he saw me Stu grabbed me by the arm, so hard that I cried out involuntarily. "You stupid little bitch," he hissed, shaking me. "How could you let this happen? How?" He drew back his arm and slapped me as hard as he could, and I would have fallen if he hadn't been holding me. "I ought to beat the shit out of you."

"What's stopping you?" I cried. "Why should today be different than any other day?"

I closed my eyes, trying to prepare for the next blow, and when it didn't come I opened them again and looked at him fearfully. Stu smiled at me with that blend of lust and cruelty, and once again I hated him. He had planted this seed inside me, and now he was blaming *me* for it, as though I had done it to spite him.

Stu dragged me into the living room and threw me on the couch. "Believe me, I'd like nothing better, but you have to take care of this. Right fucking now."

"What do you mean?" Dread wrapped loving arms around me and squeezed, and I began to feel lightheaded. "Can't we talk about this, Stu?"

He stared at me as though I was out of my mind. "There's nothing to talk about," he told me harshly. "You're getting an abortion."

"What?" I couldn't believe the utter finality with which he spoke. "I have a say in this, too. This is a baby we're talking about."

Stu came over to me and grabbed my shoulders, pressing them into the back of the couch.

"This is *not* a baby," he ground out through clenched teeth, his face inches from mine. "This is a mistake. One that you made, and one that you're going to fix."

"Stu, you can't *make* me have an abortion!"

I was certain that in this I was finally right. He might be able to hurt me, but he couldn't make me take something from my body just because he wanted it gone. He glared into my eyes, his own black and empty, and I wondered if I had imagined him telling me that he would try not to be so hard on me.

"Oh no?" he said in a dead, emotionless voice. He might have been a serial killer, looking at his latest victim with no more regard than a normal person would have shown a fly. "How about if I do it for you?"

I stared back at him, absolutely frozen, unwilling to believe he could *think* such a terrible thing. "You're just trying to scare me," I managed to get out at last, and Stu shook his head very deliberately, first one way, then the other.

"Believe me, Angie, if I wanted to scare you, I'd have you on your back on the kitchen table right this goddamn minute, and then I'd ask you where I could find a coathanger. I'd do it without a second thought. You know I would."

I tried to pull away from him but he held me tightly, and the terror that filled me was bigger than the entire world. "Oh God, Stu, please – "

Stu slammed his hand over my mouth. "Enough talking. What'll it be, Angie, me or the clinic?"

He's crazy, he is he's fucking crazy oh God help me please –

Stu shook me. "Well?" he demanded, and I broke the paralysis that held me prisoner and pushed him away. I got to my feet and darted away from him.

"You're *not* going to make me do this!" I screamed, and his face darkened with rage.

"Get over here, Angie." The look on his face promised more than pain; it promised torture and death, and I had never been so frightened. "Get over here right now or you'll be seeing the sun come up from a hospital bed. I guarantee you that."

I knew he would catch me if I tried to run, and the hopelessness that washed over me sapped all my strength. "Stu, just listen to me," I pleaded. "Think about what you're saying. This is our baby – "

In seconds Stu was across the room and in front of me. "THIS IS NOT A BABY!" he roared, and his fist flew out and connected with the side of my head. I dropped to the floor, the explosion of pain behind my eyes stealing my breath, and Stu kicked me savagely in the side. "Goddamn it, you're going to LISTEN to me!"

He continued to kick me until I was shrieking and begging him to stop, and when he had exhausted himself, he did. My entire body was in agony, and I lay curled up on the floor, ready to agree to anything if he would just stop hurting me.

When I dared to look up Stu was sitting on the couch with the Yellow Pages in his lap, and as I watched, he leafed through the pages until he got to the one he wanted. Then he picked up the phone and punched in a number.

"I want know how to go about getting an abortion for my girlfriend," he said to the person on the other end, and I buried my head in my arms and began to cry.

Chapter Forty Two

Stu made an appointment for a consultation, smoothly explaining that I was too upset to do it myself. He acted the part of the concerned, sympathetic boyfriend very convincingly, and when he hung up the phone he looked at me, calm and satisfied now.

"There, Angel. You see how easy that was?" For him it was over: problem solved. For me the nightmare was just beginning, and I would have the rest of my life to cope with the guilt and regret.

"I can't believe you're going to make me do this," I whispered. "It's murder."

Stu laughed derisively. "Oh, come on, Angel. Don't you think that's a little dramatic? Murder? I don't think so. It's just a neat solution to a messy problem."

I sat up, ignoring the stabbing pain in my back and sides, and glared at him with real hatred. "That's easy for you to say," I told him bitterly. "It's not your body that's going to be vacuumed out. It's not you they're going to take a … a baby from."

I collapsed back onto the floor and burst into tears. I told myself fiercely not to think of it, because if I did I would slide down and down to the bottom of a dark place from which there was no release. Stu came over to me, squatting beside me and placing a hand gently on my hair. I cringed at his touch.

"It's better this way, Angel," he said softly. "You'll see."

I shook off his hand and sat up again, moving away from him. "Better for who?" I demanded, and Stu seemed taken aback at the anger in my voice. "Better for you, maybe. No embarrassing explanations, no admitting you made a mistake, no responsibility. But what about how *I* feel? When do you ever think of *my* feelings, Stu? No, don't answer that, I can tell you. Never. Who cares, right? I'm just the resident punching bag. When I'm not the resident slut."

I looked him right in the eyes during this entire speech, and when I had finished my gaze slid away from him to the floor. I expected him to explode again, but I didn't care. I felt like I would never care about anything again.

It doesn't matter. It just doesn't matter. Maybe if you tell yourself that enough, you'll start to believe it.

To my surprise, Stu didn't get angry. When he took my chin in his hand and raised my face to his, the expression on his face was one I had never seen before: he looked *hurt.*

"Don't say things like that, Angel," he said pleadingly, and I looked at him in astonishment. Who was *this*, now?

"Don't say what, Stu?" I asked him wearily. "I'm only saying what you've already told me. 'You don't stand, Angel, you lie on your back.' Ring a bell?"

Stu leaned forward and took my face in his hands. He looked earnestly into my eyes, and I fought the hypnosis of that look, fought it with everything in me. "You're everything to me, Angel," he whispered, and my treacherous heart, not caring about the fear, the pain, or the anger, sang at the sound of those words. "You hear me? *Everything.*"

He kissed me, one hand firm against the back of my neck, and I felt myself wavering, longing to give in to the transient love in his touch.

You're as sick as he is if you fall for this bullshit, Angie! My mind screamed at me, but my heart replied, uncaring: *He loves you, he loves you, he loves you …*

I tried not to kiss him back, but his lips were insistent, and I couldn't help it. When Stu finally broke the kiss I began to cry again.

"How can you say something like that?" My voice trembled, the anger having melted into misery and heartbreak, and I cursed the weakness in my heart and my body that wouldn't allow my mind to hold fast to that lifesaving emotion. "Don't you know what you're doing to me, Stu?"

Stu cupped the side of my face in one palm. "I'm sorry you're hurting, Angel, but you bring this on yourself. I've told you so many times – you need to do what I want, and then I won't have to hurt you. And the abortion – you know it's the only thing to do. You know it as well as I do."

He said all this to me very seriously, and my mind teetered again, wanting to slip into that nowhere place where none of this would matter. I struggled to hold on, thinking: *Survival, Ang. Just think survival. If you try to understand things his way, you'll go crazy and he'll win.*

"Do you need me, Stu?" I asked, and the corner of his mouth turned up in that half smile that drove me wild. He crushed me to his chest.

"God, you know I do, Angel," he told me in a low, passionate voice. "I can't breathe without you. I spend every minute of every day waiting to see you, and every time I touch you I never want to stop. I can't believe how lucky I am to have you love me, Angel. I couldn't live without it. That's how much I need you."

I was speechless at this outpouring of emotion, and I pulled away and stared at him, overcome. His eyes told me everything, and I reached out and touched his face.

"Really?" My voice was barely there, but he smiled at the question.

"Really." Stu got to his feet and held out a hand to me. "Come upstairs with me, Angel. I want to make love to you."

I took his hand and allowed him to pull me to my feet. As we went up the stairs I pretended I was the heroine in a romance novel, where love conquers all and everyone always lives happily ever after.

Chapter Forty Three

Stu stayed with me that night. We spent a quiet evening watching a movie, and when we went to sleep we were so wrapped around each other that I couldn't tell where he left off and I began. I couldn't remember ever feeling so loved, and if it didn't quite erase my fear of the coming appointment, it went a long way toward soothing the hysterics that had consumed me earlier.

He was such a paradox. So cold and brutal one moment that I felt he could kill me and not lose a night's sleep feeling guilty; so intense and loving that he seemed to want to swallow me whole the next. Either way wasn't comfortable, but I definitely preferred the loving to the hurting. I didn't doubt that Stu did love me, but it was a frightening love, so inextricably entwined with pain that it was hard to tell the two apart.

I woke that Sunday morning with him sleeping beside me, and for a few moments I just lay quietly and studied his face, taking the opportunity to really look at him without fear. His features were relaxed: long eyelashes brushed cheeks flushed with sleep, his mouth was soft and vulnerable without the anger making it hard and thin, and his dark hair was tousled around his face like a little boy's. I felt a rush of love take hold of me and I reached out and brushed a lock of hair from his forehead with gentle fingers, wishing with all my heart that things were different between us; that *he* was different.

I want so much to love you, Stu. Why can't you just let me?

Stu stirred and turned over onto his back, and I propped myself up on one elbow and let my eyes caress the rest of his body. His shoulders were broad, but not overly so, his chest finely muscled with very little hair. His arms were long, tapering to those strong hands with their slender, supple fingers, and I stared at them for a moment, fascinated: it was unsettling to think that those hands could bring me so much pleasure one moment and such great pain the next.

His skin was smooth, a wonderful deep cream shade, and I had to resist the urge to press my lips to the firm skin of his belly, pulled taut by the way he was lying. There was so much I wanted to know about how to please him, but I didn't think he would ever let me do it. I was also curious about what was under the blanket that covered his hips, but the thought of exploring *that* brought a furious blush to my cheeks.

"Like what you see?" Stu asked lazily, and I jerked my gaze up and found him watching me with an amused smile on his face, his arms folded casually behind his head.

"Uh – yeah," I stammered, acutely conscious of my red face. "You're beautiful." I leaned over to kiss him and he wrapped his arms around me, kissing me back with enthusiasm. After a moment I pulled back and looked at him, enjoying the unaccustomed pleasure of being on top.

"Stu," I said hesitantly, "could I … touch you?"

Stu lifted one eyebrow, and his smile widened. "I don't know," he said. "That depends on where."

I felt my face grow warm again and I shook my head. "Never mind." I slid back down beside him and pillowed my head in the crook of his arm.

Stu chuckled and reached for my hand. "I love it. In some ways you're still a virgin, Angel." He drew my hand under the blankets and placed it on his erect penis. "Is this what you wanted to touch?"

I gasped out loud as my fingers felt smooth, warm skin that was soft yet rigid, and when I explored the length of him I heard his breath catch. My fingers went from the tip, with that soft pad and small, sensitive opening, down the shaft, where the bulging veins stood out prominently, to the junction of his thighs, where I carefully explored the loose sacs that held his testicles. His hesitant yet proprietary touch seemed to really excite him, and when I wrapped my fingers around his penis and squeezed gently, Stu groaned out loud and his hips bucked in a gesture I knew very well indeed.

"Wow," I breathed, looking at his flushed face and half closed eyes and feeling an amazing bolt of desire shoot through me. Stu pushed himself up on one elbow and reached for me, and I felt lust take over as I pushed him back down.

"It's my turn," I whispered, and I let instinct guide me as my hand began a rhythmic motion, my fingers tightening and loosening, tightening and loosening, as I pumped gently up and down. Stu's hands reached out and clutched handfuls of the blankets, and his hips moved in time with my hand.

"Oh Jesus, Angel," he moaned, and another electric shock of lust started at the top of my head and finished between my legs, making my breathing uneven. I continued what I was doing, watching the expression on his face twist into what looked like agony, and after an endless moment he threw back his head.

"God, I'm going to come," he said in a strangled voice, and his penis seemed to flex in my hand as the semen came rushing out. Stu let out a guttural cry and pushed his hips hard against my hand, and when it was over I was breathing hard, unable to look away from his face, my own body on fire. He opened his eyes and looked directly into mine, and I said the only thing I was thinking, the only thing that mattered: "I love you, Stu."

Stu put his arms around me and pulled me down beside him, holding me tightly and struggling to control his breathing. "I love you, too, Angel. I never let any girl do that before – it was amazing."

"It was amazing for me, too," I told him softly. "I loved pleasing you like that."

"Angel, there's nothing you do that doesn't please me," Stu breathed, kissing my temple, and I smiled sadly, wishing it was true. I squeezed his body with the arm I had thrown across his stomach.

"I'm glad."

We lay like that for a while, and this time when he raised himself up I let him do it, knowing what was coming and needing it, needing it so badly that it astonished me. I reached up and wound my arms around his neck, pulling his head toward mine and kissing him hungrily, and after a passionate moment Stu pulled back and looked at me, amusement on his face.

"Why, Angel," he said in a gently remonstrative tone, "if I didn't know better, I'd say you were a horny girl."

I was beyond embarrassment, wanting only to feel him inside me. I tried to pull him down to me again and he resisted easily, smiling wickedly as I began to writhe beneath him. "Stu – " I gasped. "Please …"

Stu's smile broadened, and his fingers reached between my legs and began to stroke gently. "Please what, Angel?"

My hips bucked against his hand, and I moaned. "Oh God, Stu – "

His fingers continued their teasing movements, and when he withdrew his hand I let out a cry. "What do you want, Angel?" I tried to grab his hand and he moved it out of reach. "What do you want?" he repeated, and I whispered, "I want you to make love to me."

Stu shook his head, chuckling deep in his throat. He dipped his head and placed his mouth on my uninjured breast, his tongue playing with the nipple. "I don't think that's quite it, Angel-baby," he murmured against my skin. "Come on now, what do you want?"

I turned my head toward him and looked into those dark, sexy eyes. "I want you to fuck me, Stu," I begged. "Please, please fuck me."

Stu got on top and was inside me in a single, fluid movement. I cried out as he slid into me, glorying in that feeling of fullness, of possession, of my every elemental need being met. He thrust into me roughly, and every movement created more incredible friction that went up and up and up, culminating in the most amazing explosion of sensation I had ever felt. I could feel myself contracting inside, muscle upon muscle, and as my inner walls tightened around his hardness it sent ripples of pleasure throughout my entire body.

I was hardly aware of Stu's orgasm, I was so caught up in the incredible feelings that consumed me, both in my body and in my heart, and when he collapsed beside me, panting and sweaty, his hand resting on my breast, there was no other way to cope with the overwhelming emotion than to cry.

Stu turned his head toward me, confused, and I placed one hand on the side of his face and kissed him while the tears ran between us. "What is it, baby?" he whispered, and I kissed him again and sobbed, "I can't believe what you do to me, Stu, I just can't believe it ..."

Stu wiped my tears away and smiled at me, a tender, loving smile, and what he said only made me cry harder. "Now you know how I've felt for the last two years."

This time he held me until the storm burned itself out.

Chapter Forty Four

Stu went home that afternoon, and I finally had some time to myself to think about what was to come. I felt trapped and desperate when I thought of what he was making me do, but I knew I had no choice. The thought of Stu trying to scrape the baby out of me himself was too horrible to contemplate, and remembering his face when he had threatened to do it was like recalling the face of a brutal stranger. I couldn't go to my mother, either, for the same reason: Stu's anger was certain to be terrible if she tried to protect me, and I could imagine him trying to hurt *her* with no trouble at all.

It was hard to come to terms with the fact that my gentle, wonderful lover of that morning and the enraged young man who had kicked me over and over were the same person, and once again the confusion threatened to overwhelm me.

Why couldn't I just leave him? Why didn't I have a choice about anything? I alternated between feeling furious, ashamed, and lost: furious because Stu had no right to treat me the way he did; ashamed because I allowed him to do it; and lost because of how I felt about him. If I thought about any one thing too long, I edged closer and closer to hysteria, and finally I decided to call Gin. After all, she knew everything else, and I had to talk to someone before I broke down completely.

"Hey, Angel-face," she said when I said hello, and I told her, "Please, Gin. I get enough of that from Stu."

"No problem, Ang." She sounded sheepish. "Sorry. What's up, girlfriend?"

I wondered for a second whether I should say anything, and decided to preface the news with an admonition. "I have something really big to tell you, Gin, but you have to promise you won't talk to Stu about it."

I could hear her suck in her breath, and my heart began to pound harder. "Just don't tell me he got you pregnant, Ang." I was so astonished that I couldn't say anything at first. "Oh *Christ*," she said after a moment. "I'm not right, am I?"

"Yeah, you are."

I had to hold the phone away from my ear; she was shrieking. "That son of a bitch! I'm going to fucking kill him!"

In spite of how I was feeling I had to laugh. "Stu wasn't the only one, Gin. I had something to do with it, too." I couldn't believe I was telling her the same thing I had said to Stu the day before, only in reverse.

"Oh God, you stupid, stupid children," she moaned. "What the hell are you going to do, Ang? Have you told your Mom?"

"Are you kidding? When I told Stu, he absolutely lost it."

When Gin replied her voice was flat and angry. "Don't tell me, let me guess. He beat the shit out of you."

I struggled not to cry, remembering Stu's fury and the remorseless way he had kicked me. "Not until I said it was a baby."

"*What?* What the fuck does he want to call it?" she demanded.

"A mistake," I told her bitterly. "*My* mistake. One that I have to fix."

"Oh, that's beautiful. Now I'm *really* getting mad. Just how are you supposed to do that, Ang?"

"By having an – "

It's just a word, say it, it's just a goddamn word –

(*one that's going to kill your baby*)

"... an – abortion." I forced the word out and began to cry, clutching the phone tightly and feeling despair obliterate any positive residual feelings I had had about Stu from that morning.

"Ang, you don't have to do that, you know," Gin said gently, and at the love in her voice I cried harder. Why didn't anyone understand the way my life was now? I didn't make decisions any more – hadn't she seen enough proof of that to know?

"Yes, I do," I told her through the tears. "Stu said if I didn't, he'd – " I hesitated. I didn't want to say it out loud; it would make the horror of it too real.

"He'd *what*?" Gin asked, and that edge was back in her voice.

"He said if I didn't go to a clinic, he'd do it himself."

There was a moment of absolute silence, and then Gin said, "*What did you say, Ang? Tell me you didn't say that Stu said he'd do it himself. Tell me you didn't say that.*"

Her voice was high and pleading, and I suddenly realized how much Stu was hurting her as well. Not as much as me, perhaps, but she loved him too, and it couldn't have been easy for her to hear these things.

"That's what he said, Gin. And he was serious. You should have seen the look in his eyes. He's already made an appointment for a consultation for tomorrow."

"Oh Jesus, Ang, Jesus, how in the world are you dealing with this?"

"Not very well." My voice broke, and I could barely get the next words out. "Can you come over, Gin?"

"I'm already there. See you in a few, babe." She hung up and I sagged back against the couch, letting the phone fall from my hand to the floor.

We talked for the rest of the afternoon, up in my room. Gin desperately wanted to help me in some way, to save me from Stu, and I had to tell her that it just wasn't possible.

"Come on, Ang!" she said at one point, bringing her first down hard on the pile of blankets beside her. "Stu shouldn't be able to make you do something that's against your own morals! Can't you see how wrong that is?"

"Jesus, Gin, of course I know how wrong it is!" I looked at her, and she cut her eyes away from mine, out the window at the improbable sunshine and a slice of blue winter sky. "But Stu decides everything, and you know why. If I don't do what he wants, he hurts me."

"Goddammit!" she exploded, getting to her feet and beginning to pace the room. "Why the fuck can't we go to the police?"

"Gin, I've told you this before. Because they can't protect me."

"Well, what the fuck are they for, then? Shit!" She kicked at a pile of clothing and it scattered across the floor. "This is like a bad movie!" She looked back at me, and I was startled by the passion in her eyes. "You know the ones – where people sit back and say, 'Oh, sure, like *that* would ever happen!' It sure as hell stops being funny when it starts being you."

"You said it." I grabbed a pillow and held it against my chest. "The only thing I can do is try to keep him happy. You know what the worst thing is, though, Gin?"

She sat down beside me on the bed. "What, Ang?"

"The worst thing is how good he is to me sometimes, how sweet and loving." I hugged the pillow tightly and brought my knees up, thinking of that morning. "Sometimes the things he says just take my breath away, and I wonder how he can be the same person who can kick me, and bite me, and punch me the way he does."

"God, it's so hard to hear that." Gin's voice was trembling, and when I looked at her I wasn't surprised to see tears in her eyes. "He loves you, Ang! Fuck! He really does! What the hell is *wrong* with him?"

I put my hand on her shoulder and she smiled at me, a heartbreakingly sad smile. "I ask myself that every day. I'm so afraid I'll never get away from him, Gin, and not just because of how he hurts me. Because I don't *want* to. I actually *want* to stay with him!" I looked down at the bed, and everything blurred through the tears that filled my eyes. "Am I as sick as he is?"

Gin reached out and put her arms around me, and I rested my head on her shoulder. "No, Ang. *No.* There's a lot about Stu to love – I'm probably the only one who knows that, but it's true. You might save him, you really might."

I lifted my head and stared into her eyes. "Maybe, but who's going to save me?"

Mom got home late that night, and I was glad I had had a chance to unload on Gin, because it was much easier to push everything to the back of my mind and pretend things were normal and that my weekend had been great. She told me about the book Ivan was currently writing, and her eyes glowed with pride.

"He says it has a good chance of being published by the University," Mom told me, and I smiled at her, happy that she had someone so positive in her life, someone who meant so much to her. It made the gulf between her and Ivan's relationship and the one I had with Stu widen into an impassable chasm, and I had to resolutely ignore my feelings of envy.

"That's wonderful, Mom," I said, and meant it. "Ivan deserves to be recognized for his accomplishments. You must be so proud of him."

"I am, Peach," she told me, and I couldn't resist.

"Why don't you two stop stalling and just get married already?" I asked, and to my amusement she actually blushed.

"He hasn't asked me, Ang," she said in a mind-your-own-business tone.

I made an impatient noise. "Why does Ivan have to do the asking? Where is that written?"

Mom looked at me seriously. "There are a lot of things you don't know about Ivan," she said. "He was married once before – "

"He was?" I was surprised. I would never have thought it; Ivan had always seemed to be the quintessential bachelor. "I didn't know that. It's hard to imagine Ivan being with anyone but you."

Mom smiled at me. "He had a whole other life before we met. His first wife died of tuberculosis. It was very hard on him."

"Wow, that's rough," I said. "Poor Ivan."

Mom nodded. "It took him a long time to get over it. He told me when we first met that he never wanted to marry again."

"But that was – what, five years ago!" I exclaimed. "Surely things are different now."

Mom looked at me indulgently, the look that said: You're so young, Ang, you're just so goddamn young.

"It's romantic of you to think so, honey, but Ivan isn't a man who changes his mind very often."

I made a face at her. "You're not eighty, Mom, and neither is Ivan. Surely you're both not *that* set in your ways. Be spontaneous!"

Mom laughed at the look on my face. "I'll try to remember that the next time I see him," she told me affectionately. "How was your weekend with Stu?"

A sappy, dreamy smile spread across my face as I remembered Sunday morning. "How do you know I spent the weekend with Stu?" I asked, trying to be coy, and she nudged me with her shoulder.

"Come on, my girl, you should see the look on your face." Mom looked at me searchingly. "He didn't spend the night, did he?"

A furious blush warmed my face, and I smiled again; I couldn't help it (*what do you want, Angel? Fuck me, Stu, please fuck me*) Before I even thought about what I was saying, the words came out: "Yeah, he did. God, he's a fantastic lover."

I clapped my hands over my mouth, horrified that I had actually said it out loud, and Mom laughed until tears ran down her cheeks. "That was priceless," she finally choked out. "For God's sake, Ang, I know the two of you are having sex. I'm glad it's good." She didn't say anything about using protection, and I was glad; I don't think I could have told *that* particular lie with a straight face.

"It's more than good," I told her. "Stu was the first, you know."

Mom smiled and gave me a squeeze. "That's sweet. What was it like?" I struggled to come up with something that wasn't an utter lie (*it was rape, Mom, actually it was rape*) and finally said: "Um, it hurt, actually."

Mom nodded sagely. "It usually does the first time. Sounds like Stu knows what he's doing, though."

She looked at me slyly, and I gave her a push, feeling a blush warm my face. "Mom! Jeez!"

Mom got to her feet, shaking her head. "Oh, for God's sake, Ang. How do you think *you* got here? I do know a thing or two about sex, for your information. Sometimes I even have it myself."

She went into the kitchen, and I went upstairs to get ready for bed. I wished so much that I could tell her about the baby, and then reminded myself that it was a moot point, anyway; it would be gone soon enough. That thought got me going again, and luckily I was able to make it to my room before the tears started again.

Just.

Chapter Forty Five

I didn't see Stu at school the next morning, and by lunchtime I was a nervous wreck, wondering if I would have to go to the appointment he had made by myself. Finally, ten minutes before the bell rang for afternoon classes, he came up to Gin and me in the cafeteria, looking moody and upset.

"Trouble in paradise?" Gin asked him teasingly, and when she got no response she pulled out the chair beside hers and patted the seat. Stu slid into it reluctantly, but he wouldn't look at me. Gin peered at him intently, and he waved a hand at her, asking in an irritated voice, "What's your problem, Gin? See anything green?"

She shrugged and took a sip from her can of Coke. "Hey, it's not me, Stuart. I'm wondering what's wrong with *you*." She spoke lightly, but Stu reacted as though she had pressed him for intimate details of our sex life.

"Nothing's wrong! Christ, you girls are always trying to create trauma, aren't you?" Gin and I exchanged glances, but neither of us replied.

Stu finally looked at me, but it was a flat gaze, without emotion. "Two o'clock, Angel." His voice was brusque. "Meet me out at my car."

He got to his feet and strode away, and Gin looked after him with a curious smile on her face.

"He's feeling guilty," she said. "Will wonders never cease."

"That was guilt?" I asked, surprised. "Looked more like he was pissed off to me."

"You don't know him as well as I do, Ang." Gin took another swallow of Coke. "I hope he fucking chokes on it."

"I don't want to do this, Gin," I told her in a low voice, turning my own can of pop around and around. "I really don't."

"I know you don't, hon," Gin said, reaching across the table to take my hand. I looked at her and tried to smile, but it was hard. "Want me to talk to him for you?"

I shook my head. "No. He'll just get mad. For him, the subject is closed."

Gin released my hand and pounded the table. Her can of Coke tipped over and began to fizz everywhere, but she didn't seem to notice. "Oh, sure! For *him*!" Kids at the surrounding tables looked at us curiously, and I gestured at her to keep her voice down. "Sorry. But this sucks, Ang! This fucking sucks so bad I can't believe it." She grabbed some napkins and began to sop up the spilled Coke.

"You're telling me." I met her eyes, and for a moment I was so glad she was on my side that I almost started crying again. "Gin, the best thing you can do right now is just stick around, you know?"

Gin nodded and took my hand again. "I'm not going anywhere."

At two o'clock I went out the back door of the school and saw Stu waiting beside his car. I knew he saw me, but he didn't look up. He flicked the butt of the cigarette he was smoking out into the snow and got into the car, sitting behind the wheel and waiting for me. My feet dragged the nearer I came to the Rambler, and I was conscious of a feeling of terror that had nothing to do with him.

How can I do this? This is my baby! Our baby!

I thought about trying to reason with Stu as I got into the car, but dropped the idea when I got a good look at his face. His expression was grim, his mouth in a thin, tight line, and his hands were tense on the wheel. I slid in beside him and closed the door; he didn't say anything. He started the car, and I could feel tears stinging my eyes as he roared out of the parking lot. Stu didn't say a word the entire way downtown, and I found myself growing more and more upset. I tried not to let him see it, but as he braked for a red light he looked over at me impatiently.

"Oh, for Christ's sake, Angel. Give it up, will you?"

I stared at him, outraged. "Give it up?" I repeated in disbelief. "*Give it up,* Stu? Oh, I'm giving it up, all right. I'm arranging to have this baby killed because it's what *you* want!"

Stu's hands tightened on the wheel. "Shut your goddamn mouth. This is the best thing and you know it."

"It's *not* the best thing for me, and don't try to say it is!" I started to cry in earnest. "Don't make me do this, Stu. Please, don't make me do this."

Stu pulled the car into a narrow alleyway and jammed the gearshift into park. He turned to me. "What was that, Angie?" he said in a quiet, deadly voice. "I don't think I heard you."

"I don't want to – " Before I could finish the sentence he slapped me hard, and my head struck the closed window.

Stu continued to look at me, his expression unchanged. "Anything else you want to say?" I shook my head and slid as far away from him as I could get, pressing myself against the door. When we got to the clinic I began to shake, and for a moment I wasn't sure I could walk. Stu came around to my side of the car and jerked the door open, almost spilling me out onto the ground.

"Let's get this over with." He grabbed my arm and began to drag me toward the clinic, and I pulled out of his grasp.

"I can walk. Stop dragging me."

Stu glared at me. "Watch your mouth, Angel, or you won't be able to walk for long."

We went in the double glass doors of the Planned Parenthood clinic and over to a receptionist behind a white counter.

"We have a two thirty appointment," Stu told her. "Angela Swanson." The receptionist tapped in my name on her keyboard, looking at her computer screen and nodding. She reached behind her and picked up a clipboard; attached to it was a sheaf of paperwork.

"Here you are," she said, extending the clipboard to me. "Please fill these out and give them to the counselor. You can have a seat over there."

She waved her hand vaguely in the direction of a number of upholstered purple chairs, and I went over to one and sat down. I began to work on the forms, filling out the blanks mechanically. Stu sprawled in the chair beside mine, looking bored. He didn't reach for my hand, talk to me, or acknowledge me in any way, and I tried to focus on anger, on what a selfish bastard he was, but all I could feel was pain.

I finished the forms, struggling not to cry the entire time, and when my name was called I looked around to see a plump woman in a gorgeous blue caftan smiling at me. Her brown hair was streaked with grey and she had kind eyes, and when I got up and went over to her she gave me a sympathetic smile.

"I'm Angie Swanson," I said, and she patted my shoulder in a motherly way.

"My name is Marla, Angie. Right this way." Marla led Stu and I through a door and down a narrow hallway to one of a half dozen cramped offices. When I stepped inside I sank into one of two chairs beside an old metal desk. I handed Marla the clipboard with the forms, twisting my hands together to still their trembling.

My baby Oh God my baby …

"You look very nervous, Angie," Marla said to me, and I nodded without speaking. Stu took my hand then, and I wanted to jerk it away and tell him where to go, but I didn't. I just sat there, feeling as though I was mired in a nightmare. "Is this your boyfriend?" Marla asked gently, and I nodded again.

"His name is Stu," I whispered, and she looked at Stu with an approving smile.

"It's nice that you're here to support Angie, Stu. A lot of guys don't want to be part of this."

Stu smiled back at her and squeezed my hand. "I couldn't let her go through this alone," he said, and I wanted to scream.

You're damn right you couldn't! That's because you know I'd never do it if you left it up to me, Stu!

Marla glanced at the papers in front of her. "It says here that you want to have an abortion, Angie. Is that right?" She looked at me inquiringly, and I wanted so much to deny it, to tell her that I didn't want to kill my baby, that Stu was forcing me to do it, but he clamped down painfully on my fingers, crushing the bones together.

"Yes," I whispered, blinking back tears. Marla frowned and leaned closer to me.

"Are you sure this is what you want to do?" she asked me. "There are other options, you know."

A tear snaked its way down my cheek and I managed to nod. "I'm sure."

Stu slid an arm around my shoulders and said to Marla, "This has been really rough on her, deciding what to do and everything. We've been talking about it for days."

Marla nodded sympathetically. "I can certainly understand how difficult this decision must have been for both of you," she said, and it was only through an enormous effort of will that I didn't break down completely. "Do you understand what's involved?"

She opened a drawer in the front of her desk and pulled out a pamphlet. "This is the procedure ..." She flattened the pamphlet out in front of me and began to explain it in excruciating detail. My face must have betrayed my inner feelings, because Marla stopped talking after a minute and looked at me with some concern.

"Are you all right, Angie?"

I managed to nod. "I'm all right. Just a bit lightheaded."

Stu kissed me on the temple, and my skin crawled; right then, I wanted to be as far away from him as I could possibly get.

"Why don't you just give us information about how to schedule it?" he asked. "I think this is a bit too much for her right now."

I closed my eyes as I heard Marla begin to tell Stu about the locations of the clinics and the various timelines, but it was all a meaningless buzz. I just wanted to go to sleep and make this all go away, if only for a little while. Finally, Stu patted me gently on the knee.

"Come on, Angel. Let's go." I opened my eyes and looked at him, and he kissed me gently. I got to my feet, and as we left the building I had to lean against him; I was feeling weak and shaky. Once we were outside, I took a deep breath of the cold air and pulled away from him. Stu looked at me resentfully. "What's with you?"

I was astounded at his insensitivity. "I don't feel like being close to you right now, that's all."

I turned and began to walk to the car, but before I had gone three feet Stu grabbed me and pulled me into his arms. His lips descended on mine, insistent and warmly caressing, and in spite of my misery there was an answering spark deep inside and I responded to him, as always.

When Stu broke the kiss at last, I looked at him in anguish. "Why did you do that?"

He smiled, a self-satisfied smile that made me long to slap him. "Because I wanted to." His voice was as smug as his expression. "I wanted to show you that I can *always* make you want me, Angel."

I pushed him away and began to run toward the car. Stu let me go, and by the time he got inside I was already huddled against the passenger side door, wishing my damned heart would just break in two and get it over with.

Chapter Forty Six

When Stu dropped me off that afternoon, he gave me the information Marla had given him and told me to call right away to make an appointment. When I got inside the house I went straight to my room and had the breakdown I had denied myself earlier. I cried hysterically and pounded the bedclothes, cursing Stu and hating myself for even being with him.

I tried to think of an alternative, another option, *anything* other than what he had demanded I do, but there was nothing. After about an hour I sat up, retrieved the pamphlets I had dropped on the floor, and reached for the phone. I punched in the number of the first clinic before I lost my nerve and told the voice that answered that I wanted to make an appointment.

"How soon can I have it done?" I asked, trying not to focus on the fact that I sounded eager to get rid of the life inside me.

"Ten days to two weeks," the calm female voice on the other end replied, and I began to cry again.

"I can't wait that long!" I said through the tears. "It'll *kill* me to wait that long! Please, isn't there something sooner?"

When the woman answered this time, she sounded considerably warmer and more concerned. "Let me see what I can do," she said, and there was a click as she put me on hold. I waited, clutching the phone tightly and struggling to slow my breathing, and by the time she came back on the line I almost had myself under control again.

"I can get you in on Thursday," she said, and, irrationally, I wanted to cry: "So soon?"

"Be here by eight in the morning, and nothing to eat or drink after midnight on Wednesday, all right?"

"Will it hurt?" I asked in a trembling voice, and when she answered, it was the voice of a mother comforting a frightened child.

"Not to much, honey. Try not to worry."

"Thank you." I hung up the phone and it rang immediately under my fingers. I was tempted not to answer it, knowing it was Stu, calling to see if I had done as he had told me, but I pressed the 'talk' button and held the phone to my ear.

"Hello?"

"Angel baby. Did you make that call?"

"Yes. The – appointment is on Thursday morning."

"Good girl, Angel." He was practically crooning, and I hated him for it. How could he not understand what this was going to do to me? "Do you want your reward now, or should I save it until later?"

I laughed mirthlessly. "Hmmm. A reward for killing a baby. Why don't you decide for me, Stu? You're pretty good at that."

There was silence for a moment, then: "Is it time for another lesson, Angel?"

For once, the implied threat didn't frighten me. "You know what, Stu? I don't care. I really don't." I felt as dead inside as my voice sounded. "Nothing you could do to me now would hurt as much as this."

"Well see about that, Angel. I'll be there at two o'clock. Be ready." Stu hung up abruptly, and I tossed the phone to the floor without even

285

bothering to hang it up. I must have fallen asleep, because the next thing I knew Mom was shaking me.

"Peach? Are you all right?" I looked up at her, and the moment I saw the love and concern in her eyes I burst into tears. All I wanted was to be a little girl again, a child she could take in her arms and soothe with her presence alone; a child whose problems would vanish in the face of her mother-magic. I sat up and hugged her with all my strength, sobbing helplessly, wishing wretchedly that I could tell her what was really wrong. Mom's arms came around me and she held me tightly.

"Oh, honey," she said softly. "What is it?"

"Just everything," I told her, my voice muffled against the front of her shirt. "Stu, Megan ... everything."

Mom held me away from her after a moment. "Is Stu still being too possessive?" I nodded. Her forehead creased into a wrinkle of concern, and she shook her head. "If things with him have you this upset, Ang, maybe you should call it off."

Oh God, I wish I could, Mom, I really do ...

"It's not that bad," I lied, plucking at the blanket. "Just bad enough to get in the way, and I can't really talk to him about it. And Meg hates him, Mom. She really hates him. We hardly even talk any more."

Mom cupped my chin in her hand and lifted my head. "That sounds bad enough to me. This relationship doesn't sound healthy. You know I like Stu, honey, but if he's making you this miserable then you should end it. Especially if it's coming between you and your best friend." Mom smiled at me. "You know what they say – men come and go, but friends are forever."

"I love them both," I said, wiping my eyes on the sleeve of my shirt. "Why do I have to choose between them?" Mom shrugged.

"That's something only you can decide, Ang. You've only been with Stu a few months. Are you sure he's worth it?"

He may not be, but I am ...

"I don't know, Mom. Everything is so confusing."

Mom hugged me again, briefly, and then got off the bed. "That's how it goes when you're seventeen, honey."

I rolled my eyes at her. "I knew you were going to say something like that. When did you get so old?"

Mom reached out and gave my head a push. "Stop being a smartass and come on downstairs. Or do you want do go out for pizza?"

This time my smile was real. "Pizza sounds good to me."

We had a good time that evening. Mom and I hadn't gone out together in quite a while, and as long as we avoided talking about Stu I was reasonably happy. When we got back to the house I deliberately pushed the dark knowledge of Thursday to the back of my mind and got some homework done. By the time ten o'clock came I was exhausted, and as I got ready for bed something nagged at the back of my mind, something I had forgotten, but I couldn't remember what it was.

Must not have been that important ...

In my dream his head was between my legs, his tongue caressing that tender flesh, and the sensations that shot through me were amazingly real. I felt myself climbing that exquisite slope toward orgasm, my breath coming fast and my fingers tangled in his dark hair, and when the ecstasy burst through me I realized I was awake, that it was really happening. My hips bucked against his mouth and I cried out helplessly, my hands tightening on his shoulders. Stu raised his head, his hands resting on my belly, and smiled at me.

"I told you I'd be here at two, didn't I?" he said softly, and bent his head to kiss my navel. As my mind cleared I asked, "How did you get in?" The door had been replaced months before, and the new one was strong enough to withstand even Stu's boots. He grinned at me wickedly.

"You're not very careful about where you leave your purse, Angel. I had your key copied." He raised himself up and lay on top of me, and I could feel his erection against me.

"Ready?" he inquired, and I wrapped my arms around his neck and pulled him down to me. I could taste myself on his tongue, musky and slightly salty, and it got me excited all over again. I raised my hips invitingly, and he slid into me. The feel of his hardness against tissue made sensitive by orgasm was incredible, and I groaned.

"Do you like that, Angel-baby?" Stu asked in a husky voice, and I pushed my hips into his.

"Oh God, you know I do – " He pulled out and I let out a protesting cry. "Stu, don't! I want you to – "

Stu kissed me hard, and I reached down, searching for him. He batted my hand away and secured both my wrists in his hands, pressing them into the mattress over my head. "You want me to what, Angel?" he asked, and I struggled against him.

"I want you to fuck me," I whispered, and he laughed, a throaty, sexy sound that made the ache inside me worse.

"I know that," Stu told me, planting tiny kisses on my neck and face. "Why don't you ask for what you really want?"

I looked into his eyes, my breath coming in short pants, and gave in. "Can I come, Stu? Please, can I come?"

His answer was to ram himself into me so hard that my head hit the top of the bed, and I stifled the scream that wanted to escape me with difficulty. I clung to him, biting his shoulder as he filled me again and again, and when I finally climaxed it was like I'd died and gone to heaven. We lay back, staring up into the darkness, both of us sweaty and panting, and I said weakly, "If it gets any better than that I don't think I can take it."

Stu raised himself up on one elbow and smiled down at me, tracing the edge of my jaw with one finger. "You're insatiable. I had no idea you'd turn out to be such a slut, Angel-baby."

"I guess you bring out the whore in me," I whispered, and he laughed and bent his head to kiss me.

"As long as you never forget that you're *my* whore," he told me, one hand caressing my breast lightly. "There *is* something you forgot, though."

A thread of disquiet wormed its way into my belly, and I looked up at him in dismay. "What?" I asked, and this time the smile on Stu's face was frightening. He looked possessive and determined, and that was never a good thing.

"You talked back to me again, Angel," he told me, running his finger around my areola, and my comfortable, sated feelings vanished, replaced by fear, that horrible, familiar fear. "I'm getting really tired of that."

I stared into his eyes; they were black and cold, and the lovemaking might never have happened. "You said you couldn't hurt any more than you were hurting," he told me calmly, and the fear turned to terror. "Why don't we just see about that?" I tried to get up and he pushed me back down, not gently.

"Don't you fucking move." Now his voice was angry, and I fought to maintain control.

"I'm sorry Stu whatever it was I said, I'm sorry oh Jesus I'm *sorry* – " Stu slapped a hand over my mouth.

"Sorry, Angel? It's too late for sorry. You need a lesson, a really good lesson." He removed his hand from my mouth and his fingers returned to my breast, tweaking the nipple. "Which one?" he said suddenly, his voice hardening, and I was utterly confused.

"What? What do you mean?" Stu's fingers pinched the nipple he had bitten lightly, and terror made me lightheaded as I realized what he meant.

"Oh God Stu no, Jesus, *NO –* "

His hand came down on my mouth again, and he dipped his head until his face was inches from mine. "Which one, Angel? Another second and I'll decide for you."

My breath rushed in and out in panicked gasps, and I shook my head back and forth. Stu took his hand from my mouth again. "Please, Stu, I can't decide that Oh God *I can't –* "

He nodded, bending his head to my chest this time. "Okay, this one, then." His lips hovered above the nipple he had bitten before, the nipple that had finally almost healed, and I said frantically, "No! Wait!" The fear made my mind a blank wasteland, and I struggled to hold on. "Not that one, Stu, please – "

"This one, then?" Stu kissed the other nipple gently, and when he looked at me expectantly I began to cry.

"Please, oh Jesus, *please –* "

"Whatever you say, Angel." Stu placed a hand over my mouth and his head dipped toward me like a rattlesnake attacking. He placed his mouth over the nipple and I stiffened, trying to prepare myself for the pain. When it didn't come I allowed myself to breathe again. Stu's mouth stayed against my breast, his hand firmly over my mouth, and I just held still, hoping against hope that he wasn't going to bite down, that it wouldn't be as bad as it had the last time …

At last he raised his head and looked into my eyes. "You know what I could have done, don't you?"

I nodded, looking back into his dark eyes, an absurd feeling of gratitude filling me. "Yes," I whispered. "Thank you for not doing it, Stu."

"Oh, that doesn't mean I'm not going to do anything, Angel," Stu told me, getting up off the bed and pulling me with him. When he bent over and reached for his pants, sliding the belt out of the loops, I told myself it was better than what he had threatened.

By the time he was finished with me, though, it didn't feel like it.

Chapter Forty Seven

For some reason, that lesson broke me in a way the others hadn't. My sense of gratitude toward Stu for not making me suffer the torture he had given me before had led me into a new well of self-loathing. At last, I truly felt he owned me, that I was his to do with as he wished, and it was as if Angie had finally vanished. I no longer knew who I was anymore, and a frightening indifference possessed me that hadn't until now. I realized that I was sliding down to the bottom of a dangerous abyss, but I was helpless to stop it.

I avoided Stu for the next two days, ducking out of classes before he could get to me, not going to the ones we had together, and refusing to take his phone calls. He came to the house once, but when I told Mom that I didn't want to see him and she said as much to him, what was he going to do? He had presented himself in a very favorable light to my mother, and I doubted if he wanted to screw that up now.

Finally, on Wednesday morning he cornered me at my locker, and to my surprise, he wasn't angry. If anything, he looked desperately worried. A week ago that would have been enough to bring hope to my heart, but now there was nothing.

"Where the hell have you been, Angel?" Stu stood directly in front of me and placed his hands on either side of my head on the locker above me so there was nowhere for me to go. I looked at him without emotion. I didn't care if he was angry; I didn't care if he was worried, or upset, or frightened. My feelings for him had vanished in the fear and misery of what would be happening the next morning, and it was as if none of the tender moments we had shared had ever happened. I just wanted him to go away, to fall off the ends of the earth, to die in some slow and painful manner, the way he was killing me.

"What do you care?" I answered him dully, and Stu took my chin in his hand and tipped my head up until I was looking into his eyes.

"I care," he said softly. "You wouldn't believe how much."

I let out a bitter laugh. "Yeah? You've got a hell of a funny way of showing it, Stu. Just leave me alone."

He leaned in to kiss me and I turned my head. "Angel, don't." His voice actually trembled, and I looked at him in astonishment.

"Don't what?" I asked, fascinated in spite of my antipathy.

"Don't shut me out," Stu begged, and at his tone – a lost and frightened child – a twinge of emotion was born. I cast it aside fiercely, reminding myself of the humiliation that had occurred less than two days before.

"Shut you out?" I repeated incredulously. "I couldn't shut you out if I tried. What the hell are you talking about?"

The bell rang at that moment, but we both ignored it. Other students looked at us curiously as they passed, but I ignored them, too; I had more important things to worry about. Stu pulled me into his arms and held me tightly, and I remained rigid in his embrace, refusing to give in to this new display of emotion. It was too mercurial, too temperamental in nature, for me to really believe that he felt it at all.

"I need you, Angel," Stu whispered into my hair. Sarcastic words sprang to my lips, but I didn't let them out. I just stood there in the circle of his arms, indifferent, waiting for him to release me. After a moment he looked down at me, his eyes full of tears.

"Please, just kiss me," he said in a yearning voice, and I fought the sudden, fleeting urge to make him feel better. I stood on tiptoe and pressed my lips to his obediently, but for all the passion I showed I might have been kissing my own brother. Stu pulled away from me and I expected him to be angry, but his eyes still retained that misery, and it confused me beyond all understanding.

"Stu, what's wrong with you?" I asked, and he looked relieved that I had finally shown some interest.

"Come on." He pulled on my arm to get me to go with him, and I followed him out the back door and over to the Rambler. When we reached it I stopped walking and stood my ground.

"I'm not getting in."

Stu said it again, the word he never said, and once more that confusion washed over me. "Please, Angel, get in. Please." His eyes were dark with emotion, totally devoid of threat or anger, and I cast aside my better judgment and opened the passenger door.

What if it's a trap, Ang? You really are a fool, aren't you?

Stu got in on the driver's side and sat behind the wheel silently, staring at his hands. I studied him curiously; he looked as if he was about to cry.

"What's going on?" I forced my voice to remain calm and emotionless, and when Stu turned to me his expression was anguished.

"I feel like I'm losing you," he said, and the pain in his eyes touched my heart in spite of my earlier lack of feeling. He leaned toward me and cupped my chin, pulling me forward and kissing me gently.

I pulled back and stared at him suspiciously. "Stu, this is crazy. I've never seen you like this."

"I've never felt like this." His tone was so honestly bewildered that my heart went out to him, and that cold, practical voice in my head said immediately: *He makes more than your heart ache and you know it, Angie. Don't be an idiot.*

"How do you feel?" I spoke hesitantly, still not completely trusting this new vulnerability, but when Stu answered it was with the same childlike confusion.

"Like I can't breathe." He looked down at his lap, clearly overcome. "I'm scared to death. I don't know what to do."

A tear rolled down his cheek and my control broke. I slid across the seat and put my arms around him, and he clung to me. I found myself whispering nonsense words of comfort, as though he was the child and I was the mother who wanted only to make her little boy's pain go away. We sat like that for a long time, and when Stu finally pulled away from me he looked embarrassed and ashamed.

"Don't, Stu," I told him, putting my hand on his thigh. "It's all right to tell me how you feel. It makes me feel better, actually."

He smiled and kissed me again, a passionate kiss that spoke of his need. "I love you so goddamn much, Angel," he said. "I don't deserve you."

You're so right about that, Stu.

I took his hand and pressed a kiss into the palm, telling myself to enjoy the moment while it lasted. Stu looked at me with eyes now dark with desire rather than pain.

"Can we go back to your house?" he asked, and the passion that warred with the insecurity in his voice undid me completely. I just nodded, leaning against him while he started the car.

Chapter Forty Eight

I hardly slept at all that night, and by six o'clock I gave up completely. I grabbed the phone and punched in Stu's number. It rang three times, and I heard his abbreviated greeting: "This is Stu. Leave a message." I hung up and tried again with the same result.

Where the hell would he be at six o'clock in the morning? Oh Lord, don't tell me he isn't there ...

I made myself wait twenty minutes, praying the entire time that he had been asleep, or in the bathroom, even jerking off, anything other than the terrible suspicion that began to dawn in my mind: that he wasn't there at all. I realized I had no way to get to the clinic, and I cursed myself for a fool because I had assumed that Stu was going to go with me. It had never even occurred to me to wonder if he would, and I had to push away the hysterics that wanted to surface and reduce me to a screaming wreck.

It's a little late for that! Forget crying – you have to think about what you're going to do.

I picked up the phone again and punched in the number of Gin's cell, hoping she would answer. To my relief, I heard her voice, small and distant with sleep, on the second ring.

"'Lo?"

"Gin? It's Angie." My voice began to quaver, and I bit down hard on my lip.

"Ang?" Gin sounded wide-awake now, and concerned. "What's wrong?"

I took a deep breath and fought for control. "Today is the day I have the – " I had to force the word out, " – abortion, and I can't get seem to get hold of Stu. Will you come with me? I don't want to do this alone."

"Tell me I'm not hearing this." Gin's voice was shocked and unbelieving. "He made you schedule the goddamn thing, even though he *knew* how you felt about it, and now he's not even around to take you? Do I have it right?"

"Yeah." I congratulated myself on not crying. "He never did tell me that he was going to go with me, Gin. I just assumed – "

"That he'd be fucking human enough to support you through this?" Gin's tone dripped with contempt. "Goddamn it, I'm going to kill him." She was silent for a moment, and then added hastily, "Of course I'll go with you, hon. I'll be right there."

"Thanks, Gin."

I dressed quickly and ran a brush through my hair, went into the bathroom to brush my teeth, and then grabbed my purse and went downstairs to wait for Gin. The morning was cold and dark, and it felt like snow in the air. I shivered and pulled my coat more tightly around myself, and when I heard the chugging sound of the Beetle's engine I went to the end of the walk and looked up the street. Gin pulled up to the curb, and I opened the door and got in, smiling at her gratefully.

"Thanks for coming."

She reached over and squeezed my hand. "I'm glad you called me, Ang. I'll be right there beside you the whole time, I promise." I swallowed hard and squeezed her back, and she put the car in gear and pulled away, into the snowy street. "Then I'm going to fucking kill him."

The radio played softly as we drove across the city to the clinic, and I looked at the deserted streets, powdery with newly fallen snow, with a blank kind of fascination. It was as if the city slumbered under a light blanket of white, resting up for the busy day ahead. There was very little traffic, and we arrived a half hour early. I realized that I was scared to death, and after she had parked the car I looked at Gin, trying desperately not to cry.

"I don't want to do this," I whispered, and then the tears did come. She held me while I cried, and when I pulled away and wiped my eyes, it was time to go in. Gin held my hand when we walked inside, and I saw that the glass behind which the receptionist was seated was bulletproof. It only made me feel more frightened, and Gin had to give the woman my name. She let us right in, gave me a hospital gown to put on, and directed me to a changing room. I folded my clothes neatly and left them on a bench in the tiny cubicle, and when I came out the same nurse led me into a treatment room. All the equipment, so shiny, sterile, and frightening, made me draw in a sharp breath, and the smell of disinfectant lingered in the air. I tightened my hold on Gin's hand and she whispered, "It's okay, Ang. Just don't look. I'm right here."

The nurse helped me up onto a narrow metal table covered with blue-green drapes, and I lay there feeling exposed and vulnerable, trying not to shake. All of a sudden I felt a sharp sting in my arm, and I realized I had been given a sedative. I looked over at Gin as time slowed to a swimmy crawl, and my fears melted away as the relaxing effects of the drug took hold.

"Don't leave me, Gin," I said, and my voice seemed to be coming from far, far away. She smiled at me and patted my shoulder reassuringly. "Not a chance, babe."

Reality faded in and out; first I would be aware of one thing, then another. Dimly, I felt someone raise my knees, and I jerked a little as blunt fingers probed my cervix; my gown was pushed aside and something cold and sticky was placed on my chest. I heard voice murmuring in low, urgent tones, and I could only catch meaningless snatches of conversation:

" – look at this, it's barely healed – "

"What the hell happened to her, Christ – "

" – bruises everywhere, this looks like a *shoe* – "

Then a low humming noise began and something was threaded between my legs and placed deep inside me. I felt a sudden, awful cramp seize my lower belly and expand into a horrible pulling sensation. The pain grew and grew, and I began to moan and twist on the table while the humming droned on and on. I heard Gin's voice, strident with anger: "Jesus, can't you see she's in pain? Give her something!"

A disapproving voice murmured and I felt another sting in my arm, and then blessed darkness closed around me and blotted everything out. I descended into it willingly, hoping I was dying and that it would all finally be over.

When I swan back to consciousness I was lying on a gurney with the metal sides up, narrow and hard but infinitely more comfortable than the table had been. There was a warm blanket pulled up to my shoulders, and I became aware of a constant, steady ache in my lower abdomen. I reached down and placed my hand there.

My baby … my baby's gone …

An overwhelming feeling of grief seized me and I closed my eyes again. I felt a light touch on my shoulder and opened them again to see Gin's face,

"How are you, princess?" she asked gently, leaning over and kissing me on the cheek. "Never mind. What a stupid question."

"You're still here." I was still groggy from the sedation and my throat was dry; the words came out hoarse and scratchy.

"Of course I am." Her eyes were bright with tears, and I smiled at her. "Listen, Ang, I need to tell you something – "

Before she could say anything else I heard a door open and suddenly a doctor was looming over me, peering at my face with intense professional concern. "Miss Swanson?'

I nodded slowly and he smiled at me; it transformed his face from grim to friendly, and I told myself to stop being paranoid. "Can I go home yet?" I asked, and he shook his head.

"Not quite yet." He pulled up a chair and sat beside me. I was aware of Gin in the background, hovering worriedly, and all of a sudden I was frightened. "My name is Eric Traynor," the doctor continued, "and I need to talk to you about some things we came across during your procedure, Miss Swanson."

"Is something wrong with me?" Instantly I was filled with anxiety, and the grogginess vanished. Dr. Traynor put a reassuring hand on my shoulder.

"No, nothing resulting from the abortion," he said, and I cringed at the sound of the word. "These are things my staff and I noticed while we were prepping you for the procedure."

"What do you mean?" I whispered, but a black suspicion belied my words, and the resulting fear stole my breath.

"We noticed a lot of injuries on your body, Miss Swanson." Dr. Traynor's expression was grave, and I was grateful when Gin came up beside me and took my hand. "Injuries that are consistent with abuse. I'm particularly concerned about the bite mark on your nipple. It looks quite serious."

Gin drew in a horrified breath, and I could only stare at Dr. Traynor, unable to say a thing. He seemed to sense how afraid I was, and he smiled at me gently.

"Please don't be afraid. Our records are held in the strictest confidence. They aren't even available to hospitals." I must have looked relieved, because he continued, "Can you tell me who's been hurting you?"

"My boyfriend," I whispered, feeling so ashamed that I wanted to die.

"How long has this been happening?"

I raised one shoulder weakly. "Six months, I guess. You're not going to call the police, are you?" The fear that accompanied that thought was overwhelming, and I could feel panic closing in. "Please, don't call the police."

Dr. Traynor looked into my eyes, and I could feel his sympathy. "Because you're under eighteen, Miss Swanson, I'm afraid I'm bound by law to contact child welfare authorities. There's a social worker on her way here right now."

I clutched Gin's hand and began to cry, and the only thing I could think was: *I'm already dead. I am; I'm already dead.*

Chapter Forty Nine

When Gin was finally allowed to take me home it was late afternoon. I spoke to the child welfare worker, a calm and understanding woman named Margie Sullivan, but I wouldn't tell her Stu's name, and my eyes warned Gin not to do it, either. I didn't give her any reason for my lack of cooperation and she didn't press me, but I could sense that there was a lot more she wanted to say. She asked to see the injuries that Dr. Traynor had talked to her about but I refused to show her. She outlined the options that were available to me and gave me a card with her name on it, and it wasn't until she had gone that I realized how frightened I had been.

Eric Traynor wasn't the least bit apologetic about contacting social services, and he didn't seem to understand why I hadn't told Margie Sullivan anything. I avoided speaking to him, and after Gin and I were alone I dressed quickly and told her to take me home. I didn't want to spend another second in the place that had taken my baby, and the thought that someone other than Gin and Megan knew what Stu did to me, someone *official*, scared me so much I was afraid to even talk to Stu. I was sure that once he heard my voice, he would know, and I didn't even want to imagine how great his fury would be. Dr. Traynor gave me a prescription for some painkillers and told me to expect quite a bit of bleeding that day and the next, but that it would taper off gradually.

On the ride home I sat back and closed my eyes, riding out the cramps that came and went in gripping waves. At last Gin spoke to me.

"Why didn't you tell the social worker Stu's name, Ang? Don't you want this to stop?" A feeling of utter despair washed through me. Gin was the one person I had believed truly understood the dynamics of my relationship with Stu, but now I wondered.

"I can't believe you're asking me that," I said to her, the endless weariness of this hopeless situation sapping all my energy. "Gin, he'd kill me if anyone talked to him. I'm not kidding – he really would. I don't even want to think about how angry he'd be if social services called him."

"I don't think so," Gin replied, but she didn't sound sure at all. "I've known Stu for six years. I have trouble believing he's capable of that."

"I don't." I looked at her resentfully. "You don't see the look in his eyes right before he kicks me. You don't see his face when he punches me or pulls my hair out."

Gin winced and looked away from me, back at the snowy road, negotiating the afternoon traffic. "God, that's horrible, Ang. That's so fucking horrible."

I relaxed against the seat again and close my eyes. "You have no idea. Let's not talk about this, okay? I feel shitty enough already."

"Sure, princess. I'm sorry." Before I knew it she was pulling the rusty old Beetle up in front of my house, and I opened my eyes and smiled at her.

"Thanks for being with me, Gin."

Gin reached over and hugged me. "If you need anything, Ang, anything at all, you call me, okay?" Her eyes glistened with tears, and I thought: *It should be me who's crying. Isn't it always me who cries?*

"I will." I opened the door and got carefully out of the car, and a rush of blood left me that made me feel weak. "See you, Gin."

I slammed the door and she waved. "Count on it. Bye, princess."

She drove off and I went slowly up the driveway, my belly cramping, feeling woozy. I went right to bed, feeling like I could sleep for the rest of the week. Two hours later the phone woke me, and I picked it up, trepidation jumping into my throat.

"Hello?"

"Jesus, Angel, where the hell have you been?" Stu's voice was equal parts anger and panic, and I felt nothing, absolutely nothing. I didn't care if he was frantic, I didn't care if he was furious; I was as empty as a hollow gourd, and I knew I'd never be completely filled again.

"It took longer than I thought, Stu," I said in a monotone. "I was sleeping. I'm exhausted." A dim part of my mind demanded to know why I wasn't asking him where the hell *he* had been, but I ignored it: it didn't matter now.

"I've been really worried about you, Angel-baby." He sounded hesitant, and I said automatically, "You're sweet, but don't worry. I'm just tired."

"I'll let you get back to sleep, then." Stu sounded as if he wanted to say more, but I didn't give him the opportunity.

"Okay, Stu. I'll talk to you later." I pressed the 'end' button and dropped the phone on the floor, turning over and going back to sleep.

I woke again sometime later feeling sticky and uncomfortable, and when I sat up and waited for my head to clear, I realized that I was bleeding heavily. I raised the covers and looked down and the bright red stains on the sheets raised a vague feeling of panic.

I should have changed that napkin before I went to sleep … Mom's going to kill me when she sees these sheets!

I rose from the bed carefully, feeling a rush of blood leave me that made me wince. I made my way unsteadily to the bathroom to clean up. The blood was flowing with terrible heaviness; the pad I was wearing was saturated, and my thighs were covered in blood that had dried to a brown haze. I stepped gingerly out of my panties and got into the tub, running warm water and scrubbing the blood from my skin as well as I could. By the time the tub was half full it had changed to a sinister maroon color, and I had begun to feel lightheaded and nauseous. I realized dimly that I was hemorrhaging, and I knew I had to get to the phone.

I climbed out of the tub with difficulty, watching with detached interest as the blood flowed down my legs and onto the bathmat. I grabbed a towel and stuffed it between my legs, walking awkwardly across the hall to my bedroom. The trip seemed to take more strength than I had, and I sank down on the bed for a moment to rest. I wanted so much to lie down, but I made myself reach for the phone and almost fell off the bed as what little blood there was in my head left in a rush. I raised the phone to my face and struggled to focus on the buttons. I managed to press the 'talk' button and punched in Mom's work number out of instinct.

"Good afternoon, Dyer, Dyer, Chamberlain and Foster, how may I help you?"

"Joy Swanson, please," I whispered through lips that felt cold and stiff.

"One moment, please, I'll connect you."

It seemed to take a lifetime, but finally Mom answered, sounding cool and professional.

"Joy Swanson. How can I help you?"

305

"Mom?" Speaking was a great effort, and the moment she heard me Mom's voice filled with panic.

"Angie? What's wrong?"

"I'm bleeding, Mom, "I managed to say. "I'm bleeding an awful lot, and I'm so tired ..."

Her answer was hard and strict, and she issued terse instructions that managed to penetrate the haze. "Stay on the line, Ang. Stay on the line and talk to me. I'm going to get someone to call 911 and get an ambulance there right away." I didn't respond, and her voice lost its stern edge and rose into terror. "Angie? Baby, can you hear me? Talk to me!"

"I hear you, Mom." The phone began to slip through my nerveless fingers; I couldn't seem to make them hold on. "I'm just going to lie down ..."

I fell over sideways on the bed as the phone dropped to the floor, and the last thing I remember thinking was how good it felt just to let it all go ...

I heard a terrible wailing noise as I woke up, and my body was bouncing around in a way that made me feel sick. I struggled to open my eyes, hearing snatches of a strange conversation:

" ... blood type? I'll start an IV."

" ... Mom says she's O positive. Hang one unit ... "

" ... bleeding like crazy. We got any extra?"

I felt something being pressed against my groin, and there was a sudden sharp pain in my arm that made me cry out weakly. My eyes finally opened and I realized that I was in an ambulance with the siren on, the wailing echoing in my ears, sending its sharp warning into the late winter afternoon.

I looked up and saw a red bag of blood suspended above my head, and my gaze followed the tubing attached to it down a metal pole and into a large needle embedded in my wrist. I saw a blond young man hunched over my arm, taping down the IV needle he had just inserted. The other paramedic noticed that I was awake and bent over me. She was an older woman with curly red hair and a stocky, mannish build.

"Hi, Angie," she said with a smile, and I frowned: how did she know my name? "How are you feeling, honey?" It was difficult to focus and my eyelids fluttered. I was overwhelmed with the sudden need to sleep, and talking seemed impossible.

"Angie?" the paramedic said loudly, shaking my shoulder gently. "Stay with me, hon."

I opened my eyes reluctantly. "I'm so tired ..." The young man finished with my arm and moved away, and the woman sat down beside me.

"I know you are, but I need you to stay awake, okay? What happened?"

I struggled to remember; everything seemed so hazy and far away, and the incredible fatigue dragged me father and farther down. A strong cramp suddenly twisted my insides, and the pain brought back the terrible events of the morning.

"I had an abortion ..." I whispered, and the woman nodded. She turned to her partner and he stated matter-of-factly, "I figured it was something like that."

The spasm of pain passed, and I began to fade out again. This time the other paramedic's voice was a sound without meaning, and when the blackness took me again I surrendered to it eagerly.

Chapter Fifty

Bright lights stabbed my eyelids, and I heard someone calling my name.

"Angie? Wake up, honey. Come on now, wake up." I felt a cool cloth soothe my forehead, and the voice said again, "Wake up, Angie. Wake up."

I was floating in a languid space, fighting against my own body to open my eyes, when an irrational feeling of terror seized me. My eyes flew open as adrenaline rushed through my veins, and I began to twist my head from side to side, needing to escape. A gentle hand descended on my forehead, and the same calm voice spoke.

"It's all right, honey. It's all right. Breathe, that's it, nice deep breaths." I tried to obey the voice, but my chest felt tight and constricted. Two prongs slid into my nose and cold, pure air filled my nostrils. "That's it, breathe."

This time I could breathe, and as I became more aware of my surroundings I felt my heartbeat return to normal. Things jelled all the way together and I managed to focus on the face of a smiling nurse.

"Welcome back," she said, and I had a crazy urge to laugh.

"Where am I?" I asked her weakly, trying to cough. My throat felt scratchy and sore, and the words came out in a raspy whisper.

"You're in the recovery room," the nurse informed me. "You just got out of surgery."

Surgery? What surgery? I already had the abortion, didn't I?

My confusion must have shown on my face, because the nurse patted my shoulder reassuringly. "Give yourself time to wake up, honey. The doctor will be in to see you as soon as we get you to a room." She busied herself taking my vital signs, and I lay still and tried to make my brain work properly.

"Where's my mother?" I asked, and the nurse turned her head and smiled.

"As soon as we move you she can come and see you." After a few minutes an orderly came in, pulled up the metal sides of the stretcher, and wheeled it out of the recovery room and down a wide hallway.

The University of Alberta Hospital was a large, open facility. A huge center area on the main floor contained gift shops, a food court, and bank machines, and radiating around it like the spokes on a wheel were the various departments with their concurrent patient wards. On the upper floors these wards included cardiology, pediatrics, and gynecology. With exposed pipes at the top of the lofty building and large panels of plexi-glass attached to waist high white metal railings, there was a sense of light and space that most hospitals didn't have.

The orderly steered the stretcher into the gynecology ward and maneuvered it into a room halfway down the hallway on the right side of the nurse's desk. A nurse came into the room and helped the orderly transfer me to the bed, and I lay back against the lone pillow and closed my eyes.

"Ang?" I heard Mom's voice and looked around. She was right beside the bed, and the second I saw her face I began to cry. She leaned over and hugged me gently, and when she spoke again her voice was rough with emotion. "Oh, Peach, what happened? I've been out of my mind ever since you called me at work." She pulled back and looked at me worriedly, and I didn't have the strength to lie.

"I had an abortion this morning."

Mom's frightened expression changed to one of shock and horror. "An abortion?" she whispered. "What are you talking about? You don't believe in abortion."

I gathered what energy I had and reached for her hand. She enfolded my hand in both of hers and looked at me with such pain in her eyes that I could hardly bear to tell her the rest. "I found out I was pregnant last week. Stu told me that I had to have an abortion – "

"*Stu* told you that you *had* to have an abortion?" she repeated blankly. "I don't understand. Why was it his decision?" Her voice began to rise, and I started to cry.

"Don't yell, Mom. Please, don't yell, okay?" She was instantly apologetic, and placed a cool hand on my forehead.

"I'm sorry, sweetheart. This is just the last thing I ever expected to hear from you. Why didn't you tell me? And why was this Stu's decision, Ang? It's *your* body."

"Stu decides everything, Mom." I braced myself. I didn't know how much I was going to tell her, but I knew she wouldn't like it no matter what she heard. Mom closed her eyes briefly, as though she was trying to prepare herself, and I knew an instant of pity for her that surprised me. "Stu controls everything. It wasn't even my choice to go out with him."

Mom stared at me. "*What?* That's crazy, Ang. What do you mean, it wasn't your choice? What did he do to get you to go out with him?"

I took a deep breath. "He raped me, Mom. The night of the party I had, the first time you let me stay alone, he told me he was going to have sex with me, and the next day he came back and ... he did."

Mom looked at me as though I was raving like a maniac. "He raped you? Oh my God, Ang, did you just tell me that Stu *raped* you?"

I brought my hand to my mouth and prayed for the strength to tell her the rest without breaking down completely. I nodded. "Yeah, that first time it was rape. Stu told me that if I went to the police he'd make me sorry."

To my dismay, the fury began to build in her eyes, and I tried to continue but she raised her hand abruptly, that gesture from my childhood that meant "Just a goddamn minute!"

"He'd make you sorry." Mom repeated the words in a flat voice, and when she looked at me it was as though I wasn't even there. "He's the one who'd going to be sorry, Ang. I guarantee you that."

"Mom, stop."

She raised her eyebrow at me, and I could tell she was struggling to hold onto her temper. "*Stop*, Ang? No, *you* stop. Why would you stay with a boy like this? *Why?*"

The moment had come, and I was surprised at how easily the words came out. "Stu hits me, Mom. A lot. I'm scared to death of him."

Mom's eyes grew huge, bottomless, and she brought her hands to her mouth like a terrified child. I had to look away; it hurt too much to see that.

"Right from the beginning he's been hurting me," I continued, knowing I had to tell her the entire story. "When I threatened to go to the police, he punched me and rammed my head into my bedroom wall. Whenever I do something he doesn't like, he gives me what he calls 'lessons.' "

It was spilling over the barrier, that barrier I had somehow managed to keep in place until now, and I couldn't have stopped if I had wanted to. "The lessons are the worst, Mom. Stu's used a belt on me, he's kicked me, he's pulled my hair out, and he bites me."

I forced myself to meet her eyes, and the expression on her face was a mirror of what mine must have been every time Stu hurt me: horrified, ashamed, and afraid. Mom made a choked sound in the back of her throat and turned away, and for a moment I thought she was going to be sick. She sagged against the bed, and when I realized she was crying my heart broke cleanly in two, as if it had only been waiting for something like this to kill it completely.

"Mom," I said. "Mom, please, don't cry, please – "

She turned to me, and at the look on her face I began to cry myself. "Why didn't you tell me?" she managed to say. "Why, baby?"

I held out my arms, and she sat on the bed beside me and leaned over to hug me. "I was scared," I told her. "I was scared for me, and I was scared for you. I still am."

Mom held me away from her and we looked at each other, each of us with wet faces. "You don't have to be scared anymore," she said quietly. "We're going to get a restraining order to keep him away from you."

Panic started to rise inside me again. "Mom, you can't seriously believe that will work. Stu is obsessed with me. He *worships* me. And his anger is just as strong as the love. A piece of paper will never keep him away from me. He's told me that if I try to leave him, he'll kill me."

"Oh my God, Angie!" Now Mom sounded angry again, and I found myself getting defensive.

"How could I love a guy like this, isn't that what you want to say?" I glared at Mom, and her face crumpled.

"I don't understand it, Ang. He seems like such a … normal person. I like him, you know that. At least I did."

I lay back carefully against the pillow. "That's the worst thing of all. I love him. He hurts me all the time, and he's not sorry, but I love him anyway. What's wrong with me, Mom?"

312

I looked at her pleadingly. Mom leaned over and cupped my face between her hands. The gesture made me think of Stu, and I started to cry again.

"There's nothing wrong with you, baby. As soon as you get away from him, you'll find out you never loved him at all."

I looked at her in dismay. "You're not getting me, Mom. I love Stu. I mean it – I really love him. And he loves me. I know how crazy that sounds, but he does."

Mom shook her head. "No, Angie. When a man loves a woman, he doesn't beat her up. Don't try to tell yourself that what Stu feels for you is love. You said it before – it's obsession, not love."

"Mom, I'm tired." I turned my head away from her and closed my eyes. "I don't want to talk about this anymore, okay? Not right now."

"Okay, Peach." Mom's hand was gentle against the side of my face, and I reached up and placed my own on top of it. "But I'm not letting him near you."

I turned to look at her. "You can't do that."

Mom looked incredulous. "Of course I can. You're my daughter! He's done! Finished!"

"Mom, you can't decide that for me," I told her patiently. "I still love Stu, even if he's abusive. And I still want to see him."

"Angie – "

I held up a hand; it seemed to weigh a thousand pounds. "Mom, please. I can't do this right now. I can't handle it. I don't want Stu to know that anyone knows. Not right now. Okay?"

I closed my eyes and tears ran down my cheeks. "Don't you think I hate myself for wanting him? I do, believe me. I really do. I have from the very beginning. But I need to see him. God knows why, but I do."

I opened my eyes and found Mom looking at me with an odd sort of compassion. She nodded, and then leaned over and kissed my cheek. "Okay, Ang. For now. But *only* for now, you hear me? I'm going to come up with some kind of a plan. We have to get you away from him."

"Will you call him?" I asked. "And tell him what happened?"

I expected her to explode at the request, but a grim smile curved her lips. "You know what, Ang? I'd be glad to. And I'm going to twist the knife until he screams."

I didn't have the strength to protest, and to tell the truth, I didn't really want to, anyway.

Chapter Fifty One

Mom insisted on staying at the hospital; nothing I said would persuade her to go home. She did agree to at least go down to the cafeteria, and after she left my room I was relieved. The emotion we had just shared was almost too much for me, and I knew I still had to get through seeing Stu as well. I was feeling vulnerable and terrified, certain he would know the second he looked at me that I had told, that someone else knew about his terrible cruelty.

I didn't have to wait long. Shortly after six he appeared in the doorway, and I was so frightened at the sight of him that I couldn't even smile. Stu looked at me for a long moment, his dark eyes taking in the IV stand and my pale, emotionless face, and something seemed to break in him. He came over to my side and took my hand, and I managed to smile at him weakly.

"Hi, Stu," I said, and he didn't reply. He held my hand up to his lips and began to cry, and I looked at the top of his head, feeling that irrational pity surge through me at the harsh noises he was making.

"I'm sorry, Angel," he choked out. "I'm so goddamn sorry that I made you do this, I'm sorry I wasn't there with you, I'm such a fucking coward ..." Stu sat on the bed beside me, still holding my hand tightly, pressing it to his cheek as though he never wanted to let it go.

At last I sat up carefully and put my arms around him, feeling that frustrating pull of emotion: tenderness and repugnance, pity and hatred, hope and revulsion. He raised his head and looked at me with wet, utterly naked eyes, and I truly didn't know how to feel.

"I'm all right," I finally told him, and he took me into his arms and held me tightly.

"When your mom called I almost went crazy." His voice was trembling, and for a vicious moment I was glad. "Jesus, Angel, if anything had happened to you I would have killed myself."

I pulled away from him, wincing at the pressure on my abdomen. "Don't say that."

Stu leaned forward and kissed me. "I'm serious. Without you I'd have nothing. There'd be no reason for me to live."

A shiver traced its way down my spine, and I felt like a prisoner of his love for me. I managed to smile and touched his cheek with one finger. "Well, I'm still here, so stop talking that way. I'm going to be all right, Stu."

"Are you?" he asked pleadingly, and something in his eyes cried out to me in a voice I didn't understand. I nodded and drew his head down on my chest, and he held me tightly once again, a confused and frightened little boy.

"Yes, I am," I said. "I have to tell you something, though." Stu raised his head and looked at me, and I prayed that this mood would affect his response. "When the doctors and nurses at the clinic saw the … marks on me, they called child welfare."

Immediately a watchful, suspicious expression came over his face, and I hastened to reassure him. "I didn't say anything, Stu. They looked at me while I was sedated."

Stu sat back and regarded me speculatively, and the fear began to wind itself around me. "Really. And what was it they saw, Angel?"

A thin blade of anger cut me to the quick, and I was glad to show him. I reached down for the edge of the hospital gown, gathering the folds in my hands and lifting it up and over my chest. I just sat there silently, and when Stu got a good look at my nipple, the fading bite marks, and the spectacular bruises all over my ribcage his expression changed yet again: this time he looked horrified.

"Jesus Christ," he breathed. "Did I do that?" His eyes met mine, wide and frightened, and I nodded without speaking; he already knew the answer, anyway.

Stu turned away from me, gripping the side of the bed so tightly that his knuckles were white. When I saw his shoulders begin to shake I knew he was crying again, but something deep inside told me to leave him alone, that this time he needed to go down that painful road alone.

"God, I'm a fucking animal," he sobbed, and I resisted the almost overwhelming urge to hold him and deny it.

He is an animal! You know it, Angie, you know it better than anyone, so just keep quiet! He needs this. Let him suffer for a change!

When Stu finally turned back to me the shame in his eyes was palpable; he couldn't even look at me. I reached under his chin and raised his head the way he always did to me, and when his gaze met mine I looked at him seriously. "Stop hurting me, Stu," I entreated him softly. "Please, just stop."

"I don't know if I can." His voice was so low that I had to lean forward to hear, and when his words sank in I pulled away from him.

"Then I won't stay with you. I can't. You're going to end up killing me."

Stu seized my shoulders. In an instant the remorse had vanished, replaced by anger. "Don't you fucking say that." He jerked me forward, and I cried out as I felt a stabbing pain deep in my abdomen. "You *belong to* me, Angel. What I own, I keep. Understand?"

I nodded, and this time it was my eyes that filled with tears. "I understand."

Stu pressed his lips to mine in a gentle kiss. "That's a good girl. Tell me, Angel."

I closed my eyes and kissed him again. "I love you, Stu."

And the worst of it was, I did.

He was still sitting beside me on the bed holding my hand, and we were talking quietly, when Mom came back into the room. Stu's back was to her, and the moment she saw him a look of such hatred came over her face that I was chilled. I met her eyes and shook my head, and Stu's frowned. He looked behind him, and by the time he saw Mom her expression had smoothed out. She was a good actress; I had to give her that.

"Hi, Mrs. Swanson," Stu said, and Mom walked across the room toward us.

"Hello, Stu," she said quietly, and what Stu said next astonished me.

"I'm really sorry about this. Angie and I should have talked to you."

Mom hesitated before replying, and we exchanged glances. She looked back at Stu. "I wish you had," she said. "When Angie called me right before the ambulance came it scared me to death. She could have died, Stu. Do you realize that?"

Stu nodded slowly. "I should have been there. I'll never forgive myself for that."

In spite of what she had said before Mom's eyes softened, and she put a hand on his shoulder. "Thank God she didn't."

"Mom, why did I have surgery?" I asked, and she looked at me reluctantly.

There's something wrong … something she hasn't told me yet …

When Mom told me the pity in her eyes was bottomless, and I was suddenly frightened.

"You had to have a hysterectomy, Peach. It was the only way to stop the bleeding. I'm so sorry."

It took me a moment to understand, and beside me, Stu stiffened. "A hysterectomy?" I whispered, and Mom nodded.

"Yes, honey, I'm afraid so. I'm sorry, Ang."

I pulled my hand out of Stu's and brought them both to my eyes, and the pain that ripped through me was like nothing I had ever known. I would never be pregnant again, never give birth, never have a child of my own, a child that had come from my body. For a minute I couldn't even breathe, and the atmosphere in the room became charged with tension.

Finally, Stu spoke. "Jesus, Angel, I don't know what to say – "

I lowered my hands and looked at him with real hatred, and the misery inside me exploded. "Get out!" I screamed, and the effort made my abdomen ache horribly. "Get out! I don't want to look at you, I don't want to talk to you, just GET OUT!"

Mom took Stu's elbow and pulled him gently to his feet. "You should go now, Stu."

He left the room without another word, and I collapsed. Mom came over to me and held me, and I cried until there was nothing left inside me, nothing at all.

Chapter Fifty Two

I slept badly that night. My dreams were full of frightening images of Stu and the lessons he was going to mete out for my anger. I kept trying to tell him how upset I had been, but he never seemed to hear me. He just grew larger and larger until he blotted out everything else in the world, and when I jerked awake in the pre-dawn darkness, sweaty and terrified, I didn't want to close my eyes again. I managed to turn over, but only by pressing my hand against the thick bandages that covered the incision on my belly, and a wave of depression swept over me as I remembered what had happened to me.

Barren. I'm barren. And it's all Stu's fault.

I wanted to hate him, *just* hate him, feel loathing and nothing else. I wanted that hate to destroy the love, to burn it to ashes from which nothing could ever be resurrected. I couldn't, though, and it made me want to scream. All I had to do was remember the look in his eyes and the way he had cried (*God, I'm such a fucking animal*) and my heart contracted; all I had to think of were those hands and the way they caressed me, and the feel of him inside me, and my body cried out for him. Even though I hated myself for it, I loved him, and I was at a complete loss as to what I should do.

The door opened a crack, letting in a slice of fluorescent light, and a nurse entered the room, silent on rubber-soled shoes. She was pushing a portable blood pressure monitor and carrying a digital thermometer, and I let her carry out her routine checks, watching the room gradually lighten as the sun rose.

"Would you like some pain medication?" she asked, her braids swinging forward as she bent over to retrieve the blood pressure cuff.

I nodded. "Please." She nodded and left the room, returning moments later with a syringe. She injected its contents into my IV line, and almost immediately a blessed feeling of lethargy began to overwhelm me. I was asleep within minutes, and this time there were no dreams.

When I woke again the room was bathed in sunshine and Mom was sitting in a chair across from the bed, reading a magazine.

"Hi, Mom," I said, and she looked over at me with a smile.

"Hi yourself, sleepyhead."

I stretched my arms over my head and yawned. "What time is it?"

Mom glanced at the clock on the wall. "Ten thirty. I told the nurse not to wake you for breakfast."

I turned toward her, grimacing as the muscles in my abdomen protested fiercely. "How long have you been here?"

"Since about eight," she answered, coming over to kiss my forehead. "Did you sleep all right?"

"So so," I told her. "Bad dreams for most of the night."

"I can imagine." Mom brought her chair over to the bed and sat down beside me. "I've been thinking about what we should do, Ang."

I wished I had confided in her to begin with; her determination to put an end to it made me feel so much safer. At the same time, however, the prospect of not being with Stu made my heart ache. No matter how I thought about it, the situation was painful and confusing.

"What do you think we should do?" I asked.

"I think we should move."

I gaped at her. "What? Don't you think that's a little extreme, Mom?"

"Extreme?" Mom looked back at me in disbelief. "Angie, what Stu did to you is extreme, and if you're right about what he would do if you tried to break up with him, the only solution is to go where he can't find you."

I felt as though my life was spiraling out of control again, and I struggled to find an anchor. "Leave all our friends, our house, my school, not to mention your job? There must be another way."

"What way would that be?" Mom asked sarcastically. "Stick around and let Stu kill you?"

"Jesus, Mom – "

She cut me off by grabbing my shoulders. "You don't seem to understand, Ang. I spent all last night on the Internet researching battered women, and what I found scared the hell out of me. Do you know how many women who stay in abusive relationships end up dead? You're *not* going to be another statistic. I'll kill him before I let that happen."

Her grip on my shoulders grew tighter, and the intensity in her eyes began to frighten me. I tried to pull away but she held me fast. "The hell with the house, my job, and your friends. I'm only interested in protecting you from Stu. Do you get it, Ang? Do you?"

Mom shook me, and suddenly the reality of it overwhelmed me, rushing over my head in a suffocating wave, trying to drown me in sorrow and fear. My entire life had been turned upside down, and all because of a boy I hadn't even chosen to be with in the first place. Mom must have noticed the fear in my eyes, because she let go of me and patted my face.

"I'm sorry, Peach. I didn't mean to scare you."

I smiled at her halfheartedly. "I've been scared for six months, Mom. It's nothing new."

She exploded at that. "Oh God, Ang, I could *kill* him when I think of what you must have been going through! I wish you had told me, honey. I really do." She cupped the side of my face in one hand and I swallowed hard against the tears.

"I already told you, Mom. I couldn't. And in a weird sort of way, I guess I wanted to protect Stu. I don't understand why, but I did." I looked at her in misery, and I could see that she was trying not to cry, too. "Why do I love him? *Why?*"

Mom lifted one shoulder tiredly. "I don't know. Stu does have some good qualities." It surprised me to hear her admit it, but then she continued: "But he's unstable, and he abuses you. You can't stay with him, Ang. You know that, don't you?"

I began to cry. "I know. But I don't want to leave him, either."

Mom put her arms around me, and I clung to her. She held me for a moment and then sat up again. "I'm going to send you to Ivan for a week, and while you're there I'm going to work out the details. I've booked you on a nine o'clock flight to Calgary tomorrow night."

"Okay," I said dejectedly. "This really sucks. I'm supposedly the victim here, and I have to run away. It's so unfair."

"You're *definitely* the victim, Ang." Mom's voice was inexorable. "Never forget that. Nothing you did could ever justify what Stu has done to you."

"Did you talk to Ivan?" I asked, and she nodded.

"I didn't tell him everything, just the part about the abortion and the complications."

That word again, sounding so foul to my ears. Suddenly it was important for her to know that I hadn't been a willing participant, that I hadn't killed my baby of my own free will.

"Mom?"

"What, Peach?"

"I didn't want to have the abortion." My voice began to quaver, and Mom took my hands in hers. "He made me do it. I didn't want to kill the baby – "

I couldn't finish, and I pulled my hands out of hers and covered my face, crying; it seemed that my supply of tears was endless. Mom leaned over and kissed me gently on the forehead.

"I know, Ang. More than anything else, I know that."

Mom went back to work after lunch, and I went into the bathroom and took a sponge bath when she had gone, trying to at least *feel* clean. Every movement was an effort, and as I ran the damp washcloth over my body I was aware once again of what Stu had done to me. I decided that Mom was right. I did need to get away from him before he destroyed me, but at the thought of never seeing him again my heart cried out in agony. I wondered whether I could ever feel truly safe again, and whether I would ever be able to trust another man. From where I was at the moment, it seemed impossible.

I washed my hair as best I could and was sitting on the bed combing out the tangles when I heard a noise from the doorway. I turned around quickly, instantly sorry when a fist of pain slammed into my abdomen. My heart jumped when I saw Stu leaning against the jamb with a lazy smile on his face. He sauntered into the room and sprawled in the chair next to the bed.

"Hey, Angel-baby." I continued to comb my hair, glad I had something to focus on besides those dark eyes.

"Hi, Stu. What brings you here?"

Stu left the chair to sit beside me on the bed, and he slipped his arms carefully around my waist and kissed my neck possessively. His hand reached up to cup my breast, and a shiver snaked its way through me that wasn't entirely unpleasant.

"What a stupid question," he murmured, his breath tickling my ear. "I had to see you. I'm missing you, Angel." Warmth filled me at that, and I melted against him.

"Are you?" I tried to keep my voice cool and steady. "I thought you'd be mad after the way I yelled at you last night."

I could feel it when Stu shook his head. "You had every right to be upset. Christ, I'm mad at myself. If it wasn't for me, this never would have happened."

I told myself not to put any faith in these words, but my heart sang anyway: *There's hope, there really is, don't give up on him ...*

"I love you, Angel." Stu pulled away from me and looked into my eyes. "Do you still love me?"

I nodded, and couldn't help smiling at the insecurity in his eyes. "Of course I do."

Stu smiled and leaned forward to kiss me. "I really *am* sorry, Angel. Do you believe me?"

I placed my hand on the back of his neck and kissed him back. "I believe you. And you're going to have to miss me some more, you know."

His eyes narrowed. "What are you talking about?"

"Mom's sending me to Ivan's for a week," I told him. "I guess she thinks I need to recover somewhere else."

Stu took my chin in his fingers, and a ribbon of fear would its way through me. "What have you told her, Angel?" he asked softly, but the menace behind the words was unmistakable, and I prayed that I could convince him.

"Nothing. Child welfare won't tell her anything either, because I'm over sixteen. They need to have my consent." I couldn't resist adding: "Your secret is safe with me, Stu."

His fingers tightened on my chin, and I told myself to shut up; I was pushing my luck. "Watch your mouth, Angel."

I pushed down the anger that rose up in me and leaned toward him, kissing him softly at first but then with increased urgency. Stu put his arms around me and held me tightly, and when we broke apart at last his eyes were heavy and his breathing was unsteady. Desire had kindled in my belly as well, and I placed a hand between his legs, my fingers brushing his erection.

"Jesus, Angel, don't," he said. "I'm so goddamn horny for you right now – " His hand closed over mine. "I mean it – stop it or I'll fuck you right here."

"You can't," I told him softly, running my index finger over his lower lip. "I'm an invalid, remember?"

Stu groaned and his hands caressed my breasts feverishly. "How am I going to last a week without fucking you?" he asked, and I smiled at the frustration in his voice. I pushed his hand away and began to massage his thigh, my fingers reaching higher and higher until I was touching the bulge that strained against the zipper of his jeans.

"Stop it," he pleaded hoarsely. "You're making me crazy."

At that all the common sense left my head, and I got carefully off the bed and went to the door. I closed and locked it and turned to look at him, smiling at the need in his eyes. Then I returned to the bed and placed my hand against his chest, pushing him onto his back.

"What the hell are you doing?" Stu asked me, and I placed a finger over his lips with one hand and reached for the button on his jeans with the other.

"Shhhh." I got the button undone and slowly eased his zipper down, pushing it apart with my fingers and reaching inside the vee to stroke his erect penis. I curled my fingers around it and he gasped out loud, arching his back and saying in a strangled voice, "Christ, Angel – "

My hand began to move up and down, slowly and rhythmically. Stu's hips rose up to meet it and he began to make helpless, guttural noises deep in his throat. A thrilling sense of power filled me and I squeezed him harder, pumping faster and then slowing down, bringing him to the edge of orgasm again and again. Finally, after about ten minutes, he was begging. "Please, Angel …"

I smiled to myself. "What do you want, Stu?" I whispered teasingly, and he groaned, "I want to come, oh Jesus I *need* to come – "

I leaned over to kiss him. My hand began to move faster and harder, and this time I didn't stop. As the climax seized him the semen shot onto his stomach and Stu cried out as if he was in pain. I watched his face, his passion setting my own body on fire.

At least I have some control! You're not totally in charge, Stu.

Immediately the sarcastic voice in the back of my mind responded: *Pity it doesn't hurt him the way his control hurts you, isn't it?* I ignored it and bent to kiss him again.

"Better?" I whispered in his ear, and Stu said breathlessly, "Christ Almighty. All kinds of better."

I pulled several tissues from the box on my bedside table and wiped his stomach. He looked at me so tenderly, with such love in his eyes that out of nowhere unbearable sadness filled me and I began to cry. I turned away from him, sobbing, and Stu sat up and wrapped his arms around me.

"Angel? What is it, baby?" I cried harder, wanting to push him away, wanting to hold him and never let go, hating him and loving him at the same time.

"Why can't this be the way it is?" Stu squeezed me tightly, and I knew he knew what I meant. "*Why?*"

I continued to cry in racking sobs and he held me, his silence telling me everything I needed to know.

Chapter Fifty Three

After Stu left I lay back on the bed, trying to think past the clamoring in my body. Satisfying Stu had brought out a need in me I would have thought impossible given what I had just been through. I castigated myself for surrendering to him yet again, yet all I wanted was for him to touch me the way I had touched him. Finally, after the fire burned down to embers and my head cleared, I felt that denigrating self-hatred for allowing my physical impulses to take over my common sense. My mind told me I should be withdrawing from Stu, objecting with ever fiber of my being when he got close to me, but my body ached for him and my heart stubbornly insisted I loved him.

Goddamn it, Angie, that's not love! Where's the mutual respect, the common interests, the intimate knowledge of each other's thoughts and feelings? Stu abuses you! He abuses you and he doesn't regret doing it! If you think that's love, you're as sick as he is!

I said all this to myself in my best no-nonsense inner voice, but my heart had a will of its own, remembering Stu's vulnerable pleading, his tears and apology, and the sincerity of his voice when he told me he needed me.

That's love, my heart insisted. *That's love, and you know it.*

The more I wrestled with my feelings, the more confused and miserable I became. *Why can't I just focus on what he's done to me? Why aren't the abuse, the abortion, and the hysterectomy enough to make me hate him? How can I possibly let him touch me after what's happened?*

I was on the verge of tears when I heard a light rapping at the door, and I turned over slowly and looked to see who was there. When I saw Margie Sullivan, the social worker that had spoken to me at the abortion clinic, my heart sank. The fear came rushing back as she came into the room, and suddenly my confusion disappeared; all I could think of was that I shouldn't say anything, I wouldn't, I *couldn't*.

"Hi, Angie," the short, dark-haired woman said, stopping beside the bed. "I'm Margie Sullivan. Do you remember me from the clinic?"

"I remember you. What do you want? I've already said everything I'm going to say." I tried my best to come across as defiant, but all I could see in my mind's eye was Stu's eyes when he was angry – those icy, terrifying eyes. Margie sat down in the chair beside the bed.

"You're very afraid, aren't you?" she said, and I stared at her. Was I such an open book? Margie waited patiently, and finally I nodded.

"I'm scared to death," I admitted in a low voice. "If my boyfriend saw me talking to you he'd – " I stopped abruptly, aware that I had almost said too much.

"He'd hurt you?" Margie finished for me and once again I nodded, feeling that demoralizing shame.

You deserve it, you know you do …

"I can't talk to you!" My voice was a desperate whisper, and Margie leaned forward, looking at me intently.

"Angie, listen to me. I heard about the extent of your injuries from Dr. Traynor. This young man has hurt you very seriously. Don't protect him."

"I'm not protecting him!" I cried. "I'm protecting *myself!* If he knew I told you anything, anything at all, you don't know what he'd do to me!"

"Isn't what he's already done enough?" Margie's voice was calm, but she spoke with the passion of experience. "You can't stay with this boy. Eventually he's going to end up killing you."

I pressed my hands to my ears like a recalcitrant child, trying in vain to shut out the implacable sound of her words. "Not if I don't say anything! He loves me! I *know* he loves me!"

"Angie, abuse is not love." Margie's voice continued to reach me, even though I tried not to listen. "He may tell you how much he loves you and he may even believe that he does, but when a man truly loves a woman, he doesn't beat her up."

I took my hands away from my ears and looked at her, and the misery welled up and came out in one question, the only one I had wanted the answer to since this hideous affair began. "Why does he do this to me? He tells me he loves me – he tells me he can't live without me. *Why* does he feel like he has to hurt me?"

Margie reached out and placed a gentle hand on my arm. "I don't know, Angie. For most of these men, it's a way of controlling the woman they're with. A lot of the time it's because of fear, fear of losing that control, or fear of the woman leaving."

I was surprised at her words. "That's what my friend Gin says. She told me that the more Stu loves me, the more out of control he feels, and the angrier it makes him."

Margie nodded. "I've seen this pattern of behavior many times. Unfortunately, there's one thing that seems to be consistent, and that's the escalation of the abuse. It's gotten worse over time, hasn't it?"

I felt like she could see into my head and look at all the terrifying memories of the times Stu had punched me, kicked me, used his belt on me, and bitten me. I nodded. "Yeah, it has. What can I do?"

"You need to contact the police. Right away."

I shook my head vehemently. "They can't protect me. They might arrest him, but they wouldn't be able to put him in jail. He'd find me, and then – "

"Angie, I can put you in a safe house," Margie interrupted. "Actually, since you're under eighteen, technically I could place you in foster care." She looked at me seriously. "The point is, there *is* help available. Women do get away."

"What if they don't want to?" I asked, and she looked dismayed. "I love him, Margie, I really do. I don't want to leave him."

Margie sighed, the weary sigh of a woman who has heard this too many times before. "Angie, how you feel about him doesn't matter. The violence is what matters, and what it's already done to you. Staying isn't an option, can't you see that?"

"He told me he was sorry about the abortion," I said desperately. "He's never said anything like that before. Maybe it means he's changing." Even as the words left my lips there was a part of me standing outside myself, watching in disbelief.

Do you have a fucking death wish? Are you hearing yourself?? Let this woman help you before it's too late!

"Angie, please listen to me." Margie leaned forward again and looked at me earnestly. "This young man has some very serious problems, and you can't make them yours. Don't you understand that your life is in danger?"

"I don't believe that." I refused to look at her, turning my head and staring at the blank wall beside the bed. "He loves me. He would never kill me. Never."

When I felt Margie's hand shaking my shoulder I looked at her resentfully. "He won't mean to, but it may happen." Her voice was stern and uncompromising; the sympathetic social worker had vanished, replaced by a woman on a mission. "No woman ever thinks the man she loves would kill her, but I've seen it more times than I want to remember."

"Stop it!" I brought my hands up to my ears again, and my voice rose into a scream. "Get out! I don't have to tell you anything! Just get out!" I turned away from her, and after a moment she spoke.

"All right, Angie. I'm going to leave you my card, and I hope you'll contact me. Thank you for talking to me."

I heard her walk from the room, and when I was sure she was gone I began to cry, so hard that when the nurse came in she hurried out again to get me a sedative.

I slept for a long time, worn out by the stress of Margie's visit. I woke to a nurse shaking me gently, and I looked up at her sleepily.

"Angie? Dr. Thorwell would like to talk to you for a minute, okay?" I nodded automatically; most of what she said was lost in the haze, and I struggled to full awareness. A middle-aged man in a white coat appeared by the side of my bed. He had grayish hair that curled over his collar and wire rimmed glasses, and he carried a clipboard. He smiled at me.

"I'm Dr. Brian Thorwell, Miss Swanson. I've been called in by Dr. Soloman for a plastic surgery consult." I frowned at him, still not entirely awake.

"Plastic surgery?" I repeated faintly, and he glanced at his clipboard.

"Yes, about your nipple." Humiliation rushed through me when I realized what he meant, and I had to resist the urge to bring my hand up to my breast. "Dr. Soloman told me that you have fairly extensive injuries to your left nipple that might require reconstructive surgery. May I take a look?"

"Sure." I pushed back the blankets and raised my hospital gown, looking away as his fingers gently probed me. Finally he told me to lower the gown, and I did so thankfully. Dr. Thorwell scribbled on his clipboard for a moment, and when he looked at me his eyes were dark and serious.

"That's a nasty injury, Miss Swanson. How did it happen?"

Caught by surprise, I found myself blurting out the truth. "My boyfriend. He – bit me." Dr. Thorwell's eyes widened in shock, and I felt a moment of vicious satisfaction – he had asked, hadn't he?

"How terrible," he said quietly. "I'm so sorry." I pressed my lips together and willed myself not to cry. "It appears that on the nipple there is substantial tearing away of the areola," Dr. Thorwell continued. "I can attach it and reshape the nipple, but you won't be able to breastfeed."

"That's not a problem," I said as tears stung my eyes. "I had a hysterectomy yesterday."

Dr. Thorwell looked uncomfortable. "I'd recommend going ahead with the reconstruction," he said after clearing his throat awkwardly. "Otherwise you'll lose a lot of sensation in the nipple."

Well, we wouldn't want that, would we?

Stop it, Angie. The man's only trying to help.

"Okay, when would you like to do it?" I asked him, and Dr, Thorwell glanced down at the clipboard for a moment before answering.

"Within the next two weeks," he told me. "I'll have my nurse give you a call to arrange a date for surgery." I nodded.

"Thank you, Dr. Thorwell."

"You're welcome, Miss Swanson." He turned and walked across the room but stopped when he reached the door. Turning back to me, Dr. Thorwell said, "Is there someone helping you with your situation?"

It was hard to speak past the ache in my throat. "Yes," I told him, blinking back tears. "Thanks for your concern."

Dr. Thorwell smiled at me gently. "Not at all." He left the room, and I lay back against the pillow, wondering why it was that everyone was so eager to help me when it was already too late to do anything at all.

Chapter Fifty Four

I drifted off again after Dr. Thorwell left. I was sound asleep when I felt something tickle my ear, and I reached up blindly, trying to brush it away. I felt it again, a delicate touch that woke me further, and when I stirred and opened my eyes Stu kissed me gently and I responded instinctively, reaching up to put my arms around his neck. He slipped his arms around me and lifted me toward him, and I found myself wrapped in a protective embrace that felt so good I never wanted it to end.

"Hi," I said softly. "That sure is a nice way to wake up."

Stu kissed my temple and rocked me back and forth. "I'd like to wake you like that every day for the rest of my life."

The sweet words cut me to the quick. It was if there were two Angies and two Stus: one couple was certain to live happily ever after and the other was trapped in a nightmare.

"You're sweet," I said, and smiled into his eyes. Stu gave me a lopsided smile and released me, sitting beside me on the bed.

"Just call me Prince Charming," he said, embarrassed, and I smiled.

"This is a nice side of you. It's pretty romantic."

Stu shrugged. "I have a lot of sides. I'm a complicated guy, Angel."

I looked at him, his dark hair brushing the collar of his coat, his eyes serious, and decided to try one more time. My heart wanted to believe that some kind of relationship could be salvaged, but the realistic side of me sat back and waited, knowing I was a credulous fool.

"Stu, do you think you could stop hurting me?" I asked him, taking his hand and holding it in both my own. Stu looked away from me, down at the floor, and it took him a moment to answer.

"I don't think so." I didn't know what I had expected, but it wasn't such naked honesty. I couldn't answer; I just looked down at our linked hands and my vision doubled, then trebled as my eyes filled with tears. "I need to hurt you, Angel. It's the only way I can make you understand."

I looked up at that, one lone tear falling on the back of his hand. "Understand what? What can you possibly need me to understand that justifies the way you treat me?"

Stu took my shoulders in his hands. "I need you to understand that you belong to me. That you can never leave me."

I resisted the urge to jerk away from him, trying desperately to make sense of his twisted way of thinking. "You don't decide whether or not I can leave you, Stu. That's not the way a real relationship works. One person can't own another."

Stu shook his head, and anger began to dawn in his eyes. "You belong to me, Angel," he said. "When I hurt you, it helps you to understand that. It helps you understand how I want you to behave."

"It doesn't help me understand *anything*, Stu!" I wrenched my shoulders out of his grasp, wincing at the pain in my belly. "It's horrible for me! It makes me think you hate me. It makes me hate *myself* for being with you. Do *you* understand that?" I looked into his eyes, but there was no answering spark, nothing that told me that what I had said made any sense to him.

"All I understand is that I can't live without you," he told me. "And if I have to hurt you to make you stay with me, I will."

Stu looked at me expectantly, and I burst out, "That's crazy, Stu! You don't abuse a woman until she's *afraid* to leave you! You're supposed to treat her right, so she *wants* to be with you."

I couldn't believe we were having this lunatic conversation. Part of me wanted to just go crazy and join him so I wouldn't have to deal with the frustration and pain anymore. I couldn't, though; I had my mother's instinct for survival.

"Don't you *want* to be with me, Angel?"

There was an undercurrent to Stu's voice that I recognized all too well, and I took his hand again, my own shaking. "When you're good to me there's no one in the world I'd rather be with. But I can't stay with you if you're going to hurt me. I can't."

"You don't seem to understand, Angel." Stu seized my shoulders again, and now his eyes were black and depthless, focused inward, on his own need and nothing else. "You don't have a choice about staying with me. You're with me. You're mine. And it's going to stay that way."

"Stu, stop it!" It was like he was an emotionless stranger, someone I didn't even know. "I do have choices, whether you like it or not!"

Stu fingers tightened on my shoulders, his nails digging into me through the thin cloth of the hospital gown. "You know, Angel, you're right. You do have one choice." His eyes glared into mine, and it took all the self-control I had not to scream. "You can stay with me, or I can kill you. Which will it be?"

An icy horror filled me, and for a moment I couldn't speak. "You don't really mean that," I breathed. "You're not serious – "

"I've never been more serious about anything in my life," Stu said. "And while I'm being honest, let me tell you something else." He pulled me forward until his lips were at my ear. "It turns me on to see you beg and cry. I love seeing the marks on your body that I put there. Then I know I have complete control over you."

I collapsed against him, sobbing, and Stu put his arms around me. "I love you, Angel," he murmured. "I'll love you forever."

I wanted to surrender to the counterfeit safety of his embrace, but I wouldn't let myself. After a moment I raised my head and looked at him. "What if it were you, Stu? What if I told you that you had to accept constant pain as a condition of loving me? What would *you* do?"

I expected him to lose his patience, but he continued to look at me without expression. "Good question, Angel. I'm going to show you the answer."

Stu got to his feet and shrugged out of his jacket, letting it fall to the floor. I started to shrink away from him but stopped when he made no move to touch me. Instead, he pulled the turtleneck shirt he was wearing out of the waistband of his jeans and over his head in a single graceful movement. I stared him, confused.

"Stu, what are you doing?"

He turned around, presenting his back to me. "Answering your question, Angel. Take a good look."

He moved closer to me and I looked carefully at the skin of his back. It was crisscrossed with thin white scars, prominent despite the fact that they had obviously been there a long time. They stretched from the tops of his shoulders to just above his waist, and most of them had a ladderlike appearance. It occurred to me that this was what happened to scars when a person's body grew and the scar stretched, which meant they must have been put there when he was quite young. I reached out and touched his skin gently, and Stu flinched.

I was suddenly filled with sadness and pity, but those emotions didn't absolve him of imprisoning me in the same cage of pain. Stu turned around and looked into my eyes.

"See, Angel? Pain *is* love." The fear that filled me this time had nothing to do with his fists. It was fear of the whole person, of the sickness that had been in his head for God only knew how long.

"Stu, who did this to you?" I asked him in a whisper, and he shrugged, as if the question was irrelevant.

"My mother." His eyes never left my face; they burned into mine, and I couldn't tear my gaze away.

"Oh God, Stu, why?" I couldn't imagine a child doing anything bad enough to warrant such abuse.

Stu shrugged again. "How do I know? Because she hated me, I guess. All I know is that it was the only attention I ever got from her."

"That doesn't mean you have to be the same!" I cried, and Stu placed his palms on the bed and leaned toward me, forcing me backward on the mattress.

"Don't say anything like that again. *Ever.*"

I nodded frantically. "Okay, I'm sorry. But I'm sure your mother didn't hate you, Stu."

"Correction, Angel. She *was* my mother. I don't have a mother. Not anymore."

I remembered what Gin had told me (*they just left one morning and he woke up alone*) and pity squeezed my heart again.

"I'm so sorry that happened to you, Stu." I spoke gently, and his expression wavered between irritation and agony for an endless moment. Behind the anger I thought I could see the boy he didn't want to be, the frightened boy that he probably still was, and I wanted to take him in my arms and soothe him. Stu pulled back from me and bent over to pick up his shirt, pulling it over his head. His hair emerged all tousled and full of static, and it made me smile; he looked like a little boy. Stu ran his hands indifferently through it and came over to me.

"What's so funny?"

I shook my head, my smile fading. "Nothing. Nothing about this situation is remotely funny, to tell you the truth. I guess I can understand why you hate women, though."

He looked surprised. "I don't hate women. I could *never* hate you. You're the best thing that ever happened to me, Angel." Stu cupped my face between his hands and kissed me, and sorrow twisted inside me like the blade of a dull knife.

Oh God, Stu, I wish I could believe that …

Chapter Fifty Five

Shortly after Stu left Mom came back, and I didn't mention my conversation with him. I knew it would frighten her even more than she had been already, and I felt badly enough for getting her involved in the first place.

"Was Stu here?" she asked as she took off her coat, making a poor attempt to speak lightly.

"He just left." At the look on her face I said, "Mom, don't start. Please, just don't."

"I can't help it, Ang." She sat down in the chair next to the bed. "I don't want him touching you. I don't even want him *near* you." Her words provoked an immediate mental image of me in Stu's arms, and I had to take a deep breath.

"I understand that, believe me. But this is so hard for me. I don't think you know how hard."

"Oh, Ang, I know it is." The sympathy in her eyes was almost too much to take, and I looked up at the ceiling. "But we have to get you away from him, sweetheart. For your safety."

"I know." I turned carefully onto my side. "I'm trying and trying to understand why Stu thinks the way he does, but I just don't, Mom. I

342

can't. His mother beat him when he was younger – he has scars all over his back - but why does that mean he has to do the same to me?"

I looked at her pleadingly, as if she had the answer and was waiting to give it to me. Instead, a look of reluctant sadness came over her face and she moved her chair closer to the bed, reaching out and touching the side of my face.

"I don't understand it either, Peach. I would think that if Stu went through such a horrible time himself the last thing he would want to do is hurt you, but that's me. I think there are dynamics here that we're not aware of."

I pillowed my head on my arm and sighed. "I don't want to be aware of anything. I just want him to stop."

Mom leaned forward and put her hand on my other arm. "He won't. Not without a lot of therapy, and a lot of commitment. You need to accept that, Ang."

"I'm trying." I looked up at her, and my expression prompted her to take my hand. "But I love him. I really do. I love the part of him that's good to me, that cherishes me. Does that make sense?"

"I suppose so," Mom said. "But I'm the mother bear, so I can't be very objective."

I smiled at that. "You sure are."

I heard a noise from the doorway and looked over Mom's shoulder to see Gin and Megan. "Hey, guys! Come on in." They entered the room hesitantly, and Meg said, "If this isn't a good time, we can come back – "

Mom got to her feet. "I need to go and get a coffee anyway. You girls visit." She leaned over and kissed me on the forehead. "I'll see you in a while, Peach."

After she had left the room, Gin looked at me quizzically. "Peach?" she asked, and I felt myself turn red.

"Childhood nickname," I explained briefly, and she smiled.

"At least it's not as bad as – "

I interrupted her. "You don't have to say it, Gin."

Meg looked at both of us, shaking her head. Then she came over to me and hugged me carefully. I hugged her back, suddenly realizing how good it was to see her, to see both of them. Meg sank into the chair Mom had vacated and Gin dragged another one across the floor.

"Holy shit, Ang," she said with her customary directness. "What the hell happened?"

"I started to hemorrhage after you dropped me off. I barely made it to the phone. Mom called an ambulance, and it brought me here."

Meg's eyes were huge, and she asked breathlessly, "What was it? What was wrong?"

I lifted one shoulder in a shrug. "I don't know. Apparently I went right to surgery." Meg brought one hand to her mouth, and I forced myself to tell her, hoping I wasn't going to cry yet again. "They had to do a hysterectomy."

"Oh Jesus Christ, Ang." Gin reached out and took my hand, and the sorrow in her eyes undid me. "Oh God, princess, I'm so sorry, I'm so goddamn sorry …"

I did cry then, and she held me until the tears tapered off and I was under control again. "If I didn't have a reason to hate him before, I sure as hell do now," Megan said in a low, furious voice, and I shook my head.

"What's done is done, Meg. I can't change it now."

"But you didn't want this in the first place!" she cried, looking so upset that I had to fight an absurd urge to apologize to her. "And now you'll never be able to – "

"I don't thing she needs to hear that right now, Meg," Gin said. "I'm sure it's occurred to her more than once."

Meg subsided. "You're right. Sorry, Ang. But who's going to make sure *Stu* pays? Goddamn it, this is so fucking unfair!"

I smiled weakly. "Fair's the last thing it is," I told her. "But my relationship with Stu up until now hasn't been exactly equal, so what should I expect?"

"To be treated like a human being!" Meg said bitterly. "To be loved and safe."

I swallowed hard. "You know Meg, I appreciate your righteous indignation, but it's not making me feel much better."

"I'm sorry," Meg said again. "I just hate Stu. I fucking *hate* him, and I want him to suffer some consequences for what he's done to you."

"And what would those be, Meg?" Gin asked, and at the edge in her voice Meg looked at her incredulously.

"Don't tell me you're *defending* him!"

Gin shook her head. "No, I'm not. But I've known him a long time, and I know a lot of his history that you two don't."

Meg was incensed at this. "I don't care what his fucking history is! *Nothing* gives him the right to beat the shit out of Angie! And nothing gives him the right to *force* her to have an abortion! *Nothing!* "

"Meg." She looked over at me, her face red and her chest heaving. "Calm down. This isn't really helping."

"So, does your mom know?" Gin asked, and I nodded. "Yeah. I finally told her what was really going on. She was pretty upset."

"Yeah, I guess." Again, Megan's tone was bitter, and I raised my eyebrows at her. "Come on, Ang! I can't even imagine what it was like for her to hear what Stu's been doing to you!"

"What does she want to do?" Gin asked quietly, and I was grateful for her calmness; it helped to offset Meg's fury.

"She wants to move."

Meg's face crumpled, and she brought her hands up to her eyes. "I don't fucking believe it. Now he's taking you away from *us*?" She began to cry, and Gin put a comforting arm around her shoulders.

"I figured it might be something like that." I looked at her inquiringly – *why?* – and she elaborated: "He's not going to stop, Ang. This isn't something he can control."

I was amazed. It was the very thing that Margie Sullivan had told me – how did she know? Gin interpreted my look correctly and smiled in a sad way. "My mom's husband used to beat her up all the time. She'd take it and take it, tell me he'd change, that he didn't mean it, that he really *was* a good man, until one day he put her in the hospital. She never came out of the coma."

I was filled with an icy sense of terror. "Why didn't you tell me?" I whispered, and she answered, "Why, Ang? To scare the shit out of you? To make you feel even more hopeless than you already do? I think your mom has the right idea. You need to just get away from Stu. It doesn't matter how you feel about him, princess."

"I know. Mom's sending me to Calgary for a week, to see Ivan. Then she's going to make plans."

"Are you guys going to move there to be with him?" Meg asked, and I shrugged.

"I don't know. It might not be far enough away."

"You have a point," Meg said. "Antarctica wouldn't be far enough away."

I felt a sudden stab of anger. "You know what, Meg? This is going to be the hardest thing I've ever done. I love Stu, and I love you guys. It's going to hurt like hell to leave all of you."

Meg looked at me, and disbelief and guilt fought for control of her expression. "I'm angry and upset, Ang. I don't mean to take it out on you. But I don't understand how you can love him. I just don't."

"I hope you never find out."

We fell to talking of other things then, but as hard as we tried to ignore it, the spectre of Stu hovered around us. Even when he wasn't with me, he was still there, all the time, and I found myself wondering if that would ever change.

Chapter Fifty Six

The next day passed slowly. I tried to rest but grew bored, and I had too much time to think. My conversation with Stu kept running through my mind, and no matter how much I tried to convince myself that he could change, that *we* could change, that nasty little voice in the back of my mind never hesitated to try to disabuse me of such a foolish notion.

Come on, Angie! When you asked him if he could stop, he said, "I don't think so." Remember? "It turns me on to see you beg and cry?" What does that tell you?

When Stu finally showed up I had just had myself a good cry, the beginning of my acceptance of leaving him, and when he saw my red eyes he looked concerned.

"You've been crying," he observed, sitting on the bed and placing a possessive hand on my breast. I smiled at the touch of his hand, but my heart still ached with unbearable sadness.

"Just thinking about yesterday," I said, and his brow contracted in confusion.

"Yesterday?" he echoed, and I sighed inwardly; how I wished it were that easy for me to forget.

"You told me you can't stop hurting me, and if I try to leave you you'll kill me." My voice was flat, and for a moment Stu looked almost regretful.

"If you do what I want those things won't happen, Angel." He leaned over and touched my lips with his, and I fought back a bittersweet rush of emotion.

"It's so unfair, Stu," I finally said. "Why do I have to be perfect? What about you? Shouldn't there be some punishment for *you* for hurting me?"

Stu shook his head with a tolerant smile. "Now you're just being silly."

Silly? Silly?? So being held responsible for your actions is silly? Give up, Angie. You'll be gone soon enough.

"Kiss me," I begged him. "Just kiss me, okay?"

Stu obliged, taking me into his arms and kissing me over and over, until my head spun and I couldn't think rationally any more. I wanted to stay in that space, unfocused and breathless with desire, and let it obliterate everything else. I clung to him, kissing him back with frenzied passion.

"Jesus, Angel," Stu gasped, pulling away from me. "When you kiss me like that I can hardly control myself."

A thrill of satisfaction shot through me and I smiled at him, my entire body tingling. I lay back against the pillow and took his hand in mine, guiding it under the covers and between my legs, where his fingers explored my slippery wetness. I watched his face; his eyes closed and he groaned, and when his fingers found their way inside me it was my turn to gasp. I kept my hand on his wrist, pulling his fingers out of me and placing them on my exquisitely sensitive clitoris.

"Keep touching me, Stu," I whispered, and his fingers began to move, sliding across that sensitive bud over and over again. It was torture not to lift my hips, but every time I tried the pain would rear its head, and eventually I surrendered my body to him, moaning as the pace of his fingers quickened and orgasm approached.

"Do you want to come, Angel?" he asked me, and I could barely get the words out.

"Can I, Stu? Please?"

Stu leaned over to murmur in my ear. "Come on, Angel-baby," he entreated softly. "Come for me, that's it, come for me – "

Suddenly I was up and over the peak, and the waves of sensation washed over me again and again. The pleasure intermingled with pain as my stitches pulled, but it was what I had wanted, what I had needed …

Stu brought his fingers to his mouth and tasted them, and the sight of that made another sweet contraction surge through me. "That was one of the sexiest things I've ever seen," he said hoarsely, leaning over. I expected him to kiss me, so when he drew the blankets away and pulled up my hospital gown, I said, "Stu, what are you – "

When his mouth touched my vulva and his tongue flicked out and caressed me, my hips bucked involuntarily and a bolt of pain slammed into the pleasure. "Owww, Stu, don't – "

He paid no attention, but continued to taste me, caress me, tease me, until another orgasm seized me and I let out a cry that was more of a scream. Stu put a hasty hand over my mouth and raised his head. "Shhh, Angel," he whispered. "Are you trying to get me in trouble?"

He gave me a final kiss and sat up, pulling the blankets back up just as a red haired nurse walked into the room. "Angie? Are you all right?"

Stu wiped his mouth with the back of his hand, and all I could do was smile at the nurse foolishly. She grinned knowingly and turned and walked out, and my face burned. Stu gave me a wicked smile and his hand reached out to caress my breast gently; he knew which one to touch.

"You need it as much as I do, Angel," he told me. "Maybe I should start calling you Angel-slut."

"I'm going to miss you like crazy," I told him. The words came out unexpectedly, and for a moment he looked as pleased as a child on Christmas morning. He leaned over, his hands on either side of my face, and kissed me, a long, slow, passionate kiss that fanned the flames again, those flames that were never really extinguished.

"That's not even half as much as I'm going to miss you," he whispered, and I smiled and cupped the side of his face in my hand.

"Why Mister Black," I said teasingly. "That was almost mushy."

Stu grinned and kissed me again. "You bring out the sappy romantic in me," he said, and for some reason it was one of the sweetest things he had ever said to me.

"I love you, Stu."

I looked into his eyes, and he placed his head on my chest. "I love you, too, Angel. More than I could ever tell you."

I held him, inhaling the clean scent of his hair. We stayed like that for a moment, and when Mom came in she rolled her eyes. "Don't you two ever get enough?" she teased, although I could see the anxiety behind her purposely calm expression.

Stu raised his head and smiled at me gently. "Not in a million years," he said, and it was a struggle not to cry.

"I didn't know you were such a romantic, Stu," Mom said lightly as she came over to the bed and dropped my suitcase beside it.

Stu looked embarrassed. "It's just how she makes me feel," he said, and for a second there was something soft and fond in Mom's eyes.

"That's nice," she told him, and Stu got to his feet.

"I don't know how I'm going to take it, but I'll see you in a week, Angel."

He leaned over and kissed me, whispering in my ear afterwards. "When you get back I'm going to fuck you until you can't stand up." A rush of desire began at the top of my head and swept through my body, and my breath caught in my throat.

"Behave," I whispered back, and he caressed the side of my face.

"With you around?" he said with another smile. "Not a chance. I love you, Angel."

"I love you, too."

"Have a good time," he told me, turning to Mom. "Nice seeing you again, Mrs. Swanson."

"You too, Stu." Mom looked uncomfortable, as if she knew she was lying, but Stu didn't notice. He left the room, and I watched him, that long, lazy stride making my head swim. Mom looked at me after he was gone.

"Wow," she said. "I can see why he sweeps you off your feet." I smiled, but it was a melancholy smile.

"You're not helping when you say like that," I told her, and she said, "Sorry, Peach. It's such a mystery to me – he seems like such a together kid. I can't imagine him ... doing what he did."

She didn't want to be specific, and I couldn't blame her. I didn't want to say it out loud, either; it made the situation too real.

Chapter Fifty Seven

We didn't talk much on the way to the airport. I was lost in thoughts of Stu, trying to come to terms with the fact that we were moving, that he would be out of my life, perhaps forever. I tried to focus on the abuse – on my tender abdomen, my nipple, on the fear that had been such a constant part of my life – but I couldn't seem to get past the love in his eyes and the tenderness with which he had touched me.

Why does it have to be this way? Why?

My cynical inner voice answered immediately: *Stop weeping and moaning and get back to reality! If you don't leave him, Stu's going to kill you. You understand that, don't you?*

My heart didn't understand, not at all, and in spite of that sensible side of myself my eyes filled with tears. I jumped when Mom patted my thigh gently, turning my head so she wouldn't see me cry.

"Penny for your thoughts, Peach."

Before I could stop it the truth came out, and it was actually a relief. "I don't want to leave him, Mom. I really don't."

Mom squeezed my thigh. To my surprise, when she spoke her voice was calm and understanding. "I know, honey, but I can't let you stay with him. I *won't* let you stay with him. Stu has some very serious problems. I'm trying really hard to respect your feelings, but if you want to know the truth – "

Mom cut herself off and I filled in the rest of her unfinished sentence, fairly certain of what she had been about to say. "You want to kill him, right?" I looked over at her, and for a moment she was a stranger, her face hard and unforgiving.

"Not right away." Her voice was as cold as her expression, and I shivered.

"I guess I can understand that." I wiped my eyes and placed my hand over hers. "Why do I feel like this, Mom? Why can't I feel more like you?"

"Because to a certain extent, Ang, I think Stu has you believing that what he does to you is your fault."

My mouth dropped open and I gaped at her. She understood! How was that possible? "How did you know that?" I whispered, and Mom squeezed me again.

"I've done some research. It was something I studied in university. I wanted to understand how people could do that to each other, especially to the person they claim to care the most about."

"Is this personal, Mom?" I asked, and when a light flush stained her cheeks I knew I'd hit the nail on the head. "Not with you and Dad, or you and Ivan, but maybe with Grandpa …?"

Mom nodded. "I don't really remember much of it – actually, I think I blocked it out – but there was a lot of screaming and crying, and my mother had more 'accidents' than anyone I'd ever seen."

"Oh, Mom, I'm so sorry." I felt miserably guilty, as though I'd added to her burden by deliberately hooking up with a monster. Mom looked over at me and smiled; it was her again, the mother I knew, the source of all my comfort, and I was glad.

"Peach, it happened a long time ago, and it has nothing to do with Stu. I just want better for you than my mother had. And I'm going to do everything I can to make sure you get it." She took the turnoff to the airport, and as the newly renovated building got closer I found myself becoming more and more reluctant.

Get over it, Angie! You have to leave him, and this is a good start!

After we parked the car and were on our way into the terminal, I looked at Mom and tried to smile. "Thanks, Mom," I said, and she patted my cheek. "For what?"

"For the way you're dealing with all this. For letting me have the room I need to let him go."

Mom smiled at me gently. "I hate him for what he's done to you, Ang, but I also know how you feel about him. It's better to let you make your own decision – then you won't end up hating *me* for it."

I was amazed that she was able to be so objective, but then, my mother had never been an ordinary woman. I just hoped that one day I would have the strength that she did.

I tried to think of other things on the short flight to Calgary, but thoughts of Stu kept intruding. I made myself remember him biting me, slapping me, and kicking me, but for every negative, frightening memory there was a sweet glimpse that confused me beyond all understanding. I realized that this time away was going to be very important, and told myself to make good use of it. When the plane touched down in Calgary another feeling swept through me: anticipation. It had been far too long since I had spent any time with Ivan, and I walked toward the gate, my spirits rising.

I spotted Ivan immediately. He was standing right in the front, craning his neck anxiously, and when he saw me his face broke into a huge smile. I rushed over to him and he held out his arms, and when they enfolded me the feeling of protection, of safety, of absolute love and acceptance, was so strong and so right that I dissolved into tears.

I had promised myself I wouldn't cry, but in the face of all that emotion I couldn't help it. Ivan held me tightly, kissing the top of my head again and again, and finally I pulled away and gave him a watery smile.

"All I seem to do these days is cry," I said apologetically. "It's wonderful to see you, Ivan."

Ivan cupped my face in his large, warm hands and placed a gentle kiss on each cheek. "And I am so happy to have you here with me, my Angie," he said to me in his low rumble. "With me you will be safe."

That almost got me going again, but I bit my lip and staved off further tears by asking: "So, what do you have planned for me?"

Ivan removed the cloth bag from my shoulder and heaved it over his own. We began to walk toward the baggage carousel. "Let us see," he said, pretending to think hard. "I have the gourmet meals, the soft bed, and perhaps ... the opera?" His eyes twinkled and I took his hand and squeezed it.

"You're too good to me," I told him, and he stopped abruptly and turned to face me.

"I am not too good to you, my Angie," he said to me, his voice so gentle that I had to look away to avoid bursting into tears. "This is only what you deserve, my darling. This, and so much more, after what you have been through."

I took his hand again and we resumed walking. "This young man, does he know where you will be?" Ivan asked, and I said, "He knows I'm in Calgary, but not where. I gave him the phone number – I hope that's all right. He was actually okay with me going."

Ivan looked at me closely. "He decides these things, does he?"

I shook my head with a laugh that sounded forced, even to my ears. "Mom decided I should come here, Ivan. You know that."

Ivan didn't disagree, but he gave me a penetrating look that made me uncomfortable.

"Well, I am happy she did," he declared, and warmth spread through me. "We have not had enough time together, you and I."

I looked at him and smiled. "How did Mom get so lucky?" I asked him, and Ivan laughed out loud.

"I do not ask myself that question, my Angie," he told me, delighted. "I believe it is I who am the lucky one, for I have two for the price of one."

It was my turn to laugh, and as we left the terminal for the parking lot, I sent a prayer of thanks heavenward that I was lucky enough to have this man in my life.

Chapter Fifty Eight

It didn't take long to get settled in Ivan's huge, disorderly apartment. It was truly a unique home away from home; Ivan was a scavenger and a packrat – although he referred to himself as a "collector" - and the walls, shelves, and closets of his apartment were full to bursting with fascinating finds.

There was no rhyme or reason to any of it. An eclectic collection of artwork competed for space on the walls, and piles of dusty books, sheets of ancient music, and other assorted bric-a-brac was everywhere. Ivan had unusual items of every description, from authentic African spears to Egyptian statuary, and everywhere the eye rested there was something interesting.

His furniture was old and comfortable, usually purchased second hand, with colorful throw rugs and half dead plants for accents, and the television was covered with a thick layer of dust because he never had the time or inclination to watch it.

I stowed my bag in the cluttered guest room and came out to find him making tea. I took a look around the kitchen, wincing. A typical bachelor's room, it was awash in dirty dishes and the grease was so thick on the stove that I could have drawn a picture in it.

"I can see you need a woman's touch," I said with a grin.

"You are not to lift a finger!" Ivan declared. "You are here to rest, my Angie."

I began to clear the dirty dishes from the table; some looked as though they had been there for a week. "I can rest better knowing the kitchen is clean," I told him. "Now shoo."

Ivan smiled and kissed my cheek. "I will go and call your mother. She will want to know that you have arrived safely."

He left the kitchen and I tidied quite happily, glad to have something to do. I could hear Ivan in the living room, greeting Mom effusively, and I hoped that if she and I moved here it would be to live with him. I finished loading the dishwasher and searched under the sink for some soap, appalled at the condition of the cupboard. I resolved to try and organize things for him in the following week: housekeeping therapy. I finally found the soap and started the dishwasher, and I was just finishing with the countertops when Ivan came back in. He threw up his hands in a dramatic gesture.

"It is a different room already!" he exclaimed. "You are truly an angel, my Angie. Perhaps I should call you my Angel."

My pleased smile faded. "That name is already taken." At his look of confusion, I explained, "That's what Stu calls me."

Ivan nodded. "Well, in that he is correct, at least. You are indeed an angel, my darling."

I smiled and gave him a kiss on the cheek. "This Angel is tired," I said. "I think I'll go to bed, if you don't mind."

"Not at all," Ivan said. "To bed you should go. Sleep well, my Angie."

"Good night, Ivan."

I crossed the living room and went into the spare room, closing the door behind me. My bag was on the bed, and I opened it and dug around inside for pajamas. I found a top and pulled it out, and as I did so my fingers touched something hard. It was a book, tucked in at the very bottom of the bag, and I pulled it out, curious. I looked at the cover and a hot feeling of shame swept over me: <u>When Love Hurts: Battering in Adolescent Relationships.</u>

I read the title again and again, trying to connect it to myself, anger rising inside, and at last I raised my arm and threw the book as hard as I could. It struck the opposite wall and landed on its spine in a riffle of pages, and I sat on the bed and buried my face in my hands, feeling like a statistic, like a fool, like a *freak*. The tears had barely begun when there was a light tap at the door, and I raised my head hastily, taking a deep breath and struggling to compose myself.

"Yes?"

Ivan poked his head in the door. "Your young man is on the telephone, my darling. Should I tell him that you have gone to bed?"

I shook my head, holding out my hand for the phone. "No, it's all right. I'll talk to him." Ivan stepped into the room and handed me the cordless phone, and I thanked him as he left. I brought the phone to my ear, eager to hear his voice and hating myself for it.

"Hi, Stu."

"Angel-baby." At the sound of the name only he had ever called me, a ripple of desire wound its way lazily through me, and I realized that even this far away, he still owned me.

"I'm missing you already," Stu said in a husky voice, and I smiled.

"Are you?" My voice was a soft whisper, and I could almost hear his smile when he replied.

"Of course I am. I can't stand not seeing you, Angel. You're everything to me." That sent a little shock through me.

"Really?" I asked, and this time he chuckled, a warm sexy sound that sent a shiver up my spine.

"Really. I've never loved anyone but you, Angel. I never will, either."

"Wow," I breathed. "Stop it, Stu, you're making my head swim."

"Good. Don't forget that you belong to me. Just because we're apart doesn't mean anything is different, Angel."

The possessive tone of his voice both frightened and pleased me, and I didn't know what to say.

"Angel?"

"I'm still here, Stu."

"I wish you were here." His meaning was unmistakable, and the desire inside me began to clamor more insistently. "You know what we'd be doing if you were here, don't you, Angel?"

"What would we be doing, Stu?"

"I'd be making love to you," he answered, and at the tender sound of the words it was suddenly hard to believe he had ever hurt me. The answer surprised me, and for a moment I grew lightheaded. "I'd be touching you all over, kissing you everywhere, and you'd be begging to have me inside you."

"Don't, Stu," I said, breathless. "I feel like I'm going to faint."

"Wait until you get back," he promised. "I'll make you faint." I gasped as a shock of desire blazed through me.

"I have to go, Stu. I'm really tired, and I want to go to sleep."

"Don't you touch what's mine, Angel. You understand me?"

"Yes," I said unsteadily. "I'll save it for you." Another chuckle, this one pleased and approving.

"You'd better. Good night, Angel-baby. I love you."

"I love you, too. Good night, Stu."

I hung up the phone and sat still for a moment, replaying the conversation in my mind. Then I changed into my pajamas, climbed into bed, and cried myself to sleep.

Chapter Fifty Nine

I had a wonderfully relaxing week with Ivan, and as the days passed I got to know him in a way I never had before. He was witty and observant, with a wonderful sense of humor that managed to pull me out of my darkest moods. I visited him at the University of Calgary and insisted on sitting in on one of his lectures. I thought he was a passionate and eloquent teacher, and my heart swelled with pride as I listened to him speak.

Ivan took me out to dinner one evening to an impossibly expensive restaurant, and we giggled together over a menu that neither of us could read a word of. We spent a lazy, surprisingly mild November day at the zoo, and his knowledge of animals and their habits amazed me. I managed to really relax for the first time in months, and by Thursday evening I was feeling regretful that it had to end, that I had to return to Edmonton and all the complicated issues that faced me.

Stu hadn't called since that first night, and even though I castigated myself for it, I found myself missing him terribly. It was as though we were bound together now, and without him I felt a little lost, not quite myself. I knew this was unhealthy, but it didn't change the fact. In spite of my misgivings, when I thought of being in his arms again my heartbeat would quicken and I would feel a yearning that was undeniable.

Ivan and I were settled in his living room that last night – a considerably cleaner room than it had been on my arrival – with a fire in the fireplace and mugs of hot chocolate in hand, when I finally decided to tell him what had been happening to me. I was staring into my mug, wondering where to start, when he spoke gently.

"I know what this is, my Angie."

I looked at him in surprise. "What what is?" I asked, and Ivan placed his hand briefly against my cheek before answering.

"I know this young man, he has been abusing you." His eyes were serious but very kind, and the understanding in them caught me completely by surprise.

"How did you know?" I whispered, and he smiled, a sad, poignant smile I had never seen on his face before.

"I speak very seldom of my family, my Angie." I realized it was true; I had no idea if he had siblings, or if his parents were still alive. I merely nodded, and he continued, looking down at his own hands, hesitant, as if the words hurt coming out. "My father, he was a very harsh man. He did not hesitate to use his fists to get a point across, and although my brothers and I were beaten also, he most often hit my mother."

Ivan looked at me, his eyes filled with immeasurable sadness, and all I could do was stare back at him, shocked. "He beat her more and more often as the years passed, and I would try to intervene, to spare my mother this pain, but eventually I learned that interfering would only make it worse for her, so I stopped. My mother, she did not complain, and she did not leave him, but I would hear her in the night, how she cried and moaned, and it hurt me, my Angie. How it hurt me." Ivan looked at me again, and I was astonished to see that his eyes were full of tears.

"Ivan – " I began, and he held up a hand to stop me.

"Please, my darling, let me say what I must say. I know too well that look I have seen on your face – that look of sadness, as if all the light has been stolen from your world, that look that says you are afraid. It is the look I would see on my mother's face when she would think no one was watching. I cannot tell you how it hurts me to see it on your beautiful face, my Angie."

By now the tears were running down Ivan's cheeks, and I was filled with an unbearable combination of gratitude and guilt. I was glad he understood what I was going through, but at the same time I hated myself for forcing him to relive what surely must have been the most painful of childhood memories.

"Oh, Ivan," I said as tears filled my own eyes. "Why did I think I had to hide this from you?"

I reached for him then, and he held me while I sobbed out the story. Ivan listened quietly, saying nothing until I had finished, and when he was certain I was done he took my face in his hands and kissed me solemnly, first on one cheek, then the other.

"I am going to take this burden from you," he told me. "I must tell you something very important, but it is vital that you do not tell your mother."

I wondered what he could possibly mean, and his next words took my breath away.

"I am going to ask my Joy to marry me. She will say yes, and you will both move here, to Calgary, to be with me. If this is not far enough, we will go as far as we must to make sure that this young man no longer hurts you."

I must have been gaping at Ivan like a fool, because he asked almost shyly, "This is a good plan, yes?"

I threw my arms around his neck, such joy flooding me that I could hardly contain it. "I think it's the best plan I've ever heard!"

Ivan laughed deep in his throat, hugging me tightly. "I am so glad," he said, releasing me and smiling. The phone rang at that moment and Ivan glanced at the clock; it was half past midnight.

"Let me get it," I told him. "It must be Stu."

Ivan raised an eyebrow and handed me the cordless phone. I pressed the 'talk' button and held it to my ear. "Hello?"

I got up from the couch and went into the kitchen, a mixture of fear and excitement coursing down my spine when I heard his voice.

"Angel-baby."

I held the phone with both hands and leaned against the counter, suddenly feeling weak. "Hi, Stu. Why are you calling so late?"

"God, I'm missing you," he said, and a shiver ran through me at the naked yearning in his voice.

"Are you?" I whispered, smiling a foolish little smile.

"You have no idea," he told me. "You're all I can think about, Angel. When the hell are you coming back? I can't take this much longer."

"How does tomorrow sound?" I asked, and his pleased chuckle sent another shiver down my spine.

"Are you healed?" Stu asked me in a sexy whisper, and I closed my eyes, knowing I was lost.

Ang, what are you doing? What were you and Ivan just talking about?

"Pretty much," I told him, my tone all innocence. "Why do you ask?"

"Because I've got a job for you to do." He was almost growling, and I laughed.

"Oh? What would that be?"

"To lie on your back so I can fuck you until you can't stand up." His words sent an amazing rush of lust sweeping through me, and I had to catch my breath.

"Don't know, Stuart," I said in a prim, touch-me-not voice. "Good girls don't fuck."

"You're not a good girl, Angel," Stu said immediately. "You're a slut. *My* slut. You want it as much as I do."

"I know," I confessed. "What the hell have you done to me?"

"Just brought out what was there all along," Stu told me, amused. "When will you be here tomorrow? Christ, tell me it'll be in the afternoon."

"I'll try to arrange it."

I was conscious of Ivan in the next room, and I hoped he wasn't listening. My conversation with Stu seemed like a rejection of everything he had told me, and I was suddenly filled with shame.

"Why do I want you so much, Stu?" I asked him in a small voice. "Why do I want you when you cause me so much pain?"

"Because you belong to me, Angel-baby," he answered. "You belong to me, and you know it. Call me the minute you get home."

"Tell me how much you love me, Stu." I needed to hear the words; it was so important to know that what he felt was more than lust, that I was worthy of some higher emotion.

Stu chuckled again. "I'm going to show you how much. Tomorrow. Get some sleep, Angel. You're going to need all your strength."

He broke the connection and I pressed the off button, confusion rushing around inside me. I felt as though I had betrayed both myself and Ivan: how could I be happy at the thought of getting away from Stu, but need him so desperately at the same time?

Oh, Angie, you need to get away from this guy. You need to get away from him before you don't want to at all.

366

Chapter Sixty

Ivan had three lectures to give the following day, and I was left at loose ends with too much time to think. I cleaned the apartment to give myself something to do, but the entire time I moved on automatic pilot, feeling increasingly confused and angry with myself. I had no pride, no self-control, no will of my own, and it made me question my own morals. What kind of girl felt this desperate lust for a guy who brutalized her at every opportunity?

In spite of my annoyance at Mom for putting the book into my bag, I took out <u>When Love Hurts: Battering in Adolescent Relationships,</u> and what I read didn't make me feel any better. It seemed that I had now accepted my role as a victim, and that I blamed myself when Stu attacked me. These things had already occurred to me, but to see them down on paper solidified my status as Stu's possession, at least in my own mind. I grew more miserable as the day wore on, and by the time Ivan got back the apartment was positively sparkling; the darker my thoughts grew, the busier I seemed to need to be.

Ivan looked around in amazement, sweeping me into his arms. "I will need to have you come back every week!" he said, laughing.

"No you won't," I told him with a smile. "Soon I'll be here all the time, remember?"

"So you shall," Ivan declared. He clapped his hands together twice, briskly. "Come! Let us be on our way! I am anxious to see my Joy!"

I went to the spare room to get my things together, feeling the same way about Stu but knowing I shouldn't. The ride back to Edmonton seemed short; I hadn't slept very well the night before and I dozed for most of it, staring gloomily out the window when I wasn't napping. Ivan seemed to understand that I didn't want to talk, and he tuned the stereo to a classical music station, occasionally singing along with the opera selections in his rich baritone.

The closer we came to the city the more nervous I became, and by the time Ivan pulled into our driveway I was ready to jump out of my skin. Mom came out to meet us, kissing Ivan lightly and asking me about my week. I told her quite truthfully that I had had a wonderful time, and I winked at Ivan as I said that he and I had certainly had some interesting conversations. Ivan frowned at me and I gave him a grin and left them to go into the house, intending to take my clothes upstairs and put them in the washer.

I stopped in the living room before climbing the stairs, looking around as if I were seeing everything for the first time. As my eyes traveled over the home Mom and I had created tears stung my eyes and sadness pulled at me, trying to take me down into that dark and hopeless place from which there was no escape. I shook off the feeling impatiently, telling myself that it was likely we would have moved anyway. Ivan's career was far more important to him that Mom's job was to her, and I knew she would leave it in a second to become his wife.

I smiled to myself as I went upstairs with my bag, picturing the look on Mom's face when Ivan proposed. I started a load of laundry and went into my room, heading straight for the cordless phone. A tingling began in my belly and spread as I punched in his number, and when Stu answered it flamed higher and I was overcome with need.

"Hi, Stu," I whispered. "I'm home."

"I'm leaving right now. Be ready."

I hung up and turned toward the mirror to brush my hair. I couldn't help but notice the flush on my cheeks and the desire in my eyes as I worked on my hair, and a smile kept forming and reforming on my mouth. I changed my clothes, examining my incision gently before I pulled on a fresh pair of jeans. It had healed amazingly quickly, and hardly hurt at all. I grabbed a tee shirt blindly, not really caring what I put on, and the desire inside me grew as I caught my hair up behind my head in a ponytail and slipped pretty earrings into my ears.

I went downstairs to join Ivan and Mom, stopping at the foot of the stairs to look at them fondly. Ivan was sitting with his feet propped on a comfortable footstool, and Mom's feet were in his lap. As I watched he began to massage them, tickling every now and then just to make her laugh. I cleared my throat, smiling when they both looked over at me,

"You two make a cute couple," I said, and Mom smiled. "I'm going out for a while, okay?"

Her expression tightened and she narrowed her eyes. "With Stu?" she asked, and I nodded; just the sound of his name made me weak.

"Mom, he doesn't know that you know anything," I said. "I can't very well refuse to see him, or he'll know something's up."

Mom looked at me intently, and I felt my face grow warm. "What?"

"That's not it and you know it," she told me. "You want to see him, don't you?" I nodded, and shame swept through me. Ivan squeezed Mom's foot.

"Do not be too hard on her, my darling," he said gently. "This is a very difficult situation, yes?" At Mom's reluctant nod, he continued, "We must not make this young man suspicious."

"That's great, Ivan." Mom took her feet out of his lap and moved away from him. "Somehow I don't think that'll make me feel better when he beats the shit out of her again." She looked at me, eyes snapping. "Ang, forget it. I can't let you – "

Desperation rose inside me, and I said, "Mom, you have to. If Stu gets angry he *will* hurt me. If I keep him happy, he won't."

"Goddamn it!" Mom pounded the couch with one fist, and Ivan slid over and put his arms around her. She tried to resist but he tightened his hold until she relaxed against him.

"Please, my Joy. We must do what we have to."

Mom looked at me again, and that horrible guilt rose up inside me again when I saw that her eyes were full of tears. "I feel like I'm sending you in with the lions," she said, and I went over to her and kissed her cheek. I could hear Stu's car outside, and I wanted to get to the door before he came in.

"Try not to worry," I said, and she rested her head on Ivan's shoulder, closing her eyes. I turned and left the room, crossing the kitchen quickly and looking out the back door. When I saw Stu coming up the walk, brushing newly fallen snow from his hair, my stomach did a slow somersault, and when he opened the door I stepped right into his arms, realizing that I had been waiting all week to do it.

Stu crushed me to his chest and kissed me hungrily. The depth of his passion overwhelmed me, and I couldn't catch my breath. He kept kissing me, running his hands up and down my body, and when he finally pulled away his face was flushed and his breathing unsteady.

"Jesus, Angel," he said, and his eyes were dark and sleepy with desire. "I can hardly stand up. Don't you ever go away for that long again. I can't take it."

I brushed aside the stab of anxiety his words provoked and wrapped my arms around his waist, pulling him closer to me, our bodies tight against each other. I could feel his hardness and I pushed my hips into his, feeling delirious with lust. I stood on tiptoe to whisper in his ear.

"Take me somewhere, Stu. Take me somewhere and fuck me."

To my delight, he actually shuddered, and then held me away with a groan. "For Christ's sake let's go," he said hoarsely. "Or I'll rape you right here on the kitchen floor."

He practically dragged me out the door, and as I got into his car I abandoned all control and gave myself up to the torrent of feelings he always unleashed in me.

Just for tonight, I promise. I want to love him just for tonight.

Chapter Sixty One

Stu didn't speak on the drive to his house, and every so often I would glance over at his profile, his eyes dark and intent as they focused on the road. My eyes caressed the line of his jaw and the slight curl of hair at the nape of his neck, and the sight of his slender fingers gripping the wheel sent a shock of desire through me. Stu looked over at me and the corner of his mouth turned up.

"What are you thinking about, Angel?"

I reached out and brushed the hair back from his forehead, and he smiled. "I was just thinking about how good you're going to feel inside me," I told him softly, and he gripped the steering wheel more tightly.

"Stop it." Stu's voice was a low growl, and it was my turn to smile. "Unless you want me to pull this car over and throw you in the back seat."

"Don't tempt me," I said in a teasing voice, sliding my hand up his thigh. When my fingers touched the hardness beneath his zipper Stu twisted the wheel sharply and the car skidded over to the side of a street about a block from his house. He jammed the gearshift into park and turned to me, his eyes dark with lust.

"Get in the back."

My stomach leaped and I looked at him in shock. "What?"

Stu took my chin in a hard grip. "You heard me. Get in the back. *Now.*"

I got out of the car and opened the rear door, sliding onto the back seat. Stu didn't bother with the door; he vaulted over the front seat and grabbed me, pushing onto my back and slamming his mouth down on mine. His hands reached for my zipper on my jeans as he kissed me, and he undid it skillfully and pushed the jeans down to my knees. Stu tore his mouth from mine.

"Get these fucking jeans off."

I pushed the jeans down to my ankles and worked them off with my feet as he made himself ready, and when he got between my legs Stu looked down at me with a half smile.

"I told you, didn't I?" I nodded, my breath coming in short gasps, and my hands slid up his bare hips. I tried to pull him down to me, inside me, but he resisted easily.

"Ask me, Angel," he ordered, and the words came out automatically: "Can I come, Stu? Please, can I?"

Stu's answer was to drop on top of me and thrust into me almost angrily, and the feel of him filling me was indescribable. He began to move his hips, and as he slid in and out, faster and harder, I wrapped my arms around his neck and pulled his head down to mine, kissing him over and over. The sensations mounted, and as my breathing became labored he murmured in my ear, "Are you going to come, Angel-baby?"

I managed to gasp, "Can I?" and when Stu nodded I bucked my hips, our bellies slapping together, and he brought me up and over that exquisite peak while I cried out again and again, clinging to him helplessly and never wanting to let go.

When we got to his house Stu took me straight into the bedroom, closing the door behind us. He had a set, determined look on his face, and I felt a tremor inside that had nothing to do with lust. Stu shrugged out of his coat, letting it fall to the floor, and sat on the edge of his bed. He looked at me with cool, remorseless eyes. "Take off your clothes, Angel."

I looked at him in dismay. "Stu, what – "

"Shut up. Just do what I tell you."

I took off my coat, biting my lip to keep from bursting into tears. *Why does he always do this? Can't it ever be good between us?*

I placed my coat beside Stu on the bed and began to undo the buttons on my shirt. Stu just sat and watched me, biding his time, his intention clear, and I grew more and more upset as I removed the rest of my clothes. When I stood in front of him naked and vulnerable, he patted his thighs with the palm of one hand. I knew what he meant, and I came over to him and laid myself across his knees, struggling not to cry, waiting for the pain.

Stu brought his hand down on my bare buttocks as hard as he could, saying at the same time, "I missed you, Angel." He kept hitting me, and with every blow he said something else: "I can't go that long without seeing you; I need you; don't you *ever* fucking leave me again ..."

Every time Stu brought his hand down he seemed to grow angrier, and at last I began to cry and beg him to stop. He ignored my pleas and kept going, oblivious to his own pain, which must have been considerable given the strength of the blows. I began to twist and squirm in an effort to get away, and he lost his patience and pushed me from his lap onto the floor.

"Goddamn you, Angel ..." He stood over me and I sobbed helplessly, my face buried in my arms, the agony in my heart much worse that the pain in my body.

What did I do? What the hell did I do now??

Stu bent down and grabbed me by the upper arms, jerking me roughly to my feet, and I looked at him in mute anguish, knowing better than to say anything. He pulled me forward, kissing me hard, and I clung to him, hating myself for seeking comfort but needing it, needing to know he loved me, needing to believe that in spite of the pain I was everything. Before I could stop them the words spilled out of me: "What did I do?"

Stu held me tightly, almost desperately. "You went away," he whispered into my hair, and I tried to understand his anger, but couldn't. He held me away from him and looked into my eyes, giving me a little shake. "Don't you ever fucking do that again, Angel, you hear me?"

I nodded, still crying. "I hear you," I managed to say. "I won't, Stu, I promise, I won't go away again…"

Stu pulled me to him again, so close I could hear the beat of his heart. "Good." His voice was calm now, his arms safe and loving. "Lesson over, Angel-baby. I love you."

"I love you, too."

God help me, I really do.

Later, on the way back to my house, I was silent and low, wondering how in the world I was going to be able to let him go. I knew I had to, that what he did to me was wrong, but as much as I wanted to hide it, tear it out of myself, or run away from it, there was a tiny part of me that craved the fear, that wallowed in the pain. Every time he hit me it meant he loved me more, and the pain and love had become so inextricably entwined that it was impossible to tell one from the other.

I knew I had to get away from Stu for this reason more than anything else. I knew that the more I accepted his behavior the worse it would get, but no matter what I told myself, my fickle heart wept inconsolably.

When Stu pulled the Rambler over to the curb in front of my house, I leaned over and kissed him. He placed a hand on the back of my neck, turning the kiss into something urgent and sweet, and when I finally pulled back he smiled at me. I touched his mouth, tears flooding my eyes.

"Will I see you later?" I asked him, and Stu smiled at me again and ran a gentle hand through my hair.

"You'll see me forever," he said softly, and kissed me again. I opened the door and got out of the car, taking a last look at him before I went inside: his hair was tousled around his face and his eyes were dark and serious. I gave him a little wave, and as he drove away my heart contracted yet again, leaving me wondering which pain was worse and knowing I didn't really want to know the answer.

Chapter Sixty Two

I woke the next morning with the same sense of sadness, and for a while I just lay in bed, thinking about Stu and feeling pulled in two opposing directions. One part of me hated him, hated the violence and myself for accepting it, and the other loved him with a desperation bordering on obsession. He defined me in a way I couldn't put a name to; it was as if he was a virus in my blood, something lethal but so much a part of me that to take it away without killing me would be impossible.

What's there to love about him? That brutally critical voice spoke up, trying to force me to acknowledge reality. *He's controlling, sadistic, and he gets off on hurting you! That's not love, Ang. Pain isn't love. Jealousy isn't love. Even great sex isn't love. Does he respect you? Protect you? Feel pride in what you do?*

This all made perfect sense, but unfortunately my heart wasn't interested in common sense. It only remembered the need in Stu's voice when he told me he thought he was losing me, the passion he never hesitated to show me, and the tenderness I saw in his eyes every time he thought I wasn't watching. My heart remembered the reverent way his fingers caressed my body, the way he clung to me in his release, and the pain he had shared with me when he had shown me the marks on his back.

Oh, but you have your own scars now, don't you, Angel?

The way that inner voice drawled his name for me made me cringe, and I had to resist the urge to scream out loud at it to go away, go *away*, fuck off and leave me alone.

What are they, badges of honor? Proof of his everlasting love? Get real. He beats you up. I don't care what he says. Love is NOT pain, and you fucking well know it.

I got out of bed and tried my best to ignore the inner debate, but I knew deep inside that it would go on until we finally left Edmonton for good. I went into the bathroom and took a long, hot shower. When I stepped out of the tub I toweled off carefully, looking at the red line of the incision on my abdomen, just above my pubic hair. It was healing nicely, and likely wouldn't leave a noticeable scar. I couldn't say the same for my breast, unfortunately, and as I stared at my misshapen nipple I thought of the surgery to come and shuddered. I wrapped myself in a towel and headed across the hall to my bedroom, and when I was dressed I went downstairs and found Mom and Ivan sitting in the kitchen. Ivan looked up from his paper and I grinned at him. An answering smile creased his bearded face and he nodded emphatically.

"I have been waiting for you to get up, my Angie," he said with a knowing wink, and excitement shot through me: he hadn't asked her yet. I went over to Ivan and kissed him on top of the head, where his black hair was beginning to thin.

"That's very sweet, Ivan," I told him, and Mom looked at both of us, confused.

"What in the world are you two talking about?" Before either of us could answer she looked at me narrowly. "What time did you get home, Ang? We were up until two."

I shook my head at her, giggling. "Forget that right now, Mom." Out of the corner of my eye I could see Ivan stand up, and I bounced up and down on the balls of my feet.

"Forget it?" Mom demanded, looking annoyed. "Angie – "

Ivan pushed me gently out of the way and knelt down in front of Mom with a flourish, one knee propped like a singer in a minstrel show.

Mom looked at him with a skeptical frown. "Ivan, what the hell are you doing?"

Ivan took her hand and kissed it gently, and I felt tears begin to sting my eyes. "What I should have done so long ago, my Joy," he said, and as Mom's eyes widened and understanding began to dawn he said it; he finally said it. "My dearest Joy, will you be my wife?"

I watched an expression of stunned happiness spread across her face, and Mom threw her arms around Ivan's neck. "Oh, God, Ivan, of course! You know I will!"

Ivan got to his feet and took Mom into his arms, and as they kissed passionately I looked away, feeling like I should be somewhere else. Mom looked away from Ivan toward me, her face radiant.

"You knew!" she exclaimed, motioning me forward. I nodded and came over to her and Ivan, putting one arm around each of their necks and squeezing.

"Ivan told me a few days ago," I said to Mom. "He swore me to secrecy." I looked at Ivan and smiled, and I could feel my lips trembling. "It's going to be so wonderful to have a father," I whispered, and he let go of Mom to hold me tightly.

"You have been like my own since I first met you, my darling," he said to me in a choked voice.

"Gee, I hope I'm not interrupting." We all looked around, startled by the hesitant voice, and I saw Megan at the back door, looking at us curiously. I went over to her, still smiling.

"Ivan just asked Mom to marry him," I told her, and Meg's face lit up.

"That's great! Congratulations, Mrs. Swanson! Congratulations, Ivan!"

"Thanks, Meg," Mom said. "It's nice to see you. You haven't been around much lately."

"I can't stand Stu," Meg said, and her voice was bitter, with an underlying sadness that tore at my heart. "I can't stand seeing what he's doing to her – " She broke off abruptly, giving me a quick glance, and the cautious wariness in that glance hurt more than I would have believed.

"I know how you feel, Meg," Mom said in a quiet voice. "But I'm trying to understand it. For Angie's sake."

"There's nothing to understand!" Meg cried. "He's an abusive *bastard*! That's it! The end!"

Anger shot through me and I struggled for a moment with my temper. "You don't know him, Meg."

Meg looked at me in disbelief. "Ang, do you hear yourself? I don't have to know him! I don't *want* to know him! That's the *last* goddamn thing I want! I just want you away from him!"

I had to take a step away; the maelstrom of emotion churning inside was making me feel more than a little crazy. "Excuse me," I said in a tight voice, and walked into the living room, my breath coming in panicky gasps.

Oh God, this is going to kill me ... it is, it'll just keep at me and at me until I break into a million pieces ...

I sank down on the couch and gave in to my raging feelings, pounding my fists on the nubby fabric and crying in hysterical sobs. There was no answer, no solution, nothing at all that would make everyone happy. No matter what decision I made, the rest of my life was going to be a long, hard road, and I wailed at the injustice of it, feeling like the despair and frustration were strangling me.

I jumped as I felt a gentle touch on my shoulder. Meg put her arms around me, and her tears mingled with my own as we both struggled to release some of our anguish, each without hurting the other.

Chapter Sixty Three

I was nervous about seeing Stu at school the next day. I had lain awake most of the night, the debate raging endlessly inside me, consumed with misery. I was unable to fully commit to either option, and the thought that I didn't actually have a choice made me feel both relieved and desperate. I didn't know how I was going to hide these feeling from Stu until I left, and I told myself that trying to create distance between us might be the answer. I knew he would be angry, but it wouldn't compare to his rage if he found out I was moving, and I forced myself to start that very morning.

I was standing at my locker talking to Megan when Stu sauntered up to us. My heart leaped, and I tried to ignore how good his hair looked and how much I loved his lean, slim-hipped body. He slid his arms around my waist and murmured in my ear, "Hey, Angel-baby." It was so hard not to melt against him, but I made myself pull away and touch his lips lightly with mine.

"Hi, Stu." He raised an eyebrow at me, and I didn't miss the shadow that crossed his face.

Oh God, I don't think I can do this, I really don't –

"Why the cold reception?" he asked, and I smiled with what I hoped was fond tolerance.

"It's not cold," I said. "I'm just a little nervous about classes. I'm pretty far behind, and lately I've been *the* source for idle gossip."

Stu chuckled and slipped an arm around me, his hand deliberately brushing my breast. I looked up at him and smiled, a real smile, my heart in my eyes, and Stu briefly caressed my cheek before kissing me long and deeply.

Meg slammed her locker door, made a disgusted noise, and walked off. Dimly, I heard someone passing by say, "Jeez, you guys, get a room!" but I ignored it, lost in the feeling of Stu's mouth devouring my own. When he finally broke the kiss, he smiled at me and whispered, "Wanna ditch class to go back to my place? I've got something with your name on it."

I laughed softly and shook my head. "I can't. I've got to get caught up."

Stu looked at me in a speculative way that made me a little uneasy. "You know if I really want to, we'll go, don't you, Angel?"

A chill ran through me at that and I nodded. It was time to play the victim, a role I now slipped into with no effort at all. "I know. Please, Stu, let me stay here. I'm going to get in trouble if I miss any more classes."

Stu took chin in his fingers, still looking into my eyes, and I prayed that my face wasn't giving anything away. Then he relaxed his grip and bent his head forward to kiss me lightly. "Go on. I'll see you later."

Relief swept over me and I smiled at him gratefully. "Okay. See you later, Stu." He walked away and I turned back to my locker and pulled out the books I needed for my next class.

The rest of the morning passed uneventfully, and when I finally caught up with Megan again, in the girls' washroom just before lunch, my melancholy feelings had returned. She looked at me as we both stood in front of the mirror over the sinks.

"What's up, Ang? Stu being Stu?"

I shook my head and took a brush out of my purse. "No, nothing like that. I almost wish he'd do something. Then at least I'd feel better about leaving."

Meg looked at me like I was crazy. "I don't understand how you can feel anything for him."

I shrugged. "I don't know why I do, Meg. I just do. He does something to me – "

"Yeah, he does something to you, all right," Meg interrupted. "He leave you black and blue."

I glanced around quickly, and to my relief there appeared to be no one else in the washroom. "Meg, be quiet!"

She made a face at me. "The truth hurts," she muttered, and the offhand comment was like a slap in the face. Meg must have seen it in my expression, because the next moment she was hugging me and apologizing.

"I just hate him," she said, and I nodded; I didn't blame her. I knew if the situation were reversed, I would feel the same way. "So, when are the movers coming?" she asked, and I put away my lip gloss.

"Thursday," I told her, waiting for her to finish with her mascara. "We're not even sure if Calgary is where we're going to end up. Ivan doesn't think it's far enough away."

Meg tossed the tube of mascara into her purse and slung it over her shoulder. "Siberia isn't far enough away," she said, and I smirked at her.

"Ha, ha. You're a real comedian."

We left the washroom and headed for the cafeteria. Gin was already there and Meg and I joined her, digging into the lunch bags we had brought with us. Before long we were immersed in gossip and I was thinking how nice it was to talk about someone else for a change. I was laughing at something Meg had just said when I noticed that Gin wasn't paying attention. She was staring at the entrance to the cafeteria, shock evident on her face, and I said, "What, Gin?"

Gin looked at me, and when I saw pity mixed with the shock in her eyes a sudden feeling of dread possessed me. "Ang, maybe we should — "

I followed her gaze, and when I saw what she had been looking at the sandwich fell from my hand onto the surface of the table and my breath caught in my throat. Stu was standing in front of the double doors, a casual arm slung around Delaney's shoulders. His eyes searched the room until he found me, and when he was certain I was watching he bent his head to her and kissed her, once, then again. She reached up and slipped an arm around his neck, and his hand slid down her back and squeezed her behind, exactly the way he always squeezed mine.

Something splintered and cracked inside me, and I felt all the blood leave my face in a rush. The most intense agony I had ever felt filled every cell in my body; all the physical pain was nothing, absolutely *nothing*, compared to the anguish that was breaking my heart.

After all Stu had done to me, after all the times he had made it clear he possessed me, after he had protected me from this *same girl*, there he stood, right where he knew I could see him, kissing her in front of me. I knew that Gin and Megan were watching me and waiting to see what I would do, and I got to my feet so suddenly that my chair tipped over.

"Ang?" Meg said in an urgent voice. "Don't — "

I turned on her, and she shrank from the sudden fury in my eyes. "*Don't?*" I repeated in a breathless, faraway voice. "Don't what? Kill him? No. Oh, no, I don't think so, oh no ..."

I left the table and strode across the cafeteria, the anger misting my vision with red. Delaney looked at me as I approached, and the smug expression on her face made me want to pull every spiky hair from her head. I ignored her entirely, however; the only thing I cared about at that moment was letting Stu know exactly how I felt. He looked at me impassively, a slight smile on his face, and before I could lose my nerve I drew back my hand and slapped him across the face as hard as I could. The sound echoed like a pistol shot, and instantly the cafeteria grew silent as everyone around looked at us in fascination.

Stu's head snapped back and he put a hand to his reddening cheek and stared at me in astonishment. The look of stunned surprise on his face was almost comical.

"You fucking bastard!" I screamed, oblivious to the buzz of shocked whispers that now surrounded us. "If you want her so much, you can have her! You two deserve each other!"

I pushed past them and began to run, crying and hating myself for it. I managed to make it to the girls' room and pushed the door open so hard that it slammed against the outside wall before closing again. I gripped the counter in front of the sink and bent my head, crying so hard I felt nauseous.

After everything he's done ... after everything he's put me through, this is how he treats me ...

My sarcastic inner voice spoke up at once: *Oh, for Christ's sake, Ang, what were you expecting? Moonlight and roses? He treats you this way because he knows he can. Period.*

At that brutal, unwanted honesty I wailed out loud, sliding to the floor and sobbing until I couldn't catch my breath. The door banged open again and Stu charged into the room, coming over to me and jerking me to my feet. For once I wasn't afraid, and I pulled away from him, still crying.

"Don't you fucking touch me!" I yelled, and that expression of unaccustomed surprise crossed his face again. "You have no right, after what you did!" I looked at Stu in agony, and he actually backed up a step. "How could you do that, Stu? How could you do that to me?"

I covered my face with my hands, feeling as if I was dying inside. The next thing I knew Stu's arms were around me and his breath was warm in my ear. "You're right, Angel." His voice was low and ashamed. "I'm an insensitive prick. I'm sorry."

I looked up in amazement, twisting around to see his face. "You are?"

He smiled at me sheepishly and nodded. "Yeah. That was a pretty lousy thing to do. I don't give a shit about her, you know that. You're the only girl I care about."

I turned around in his arms and kissed him. "Thank you for saying that, Stu."

Stu looked at me seriously, and his smile faded. He brought his hand up to his cheek, where the red marks of my fingers stood out plainly. "Now, about that slap …"

"I was upset, Stu," I told him. "Think of how you would have felt – "

Stu's grip on me tightened, and his eyes hardened. "What have I told you about hitting me, Angel?"

It had all changed in an instant, and I wanted to scream. Before I could answer the bathroom door slammed open again, startling both of us, and when we looked, Delaney was standing in the doorway, incredulous.

"I don't believe this, Stu!" she cried. "She fucking *hit* you!"

I tried to twist out of Stu's arms, but he correctly interpreted my intention and held me tightly.

"You're lucky it wasn't you," I said in a low, threatening voice. "You wouldn't be walking right now, you *slut*."

Delaney's expression hardened into something vulpine and frightening, and I could see her hands clench into fists. Then her expression smoothed out, and a curious triumph came over her face as she looked at Stu.

"Why do you care about the little prom queen anyway, Stu?" she asked sweetly. "I mean, she's not going to be around much longer."

Stu's hands tightened on my arms, so hard that I gave an involuntary cry of pain.

"What the fuck are you talking about, Del?" His voice was ice, colder than I'd ever heard it, and I had to fight against the terror that wanted to spirit me away to a place where none of this would ever matter again.

She doesn't know ... how could she possibly know?

"I heard her talking to her little friend earlier," Delaney told him with obvious enjoyment, smirking at me. "She's moving to Calgary with her mommy."

Stu swung his head around and trapped me in a lethal gaze, his eyes blazing. "Is it true, Angel?" he hissed at me, and I was totally unable to respond. His fingers bit into my shoulders cruelly, and I could see my life slipping away before my eyes.

Oh, Delaney, you stupid, stupid bitch ... you killed me, you just killed me ...

I was too terrified to speak, and I could only shake my head helplessly. Stu suddenly released me and turned to look at Delaney, and she began to back away when she saw the look on his face. "You remember that saying about killing the messenger, Del?" Stu asked softly, and her eyes widened. "I'd get lost if I were you."

Without a word she turned and ran, and Stu spun around and slapped me so hard that I lost my balance and fell to the floor. He bent and grabbed a handful of my hair, pulling me to my feet, and I shrieked as the roots tore.

"Oh, Angie," Stu said in a quiet voice more frightening than any shout, "you have so much to learn. And I'm going to take all the time I need to teach you."

He let go of my hair and grabbed me around the waist, wrenching my left arm up between my shoulder blades. He brought his other hand up and seized my breast, pushing me back against his chest. "This is going to be the hardest lesson you've ever had," he murmured in my ear, and whimpering sounds began to escape my lips. "I'm really going to enjoy it."

His fingers grasped my nipple and tightened relentlessly, and I shrieked. Instantly Stu slapped his hand over my mouth. "Let's go." His voice was inexorable, and I began to cry helplessly. "And if you try to run, scream, *anything*, I'll make you sorrier than you've ever been in your life. Understand?" He released me and my hand came up instinctively to cradle my breast.

"Stu, please," I begged. "Let me explain – "

Stu slapped me again, viciously, and I stumbled and nearly fell. He grabbed me by the shoulders and pulled me forward until my face was inches from his. "Shut the fuck up and let *me* explain something to *you*. Do you remember what I told you, Angie? You can stay with me, or I can kill you. You try to leave, and I'll do it. You know I will. I'll fucking *kill you* before you leave me. Are we clear on that?"

I nodded frantically, tears dripping from my chin to the floor. "Yes, yes, I understand," I whispered. "You won't have to, Stu, I won't leave you I swear I won't – "

He slapped me again, harder than ever. "You're right," he said in a calm voice. "You aren't going to be able to. Not when I'm done with you."

Stu began to push me toward the door, and the world suddenly went gray and all the feeling began to leave my legs. My knees buckled and I started to fall, but he jammed my arm up between my shoulder blades again and the pain jarred me back to reality.

"Walk."

His voice held a promise of more pain if I resisted, and I obeyed him, walking in front of him through the school and out the back door to the parking lot, wondering the entire way if this was my last day on earth.

Chapter Sixty Four

I was so frightened that I didn't even look at Stu on the short ride to his house. I huddled against the passenger side door, my mind blank except for a fracture of prayer: *The Lord is my shepherd, the Lord is my shepherd ...*

When we reached his house Stu pulled the Rambler halfhazardly into the carport and shut off the engine. He came around to my side of the car and wrenched the door open, reaching inside to jerk me out. For no reason at all I wondered where his mother was: *Does he even have a mother? All this anger had to come from somewhere ...*

Then the thought fell away as Stu opened the side door and pushed me into the house. I went sprawling on the dirty linoleum, lightheaded with fear. I got to my feet as he slammed the door shut and locked it, and I backed away from him with my hands held up in front of me.

"Stu, please ..." I had to force the words out through trembling lips. "I don't want to die, please ..."

Stu's mouth curved in a smile that in another lifetime would have kindled heat in my belly. "You're not going to die, Angel," he told me gently. "Not if you take what I have to give you."

He closed the distance between us and took me into his arms, kissing me over and over. I pressed myself against him, trying desperately to believe that he wasn't going to kill me, that I would make it out of this house alive.

"Tell me," he whispered, and I choked out, "I love you, Stu."

Stu tangled his fingers in my hair and touched his lips to my ear. "Tell me you love it when I hurt you," he said, and I began to cry harder.

"I – I love it when you hurt me."

Stu laughed, a dark chuckle that froze the blood in my veins to red ice. "Ask me to give you a lesson, Angel," he murmured, and I could barely get the words out.

"Please give – give me a lesson, Stu."

He pulled away from me and took my arm in a strong grip, looking at me with merciless eyes. We crossed the living room and he pushed me ahead of him into the bedroom. When the door had closed behind us he just stood and looked at me, and I wanted to scream at him to get on with it, to just do it, that anything was better than this terrifying wait for the pain.

"Get your clothes off." Stu's voice was low and controlled, and I thought briefly of trying to explain, but dismissed the notion; he didn't want to hear it. I began to undress, praying all the while, and when I was naked he ran his hands over my body tenderly, almost regretfully. He kissed me deeply and I clung to him, wanting to plead with him not to do this, that I loved him and would never leave him, but I didn't, knowing it wouldn't do any good.

Finally Stu pushed me away and ordered me to lie on the bed. I lay down and closed my eyes, and when I heard the sound of him removing his belt it was all I could do not to scream.

"I want you to lie still," he told me in a serious voice, and I opened my eyes and stared at him. "Make any noise and it'll be harder and longer. Understand?"

I nodded, thinking: *He's crazy, Oh God, he's so crazy why did You make me love someone so crazy?*

Stu cocked his arm and snapped the belt across my breasts with all his strength, and the fiery agony that followed made it utterly impossible to remain silent. I screamed and screamed, and he brought the belt down again and again. My skin split and began to bleed, and the sight of the blood seemed to inflame him further, giving him renewed strength. I twisted from side to side and brought my arms up, trying to shield myself, and at last, after I was hoarse from shrieking and begging him to stop, he let the belt fall to the floor.

I was covered with welts and slash marks, many of them oozing blood, and the pain was the only thing in the world. Stu sat beside me on the bed and ran his hands over my wounded body with obvious enjoyment, smearing the blood on his hands like red paint. I tried not to scream, but when he grabbed my shoulder and turned me roughly onto my stomach I couldn't help it; the blanket felt like steel wool against my broken skin.

"You don't have much stamina, do you, Angel?" Stu asked, and I cried helplessly.

Oh God I'll do anything if You'll only get me out of this I swear —

I heard Stu removing his clothes, and then he was pushing my legs apart and getting in between them. "Let's try something new." When I felt his hands on my buttocks, spreading them apart, I began to scream again.

"Stu, no! Oh God, Stu, *no!*"

I felt the tip of him pressing against my anus and without warning he pushed himself brutally inside. I felt as though I was being ripped in two: the pain was unbelievable. As he thrust in and out the tender tissue stretched and tore, and I was losing a different kind of virginity altogether, one that was never meant to be lost. Stu's entry became easier when I began to bleed, and he continued to jam himself in and out of me for what seemed like hours. Finally he gave a shuddering groan and climaxed, and when he pulled out of me I cried from the relief of it.

He left me then, and I tried to be as still and quiet as I could, hoping I would just disappear, so he wouldn't be able to hurt me any more. When he came back into the room I began to pray again, and when he put his hand on my shoulder I cringed.

"Turn over, Angel." Stu's voice was curiously gentle, and as I struggled to shift from my stomach to my back I allowed myself to hope that he was done. When I saw what he had in his hand, however, any control I had managed to achieve shattered and shrieks tore out of my throat again, mindless animal noises that couldn't possibly convey the depths of my fear. Stu waved the knife in my face, ignoring my cries.

"It's time to show the world that you belong to me, Angel." He placed a hand on my bare shoulder, and I began to struggle wildly.

He's going to kill me Oh Lord he's really going to do it save me Jesus save me —

"*Lie still.*" I obeyed Stu's command instinctively, my chest heaving and tears spilling from my eyes. Terror was the whole world and it filled my head, raving and gibbering, until there was no conscious thought left at all.

Stu pressed the tip of the knife to my right cheek and I dimly felt my bladder let go as it broke the skin. The sharp blade slid into my flesh and I could feel the skin parting, giving way under the pressure of his fingers to trace a sinister red line down my cheek. It didn't hurt at all, and I vaguely wondered why as I watched Stu's face. His expression was serious and absorbed; the same expression he had had when he had bathed me so tenderly a lifetime ago.

When Stu lifted the knife from my skin the blade was crimson, and it occurred to me that I was looking at my own blood. The thought made me feel sick with horror, and the look in his eyes as he wiped the blade on the bedclothes was one that he often had after particularly good sex. Stu leaned in close to me and touched my lips with his.

"Repeat after me, Angel-baby," he told me, and I struggled to focus; my mind kept wanting to retreat in on itself. " 'I belong to you, Stu.' "

I forced my cold lips to say the words. "I belong to you, Stu."

He smiled, pleased at my acquiescence. "Very good, Angel. 'I'll never leave you, Stu.' "

I looked at him pleadingly, my breath coming in hitches and gasps. "I'll never l-leave you, Stu."

Stu kissed me again, so softly I wasn't certain I had felt it at all. He placed one palm on each side of my face. "Do you know how much I love you, Angel?" he asked me seriously, and I managed to nod. My cheek began to throb in time with my heartbeat, and I whispered, "Yes," as every part of me blazed with pain.

"You're not going anywhere, Angel." His eyes burned into mine, and I gave myself up to him.

"No. I'm not going anywhere."

Stu took my hand and pulled me to a sitting position, and I let out a weak cry. It hurt, oh God, it hurt more than anything ever had in my life. I wanted to go home so badly; I had never needed my mother more than I did now. Stu helped me into my clothes and I cried continuously: every movement hurt more than the one before it. When I was finally dressed and in the car it occurred to me to wonder if it was really over, and deep inside I knew it wasn't.

Chapter Sixty Five

On the ride back to my house I stared out the window, unseeing, struggling against the growing apathy that urged me to give up.

No! The rational part of my mind fought back. *Fuck that, Ang! Fuck him! First you'll call the police, then you'll leave! Think about the pain!*

It wasn't hard; even the brush of clothing against my skin was unbearable, and sitting was so painful that tears had come to my eyes. As we pulled up in front of the house I saw Mom's car in the driveway, and Stu muttered under his breath, "Good. We can get this over with right fucking now."

I looked at him in sudden terror. "What are you talking about?"

Stu smiled, a smile with no happiness or warmth. It was a terrible, possessive smile, and I began to shake. "I'm talking about letting your mother know the facts."

He got out of the car and came around to my side, and I slid off the seat with difficulty. Stu helped me out, kissing me on the temple, and I resisted the urge to pull away. "I love you, Angel," he said. "It'll be okay, we'll be together. You'll see."

He held my hand as we walked toward the house, and the unreality of it kept trying to carry me away. Surely this was a movie, and not a very good one, either, because things like this didn't happen in the real world.

When we went through the back door Stu crossed the kitchen in three long strides and yelled up the stairs, "Joy! Get the fuck down here, you *bitch*!"

Shock slammed into me like one of his fists, and I couldn't do anything but stare at him in horror. I heard running footsteps on the stairs, but before my mind jelled all the way together and I could open my mouth to warn her, it was too late. Mom came running into the room, and when she saw Stu, and then me, she skidded to a stop. Her eyes fastened on my right cheek, and her hand came up to her mouth.

"Ang," she breathed. "Oh my God, Ang, what happened to you?" I began to shake my head; I still couldn't speak. Mom looked from me to Stu, and her eyes narrowed into angry slits. "Get away from my daughter, you *freak*."

Stu smiled at her; that same awful smile he had given to me when I had gotten out of his car. "Come on, Joy," he said in a tone of counterfeit courtesy. "Is that any way to talk to your daughter's one and only?"

Mom's expression curdled into hatred, and it changed her face into a mask of avenging fury. "You're never coming near her again, you bastard. Not if I have anything to say about it."

Stu dropped all pretense of civility and began to walk toward her, his hands clenched into fists. "Well, I'll have to make sure you can't say anything then, won't I?"

My paralysis finally broke and I flew toward him, catching his arm. "Stu, don't, please don't – "

Stu jerked his arm out of my grasp and turned, slapping me stingingly across the face. "Stay the hell out of this, Angel. I already enlightened you, remember?"

Mom made an inarticulate sound of rage and started forward. Stu pushed me away and smiled again. "Come on, Joy," he purred. "Come to Stu."

Mom darted forward and her fist connected with Stu's jaw before he was fully prepared. She jumped back as he swung his arm out and grabbed for her, hissing at him, "*You* come on, you chickenshit loser. I'll show you how a *woman* fights."

Stu advanced on her, his fists held loosely in front of him, and the sight of him preparing to hit her tore a scream from my throat. I rushed forward, behind him, and seized his arm again, and he half turned, swinging his other arm and punching me in the side of the head, hard enough to make me see stars. I stumbled back, and Mom took advantage of the distraction I had provided to kick him hard in the stomach.

Stu doubled over in surprise and I backed away, bumping into the kitchen counter. Suddenly I realized that the phone was right beside me on the wall, and I snatched it up and pressed the 'talk' button, then 911. Stu wheeled around when he heard the electronic beeping noises, his face distorted with fury.

"Goddamn you, Angel," he said through gritted teeth. "You just never learn, do you?" He slapped the phone out of my hand and it went skittering across the floor. Stu grabbed my arm, pulling me toward him, and punched me in the stomach as hard as he could. I bent over in agony and Mom let out a wild shriek and jumped on him. Stu threw her off easily, and she went sprawling on the floor. She was on her feet in an instant, her eyes feral, her hands hooked into claws.

"You're never going to touch my daughter again, you sick fucking *animal.*" She came toward him in a crouch, clearly ready to do some serious damage, and Stu looked at her with an expression of tolerant amusement.

"Let's talk about this, Joy," he said easily, and she screamed, "Get out of here! Get out and leave us alone!"

"You really don't get it, do you, Joy?" Stu's tone was dangerous now, and all I could do was stand helplessly when I was able, frozen with fear as I watched them. "I'll leave you six feet under without a second thought, you cunt. Angel is *mine*. And I'm not leaving without her."

This time when Mom came for him Stu was ready. He seized the fist she swung forward in a crushing grip and jerked her toward him, and the fury on her face melted into fear when he wrapped those strong, long-fingered hands around her throat.

"Stu, no!" I wailed. "I'll go with you! I'll do anything you want! Don't hurt her!"

"Shut the fuck up, Angel." Stu began to squeeze and Mom's hands clawed at his tightening fingers, her face turning red.

"Stop!" I screamed. "Stu, stop!"

That was when I heard a voice, tinny with distance, coming from the corner of the kitchen. The phone was still on, and someone on the other end was calling out. "He's killing her!" I shrieked. "Please help!"

I looked wildly around the room and my eyes fell on the knives that filled the wooden butcher block next to the toaster. I darted over to it and grabbed the biggest one, advancing on Stu. Mom was making helpless choking noises and her struggles were growing weaker, but he kept squeezing, his face red, mindless fury in his eyes.

"Stu, stop!" I waved the knife and he shook his head, still squeezing with all his strength.

"You won't do it, Angel," he said, and the confidence in his voice filled me with rage. "You wouldn't dare."

I didn't bother replying. I moved around in back of him like a woman in a dream and buried the knife in his back up to the hilt. It slid into his flesh easily; I was surprised at how little resistance there was.

Stu let out a howl and let go of my mother. She dropped to the floor like a stone, making harsh hacking noises and struggling to draw air into her lungs. Stu's hands scrabbled madly behind him, trying to grab the knife, and after a moment he fell to his knees.

"Angel?" he said in a surprised voice. "Angel – " He collapsed forward onto his face, and I went over to my mother and knelt beside her.

"Are you okay, Mom?" I asked in a trembling voice, and she coughed and again and again and finally nodded.

"Watch him," she told me in a rough whisper, and I looked over at Stu. He lay motionless, blood beginning to seep around the knife and stain the back of his jacket. He didn't move, and I stepped around him and went to retrieve the phone, picking it up and holding it to my ear.

"Hello?" I whispered in an uncertain voice. "Is – is anyone there?" Instantly a terse voice replied, "We have units on the way ma'am. Is anyone hurt?"

"You'd better send an ambulance," I whispered, and I jumped as Mom put a hand on my shoulder.

"If we're lucky he'll die before it gets here."

She took the phone from my hand and I slipped to the floor; my legs were no longer able to support me.

After the ambulance arrived and took Stu away, shock took over. I began to shake uncontrollably and I stayed on the floor, my knees drawn up to my chest and my arms tight around them, resting my forehead on my knees and trying desperately to achieve some sort of equilibrium. When I remembered the sensation of the knife sliding effortlessly into Stu's back, something inside me cracked and broke. I began to hyperventilate, my breath rushing in and out in shallow pants that made me lightheaded. I couldn't seem to get any air into my lungs, and the harder I tried the worse it became. Mom knelt beside me and put her arms around me.

"Ang?" she said in her new, scratchy voice. "Are you okay, hon?"

I didn't answer; I couldn't. The terror and guilt that enveloped me didn't leave any room for words, only the possibility of my new identity as a murderer.

What did I do? Oh God, tell me I didn't kill him please tell me he isn't dead -

I gripped my legs more tightly and began to rock back and forth, back and forth. From a great distance, I heard the back door open again and a male voice speaking to my mother, but it didn't really register; a black vortex was sucking me in and everything was getting farther and farther away. I felt a hand on my shoulder and someone said, "Angie? Can you hear me?"

If I don't answer, they'll go away ... if I don't answer, I'm not even here ...

I continued to rock, trying in vain to soothe myself with the rhythm of movement. I heard Mom's voice again, more urgent this time: "Ang? Talk to me, honey. Please talk to me."

Keep rocking. Keep rocking and hold on, just hold on ...

All at once I felt hands on my arms, prying them apart, and hard fingers burrowed under my chin, trying to lift my head. I screamed, suddenly and piercingly. Stu was back, he was here, he was going to pin me with that furious black gaze and the lesson would begin, the one he had promised would be the hardest one I had ever had. I tried to tear my arms away from the hands that trapped them, shrieking again and again.

"No, Stu! I'm learning, I swear I am, I'll never leave you I *promise* – "

Two warm, strong hands cupped either side of my face and I squeezed my eyes shut and tried to pull away.

"Angie." A deep voice said my name, once, then again. "Angie! This is Mark Hayward of the Edmonton City Police. Can you hear me?"

Slowly the words filtered in, and I opened my eyes. "Stu?" I whispered, looking into the eyes of a young man with closely cropped brown hair and a thin moustache. He removed his hands from the sides of my face and smiled at me gently, taking my hand. I tried to stop shaking but it was impossible: it was coming from deep inside and I was powerless to control it.

"Angie?" Constable Hayward said again. "Do you know where you are?"

I kept my eyes on his face, shaking my head. "Where's Stu?" I whispered. "Where did Stu go?"

Constable Hayward's expression softened, and when he answered his voice was calm and even. "He was taken to the hospital, Angie. Can you tell me what happened here this afternoon?"

I shook my head again, pushing away the memories that wanted to claw their way up to the surface of my mind and destroy what was left of my sanity. "Did Stu hurt me?" I asked in a childlike voice, and from somewhere behind me I heard Mom begin to cry.

"Yes." Constable Hayward answered me gently. "It looks like he did."

It was as if the pain had been waiting for me with claws bared, needing only that spoken permission to come out. It all descended on me at once and suddenly every part of my body had an agony all its own: my torso, arms, and legs, where he had whipped me relentlessly; my anus, where he had raped me brutally; and my face, where he had cut me with such careful consideration.

"It hurts," I whispered, and the reality of what had happened that day came rushing at me like the winds of a murderous tornado. My head whirled with knowledge that was too much for my mind to cope with, and I looked desperately into the calm blue eyes in front of me. They were the last things I saw before I fainted.

Chapter Sixty Six

When I returned to consciousness I was lying on a gurney in the University of Alberta hospital's emergency room, the drapes drawn all around me. I blinked and struggled to focus; my mind was moving slowly and time seemed to have slowed to a swimmy crawl, and I realized that I had been sedated. It couldn't quite take away the pain, though. My cheek ached fiercely and I raised a hand to it, my fingers tracing a cut that was stiff with dried blood. Terror rushed in to fill the emptiness inside, and I pushed away the memory of the blade sliding painlessly into my skin.

What did he do to me? Dear God, what the hell did he do to me?

Mom's face suddenly appeared in my field of vision. Her eyes were red and her mouth trembling, and I had never been so happy to see her. I reached for her and she held me, sobbing.

"Peach … " she managed to say after a few seconds. "Oh God, Peach, your poor, poor face …"

We cried together, and when we heard the sound of the drapes being pulled back Mom stepped away from me and wiped her eyes on the sleeve of her shirt. A man in a white coat stepped into the cubicle and I recognized him as Dr. Soloman, the same physician who had treated me only days ago. He was a tall, angular man with salt and pepper hair and a neat moustache, with a gentle manner I found reassuring. He stepped over to me and smiled.

"Angie," he said. "I'm so sorry to see you back here under such circumstances. How are you feeling?" Resentment pierced the medicated haze that surrounded me.

How does it look like I feel? I'm branded like a fucking thoroughbred!

"Everything hurts," I told him simply, and he patted my shoulder.

"Let me have a look, all right?" Dr. Soloman glanced at Mom, then back at me. "Do you mind if your mother stays, Angie, or would you like her to leave?"

I reached for Mom's hand, and she took it gratefully. "I want her to stay."

Dr. Soloman pulled down the blanket that covered me; all I had on underneath was a hospital gown. He reached around me carefully, undoing the bow at the back of the neck that held the gown together, and drew it carefully over my shoulders. I turned my head away from Mom; I couldn't look at her face when she saw what Stu had done to me. Her fingers tightened unbearable over mine and I heard her draw in her breath in a horrified gasp.

"Sweet Jesus," she breathed. "What did he do to you?"

Dr. Soloman didn't look at my nipple; he had already seen it. He examined the belt marks, doing his best not to hurt me any more than necessary. At last he pulled the gown back up and bent over my face, looking closely at the cut on my cheek.

"What was used to do this, do you know?" he asked me, and at the serious expression in his eyes I had to push away the shame again, the shame I felt would be a part of me forever, emotional proof that I had only gotten what I deserved.

405

"A pocket knife," I said in a whisper, and Dr. Soloman touched the wound very gently.

"It doesn't look too deep," he observed. "Dermabrasion should remove it, but only after it's completely healed."

"How long will that take?" I asked.

"Three and a half to four months," he replied, and the thought of wearing this hideous badge of pain for that long made me want to die.

"I'll have to ask you to turn over now, Angie." Dr. Soloman's voice was soft and sympathetic, but the reminder of the rape I had suffered brought a flood of tears. Mom helped me turn over, and I cried continuously, wishing it was all a bad dream, a nightmare from which I could awaken with a shaky sigh of relief.

Dr. Soloman examined me as gently as he could, but it still hurt like hell, and I buried my head in my arms and sobbed as his fingers probed inside me. Mom stroked my hair and murmured words of comfort and when it was over I lay still, feeling violated all over again.

"You have some significant tearing, Angie, but it should heal on its own. Soak in warm water and try to keep the area as clean as you can." Given the area that Dr. Soloman was talking about, the instructions should have been funny, but nothing about this long, crazy day had been remotely funny, and I was as far from laughing as I had ever been in my life.

"Stay on your stomach, Angie," Dr. Soloman told me as I started to turn over again. "I have to complete a rape kit for the police. I'm sorry – I know this has been terrible for you, but it's necessary in order to obtain evidence for the case against the young man."

"How is Stu?" I asked suddenly, feeling Mom stiffen beside me. "Is he alive?"

"That sick, twisted son of a bitch!" she burst out. "I hope he's dead."

I began to cry again. "That's great, Mom. If he's dead, then I'm a murderer."

She was instantly contrite, and she leaned over and kissed the top of my head. "I'm sorry, baby," she whispered. "I just hate him so much for what he did to you."

Dr. Soloman, who had been standing uncomfortably silent during this exchange, spoke.

"I'm fairly certain the young man is alive," he told us. "I don't know how he's doing, though. Excuse me – I have to go and get the rape kit."

He left the cubicle in a flap of curtain, and almost as soon as he was gone I heard another voice: Constable Hayward. I closed my eyes. Would this day never end?

"Mrs. Swanson? Angie? May I come in?"

I looked at Mom with a halfhearted shrug. "Sure."

The curtain parted and Constable Hayward stepped in, followed by a female officer with blond hair pulled back into a bun.

"Angie, Mrs. Swanson, this is Constable Dorry Grant. She's going to be taking some pictures of your injuries. I'm sorry to put you both through this, but evidence will be important in the case against Mr. Black."

When I heard him mention Stu I began to cry again. I knew that I shouldn't care where he was or how he was doing – he had tried to *kill* my mother – but I did, and there was no use in denying it. I think I hated myself for that most of all.

"Is he all right?" I asked, and I knew that Mom was struggling to understand why I needed to know.

"He's in surgery right now," Constable Grant said, and agony shot through me: *Surgery! He's in surgery because of me!*

Dr. Soloman came back into the cubicle, carrying a white plastic container. Constable Hayward back out, leaving Dorry Grant to be a witness, and I clutched Mom's hand, knowing what was coming. I heard Dr. Soloman unwrapping something, and then he drew the blanket off my body again.

"Okay, Angie, this is going to be uncomfortable, but I want you to tell me at once if anything really hurts, all right?"

"Okay," I whispered, feeling like I was marooned in a nonstop nightmare. I felt something slide into my anus and my breath caught as it probed around for a moment.

"All right?" Dr. Soloman asked, and I nodded, trying to hold back tears. I leaned my forehead on my arms, praying for this to be over. There were two more swabs, and then I heard the sound of paper rubbing together. Dr. Soloman spread my buttocks apart slightly and what felt like a brush swept across my skin for an instant.

"I'm finished, Angie," Dr. Soloman told me. "Constable Grant is going to take some pictures now."

I felt my buttocks being held apart again, and then the distinctive whirr-hum of a Polaroid camera.

Oh, that'll be a keeper ...

I suppressed the hysteria rising in my throat with an effort, knowing how much it would frighten Mom if I laughed, but the whole thing was taking on the quality of a third rate movie. Dr. Soloman moved away from me, and I could hear the snap of him removing his rubber gloves. The blanket was pulled the rest of the way off, and two more pictures were taken, and then Dorry Grant was saying, "I need you to turn over now, Angie."

Mom helped me turn over, and Constable Grant took several pictures of the marks on my legs. I braced myself and pulled the hospital gown off entirely, leaving my body totally uncovered. Dorry Grant kept her expression carefully impassive, but I knew what it looked like, and I almost wished she would make a face, or remark on how bad it was. In a twisted sort of way, it would have made me feel better. She took several pictures of my chest, and then moved the camera's pitiless eye up to my face and photographing the mark Stu had made with his knife. Mom had covered me up with the blanket and I clutched it to my neck gladly; I had never felt so exposed in my life.

Dr. Soloman smiled at me, and I smiled back; he was so kind, and had always done his best to make me comfortable. "I'm going to admit you for tonight, Angie," he said. "Just to be on the safe side."

Mom kissed me. "Good. I'll feel better knowing you're being looked after, Peach."

"Thanks, Dr. Soloman," I said, and he said, "You're more than welcome, Angie. I'll see you in the morning."

He left, and Dorry Grant turned her attention to Mom. "Mrs. Swanson, I'll need to get a few pictures of you as well," she said, and Mom nodded, her hand going instinctively to her throat, where the angry red marks of Stu's fingers still remained. She stood quietly while the photos were taken, and when Constable Grant was finished Mom gave me a tremulous smile.

"I don't know why that makes it seem more real, but it does." I nodded in perfect understanding and reached for her hand. Constable Grant placed the camera back in its case.

"Well wait until Angie is settled in a room, and then Constable Hayward and I will come and get your statements, all right?"

I nodded, suddenly exhausted. "Okay." Constable Grant left, and I looked at Mom. "I'm so glad he didn't really hurt you, Mom." My eyes filled with tears and a terrible sense of guilt ran through me. "I'm sorry, Mom," I gasped. "I'm so sorry for putting you through this – "

Mom placed her hand over my mouth, so gently. "Stop, Ang. Don't do that to yourself. None of this is your fault. It never was."

She held me then, and I felt the love she gave me and took solace in it, while in the back of my mind a voice whispered: *Don't kid yourself,* Angel. *This* is *all your fault. It's all your fault, and you know it.*

Chapter Sixty Seven

After I was taken to a room, Mom helped me get settled in the bed and we waited for Constables Hayward and Grant to return. When a nurse came to take my vital signs I begged her to find out how Stu was doing; she looked at me oddly but said she would see what she could do. Mom sighed as the nurse left the room.

"Why do you keep asking about him, Ang?" she said quietly. "After what he did, how can you possibly care?"

I pulled the blankets up to my chin, knowing I could never tell her in a way she would understand. "I don't know, Mom." I stared at the ceiling and struggled to hold back the tears. "It's like there are two of him. One is gentle and considerate and a wonderful lover, and the other one is a controlling monster. I've never known someone who had two such completely opposite sides before. I love the first one and I'm scared to death of the second."

Mom brushed the hair back from my forehead, and the smile she gave me was sad. "He's only one person, baby. One very sick person. And I hope he goes to prison for a long time."

I looked at the angry red mark encircling her neck and nodded, although my vision blurred. "So do I," I said. "I guess I have to, don't I?"

Hours later, when the police had finished taking our statements and Mom had finally gone home, I lay quietly in the darkness, exhausted but unable to sleep. My muscles still felt tight and constricted and a sick anxiety remained in the pit of my stomach, making it impossible to relax. What had happened that afternoon ran through my mind again and again, like a horror movie I couldn't turn off, and after tossing and turning for a while I reached for the pad of buttons that lay at the top of the mattress, pressing the one that turned on the light just over my head.

I sat up and swung my legs over the side of the bed, sitting still for a moment, trying to work up the courage. At last I forced myself to lower my feet to the floor, stand up, and walk the short distance from the bed to the room's small bathroom. When I opened the door and flicked on the light my heart began to pound faster and I was flooded with fear. I had been in here before, but I had shielded my eyes from the mirror, quickly taking care of business and hurrying out again.

Now, I took a deep breath and stepped in front of the mirror before I could change my mind. When I caught sight of my face, chalk white, the bruises standing out clearly, my hair hanging lank and unbrushed, my first thought before I focused on my right cheek was: *Who is that? Who is that girl?*

Then my eyes took in the mark Stu had cut into my skin, and my eyes grew wide. Carved into my cheek, limned in red and standing out like a beacon, was the shape of a heart. It was jagged and crudely made, but unmistakable for all that, and I raised my fingers and traced it, watching it blur as hot tears filled my eyes. My legs went weak and I had to grab the lip of counter at the end of the sink, lowering my head and crying in gasping sobs.

"Oh, Stu," I wept. "Why?"

"Angie?" I jumped and whirled around, almost losing my balance, and a wave of dizziness rushed over me. The nurse standing in the doorway moved forward and caught my arm, and I leaned on her as we made our way back to the bed. I sank down onto it gratefully, and she helped me get in, pulling the blankets up to my chin.

"You need to stay in bed, honey," she admonished gently. Young and pretty, she had red hair caught up behind her head in a thick ponytail, and she smiled at me and patted my uninjured cheek. I brought my fingers up and traced them over the heart, and the tears rose up in my throat again, hot and choking.

"I just looked at this for the first time," I told her, and the nurse's expression became sympathetic and concerned.

"That must have been very difficult," she said. "Who did this to you, Angie?"

"My boy – boyfriend," I said; the word was jarringly out of place now. "At least he was, until he – he …"

I couldn't continue, and I raised my hands to my face and began to cry in earnest. The nurse sat on the edge of the bed and placed a gentle hand on my shoulder. "I'm so sorry," she said. "That must have been so terrible for you."

She sat with me for a few moments, and her presence was curiously comforting. When I managed a semblance of control I asked her about Stu. "He was taken to surgery this afternoon," I said, and that irrational guilt rose up again. "Can you find out how he's doing?"

To my relief she didn't ask why, or express disapproval. She just nodded and told me she'd see what she could do. "But you have to rest, all right?"

I looked at her and tried to smile. "I can't even close my eyes. I feel as though I'll never sleep again."

The nurse stood and gave me a smile. "I'll get you something to help you relax." As I began to protest, she held up a hand. "If you take it, I'll do my best to find out how your boyfriend is doing. Okay?" I nodded reluctantly.

"Good," she said. "What's his name?"

"Stu," I told her, and the sound of his name on my lips was unbearable. "Stuart Black."

The nurse nodded and left the room on soundless loafers, and when she returned about ten minutes later she was holding a tiny paper cup and a glass of water. I sat up and she handed me the paper cup; nestled inside were two tiny white pills. I shook them into my palm and brought the hand to my mouth, and she handed me the glass of water. After I had washed them down the nurse took the glass from me and I lay back down.

"Good girl," she said. "Your boyfriend had surgery for a punctured lung, but he's doing fine. He'll be in intensive care tonight, but he'll probably be moved to a ward in the morning."

I stared at her in horror. "A punctured lung?" I whispered. "My God, what did I do —"

The nurse reached out and put a comforting hand on my shoulder. "It's all right, Angie. He'll be fine. You're the one who's really hurt. Try to take it easy."

"I did that," I said, more to myself than to her, and the guilt raked me with razor sharp claws. "I did that to him — "

"Don't do this to yourself, honey." I looked at the nurse in disbelief, and what she said next made me angry. "From what I heard, he deserved what he got."

"Go away!" I cried. "You don't understand, so just go away!" I turned over, clutching the covers and struggling not to cry again.

"Rest," the nurse said softly. "Things will look better in the morning." She left the room and I lay still, unable to believe that I had hurt him that badly.

Things will never look better. How could they? How?

A blessed feeling of lethargy began to steal over me like a soft, comforting cloud, and I was glad to give myself up to it, wanting to forget for a little while; just a little while. I drifted, finally relaxed, and when sleep came it was merciful and there were no dreams.

Chapter Sixty Eight

I woke up slowly, drifting through layers of sleep and finally opening my eyes to a room flooded with sunshine. I was immediately aware of two things: one, that I felt rested, really rested, for the first time in a long time, and two, that my entire body throbbed miserably. I got carefully out of bed and hobbled into the bathroom, and after I used the toilet I took another good look in the mirror. This time anger filled me, and I remembered Stu's words like a line from a bad play: *It's time to show the world you belong to me, Angel.*

I left the bathroom and went back to the bed, trying to hold tight to that anger. It made me feel stronger and more in control, something I needed desperately. I lay back against the pillows and tried not to move. The places where Stu's belt had split my skin were stinging, my cheek had the dull ache of an open wound, and my stomach was unbelievably tender. Sitting down was still a new experience in pain, and to avoid thinking about what he had done I stayed on my back as much as possible.

I had just settled myself when another nurse, this one short, plump, and cheerful, bustled into the room with a covered tray in her hands. She placed it on the rolling table next to my bed, pushing it toward me until the wheels slid underneath the bed and the adjustable tray was right in front of me. I sat up, wincing at the pressure on my wounded behind, and removed the cover.

"Enjoy, sweetie," the nurse said with a sunny smile, and I smiled back and thanked her, looking down at my breakfast. The two scrambled eggs, toast, and a small box of cereal disappeared like magic, and after I had washed it down with a glass of orange juice I felt pleasantly full. I pushed the tray out of the way and lay down again, feeling better than I had in days. For a moment I wondered why, give what I had just been through, but after a moment's reflection I realized what it was: the lack of that ever present, anticipatory fear. I knew exactly where Stu was, and for once he wasn't able to hurt me.

The relief that filled me was accompanied by an emotion that felt almost like happiness, and I smiled to myself as I tucked my arms behind my head. I knew I would have to see Stu once last time, if only to prove to myself that any remaining hold he had on me was broken, and I believed it was the right thing to do; it was finally time to say goodbye. I knew Mom would be upset at the idea, and I was wondering how to explain it to her when she appeared in the doorway, smiling at me. When I saw Ivan behind her I sat up, an answering smile on my face.

"Ivan!" I exclaimed. "What are you doing here?"

He was at my side in a moment, taking me gently into his arms and holding me close to him. I could hear his ragged breathing and knew he was crying, and tears came to my own eyes as I clung to him, letting the love I needed wash over me and make me clean. At last Ivan released me and stepped back, wiping his eyes with the fingers of one hand.

"My Angie – " he began, but he was unable to continue, and he hung his head and wept again, reaching up as Mom placed a hand on his shoulder. He leaned on the bed for a moment, overcome with emotion, and Mom put her arms around his shoulders and rested her chin on his back.

I saw the angry red marks on her neck, and that slammed it home to me like nothing else could have: Stu had wanted to *kill* her, and if he had succeeded a part of me would have died with her. I felt weak and shaky at that, and I lay back against the pillows, smiling at Mom. When Ivan raised his head again I said, "I love you, Ivan. I'm so glad you're here."

Ivan looked at me with wet, red eyes and placed both palms against the sides of my face in a gesture that had, for me, become his trademark. He leaned forward and placed a soft kiss directly on my wounded cheek, then kissed the other cheek, and at last he was able to speak.

"And I love you, my Angie. So very, very much. I thank the Lord above that you are safe, you and my Joy both. If I had lost either one of you I would not have wanted to go on living."

From anyone else such a statement would have sounded melodramatic and foolish; from Ivan it was heartfelt and touching, and I didn't doubt he meant it.

"You ready to get out of here?" Mom asked me, and I nodded, bracing myself.

"Not until I see Stu."

She gaped at me for a moment, astonished, and then a shutter came down across her face. I knew this was going to be difficult, and I prepared myself for a fight. "Not a chance."

Mom's voice was flat and matter of fact, as if the matter had already been decided, and I tried not to get angry. "You're not getting within ten yards of that lunatic, Ang. I've tried to be understanding about Stu up until now, but this is too much. He tried to *kill* me, for Christ's sake! What could you possibly have to say to him?"

"You know what, Mom?" My voice rose, and I told myself to keep cool; screaming wasn't going to get me anywhere. "I don't remember asking for your permission. I'm sorry if the idea upsets you, but I'm going to see him."

Mom looked at me as if I had sprouted another head that was speaking a different language. "Angie," she said in that maddeningly precise way, as if I were three instead of almost eighteen, "You don't seem to get it. *No way.* I'm not letting you near him."

I looked back at her, suddenly furious. "*You're* the one who doesn't get it, Mom!" I cried, and she looked almost comically shocked at the anger in my voice. "I've been Stu's prisoner, his *possession*, for the past six months! In spite of everything he's done to me, and what he did to you, I still love him!"

I began to cry at the look on her face – total shutdown – but I had to tell her how I felt. Honesty was the only thing I had left, the only thing that felt right in a world that had gone so terribly wrong.

"Don't you think I hate myself for feeling like this?" I sobbed, and she tried to take me in her arms but I wouldn't let her. "I should hate *him*, but I always end up hating myself! I just have to see him, Mom – I have to."

I began to cry, so hard I could no longer talk, and this time I let her enfold me in her arms. When the tears tapered off at last Mom handed me a swatch of tissues and I wiped my eyes.

"All right, honey," she said in a low voice. "I guess I really don't understand the hold he has over you."

"I'm sorry, Mom." My voice trembled, and Mom caressed my cheek and shook her head.

"Don't say that, Peach. You have nothing to be sorry for. Not one goddamn thing."

I changed into the jeans and sweatshirt she had brought from home, and I felt better when all the welts and bruises were covered up. I brushed my hair and Mom braided it, and when I looked at myself in the mirror five years had fallen off and a frightened twelve year old looked back at me through haunted eyes. We left the room and made our way to the intensive care unit, and I approached the nurses' station with apprehension. The nurse behind the counter looked up and smiled at me, her gaze sliding professionally over the mark on my cheek.

"May I help you?"

I swallowed past the dryness in my throat and asked nervously, "Has a patient named Stuart Black been moved from here to a regular ward?"

"Are you a family member?"

I stared at her, nonplussed. "Well ... no," I admitted. "But I need to see him."

The nurse, an older woman with attractive silver hair, smiled at me in a sympathetic way. "I'm sorry, dear, but if you're not immediate family I can't give out that information."

I began to cry, and she looked at me in alarm. "You don't understand," I choked. "I need to see him – I'm all he has."

The sound of the words made me cry harder, and Ivan came over and put a protective arm around my shoulders, trying to lead me away. "No!" I cried, and the other people in the waiting area looked at me curiously. "Please, I *need* to see him – "

Mom stepped over to the counter while Ivan led me to a chair. She began to speak to the nurse in a low voice, and I cried against Ivan's shoulder while she explained my situation to the woman. After a few minutes Mom returned to where Ivan and I were sitting, and when I looked up at her she nodded.

"I think they'll let you in," she said, and I wiped my eyes and tried to compose myself. I looked to my left and saw a doctor approaching us, his white coat belling out behind him as he walked. He stopped in front of my chair, a tall man with iron grey hair and a lined, careworn face.

"Miss Swanson?" he asked, and I nodded. "I'm Dr. Ward Graham, chief resident in the ICU. It's not hospital policy to allow anyone but immediate family onto the ward, but given your circumstances I'm going to allow it."

Relief flooded me. "Thank you," I whispered. I looked at Mom and Ivan. "I'll see you in a little while, okay?"

Mom nodded without saying anything and Ivan put an arm around her shoulders. I rose and followed Dr. Graham over to the pneumatic doors that led into the ICU. As we walked down an antiseptic white corridor Dr. Graham asked, "Does this young man have any family?"

I shook my head, and my heart filled with pity for Stu. "I don't think so," I answered. "Has anyone been to see him?"

"No family," Dr. Graham replied. "We can't seem to locate anyone." He stopped outside a door that led to a private room. "I can only give you ten minutes."

I thanked him again and he nodded at me and walked away. I looked at the door, sudden terror constricting my throat. I gathered my courage and pushed the door open, peering inside and seeing only the end of a bed. I forced myself to go the rest of the way inside, and I stopped when I saw him, overcome with such a rush of emotion that I literally couldn't move.

Stu lay with his eyes closed. His hair was impossibly black against the white pillow, his features relaxed, his breathing calm and even. His

421

hands rested at his sides, the fingers loose, and I had a sudden fierce urge to pick up the one closest to me and press a kiss into the palm. His chest rose and fell steadily, and the quiet hum of the machine that pumped medication into his arm was soothing. A rubber tube ran from his left side into a container hooked to the end of the bed, and I saw with horror that the liquid in it was bright red, which meant it was probably blood.

My paralysis broke and I moved closer to the bed, tears spilling down my cheeks unnoticed. I reached out with a shaking hand and brushed an errant lock of dark hair from his forehead, feeling such guilt well up in my heart that I wanted to die. Stu didn't wake, and I placed my palm against the side of his face and wept quietly, wondering if I would ever be able to really let him go.

As I watched through prisms of tears his eyes fluttered and opened, and he looked at me in confusion, as though he thought he was dreaming. He blinked several times and made a noise in the back of his throat. His hand came up and covered mine, and a faint smile curved his lips.

"Angel?" he managed to say, and I nodded, trying to smile back. "Are you really here?" I tried to stop crying, telling him, "I'm really here, Stu."

Stu's hand tightened on mine. "I thought I'd never see you again," he said in the wondering tone of a boy on his first visit to Santa Clause. I took a shaky breath and leaned over to kiss him gently.

"You probably won't after today," I told him, and the words pierced my heart. "I just had to see you before I go."

I took my hand away from his face and Stu reached out and traced the heart on my right cheek with the tips of his fingers. "Now everyone will know," he said, and I was confused.

422

"Everyone will know what, Stu?"

He smiled again, fully awake now, and pushed against the cut, making it sting. "Everyone will know that you're mine."

I backed away a few steps and stared at him, and fear began to dissolve the love, obliterate it, eat away at it like acid.

"It's over, Stu," I whispered. "You know it's over."

Stu's eyes captured mine, so cold and black, and I noticed for the first time that his left hand was manacled to the metal railing of the bed. I backed up several more steps, unable to tear my eyes away from that dark, determined gaze.

"It will never be over, Angel-baby," he told me. "Don't you remember what I told you? What I own, I keep."

"You don't own me anymore." I struggled against the fear that wanted to wrap loving arms around me and squeeze until I begged for mercy. Stu smiled at me, the lazy, insolent smile that had once been my undoing.

"You're wrong about that, Angel," he said. "You're so wrong. I can't wait to show you *how* wrong."

I turned and ran for the door, and in spite of my need to get away he stopped me with one word.

"Angel."

I turned around and looked at him one last time.

"Lessons, Angel." Stu's voice was filled with dark amusement. "There are so many more lessons."

I fled the room in a panic, garnering a startled look from a passing nurse, and when I reached the pneumatic doors I made myself walk. I pushed them open and hurried over to Mom and Ivan, and they looked at me in concern.

"What is it?" Mom asked, and I shook my head and began to walk toward the door that led out into the corridor, glad I could walk out of the hospital and leave him far behind.

"Nothing," I said. "I just want to get as far away from this city as I possibly can."

It wasn't even a week after the trial ended when Meg received the first letter.

The End